INFERNAL PARADISE
A TALE OF MALLORCA

By
Glyn Gowans

Grosvenor House
Publishing Limited

All rights reserved
Copyright © Glyn Gowans, 2025

The right of Glyn Gowans to be identified as the author of this work has been asserted in accordance with Section 78 of the Copyright, Designs and Patents Act 1988

The book cover is copyright to Glyn Gowans

This book is published by
Grosvenor House Publishing Ltd
Link House
140 The Broadway, Tolworth, Surrey, KT6 7HT.
www.grosvenorhousepublishing.co.uk

This book is sold subject to the conditions that it shall not, by way of trade or otherwise, be lent, resold, hired out or otherwise circulated without the author's or publisher's prior consent in any form of binding or cover other than that in which it is published and without a similar condition including this condition being imposed on the subsequent purchaser.

This book is a work of fiction. Any resemblance to people or events, past or present, is purely coincidental.

A CIP record for this book
is available from the British Library

ISBN 978-1-83615-232-3
eBook ISBN 978-1-83615-233-0

For Karim, who made this book possible.

ABOUT THE AUTHOR

Glyn Gowans was born in Newcastle-upon-Tyne and educated at Durham University, where he graduated in Law. After nineteen years specialising in intellectual property with a major UK law firm, he took early retirement to write. His first novel, *Gloria! Gloria!*, was published in March 2025.

PREFACE

I arrived in Palma by ferry from Barcelona in February 1998 after two delightful years residing in the heart of Bordeaux – arguably, one of Europe's most civilised cities. The previous summer, after a brief tour of all the inhabited Balearic Islands, my partner and I had identified Mallorca's relatively undeveloped south-east corner, around Santanyí, as an ideal location for transforming a 'country house' (*finca*) into a luxury hotel.

To provide ourselves with a base from which to undertake the search for a suitable *finca*, we rented a house in Ca's Concos, an unassuming village (*pueblo*) eight kilometres north of Santanyí. Later, when we penetrated the upper echelons of Palma society and revealed where we lived, laughter would erupt: apparently, it was a standing joke that Ca's Concos was the island's most unsophisticated backwater.

But this proved to be grossly inaccurate. In our neighbourhood, tucked away in elegant secluded fincas, resided a veritable battalion of international VIPs, including millionaire tycoons, renowned painters, writers and architects – even a monarch in exile. In fact, the creeping 'colonisation' of the pine-wooded hills thereabouts was a factor in the frustration of our efforts to find an affordable *finca* ripe for conversion. With many EU countries preparing to abandon their national currencies and adopt the euro from 1 January 1999, undeclared cash assets, especially Deutschmarks, were pouring into Mallorca for conversion into real estate. Overnight, prices rocketed and our plans became unviable.

Yet, I remained for eleven years, during which Spain boomed, thanks in part to becoming the largest net recipient of EU funds. Meanwhile, hard-working Mallorcans were finding it ever more difficult to afford a decent home of their own – even to rent. Their understandable anger mounted; 'foreign' residents were an obvious target. Mercifully, when enjoying the island's bars, cafes and restaurants, most 'foreigners' – whether residents or tourists – were ignorant of the insults directed at them in Catalan/*Mallorquí* by some adjacent Mallorcans.

GMG, Witham, Essex, 2025

MAP OF MALLORCA

PART I
CHAPTER 1

'I thought we'd never get out of that bloody airport,' said Mike Oakheart as his wife, Jane, negotiated the hire car through the maze of roads around Palma Airport's terminal buildings. 'Now you have to follow the signs for Llucmajor, Campos and Santanyí,' he advised, closing his window and reaching for the air conditioning controls; it was early July and almost noon on a cloudless, baking Sunday.

'Oh, Mikey, let's have some fresh air. Whenever I arrive somewhere new, I love to smell the place – the herbs, the flowers – that wonderful Mediterranean fragrance of dark tobacco, cigars and eau de cologne that permeates everything. I could smell it the instant we got off the plane. ... Strange really, with smoking banned in public buildings.'

Mike's grip on the control knob loosened. He glanced at the dashboard thermometer: it read 29 Celsius; he could feel the perspiration trickling down his back. 'It's very hot,' he said, wondering how Jane, with her milk-white complexion, could look so cool in her Burberry's ensemble of Black Watch tartan slacks and white linen sleeveless blouse.

'You'll just feel even hotter when you get out if you use the air conditioning,' Jane opined as they joined a busy four-lane motorway and headed east for Santanyí. She accelerated to 110 KPH – the maximum stated on the signs – and Mike lowered his window; the roar was deafening. Within minutes, they were crawling behind a badly maintained truck belching out thick blue smoke.

Unable to overtake, thanks to an endless stream of vehicles roaring past them in the outside lane, Jane shouted: 'I think we'd better switch on the air conditioning until we pass this effing idiot!' Insulated from the outside world, the possibility of meaningful conversation returned.

'So, this is Mallorca,' Mike said merrily, scanning a landscape of parched brown fields, drystone walls and pine trees. 'Not bad really. I thought there'd be villa developments and blocks of holiday apartments everywhere.'

'They're at the *coast*, Mikey – along with all the package holidaymakers, lager louts and– *Jesus*! What's wrong with these people? The prat in the BMW behind us is right up our arse! He's indicating, so why doesn't the bugger bloody overtake? It's bloody clear now! Well, if he's not going to–!'

After Jane had successfully passed the truck, and Mike had stopped holding his breath while the BMW flashed past them with its horn blaring and driver gesticulating homicidally, the air conditioning remained on.

'"**NAZIS 'RAUS**",' Jane intoned, reading from a stone wall bordering the motorway. 'That's the third lot of anti-German graffiti I've seen since we left the airport.'

'Yeah. Actually, I'm surprised there wasn't more security in evidence.'

'They probably don't want to frighten the tourists.'

'The plucky British, you mean? There certainly weren't many Germans in evidence, were there? Actually, I heard quite a few French voices.'

'Hmm. I think Daddy was right – the Germans always overreact to everything. They're paranoid. I mean, a few villas and shops are burned down and they get absolutely hysterical. It's not as though anyone's been *killed* – or even seriously injured. The "terrorists" have only attacked *unoccupied* homes – out of season. As for the commercial premises, they were set alight after working hours, weren't they?'

Mike nodded and thought how lucky he was that Jane's father, Sir Douglas Trench-Foot, had not pooh-poohed their trip. Otherwise, instead of driving under the dazzling blue skies of the Mediterranean, they'd now be entombed in the Trench-Foots' 'cottage' in the Derbyshire Dales for the traditional damp summer fortnight of rambles, jigsaws, crosswords and socializing with the snooty neighbours. And then there was the food: Jane's mother, Betty, insisted on cooked breakfasts, three-course lunches, afternoon tea, four- or even five-course dinners, *and* 'supper' – not to mention all those nibbles with the aperitifs! At least he managed to burn off some of the calories with his mountain bike. Still, because Douglas was a diplomat – currently 'our man' in Madrid – Jane didn't get to see her parents as much as she'd like, and the least he could do was to put up with the Derbyshire purgatory once a year. But then, just ten days ago, and completely out of the blue, had come the opportunity to avoid the annual pilgrimage thanks to Werner Stumpf – of all people! He'd apologized for the short notice, saying that at the last minute he'd decided to organize 'a very special party' and would love Mike to come – 'with Jane, naturally' – as a way of thanking him for all his legal assistance over the last year.

As Jane overtook yet another little Citroën van barely making forty kilometres per hour – she gave its aged driver a blast of the horn – Mike said: 'You don't think Werner's paranoid, do you?'

'Silly old coot! It's people like him who cause accidents. I've never seen so many of these Citroën things in all my life – and they're *all* white!'

'Hmm. ... But we're not really in a hurry, are we? I suppose the country folk hereabouts aren't ... a different pace of life.'

'Well, we did promise the Stumpfs we'd make it to their place by lunchtime – one o'clock Werner said – *quite* specific – and it's almost half past already. ... What were you saying about "paranoid"?'

'I–'

'Werner? Oh, bound to be. I told you – all Germans are. Daddy says so, and he should know.'

Jane thought of Derbyshire and the lovely Georgian house built from the local limestone. She could smell the scent of the rambling roses, and pictured her parents playing croquet on the immaculately mown lawns – weather permitting, of course! Her eyes began to feel just a little moist. She hoped Mummy and Daddy weren't too disappointed. She liked tradition as much as they did, but it wasn't every day that Mikey got invited by a client to come and stay – and not any old client, but one of his firm's most prestigious.

*

When Mike phoned his wife to say that Werner Stumpf had invited them to Mallorca, Jane Trench-Foot, as she was still known professionally at the Bar, had just returned to the Temple after a gruelling morning at the Royal Courts of Justice. As the niece of the Head of Chambers, Nicholas Trench-Foot, KC, there was some malicious gossip in legal circles that she'd got a seat there solely by reason of nepotism: after all, they were leaders in the field of patents, trade marks and copyright, and only legal high-flyers were ever considered for admission. But the truth was that Jane had both a first-class brain and a passion for intellectual property, attributes that had soon become evident to Uncle Nicholas during her university vacations, when she was permitted to sit with him in chambers.

Five years ago, when she first met solicitor Michael Oakheart, Jane fell in love at first sight. It was at a legal seminar, and, at twenty-four, she was not only the youngest speaker on the panel but also one of the prettiest women Mike had ever seen. He was three years her senior and a bright assistant with good prospects in a niche firm of London solicitors specializing in intellectual property. Mike always claimed he didn't believe in 'love at first sight', but within a year they were married and, thanks to the generosity of both sets of parents, proud owners of a small mid-Victorian terrace house in Richmond-upon-Thames.

As yet, there were no children, but there was a dog – a three-year-old Dalmatian with the pedigree name 'Marmaduke Orchestra Leader', but who answered to 'Hugo'. He was certainly Mike's dog, albeit Jane was much fonder of him than she cared to admit. Hugo was, in fact, something of a baby-substitute: although Mike worshiped him, he looked forward to the day when Jane would finally announce she was pregnant. Jane, on the other hand, was still arguing – and with some merit – that her career was at a critical phase. In truth, she was not that bothered about babies at all; so far, she'd succeeded in concealing this from Mike. In the meantime, Hugo appeared to give him almost all the outlets he required for his paternal instincts. Luckily, the widow next door, Mrs Babcock, was only too happy to look after the dog: she loved him almost as much as Mike did, and the sentiment appeared to be reciprocated.

Although their respective careers had both developed promisingly, it was clear to Jane that she was well out in front: Mike was a very good lawyer, but at thirty-two he still hadn't been made a partner. He had been told, however, that if he 'played his cards right' and didn't 'blot his copybook', he'd get the long-awaited promotion in a year's time. His problem was that he didn't blow his own trumpet loud enough; he needed a push. So, when Jane got back from court and learned of Werner Stumpf's extraordinary offer, she knew precisely what had to be done. And to be fair to her, this was before Mike had said:

'It's very sweet of you, Footy – being prepared to abandon Derbyshire and everything, but it's a tradition and I wouldn't want to be responsible for breaking it. Anyway, we'd probably never get a flight at such short notice. Mind you, it might have been a bit of a giggle meeting Lionel de Tourny. Apparently, he and his current girlfriend, Jeanne Moineau – remember? – we saw her in that incomprehensible *Three Nuts and a Bolt* – what was it called in French? ... Well, they're going to be at the party. Werner says they're neighbours.'

As Mike rehearsed all the reasons why they should head for the Midlands and not to the Mediterranean, Jane's mind was thinking fast. She could picture Tourny – so pretty – *too* pretty, perhaps – in those recent blockbusters, *Normandie* and *Dreyfus* – Hollywood nonsense, of course, but one couldn't deny that whatever the merits of his looks or acting ability, his face was currently one of the best known on the planet. Socializing with people like that would do wonders for Mike's career. And with a bit of help from her, Mike could even win him as a client – or Moineau; she was fairly well known among more discerning cinemagoers – an icon, of course, in France!

Mike was still bleating on: 'Mallorca's probably not our scene, Footy. And there's that nasty terrorism – the recent attacks by "nationalists" on German homes and businesses–'

'We're going!' snapped Jane. 'We need a change – a complete rest – *both* of us – after all these months of endless toil. We'll never get that in Derbyshire, especially as Julian and Vanessa are coming for the second week with the kids.' Julian was Jane's elder brother. 'I'll square it with Mummy and Daddy. We can visit them in the autumn – in Madrid – for a week – we haven't seen the Official Residence yet. I'll phone now. As long as Daddy says there's no danger in Mallorca – can't be, not with all the package holidaymakers flocking out there. ... You find out about flights on the web, OK? Can one fly scheduled?'

In the event, Sir Douglas said Mallorca was 'as safe as houses' in the Foreign Office's opinion, and that the Germans were 'absolute ninnies' by staying away and causing such needless damage to the island's economy. As for not seeing his daughter and son-in-law, he took on board all that Jane had said about Mike's career. He didn't tell her, however, that he and Betty had been chatting about it over breakfast that very morning: perhaps they'd been right all along – that she'd married 'a bit of a dud'; anything that might usefully push the lad's career forward should be welcomed.

'Just stay clear of branches of Deutsche Bank!' he'd joked at the end of their conversation. 'And watch out for Stumpf. I remember that when I was Deputy Head of Mission in Berlin, he'd a bit of a reputation – with young girls – the younger the better, if you catch my drift. And all those recent 'revisionist' biographies of his – well, seems the chap's getting somewhat right-wing in his old age. Of course, Michael will know all about that, I suppose – what with the court case.'

*

The motorway, which bypassed Llucmajor – Jane thought the church might be worth visiting later in the week – fizzled out at Campos. The intricacies of its ring road were successfully negotiated, and the Oakhearts were swiftly back in open countryside. Now, thirty kilometres from the airport, the traffic on the Santanyí highway had thinned considerably. Ahead, an almost empty road began to rise towards distant wooded hills. Mike noticed that their average speed was slowly but surely diminishing; perhaps Jane was beginning to relax at last.

'Try and phone Werner again,' she suggested. 'How much further is it?'

Mike looked at the maps and the extraordinarily detailed instructions emailed to them a few days ago by their host. 'Um ... eight kilometres – about five miles – to Santanyí, and the same again to Alqueria Blanca. I'll try phoning, but it seems pointless – I just keep getting one of those bloody phone-company answering machines – in Spanish. It's strange – no answer at all since we landed at Palma. I wonder where they can be.'

A few minute later, having reached a high plateau of olive groves amidst dark red earth, Mike put the mobile back in his breast pocket. 'Same bloody female robot prattling away! I hope we've got the right day.'

Clearly not listening, Jane asked: 'You don't think Werner's some kind of fascist, do you, Mikey? I mean,' she added swiftly, 'I was just thinking of something Daddy said. He didn't strike me like that – when he came over to meet you a year or so ago and took us both out to dinner. He seemed positively urbane – cosmopolitan – very broad-minded ... quite the Renaissance man.'

'Hmm? ... Yes ... *very* broad-minded.' Mike yawned; he was shattered. They'd been up since dawn to get to Gatwick and had had to walk for miles along the seemingly endless marble corridors of Palma Airport to find their luggage. And the interminable bureaucracy to procure the car hadn't helped. Nor, for that matter, had the double gin and tonic on the plane. Sometimes he wondered where Jane found all the energy.

'Right-wing? ... No, Werner's just patriotic ... proud to be German. I think he feels that the country had a kind of collective nervous breakdown starting in 1918. They began to get over it sometime after 1945. Now they're cured. That aberration can't negate the greatness of a people who've given us Goethe, Schiller, Beethoven – some of the world's greatest painters, physicists, architects, engineers, inventors. He believes that since the War the world has forgotten this, and that the Germans are themselves primarily to blame – because they fear that singing their own praises will be regarded as neo-Nazism. ... Which, of course, is exactly what happened to *him*. Hence the case against Piston-Jones and *The Times* and–'

Mike broke off. 'That sign said something like "Welcome to Santanyí". Now we have to follow signs for Cala d'Or.'

'We *must* come and visit the church here,' Jane fizzed. 'The guidebooks say it has the most magnificent Baroque organ screen. Maybe they have recitals. ... Stumpf's bound to know.'

'Hmm.'

'And there's the monastery of San Salvador near this Fela-thingy place–'

'Felanitx'

'–and a little nunnery at Alqueria Blanca. They *all* sound *very* interesting.'

'Hmmmm.' Mike could picture the two of them trudging from one historic monument to another, like mad dogs and Englishmen out in the midday sun.

'By the way, what happened to Piston-Jones? Did the damages bankrupt him in the end?'

Mike was trying to focus on Stumpf's directions. 'Hmm? ... Still holds the Microsoft Chair of Modern History at Oxford. No, *The Times* coughed up on his behalf – after all, *they* published his review of the Rommel biography.'

'The one in which he called Werner "a crypto-Nazi"?'

'And "a fascist sympathizer", "an apologist of the Third Reich", "an amateur historian" – the list of pejorative epithets was almost endless. And, of course, he photocopied and emailed great chunks of *Rommel: A German Hero* to all his academic cronies around the world to drum up support for his anti-Stumpf vendetta. Hence the copyright infringement claim, albeit the libel aspect was the core of the action.'

'But the jury only awarded Werner damages of a hundred thousand pounds?'

'A hundred and *twenty-five* thousand, plus costs – twice that amount. Yes, the damages were a bit disappointing, but I suppose the jury were swayed by the defendants' arguments that Werner didn't have much of a reputation in England to be damaged.'

'Or maybe they just didn't like Germans.'

'Possibly.'

'I wonder what his wife's like – Heidi.' Jane chuckled. 'Sorry! I can't say that name without thinking of long golden plaited hair and cowbells.'

'I wonder. He hardly ever mentions her. I gather she's younger. I think she's his second or third wife.'

'Ah, Daddy said he liked them young. She'll probably look like Claudia Schiffer, aged twenty-something – if you've ever seen pictures of her in the 1990s – and have a brain the size of a pea.'

'Don't be rotten!'

Ahead of them, bare limestone crags rising above steep wooded slopes stood out white against the cloudless sky. At their base, a massive church in a severe classical style almost overwhelmed the village of Alqueria Blanca clustered around it. Jane looked ecstatic.

'Oh, how *lovely*!' she cried. 'One would think one were in Tuscany. We *must* visit this church too.'

Five minutes later, and having taken the first turning to the left after the church and followed the signs to Ca's Concos, Stumpf's meticulous directions had brought the Oakhearts to a narrow dirt track that led from the tarmac road and disappeared into the pine-clad hills. On a post protruding from a stone wall was a rustic sign: in Gothic script, it bore the name 𝕮𝖆'𝖓 𝕻𝖆𝖚.

Mike leaned over and gave his wife a kiss. 'There you are – *Ca'n Pau*! So, who's a clever boy then? Got you here without getting lost once.'

Jane grinned impishly. 'And I got you here safely without a single bump or scratch, notwithstanding all those awful Spanish drivers. Anyway, with such detailed instructions, you'd have to be an idiot *not* to find your way here!'

'Charming!'

They kissed again, and then Jane lowered her window and finally extinguished the air conditioning. It was like opening an oven door.

'Oh, just smell that pine resin and rosemary!' she enthused as the car began to bump up the track, a dense cloud of dust trailing behind.

After ten minutes of driving through thick pine woods with just the occasional break affording panoramas of scorched pastureland and olive groves sweeping down to the distant aquamarine of the Mediterranean, the Oakhearts concluded they were lost; they must have missed a turning somewhere. Apprehensively, they passed a dilapidated farmhouse with chained, barking guard dogs and refuse in the courtyard. A few hundred metres further on there was talk of turning back. Then, suddenly, they came upon what looked like a medieval gatehouse, complete with a pointed arch and an effigy of the Virgin in a recessed niche. One of the ancient double doors was open; the other bore another Ca'n Pau sign in the same Gothic script.

Jane gasped. 'Good Lord! It's a bloody castle!'

After a moment, Mike said: 'Maybe there are two *Ca'n Paus*.'

They got out of the car, rang the old bell at the side of the arch, and entered. Beyond, shaded by tall palms, was a cool courtyard paved with pebbles; a simple fountain tinkled at its centre. Around all four sides were low two-storey stone buildings; they reminded Jane of Derbyshire and Pennine farms, except that the walls were ablaze with the most stunning bougainvillea she'd ever seen – pink, white, scarlet, purple – even orange.

'Well, it may not be a castle,' she said, 'but it certainly looks like paradise to me.'

'Christ, he must be bloody loaded! We're in the wrong profession, Footy.'

The stillness was broken by the sound of feet clattering across a hard surface. Almost immediately, a woman in her mid-forties shot out of an arched doorway to their right and bounded towards them, smiling broadly. Clad in salmon-pink culottes and a lemon-yellow T-shirt, she was of medium height with curly shoulder-length golden hair framing a kind round face.

'Hello! Hello! Hel-*lo*! *Willkomm* to the *Ca'n Pau* – the House of Peace. I am Heidi, the woman of Werner. You are Michael and Jane, yes?'

After Heidi had kissed them on each cheek, Jane said: 'What a beautiful house, Heidi, and such lovely countryside! We'd no idea Mallorca was like this.'

'Thank you! It is being just a farmhouse, and ... Oh, please excuse my English. It is not often that I speaks–'

'It's excellent!' said Jane.

'Better than our German! And do call me "Mike".'

'You are both so kind. ... Yes, I am saying it is an old farm, but Werner is doing so much to make it nice during many years.'

The Oakhearts wondered where Werner might be.

'We are so sorry we are a bit late' – Mike was talking louder and slower than usual – 'but the plane was delayed, and it took *ages* for the luggage to turn up and ... We did try to phone you – *several* times – to let you know, but–'

Looking embarrassed, Heidi raised her hands apologetically. 'I heard the phone, but Werner ... er ... he is not wanting the phone to be answered in the day – not between – you say "between"?' – the Oakhearts nodded – '... between nine in the morning and six in the evening. All our friends are knowing this. You see, we work in the garden all the day and must not be going in the house and out all the times to the phone. And the handies, er ... *mobiles*?' – she slit her throat with a finger – '... *verboten*!'

'And Werner is well?' asked Mike, winking at Jane.

'"Well"? ... *Ja, ja*! He is in the sleeping room. He was going for the siesta. In *Sommer* he always has the siesta between *halb drei*–'

'Half past two,' Jane assisted.

'Yes. We say "half way to three". ... So now he goes for it until half ... four. *Always*! But I think he is still awake. I get him.'

The word 'lunch' was beginning to loom very large in the thoughts of both Mike and Jane as they cried, 'No, no, no!', but Heidi was already trotting back to the front door.

'Come! We find your bags soon and put you all in the room. And you must drink – and eat a little.' The Oakhearts exchanged anxious glances. 'Werner and me are eating at the one o'clock, but I have bread and cheese and olives and the pig flesh for you.'

As they reached the front door, a plump woman with wrinkled olive skin and grey hair in a bun suddenly stepped out. Dressed in the traditional black of a widow, she looked prematurely middle-aged.

'Good Lord!' cried Jane, gripping Mike's arm. Immediately, she felt foolish and let go.

'*Me voy*,' the woman grunted to Heidi, without any acknowledgement of the visitors' existence. '*He terminado.*'

Heidi said something in Spanish and then turned to the Oakhearts. 'This is Margalida, the ... the ... She washes. Now she is washed up and evacuates for her *siesta*. Margalida, *nuestros invitados*, Señor Michael and Señora Jane.'

'Hello!' boomed Mike, holding out his hand.

'*Hola*!' chirped Jane.

'*Encantada*,' grunted Margalida, looking at her feet.

After Margalida had shuffled across the courtyard, Heidi said: 'She is working here for *years*. ... Werner likes her much. Her son, Mateu, works in the garden some days. I like *him*. They are living near us. Her man is dead long time.'

'Ah,' said the Oakhearts nodding.

'She looked a little ... sad,' added Jane sympathetically.

'Yes. She is not happy because always she evacuates at the one o'clock, but today she stays to finish the painting.'

They were now standing in a cool entrance hall that rose the full height of the building – to the very apex of the roof, with its bare rafters and stone tiles. It had once been the old farmhouse's living room, where animals and their owners had coexisted. Now it was incongruously paved with the same shiny, slippery marble that caused so many accidents at Palma Airport. Around three sides, a staircase curved grandly upwards to the first floor and a balcony-type landing. Although there were only a few items of antique rustic furniture, vast unframed canvases hung on the walls, each one painted in just one uniform pastel shade. There was indeed a smell of paint, and Mike wondered whether the uncommunicative Margalida had just painted them.

Immediately opposite the entrance was a large stone fireplace, and above it hung a crucifix bearing a most lifelike representation of Our Lord, complete with dripping blood. Jane was transfixed. 'Golly!' she finally managed. 'I should think you could roast an ox there!'

Heidi smiled, clearly not understanding. 'Yes, I am sorry about the paint fuming, but Werner is in your room this morning to see all is good, and there the spots on the wall are, and he is saying that he tells me to paint it many weeks past, but I am not ... remember? ... to remember. It is the old white paint of the island. ... Only Margalida knows how to make it.'

'Whitewash?' suggested Mike.

Heidi smiled. 'Yes, I think you are right. I say, "Werner, it can wait," but he is saying the room must be *perfect*. And then he finds other spots around the house. So now you have the smell and Margalida is not happy. All the windows are open and–'

'Michael, my boy! Jane!' All faces shot upwards to the landing where a bronzed Werner Stumpf, clad only in a pair of skimpy beach shorts, stood behind intricate wrought iron railings; for a man in his late fifties, his body was in superb shape. 'I was beginning to think the nation of Drake, Raleigh and Cook had lost their map-reading skills!' Within seconds, he'd bounded down the stairs and was hugging the Oakhearts, each of them receiving three kisses on their cheeks.

'There was a delay due to French Air Traffic Control,' Mike began, 'and–'

'*Ja, ja*! Wonderful that you could make it! W*on*derful! We can have a jolly good natter later ... *after* the siesta. And your parents are well, Jane – Sir Douglas and the Lady Betty?'

Mike tried not to laugh: 'the Lady Betty' sounded like a pleasure steamer. *But how come he never asks after my parents? Or are a bank manager and a housewife in Cardiff not important enough?*

'Very well, thanks. They're–'

'*Ja, ja*! I was just thinking – a few minutes ago upstairs – that if they were at a loose end, they could fly over from Madrid and stay too.' Heidi's mouth fell open. 'I'm sure they'd enjoy the party.'

'I'm afraid they're at our place in Derbyshire at the moment.'

'*Schade*! ... Derbyshire! I had a girlfriend from there. The Honourable Molly Bandy-Coutts. Do you know Crich Castle? – Lord and Lady Bandy-Coutts?'

'Er ... no. ... I must say, I can't wait to meet Lionel de Tourny and–'

'*Ja, ja*! ... Mike! Jane! You've met my lovely wife, Heidi?'

'Yes, she–'

There was a curt exchange of German between the hosts and the last vestiges of Heidi's smile dissipated.

'So! Heidi will show you your allocated space in the guest parking area on the other side of the *camino* – the lane – and then help you bring your luggage in.'

'No, no!' protested Mike, 'I can–'

'*Ja, ja*, Mike! She loves to help!' Maintaining his smile, Werner paused. 'I understand Heidi has told you that there is a *faint* fragrance of whitewash in your room. Now, you are not to worry because I only allow non-toxic paints made from natural materials in my house, just as the peasants here have made them for generations. You have nothing to fear, OK?' Without waiting for a response, he added: 'While you settle in, Heidi will lay a lunch for you of organic local produce on the terrace. We ate at *one*, as we *always* do. Then Heidi must join me for her siesta. She needs her rest. So! Now I ascend to my quarters. I will see you later. We *always* return to work at half past four.'

As Werner bounded past the hall table he tutted and snatched up a stapled booklet. 'Jesus! I nearly forgot.' He retraced his steps and proffered the document to Mike. It was headed: '**CA'N PAU – RULES OF THE HOUSE**'. Mike's eyes bulged.

'Just a few helpful tips, dear friends,' Werner explained grinning. 'You'll find life here a bit different to Richmond-upon-Thames! Hah! I've made a special translation for you. If you have any questions, I'll be only too happy to answer them – *later*.'

After Werner had disappeared from the upper landing, Heidi's smile returned. 'He works *very* hard,' she said, as if by way of an apology. 'And he is not a young man now.' The Oakhearts nodded with forced smiles. 'Come! I show you the car *Platz*, get your baggages, take you to the sleep room, and then you eat. You must be ravished – that's right? – "ravished"?'

CHAPTER 2

Hours earlier that Sunday, off the coast a few miles to the south of *Ca'n Pau*, Jaume's old wooden fishing boat rocked gently as the sun rose over a calm Mediterranean. He took four cans of San Miguel from the cool box and passed one to each of his three subordinates. Tutting, he noticed that they'd already devoured most of the bread and cheese. Oh well, to be fair, they *had* swum over from their own little boats, which, to minimize suspicion, as ordered, lay at anchor some distance away. Their exertions must have given them quite an appetite. Still, a bit of deference might have been expected: after all, he was the Supreme Commander of ENABA, the *Exèrcit Nacionalista de Balears* – the Balearic Nationalist Army.

'You like Ca's Concos cheese then?' he muttered, snatching the remaining bite-size piece. His sarcasm fell on deaf ears.

'Best cheese in all Mallorca!' crowed Antoni.

'All the best food comes from around here,' added Vicenç, '– cheese, bread, olives, *sobrasada* – and wine.'

Ricart, the other covert Sunday-morning fisherman, nodded as he crammed a thick slice of the chewy wholemeal bread in his mouth.

Jaume smiled condescendingly: Mallorca's south-east corner deserved its parochial reputation; by all accounts, Antoni's grandmother still hadn't set foot in Palma – a mere fifty kilometres away as the crow flies – and she was by no means exceptional for her generation in this neck of the woods. But then, it had been one of the last outposts to fall to the invaders. Jaume scanned the coast; it lay some two kilometres to the north, with its hinterland of wooded slopes rising towards distant jagged hills. He could remember fishing in these waters thirty years ago with his father when those hillsides were almost virgin. Now, you could make out hundreds of little white and brown dots, each one representing yet another foreigner's 'dream home'. Sometimes he prayed for an earthquake.

'Have any of you seen a patrol boat around recently?' asked Jaume as he turned and looked out to sea.

Antoni and Vicenç shook their heads.

'I saw one of the Customs' launches from Palma churning up the water a few days ago,' said Ricart, '– on the lookout for drug smugglers as usual. The *Aduana* should stick to the Straits of Gibraltar and the Costa del Sol.

That's where all the stuff from Morocco comes in – and them illegal immigrants.'

'Moroccans!' snorted Vicenç through a mouthful of cheese and bread. 'I almost miss them. Not exactly the fastest workers, but they did what they were told – respectful even. And being Africans an' all, they were used to the sun. OK, some of them might have had a couple of beers on the sly now and then, but being Muslims, you never saw them in the bars, or getting drunk and being a bleeding nuisance – not like them peasants from God-only-knows-where in the East. We should never have let them join the EU – Romania, Bulgaria ... and all them places.'

Ricart drained his beer can and slammed it down on the deck. 'Too true! The other day I had some Slovaks ... Slovenians? ... whatever – picking the aubergines on my smallholding up in S'Horta, right? Hardly a word of Spanish – let alone Catalan or *Mallorquí* – among the lot of 'em! Of course, they're so fucking poor they'll do the jobs no local would ever touch – or Mainlander come to that – and for peanuts, but Vicenç is spot on. They're nothing but trouble. They nick everything. I've even seen 'em flogging fruit and veg in the markets round here. And they drink like fish. And they're always quoting European laws and stuff at you – "minimum wages", "maximum hours" – communists the lot of 'em!'

'Well,' said Antoni, 'they *were* bleeding communists until recently, weren't they? ... If you ask me, they don't get enough to eat back home – anaemic probably. They're so *pale* when they get here – worse than the tourists!'

Jaume glanced at his watch: it was just after seven; time to make progress. It would take almost an hour to chug back along the coast to Colònia de Sant Jordi and his little holiday home. And he'd promised his wife to return in time for breakfast with her and the kids. 'Don't worry, *chicos*,' he said, attempting a smile, 'when we get independence, we'll be able to pick and choose who comes to work and live on *our* island – and the other Balearics. It'll be like old times again, and the Moroccans can return to do the dirty work on six-month visas. And when their time's up, we'll ship 'em back. You won't have hordes of drunken Romanians and Bulgarians hanging around when they've outstayed their welcome, demanding their EU "rights" – social security, healthcare, free housing – *and* education for all their brats – *and* with lessons in their own God-awful languages!'

The cheers seemed very loud on this windless morning, and the three culprits scanned the surrounding waters with guilty expressions.

'Well then,' said Jaume, '– down to business. I call this meeting of the South-East Division to order. First, I want your district reports. We'll start with you, Vicenç.'

As Felanitx was the largest town in the area, Vicenç felt more important than his two colleagues, Antoni and Ricart, who commanded the Campos and Santanyí districts respectively. But, as an inland town of little historical or architectural interest, it had barely been touched by tourism or foreign immigration until fairly recently, and even then, the scale had been relatively modest. Santanyí, on the other hand, as Ricart was prone to remind everyone, had one of the highest per capita incomes of any municipality in Spain – if not the entire EU. This extraordinary statistic, however, was solely due to its status as a Mecca for foreign millionaires, the majority German. The reason for its magnetic attraction still bemused the locals, for whom Santanyí's church and market square looked much like many others on the island – as indeed they did. And although the surrounding countryside was undulatingly pretty, it was not as scenically dramatic as Mallorca's mountainous west and north. But it had only taken one or two German plutocrats to build impressive retreats in the vicinity for a flock to follow.

At twenty-nine, Antoni was a few years younger than his fellow district commanders, which contributed to his feelings of inferiority, for Campos was the smallest of the Division's districts; nor did it possess anything like the wealth of neighbouring Santanyí. On the other hand, some of the island's least-developed coastline fell within his bailiwick, and in order to boost his morale, Jaume had once told him that if the worst came to the worst and the Mainlanders resisted the overthrow of their illegal yoke, a seaborne invasion would, in all probability, take place on Antoni's beaches. During World War II, fearful of the British, Franco had had pillboxes built all along them; luckily for Antoni, many were still intact. Apart from Antoni, however, no one in ENABA seriously believed that Madrid would ever risk anything like a D-Day style landing on the beaches of Es Trenc, or, for that matter, on any of the other long, gently shelving beaches of the Campos district.

'So, that's about it,' said Vicenç as he brought his brief report to a close. 'We've stolen another load of explosives and detonators from the quarry on the Portocolom road, the windows of the Felanitx Goethe-Institut have been smashed again, and F62 has had the health inspectors sent in for the fourth week in a row to that bloody Kraut restaurant in Ca's Concos, Potsdam. He leaked the visits to all the papers – rats, cockroaches – the lot. I don't think many foreigners will be patronizing Potsdam this summer!' With a somewhat effeminate giggle, Vicenç patted his bulging stomach.

But the others looked unamused.

'F62's you brother-in-law – the mayor, Bernardi Pons, isn't he?' asked Ricart, who, like Vicenç and so many other Mallorcan men, sported a full black beard.

Before Vicenç could reply, Jaume snapped: 'That's none of your damned business, Ricart. You know the rules.'

ENABA operated on a 'need-to-know' basis through small ring-fenced local cells. That, at least, was the theory. Mallorca, however, was not such a big island, and the problems of security were exacerbated by the intimacy between ENABA and its political wing, PANABA, the *Partit Nacionalista de Balears* – the Balearic Nationalist Party.

It was Antoni's turn to deliver his report. Unlike Vicenç and Ricart, he'd benefited from tertiary education, studying electrical engineering at a Palma technical college. In consequence, he felt he was more on Jaume's intellectual level; currently, he was a telephone engineer with *Telefónica*'s maintenance subcontractor. But there was a far deeper bond between Antoni and Jaume: they were both fair-haired and blue-eyed, and, therefore, in accordance with ancient myth, believed themselves to be true and pure descendants of the people who'd inhabited the island long before even the Arab invasion at the beginning of the tenth century. Antoni and Jaume were also clean-shaven; in truth, they looked just a little German.

'We're not much into *economic* warfare and window smashing in Campos,' Antoni scoffed. 'As I understand it, our mission is to support our "democratic" friends by using *violent* means to do what so many people on this island want and what PANABA can't yet lawfully do – get the foreigners – Mainlanders, Easterners, English, Germans – especially *Germans* – off our homeland. We have to make it so unpleasant for the bastards that they just can't wait to leave – and to dissuade others from coming. That's right, isn't it, Jaume?'

Jaume nodded. 'Absolutely.'

'I'm sure me and Ricart don't need a lesson in–'

'Let him finish, Vicenç,' ordered Jaume.

'Well,' Antoni continued smugly, 'we all know that whenever we torch another German villa or branch of Deutsche Bank, everyone down at the local bar is over the moon. It's the one thing that unites the people, whether they're socialists, capitalists, communists – whatever.'

'I know why he's rabbiting on like this,' Vicenç sniggered, '– he's got nothing to report from bloody Campos!'

'I have too! You don't read the papers, mate – or follow social media. That German *hotel rural* halfway between Campos and Es Trenc, yeah? A few weeks back we poisoned all their sheep and goats. Last week we finished off their two *burros* and the chickens. Three nights ago, their pet dogs got shot. They've had enough! They're selling up! This builder I know in Campos has already bought the place – got it dirt cheap.'

'Good riddance!' snarled Vicenç.

'*Very* dramatic,' Ricart scoffed, '– very *violent*. I bet that makes all the papers in Germany.'

'Everything counts, Ricart,' Jaume said. 'I know for a fact that Antoni and his lads took quite a few risks crawling around that hotel. The Germans had alarms, barbed wire, floodlights. And don't forget, most foreigners are much more affected by violence to animals than to property. Some – like the English – find it more distressing than violence to people.' Heads shook in disbelief. 'Anyhow, I think that what Antoni is trying to say, Vicenç, is that the more violent we are, the better are our chances – PANABA's chances – of ultimate victory. OK? ... Your report, Ricart.'

The news from the Santanyí District was impressive: no less than three German estate agents had seen their premises torched in the last fortnight and were shutting up for good. A prestigious German jeweller in the package-tourist resort of Cala d'Or had suffered the same fate, albeit the blaze had also set fire to a neighbouring bar owned by a Mallorcan. He'd get some kind of compensation; if he wanted to extend his premises and take over the German's lease, his planning application would be rubber-stamped, notwithstanding the official ban on new bars in the town.

Ricart, however, wound up with a note of concern. 'There's quite a bit of grumbling on my patch, boss, about what we're doing to the tourist trade. It's a lot of folk's bread and butter, and the promise of jam tomorrow is not much cop. They've got bills to pay and kids to feed and clothe. Even though the English are still here, the loss of most of the German market has been a bitter–'

'There's no satisfying some people, is there?' groaned Vicenç. 'They spend most of their lives whingeing about the Germans and the destruction that mass-market tourism has caused, and then when we begin to do something about it, they start moaning about their bloody bank balances! We need *quality* tourism – *fewer* foreigners – preferably not Germans – spending a damned sight more per head than the riff-raff we mostly get now. ... You know, we've got great plans for some *very* exclusive hotels in Felanitx – for real toffs – by converting a few of them big old merchants' houses near the church. Then you can demolish those concrete egg boxes that clutter the cliffs an 'all at Cala d'Or and the like.' Sighing, he added: 'I can remember when you could go down to the *calas* – in the height of summer, mind you – and have the whole place to yourself. There was bloody nothing and–'

'The transition to the new economy and society will not be easy, Vicenç,' Jaume interjected. 'Ricart is right to remind us of the problems our people are experiencing now. We have to know how to deal with that. Many of our junior troops are waiters and waitresses, barman, hotel staff.

They're rightly worried about their jobs. We can't just dismiss their concerns for the future. But people will put up with hardship if they believe it's *temporary*, and that it's necessary to destroy an evil that threatens us all *equally*. Hence the need to identify with a common enemy.'

'The Germans!' snapped Antoni.

'Precisely. And what do young people complain about most?'

'Their parents and hard work,' retorted Vicenç.

Antoni groaned. 'Christ! You're only five years older than me, but you're *so* out of touch. The cost of housing, of course, you prat – the cost of *everything* on this island!'

Jaume was nodding. 'Correct. And we have to remind everyone – like our PANABA comrades do – of the reason. Basically, there are too many people on Mallorca, OK? The German invaders have priced us out of our own homes. And before the foreigners overdeveloped our coastline, we produced almost all the basic foods we needed. Now we have to import from the Peninsula, and that's expensive.'

'So, the Germans are the cause of *all* the inflation,' said Ricart quoting the party line.

'They're the cause of *most* of our problems. That's the simple message for simple people to understand.'

Vicenç was shaking his head. 'I'm still not sure why we're not picking on the English – I mean, there are thousands of them living on Mallorca as well. In fact, they were here long before the Germans.'

Ricart and Antoni looked at each other and rolled their eyes.

'You know the policy,' Jaume answered. 'The English are not to be harmed if at all possible – or any other foreigners. And that goes for Mainlanders too ... for the time being. Otherwise, there'll be confused signals – a dilution of the hatred – and our resources will be spread too thinly. Anyway, we don't want to *destroy* the tourist industry – or suffer an economic catastrophe, with an exodus of the entire foreign population of sixty thousand. And, Vicenç, our people don't hate any foreigners as much as they hate the Germans. In fact, my friends, for all sorts of reasons nobody in the world really likes the Germans. And don't forget – in order to get our independence and to renegotiate our relationship with Europe, we'll need *international* support. And that means getting important nations on our side and exploiting rifts in the EU. Germany and France are at odds over a whole raft of issues – like ... well ... *everything* really, except trashing Poland, Hungary–'

'You're absolutely right,' said Antoni sagely, albeit his knowledge of international affairs was equally limited.

Jaume looked at his watch and frowned. 'OK, we have to wrap this up. Since stepping up the action in the spring, everything has begun to fall into place. For a start, Madrid has shown the first signs of overreacting – threatening to send reinforcements of mainland troops and to outlaw PANABA – just like it did with some of the Basque parties and the Catalans. And that dickhead Azucena – 'our' prime minister – in Madrid has started to lecture us like naughty kids. "How can those unsophisticated islanders out in the Mediterranean imagine they could govern themselves and go it alone in this big nasty world? They have to be protected from their own foolishness." So now he's insulting our intelligence. And then there are the Germans themselves. As predicted, they're beginning to fight back. Look at the formation of that new party, the "Deutsche Mallorca Bund", by that fascist lunatic, Baron von ... von–'

'Haber-Bosch,' Antoni assisted, '– Wilhelm von Haber-Bosch.'

'That's the one. We've reason to believe that he and his "DMB" followers were behind the petrol bomb attack on PANABA's Magaluf offices last Thursday.'

Vicenç looked doubtful. 'I suspect Madrid myself. Their dirty tricks people are all over the island, just like they were in the Basque country.'

Jaume shook his head. 'I wouldn't worry about them – our friends in the *Guardia Civil* have got them under constant surveillance. ... Well, as I was saying, with German reprisals our people will hate them even more. And the German government will start kicking up an even bigger fuss, egging Madrid on to crack down harder and harder – making this island into a police state – road blocks, identity cards checked on every street corner – the lot! Eventually, Madrid and the Mainlanders will get so fed up with the mess here, they'll be only too happy to wash their hands of us and give us our birthright – independence. Then it's out of the European so-called Union and goodbye to high taxes to subsidize peasant economies in the East, uncontrolled immigration and overpopulation, arrogant Germans treating *us* like peasants – and their disgusting anything-goes, libertine morality – *queers* – *transvestites*! –'

Jaume's clenched fist had crushed Ricart's empty beer can. The subordinates stared in embarrassment at its remains.

'Well,' Jaume hissed, 'no pinko, gay anti-Christs in Brussels are going to tell *us* that we can't ban pornographic filth. We'll have Catholic values back. Franco was right about something ... *many* things.'

'I heard a rumour the other day,' whispered Vicenç, 'that the Bishop of Palma is gay and lives with his boyfriend.'

Jaume appeared not to hear. 'Look, High Command has decided that it's time to step up the action and move on to "Phase 3". Things are going better than we'd expected, and now that it's July and we're at the height of the holiday season – even the Mainlanders' "king" is here at that sodding

Marivent "summer palace" lording it over us – Madrid and Azucena are at their most vulnerable. So, it's time to do something *really* big, something that will not only make the international community sit up and take notice of us, but, hopefully, will also cause that git Azucena to make a fatal mistake.' Jaume paused for dramatic effect. 'This is absolutely top secret. ... We're planning to assassinate Jordi Adrover and pin the blame on Madrid's agents. The island will erupt, lads.'

There was a stunned silence.

'But, Jaume,' Vicenç finally croaked, 'Adrover's one of *us*. He virtually created PANABA. Damn it – he's the head of the Balearic Government! Without him, the coalition would probably collapse!'

'No, Jaume's right,' said Ricart coldly. 'If the people think Madrid did it, there'll be rioting in the streets. Every symbol of Madrid's hated rule will be attacked.'

'And then we can exploit the disorder,' added Antoni, 'when they try to impose direct rule.'

Jaume was nodding vigorously. 'Anyway, we've discovered that Adrover's maternal great-grandmother was Jewish.' Ricart gasped. 'Oh, it was cleverly concealed, but sooner or later the truth would almost certainly have got out, and then we'd *all* have had egg on our faces.'

'I've got a cousin who married a Jewish bloke,' Antoni said, '– a rich jeweller in Palma. ... Well, he had a Jewish ancestor. Nice chap but my family disowned her. Personally, I couldn't see what all the fuss was about.'

'So,' Jaume continued after a brief silence, 'how do we exploit the disorder? Azucena has his sights on being elected the first "President of Europe" next year – what a joke! The Jewish-controlled media will never support a German candidate – so that's Chancellor Klipper out of the running. That Italian's too right wing. And the candidates from the little countries and the East are a joke. Which only leaves the French as the other serious contender.'

'Now, as Klipper won't stomach the idea of a French president bossing him about, he might well support Azucena – that is, if he does Klipper's bidding to protect his fellow Germans in the event of a *real* crisis here. Well, High Command have various anti-German stunts planned for the coming weeks, but I want to know if you guys can think of any opportunities in your districts to make the shit spectacularly hit the fan. I should add that although our policy has been to cause only economic damage so far, the gloves are now well and truly off.'

'How do mean exactly?' asked Vicenç frowning.

'He means we can *liquidate*,' said Ricart with a broad grin, '– at last!'

'Oh!' Antoni was not smiling: up until now, ENABA had all been a bit of a lark – like his days in the Boy Scouts.

'We have to be *very* careful,' Jaume warned. 'We don't want the sort of terrorism that provokes such a degree of outrage that we permanently alienate international support – mass carnage at the airport – that kind of thing. So, I'm thinking of a relatively small number of casualties – but *significant* ones – quality rather than quantity.'

The sun was rising rapidly, and with it the temperature. Vicenç wiped his brow with the back of a hand. 'I'm not sure I'm following you, boss.'

'Do you mean "significant" in a German sense, Jaume?' asked Ricart.

'That would be the ideal scenario – yes. If we could eliminate some German icon – a hero – a popular figure – a star ... someone whose violent demise would provoke outrage in Germany and cause the media there to howl for blood and revenge ... that kind of thing.'

'I don't think we've got anyone like that in Campos,' Antoni said gravely.

Vicenç was shaking his head. 'Nope, can't say any names spring to my mind either.'

Everyone was looking at Ricart; he was rubbing his chin and staring across the water towards his own little boat bobbing at anchor.

'Come on, Ricart,' Vicenç sneered, clearly anxious to pass the buck. 'You're always telling us about the Kraut millionaires that make up half the population of Santanyí. You must be able to bump off at least one!'

'Shut it, Vicenç!' snapped Ricart. 'You're speaking through your fucking arsehole as usual. Weren't you listening to Jaume? The target has to be a kind of German folk hero – not just fucking rich. I–'

There was a tremendous crack as Ricart slapped his bare knees with the palms of his hands. 'Got it!' he cried. 'Stumpf!'

'Got what?' asked Antoni nervously, peering at his colleague's knees for signs of a squashed insect.

'Who or what the hell is "Stumpf"?' queried a bewildered Vicenç.

'Hmm,' murmured Jaume, 'that name rings a bell. You've mentioned him before, haven't you?'

Ricart smiled. 'Sure have! Werner Stumpf – the uncrowned king of the Santanyí German colony – at least, that's what he'd like to be. One of my best agents is pretty close to him. Stumpf used to be a top journalist – war correspondent in the Middle East, interviews with all the big noises – Arafat, Saddam Hussein ... er ... Anyway, he retired about ten years ago and bought this ruin of a *finca* near Alqueria Blanca – got it for next to nothing. He's slowly tarted it up, and now it's worth *millions*.'

'Typical!' snarled Vicenç.

'Sounds a bit of a has-been to me,' said Antoni.

'Well, that's where you're wrong, *chico*,' Ricart retorted. 'Now he writes books, see, about famous Germans.'

'Oh yes,' said Jaume nodding. 'Now I remember – historical biographies and stuff.'

'You got it, boss.'

'I've read about him in the papers. He's sort of rehabilitated spectres from Germany's past, dusted them down and put them back on their pedestals – Bismarck, the Kaiser, generals from both World Wars.'

Vicenç and Antoni were none the wiser.

Jaume sighed. 'Yes, he's a good candidate, Ricart, but do you think that *his* death would really inflame the Germans?'

'Maybe not on his own, but I know from my agent's latest report that it's Stumpf's birthday next week and he's having this right posh do at his house. There'll be half a dozen guests or so, and from what I understood, they're exactly what you're looking for. There's some Nobel Prize winner – this old professor geezer. ... I think he invented a cure for some disease – my agent will know if you want me to find out. Oh yes, and there's this conductor – of an orchestra – or an opera – who's dead famous in Germany. And that German clothes designer ponce – you know, the one that does all them expensive underpants and things. And Lionel de Tourny.'

Antoni gasped. 'Lionel de Tourny? The movie star? Jesus!'

'Who?' asked Vicenç.

Over the groans, Jaume said: 'Shit! He's *French*, not German. That throws a spanner in the works.'

Ricart looked incredulous. 'French? Are you sure, boss? His villa's on "Hamburg Hill" – just round the corner from Stumpf's place. Everyone's a Kraut millionaire on "Hamburg Hill".'

There was no doubt in Jaume's mind, however, as to Tourny's nationality.

Clutching at straws, Ricart said: 'Maybe Tourny *has* been invited, but isn't going. I'll check with my agent and ...' But by the look on his face, Ricart had clearly hit another snag.

'Now what?' sighed Jaume.

'Sorry, boss, but I've just remembered the other guests – a young English couple. The woman's the daughter of the British ambassador in Madrid ... no idea who her husband is.'

'Oh well,' said Vicenç pompously, 'we can't go upsetting the bloody Brits or the Frogs, can we?'

After a few moments' silence, Jaume said: 'I'm not so sure. You know, maybe we're wrong about limiting casualties to Germans. If we really want to set the cat amongst the Euro pigeons – push people into corners and get them coming out fighting each other – then maybe we *do* need a few more important nationalities involved. If the "Brexit" British and French see their casualties as the innocent bystanders of a campaign against the hated Germans, rather than the targets, it's just possible that the Germans could get more flak than us. I'll contact High Command immediately, Ricart, and sound them out. If they give the green light, then, with Vicenç's explosives and Antoni's electrical skills, I think we could organize some pretty spectacular fireworks up at Alqueria Blanca.'

'But surely there'll be staff at the party,' Vicenç bleated, '– locals to do the serving and–?'

'Nope,' Ricart interrupted. 'For all his big talk, Stumpf's a mean bastard by all accounts. He treats his wife like a slave – they've only got *one* part-time cleaner! And her son – the cleaner's, that is – helps out in the garden a few times a week. I'll check, but I'm almost one hundred per cent sure that at this birthday bash the Stumpfs will be on their tod as usual, waiting on their guests. It's sickening! Our people could do with the extra cash – especially now with tourism in the dumps.'

A few minutes later as the meeting broke up and the three visitors prepared to return to their own fishing boats, a booming, throaty roar suddenly destroyed the tranquillity. Around a headland, some five hundred metres to the north, appeared a large shiny-white dart of a speedboat.

'Jesus!' snarled Antoni. 'If that son of a bitch goes any faster, it'll take off!'

'The bastard must be doing at least fifty knots!' cried Vicenç.

'Bet you anything it's a fucking German!' sneered Ricart. 'They're always in a hurry.'

Jaume was concerned for the safety of his beloved boat. 'If that maniac comes any closer, I'll – I'll ...!'

But when it was just a hundred metres or so from them, the torpedo-like menace swerved sharply to port and began heading southwards out to sea, making for the dramatic outline of distant Cabrera, the smallest of the Balearics.

Jaume grabbed his binoculars. 'Hah! You were right, Ricart – a German flag and four golden-tanned gits with blond hair. Why don't they–?'

As the speedboat's formidable wash hit the fishing boat broadside and caused it to roll violently, Jaume lost his balance and fell backwards into the foaming water. When he came spluttering to the surface and three pairs of arms reached out to haul him back on board, retribution burned in his deep blue eyes.

CHAPTER 3

Shaking her head in disbelief, Jane put down 'The House Rules' and stared at her naked husband curled up in a foetal position on the bed beside her. She never ceased to be amazed by how vulnerable and childlike a grown man could appear when deep in sleep. She looked at Mike's golden wavy hair and was tempted to stroke it. Their lovemaking after lunch had been heavenly. If she moved around a bit, perhaps he might wake up. ... No, it wouldn't be fair: he was exhausted. She really ought to let him sleep. He'd worked so hard over the last few months, six – sometimes even seven – days a week. ... Of course, they'd *both* worked like maniacs since they'd managed to grab that week of skiing at New Year, but Mike worried so much more than she did. He just didn't have her self-confidence, which was silly really, because he was just as able – cleverer probably, but–

'God!' she hissed. 'This room is suffocating with that stink of whitewash! ... What time is it anyway?'

She glanced at the travel alarm clock on the bedside table: just after five. Werner, no doubt, would already be back at 'work' – whatever that entailed! What an odd character! And those 'House Rules'! Talk about German organisation! That stuff about not taking food into the bedrooms because of ants! And the plan of the kitchen indicating the whereabouts of basic foodstuffs and utensils in the event that guests failed to turn up for meals at the decreed times! It was sheer madness. Their friends would never believe it ... unless the document fell into a suitcase when they left – or would Werner expect it to be delivered up at their departure? Maybe he went round with a checklist?

Which reminded her: poor Heidi was probably pottering about somewhere. It could be useful to get some gen on the old boy's party – a bit of gossip about Lionel and the other celebs – what to wear, whether they were celebrating something special. Oh, Lord, they might have to buy a bloody present! Where? ... What?

'Jesus!' she muttered. 'This stink! And the heat!' Maybe she should go for a swim instead. There was a swimming pool somewhere – a whole section on it in the 'House Rules'! '**DO NOT TAKE INDOOR TOWELS TO THE POOL. SPECIAL BLUE AND WHITE STRIPED TOWELS WILL BE FOUND IN THE POOL HOUSE. AFTER USE, PLACE IN THE WICKER BASKET** ...'

'What a fruit cake!' she sniggered under her breath. Word association made her think of Derbyshire. *Actually, a cup of tea would be lovely. God! I sound like Mummy – bless her!*

Chuckling, Jane moved off the bed. Mike stirred and rolled onto his back but didn't wake up. She slipped on some knee-length shorts and a sleeveless top – yet more last-minute purchases from Burberry's – and let herself out.

The Oakhearts' room was not in the main house but across the courtyard in what had once been a barn; Heidi had told them that Werner liked guests to have 'their own space'. From her experiences so far, Jane guessed it would prove a most propitious arrangement – that she and Mike would be doing their own thing a lot of the time. Indeed, filling her lungs with air unpolluted by whitewash as she crossed the courtyard, she suddenly recollected a conversation with Mike during their lunch *à deux*:

'I'm beginning to suspect we're substitutes,' he'd said, '– that some far more important guest – or guests – for this party dropped out, and Werner thought your credentials as "the Ambassador's daughter" would be suitably impressive.'

'What on earth makes you say that?'

'Because when we arrived, he was more bloody interested in your mum and dad than *us*.'

'Don't be ridiculous! He was just being polite – hospitable – considerate – trying to bring the family together.'

But now, as Jane entered the house and tried to get her bearings, she wondered whether Mike might have been right. After all, Werner had been ... well, almost rude – so anxious to get back to his bloody siesta! But was she being fair? Middle-aged people had their routines – look at her own parents! Werner had probably been up since the crack of dawn. By all accounts he worked very hard – writing *and* gardening. And it was hot – very hot – insufferably hot. The poor man had just been dropping off when they arrived, and ... well, he'd probably be a different character now. He'd certainly been *very* different at that dinner in London last year!

A woman was singing softly somewhere – Heidi in all probability. Jane chose a corridor that led from the hall and followed the strains. The route turned out to be familiar – the way Heidi had led them to the terrace for their 'organic' lunch. Impressionistically, Jane recollected terracotta pots of palms and succulents, vistas through open French windows of vivid green pines set against dazzling blue skies, fragrances of lavender, oleander and jasmine ... the distant buzzing of countless cicadas. Yet, although these grand reception rooms had seemed so magical only a few hours ago, now, as she retraced her steps, Jane's eye became less generous. The fact was that apart from the plants, fragrances, heat and views, they weren't very 'Mediterranean' at all. To be honest, she could imagine the furnishings in a German apartment of 1990s vintage, the first home of aspiring professionals on a tight budget. But there was one glaring incongruity – a magnificent grand piano in the centre of the living room. And on top of it stood a pair of monumental High Victorian silver candelabra.

Good Lord! Liberace would have loved this lot. ... They can't be solid silver, surely? She wondered who played – and who was responsible for the bad taste. Well, the latter had to be Werner: she couldn't imagine Heidi being allowed to move a single ornament without his consent, let alone buy any furnishings! Feeling cheated, Jane then got cross with herself for being so critical. What the hell did it matter anyway? In such a heavenly location, the Stumpfs would be mad not to spend most of their days outdoors. Maybe they just didn't give a damn about material things anymore. Good for them!

Singing a Schubert song, Heidi was browning pieces of chicken in a ludicrously cramped kitchen – about nine square metres. It was like a furnace, and Jane immediately concluded that her hostess didn't cook very often – at least not in summer.

'Hello, Heidi!'

Looking more embarrassed than startled, Heidi jumped, but the now familiar warm smile instantly appeared. 'Jane! You sleep not?'

'Too excited,' Jane lied. 'Mike's still out for the count – fast asleep. I thought I heard you singing. ... Schubert, wasn't it?'

'Er ... yes.'

Jane stared at the pile of chicken and rolled her eyes. 'Didn't you have your siesta then?'

'Oh yes – a little. Now Werner works with Mateu in the garden, and I do some cook. I love the cook.'

'*Really?*'

Heidi caught Jane's eyes encompassing her compact workspace. 'Yes, it is too small. Once this was the room to keep the food. In the old days they cook on the fire in the hall and the big oven outside. I show you later. Werner is always saying that one day we have a new kitchen, but ... well, I'm ...'

'You've learned to cope. ... Can I help?' Jane prayed: cooking was not her forte, and the kitchen was already torture.

Heidi removed the last piece of chicken from the frying pan and placed it with the others in a large casserole. 'You are very kind, Jane, but now I finish. ... You would like some tea or coffee – a cold drink?'

'Oh, you can read my mind! It sounds crazy in this heat, but a cup of tea would be wonderful.'

It transpired that the Stumpfs appeared to possess every imaginable herbal and fruit tea, many of which were prepared by Heidi herself from plants cultivated in the garden. Luckily for Jane, they also had a tin of Twining's English Breakfast.

When the tea was made, Heidi said: 'Come! We go to the sitting room. It's cooler there. I should go now to help the men remove the weeds around the olives, but I prefer to talk to you. Do you like the Black Forest cherry cake? I bakes one this morning.'

The cake was so good that Jane had two large slices, and as she slowly demolished them, Heidi opened up, giving the impression that she hadn't enjoyed a cosy chat with another living soul for a very long time. It soon became clear why she was responsible for such a delicious cake. After school, she'd been apprenticed to a pastry chef in her home city of Hamburg. She fell in love with him, and when she was nineteen, they got married. She should have known better: he was ten years older with three *Konditorei* of his own; she quickly realized he'd been looking for a wife to run them. She'd had a daughter, Anna, and ten years of penal servitude working every hour that God sent. But she'd had the last laugh: her husband ate too much of what he made and died of a heart attack. At thirty, she suddenly found herself a widow and the owner of a very reputable and profitable business.

'And you met Werner in Hamburg?' asked Jane.

Heidi smiled oddly. '*Ja* ... his apartment is near one of my shops. He comes often for my things. He was so handsome and–'

'He still is.'

'*Ja* – yes of course! Well, we see each other more and more after Manfred dies. ... It was a difficult time for Werner.'

'Oh?'

'His first woman – wife – Clara – the mother of his two children – her family owned the *Stahlwerke* ... steel factory in Essen ... very rich. ... Well, she kills herself – jumps from the balcony – of the apartment. And then he marries Sylvia – this is soon after. She came to my shops ... very beautiful – and rich too. Her father, Herr Fleck, has the big shops, er ...'

'Department stores? ... supermarkets?'

'*Ja*, Flecks Supermarkets – they are all over Germany. So, Sylvia is not happy because Werner is always travelling as a newspaper writer, and she likes the sun and sea and is not liking the weather in Hamburg. Well, she bought this house and moves here.'

'*Really*? So, *she* bought it. ... I see.'

Heidi shrugged her shoulders and sighed. 'It is so sad. She is so happy here and then she dies in the car ... car smash ... the brakes.'

'God! How awful! Where?'

'Here, on the *camino*, our little road to Alqueria Blanca. Werner found her.'

Thereafter, according to Heidi, events moved swiftly. Werner was so devastated by Sylvia's death, he could no longer hold down his job as a journalist, spending more and more time at *Ca'n Pau*. Whenever he returned to Hamburg, he and Heidi were almost inseparable. He begged her to sell up and for the two of them to settle permanently in Mallorca, but Heidi didn't want to disrupt Anna's schooling. Five years ago, however, with Anna going off to university, there really was nothing to keep her in Hamburg. So, she married Werner, sold the shops, and moved down.

'And you're happy here,' Jane queried, 'or do you miss Germany?'

Heidi's smile broadened. '*Ja*, I love it – the house, the garden, the weather. I do not think I could go back to all those clouds and rains and the long months of winter. But sometimes I think we work too hard in the garden. It is very large – too large perhaps – and there is always so much to do. And Werner wants to plant more things, which is difficult because the soil is so thin. We have to use' – she made the sound of an explosion – '... the bombs, yes?'

'Explosives? Dynamite? Good heavens!'

'*Ja*. Everything is rock here, and so little water. We have the irrigation now – at last! – but it does not go everywhere, so each day I am many hours watering plants. And then there are the plants you don't want.'

'Weeds?'

'Weeds, *ja*, and the cutting of the almond and fruit trees in the spring–'

'Pruning?'

'You say "pruning"? ... There are forty almonds and many more orange and lemon trees, so when they have the fruit, I must pick them, as Werner does not like to see them to the waste go. Every morning I squeeze a dozen oranges, and I make jam and crack and peel the almonds–'

'Oh stop! I'm exhausted just listening to all this, Heidi!'

Heidi laughed. 'Yes, there are days when I am *very* tired, but it is so beautiful in the garden with the air and smells and the sound of all the birds.' She shrugged her shoulders. 'But I don't want to spend *every* day working like a peasant. Look at my hands! Sometimes I am ashamed to show them. Werner wants the most beautiful garden on the island, I think, but *I* am thinking that my life is not to be spent just making something beautiful and valuable for his children to inherit one day – I mean *our* children – our *families*.'

'I understand. But you have a man to help in the garden – the housekeeper's son?'

'Yes, Margalida's boy, Mateu – well, now he is twenty-two. *Ja*, he works here, but only a few times a week.'

'And you do all the cooking too?'

'*Natürlich*! I love it.'

'Couldn't Mar ... Mar–'

'Margalida.'

'– Margalida help?'

'No, Margalida does not help. Werner says she can only cook peasant food and that she makes the messes with frying in oil everything and making the kitchen dirty. And she cannot serve because she is a peasant and does not know the right way to do things.'

'You could find other people – I'm sorry, it's really none of my business.'

'*Nein* – no – you are right, Jane ... but Werner says it is wasting the money.'

Jane was tempted to tell Heidi to stand up for herself, but then remembered that she was only a guest who barely knew the hosts. 'Well, Heidi, with all this work, do you ever find time to socialize – get out and see the neighbours – go to the cinema, theatre, concerts – if you have such things on the island?'

'Oh yes! Werner makes sure I get out – *every* week. There is a plan. It is on the wall in the kitchen. You didn't see it? On Mondays we always have the lunch with Professor and Frau Kommis, and our friend Helga. Professor Kommis is Nobel ... er, he wins the Nobel Prize for medicines and lives in a very big house over the hill – a very nice man – and his wife. They both love the cooking, and so does Helga, who is a painter and lives in a little house. She is not a very good painter and drinks much. So, every Monday, we have lunch at one of the three houses and we all cook together.'

'Including Werner?'

'Er ... he is ... he helps. ... And then on the Wednesdays we go to Palma and see a movie, or, if there is something at the Auditorium – a concert, ballet, opera – we go to that. Sometimes we stay the night in our little *piso* – apartment ... near the *Domkirche* ... cathedral? Werner bought it many years past. He goes there more than me. ... A few months ago, we even see Wagner's *Götterdämmerung* performed by the Barcelona Municipal Opera – in Catalan.'

Jane just managed to keep a straight face. 'You like opera?"

'Oh *ja*, but Wagner is not my favourite. I prefer Mozart. We took Margalida.'

'To *Götterdämmerung*?'

'Werner said she would be improving from the experience and that it was our duty to educate her.'

'Good Lord! Did she enjoy it?'

'She is asleep after fifteen minutes.'

They both laughed hysterically.

'And then on Thursdays,' Heidi continued, 'we always have lunch at a little cafe in Felanitx with our friend Jorgen – he is a dentist here – and his partner ... boyfriend?'

'You can say either. Perhaps "partner" is more appropriate these days.'

'So, we eat with Jorgen and Hans every Thursday ... at half past the one – *always*. The *menu* costs fifteen euros. Werner thinks it is very good. It includes wine.'

'Golly! How very ... economical.'

Jane was thinking that it all sounded horribly dull, when Heidi said brightly: 'And we go out to visit friends, and Werner is always inviting people here for the dinner. There is always the surprise.'

'Never a dull moment.'

'*Ja*, "never a dull moment". Some more tea, Jane?'

After the tea had been poured, Heidi said: 'Well, now you have to tell me all about you and Mike. Werner says little. Until last night, I do not know you are coming. Werner said he told me and that I forget everything, but–'

Jane spent some minutes apologizing for the disruption to Heidi's highly regulated routine, although, in truth, she knew that she'd no cause to. Mike would be stunned! She couldn't wait to tell him! Meanwhile, Heidi had realized her gaff and begged Jane not mention it to Werner. In any event, she was delighted to have some guests, particularly such lovely people as Mike and Jane.

Eventually, Jane got round to telling Heidi something of the Oakheart history and lifestyle. Heidi seemed enthralled, as though she was listening to a fairytale. 'You must be *so* clever,' she said after Jane thought she'd said more than enough, and began to wonder whether she should go in search of Mike. 'All those important people you meet! And the courts! It must be so exciting. And you are always eating in restaurants! How lucky!'

'Well, it's also a lot of very hard work. And *you* get to meet lots of exciting people too, Heidi. I mean, we don't have neighbours like Lionel de Tourny – or Nobel Prize winners!'

Heidi pulled a face. 'Professor Kommis is very nice man, but he is not exciting! You will meet him. And we never see Herr Tourny – he hides. So unfair! He is so beautiful. I love his films *Normandie* and *Dreyfus*. Oh, I cannot stop watching them, but Werner says they are rubbish. I often think that if I not love Werner so much, I have Lionel as a toy boy. *Wunderschön*! I climb over his wall and risk the big dogs and fall in his pool, and then he jumps in to rescue me. It is my dream!'

When they stopped giggling, Jane said: 'Well, I think he's *too* pretty. I prefer a *real* man – like Mike.'

'Me too, but it's nice to have the change sometimes!'

'I can't wait to meet Tourny. Is he shorter than he looks on the screen? They always do, don't they?'

'Er, I do not think so. I only see him once or twice – on his motorbike. I think you will be very lucky to see him while you are here.'

'But he's coming to the party, isn't he – with Jeanne Moineau, his partner – the French film star? Werner said so.'

Heidi rolled her eyes and tilted her head back. 'Werner told you *that*?' Suddenly, there was a muffled shout from the other side of the house and Heidi glanced at her watch. '*Scheisse*! It's the six o'clock already? That is him – calling me.' Her voice sounded edgy. 'Now he gets ready to go for the swim down at Portopetro. If he asks you to go with him, Jane, you must know that he always swims without the clothes. I cannot do that and he always laughs at me. We have the swimming pool – I insisted on that, at least – but he says the chemicals are bad and he never goes in it. He will only swim in the sea – twice a day from first May to thirty – *thirtieth* September. He enters the water at seven in the morning and seven in the evening.'

Jane was barely listening. 'Lionel de Tourny is *not* coming to the party?'

'*Ach*, Jane, Werner invites all sorts of people to his birthday party – writers, musicians, ministers from Berlin – and beautiful Lionel. But most of them do not accept. I think all the Germans are too frightened to fly because of ENABA. You know ENABA?'

'Yes,' said Jane sadly, 'those mad terrorists.' The Tourny bombshell had taken the wind out of her sails. Some holiday this was turning out to be!

'We get a letter from Herr Tourny a few days ago. It says, "Thank you for the invitement" – oh there's Werner shouting for me again! – "but Monsieur de Tourny and his ... his partner cannot come to the party." At least I have his autograph now! Werner wanted to destroy it.'

Jane sighed. 'So, it's a *birthday* party,' she said absent-mindedly.

'*Ja*, he is–' Heidi looked around nervously. 'Werner will kill me if he finds out I tell you, but he is sixty on his birthday.'

'*Sixty*! He only looks–'

'Shush! He is coming. He says to everyone he is fifty-something, but he still wanted it to be a special party. I said he should be honest and then the important people come, but–'

Clad only in stout boots and tattered denim jeans cut savagely short to reveal the bulk of his massive thighs, the tall golden form of Werner Stumpf appeared beyond the grand piano at the other end of the living room.

'Ah,' he blasted, '*this* is where you two are hiding!' A broad smile revealed an array of gold fillings deep within his mouth. 'And *tea*! And Heidi's magnificent cherry cake too! So, it is a real *English* tea. It is like colonial times, my dear Jane. Already you are corrupting the natives with your decadent ways!' His laugh was oddly high-pitched for such a large man with a deep voice. He strode across the room like an athlete, the sweat of hard labour glistening on his torso. Heidi began to say something, but he ignored her.

'And now, Jane, we *swim*! You can burn off all the calories. The water is wonderful at Portopetro. You will love it. Where is Mike? He must come too, and then in the car you can tell me all your news. I saw Sir Douglas on the lousy Spanish television the other evening, talking about Gibraltar. Very impressive!'

'Well, actually, Werner,' – Jane shot an embarrassed glance at Heidi – 'if it's all the same to you, I didn't sleep a wink this afternoon, and with all the cake – I couldn't resist it – wonderful! – I'm now feeling a little sleepy. I think I'll potter about here ... maybe lie down a bit before dinner.'

Werner's expression reminded Jane of a games mistress at school and her customary reaction to a convalescing pupil presenting a sick note from matron. She was just excusing herself to go and rouse Mike, when he appeared in the doorway. He'd donned a pair of shorts and Jane was struck by the whiteness of his skin.

'Hello, everyone!'

'Mikey–'

'Mike! Swim! The sea!'

'Love to, Werner! I'll just get my–'

'Mikey–'

'You coming, Footy?' Mike spied the tea things and the cake. 'Ah, so this is what you lot have been up to!'

'*Ja, ja*! My wife has sabotaged yours with her secret weapon while I toil. So, now Jane stays behind to sleep it off, and Heidi stays to do the weeding under the olives that she missed. So, Mike, it is just the men who embrace Neptune! *Vamanos*!'

Back in their room, as Mike grabbed his Speedos – the host had given him five minutes to get down to the front gate – Jane told him about Werner's non-existent party guests and his swimming habits. Mike, however, seemed maddeningly unconcerned.

'For God's sake, Footy, I've seen enough naked men in my life. Why should I give a toss if the old geezer swims in the nude? And I'm sure you've got this Tourny thing all wrong. I mean, Heidi does sound a bit batty to me. Telling you she didn't know we were coming until yesterday! Ridiculous! She's obviously got a memory like a sieve. She even forgot to get this room painted, didn't she?' He paused at the door. 'Are you sure you don't want to come?' Jane shook her head. 'Oh well, have a nice nap. You really must learn to relax, honey.'

Twenty minutes later, Jane had still to close her eyes: Mike's assumption that everything she'd learned from Heidi was some kind of inane housewifey gossip continued to irritate her as much as the smell of Margalida's whitewash. Consequently, she decided to go in search of the swimming pool after all. She ambled back over to the house, but this time there was neither sight nor sound of Heidi: presumably, she'd knuckled down to her weeding duty. And so, armed with just her costume, Jane crossed the courtyard and passed through an arch on the far side.

Beyond lay a deliciously shaded world of colourful jacaranda and wisteria trees, deep green Holm oaks, tall elegant cypresses, and yuccas of giant proportions. Beneath them, grew every Mediterranean and subtropical plant one could ever wish to see. Enchanted, Jane proceeded along labyrinthine gravel paths that meandered around the hillside, sometimes descending into rocky glades with dark pools of water lilies, and then rising again to bluffs with an old stone seat or a gazebo affording stunning views across the countryside down to distant Santanyí and its tall church tower. On and on she went, never retracing her steps.

Finally, a path brought her to the valley bottom and groves of olives and citrus trees planted in long straight rows. Sheltered from any breeze, the heat was stifling. She shook her head and sighed.

'Where the bloody hell is that sodding swimming–?'

'*Hola*!'

'Jesus Christ!'

Smoking a cigarette, an unsmiling young man sat cross-legged under an adjacent olive. All he had on were a pair of shiny blue running shorts and some very dirty trainers. A frisson of alarm shot through Jane's body as he slowly got up and emerged into the sunlight.

'*Hola*,' Jane mumbled.

'I'm Mateu, *señora*,' he said in Castilian, the standard spoken Spanish. Pointing to her swimming costume, he added: 'Are you looking for the pool?'

Never had Jane felt so grateful for studying Spanish at school. 'Yes – yes I am.' She eyed him more closely. It was no wonder that Heidi had said she liked him: he could only be about five foot nine, but he was certainly good-looking, and all that gardening, well ... His shorts were rather tight – too tight. *Don't stare!* 'I don't think it's down here, is it?'

Mateu slowly shook his head. 'You've come the wrong way.'

'Obviously.'

'It's on the other side of the house. I can show you.' He dropped his cigarette butt and flattened it. 'I've finished here anyway.'

'No – no thanks. I'll find it.'

'As you wish. ... See that gate?' He pointed to the end of a row of olives. 'That leads onto the *camino*. If you turn right, you can get back to the main entrance in five minutes. Saves you walking kilometres through Stumpf's botanical gardens.'

Cocky and sarcastic. 'Thanks – thanks very much. *Adiós*!'

As she turned towards the gate, Mateu said: 'See you around. By the way, you speak Castilian well for a German.'

'That's because I'm English.'

'Oh! Well, that explains it.' He managed a smile at last – and then laughed; he had dazzlingly white teeth.

When Jane reached the gate, she finally looked back, pretending to admire the scenery. But to her surprise, Mateu was nowhere in sight. Hot and dehydrated, she wished she'd gone with Mike after all. He'd been right: how provincial could one be, fretting over a sixty-year-old man's skinny-dipping?

To the right, the twisting dirt *camino* rose steeply up the valley side. Laboriously climbing it, she recalled Heidi's revelations of how Werner's second wife had died ... Sylvia? *A wrecked car smashed against a pine tree or stone wall – perhaps here – at this very spot – with a beautiful woman crushed against the steering wheel, her clothes bloodstained, Werner bending over her. Did the local police discover that his first wife had also–?*

A tremendous explosion of sound stunned Jane as something shot around the bend just ahead of her. It was the sight of the black helmet with its sinister opaque visor that transfixed her, like a rabbit caught in the beam of a car's headlights. Then tires were screaming as the massive motorbike skidded down the hill towards her.

*

'Are you sure you don't want to have a drag?' asked a smiling Lionel de Tourny as he offered Jane the spliff again. 'It will help calm your nerves.' He was kneeling in front of her with a piece of bloodstained cotton wool in one hand and the slowly burning spliff in the other.

'No thanks,' Jane said appreciatively, not wanting to admit that she hadn't smoked anything like that since taking her Bar finals. 'I'm fine now – *really*.' She was unable to resist staring into his sparkling blue eyes; they were hypnotic.

'OK.' He put the spliff back on the ashtray and began rubbing some antiseptic cream on her scratched knees again.

Jane squirmed.

'Sorry! ... Would you like some paracetamol? I should have asked before.'

'Um, no thank you. I'm all right – *really*. It was very kind of you to bring me here for first aid. I could have easily walked to *Ca'n Pau*.'

'It was the least I could do. I'm truly very sorry about the accident. It's just so unusual to find anyone walking along the *camino*.'

'Please stop apologizing. It was all my fault – ambling in the middle of the road, not looking–'

'You always drive too fast on that bloody bike,' hissed Jeanne Moineau. 'It will be the death of you one day – like James Dean.' She was sprawled just a few feet away on one of three original art nouveau sun loungers, a Gauloise between her lips.

Lionel sighed. 'He wasn't killed on a motor bike.'

'You have a lovely villa,' Jane chirped, scanning the vast covered terrace. *God! How trite! I must sound like a star-struck schoolgirl.*

'It's his parents',' Jeanne sneered, rolling her eyes. Rising languidly, she removed a bottle of Krug from the ice bucket at her side and topped up Jane's glass. 'This is what will calm you down, *chérie*,' she said, stroking Jane's arm, 'not *that* stuff. ... By the way ... *Jane*, do you speak *our* language, or are you a typical Anglo-Saxon girl?'

'*Your* language?'

'*La langue française*!'

'Ah.' In perfect French, Jane added: 'What exactly do you mean by "a typical Anglo-Saxon girl"?'

'*Oh là là!*' cackled Jeanne, '– an English freak!'

'Don't mind her,' Lionel said, inhaling the last lungful of smoke, 'she's just jealous because she's so unpopular in the States.' Jeanne pretended to pout as Lionel kissed her on the cheek before sitting down on the other sun lounger.

Ever since the Mallorcan trip had been arranged, Jane had spent almost every spare moment trawling the Internet for information on Tourny and Moineau – and what a lot of websites there were! But as a successful lawyer, she knew the value of thorough research. Accordingly, she was aware that the relationship between the two stars was reputed to be 'volatile'. Frankly, as she now looked from one to the other, she wondered what could possibly be the attraction between them. For a start, although at twenty-five Lionel was ten years younger than Jeanne, he looked more like eighteen, and she could easily be mistaken for fifty; her notorious chain-smoking and love of the old vino clearly had a lot to answer for. And while she'd been appearing in avant-garde French films since she was fifteen – the sort of films that won prizes at obscure European film festivals but which no distributor in the English-speaking world would touch with a barge pole – Lionel had horrified his native land by allowing himself to be seduced by Hollywood.

As the son of a titled Paris banker and his Liechtenstein aristocratic wife, Lionel had enjoyed a cosmopolitan upbringing that had finally led to spasmodic attendance at an art history course at the Sorbonne. He'd been 'discovered' by an advertising agency in a student production of *Le Malade Imaginaire* in which he'd had a walk-on part; various commercials for cologne had followed on French TV. Then the Hollywood scouts had spotted him. Now, with just two movies under his belt – as opposed to Jeanne's twenty-two – he was a global megastar. The fact that both blockbusters had a French theme had not, however, mollified Jeanne – nor, for that matter, her country's critics. But then the 'true story' dramatized in *Dreyfus* – the wrongful conviction in 1894 of Alfred Dreyfus, a thirty-five-year-old Jewish army officer, for selling military secrets to the Germans and his imprisonment on the infamous Devil's Island off French Guiana – had been interpreted by Hollywood with much poetic licence. In particular, almost every French citizen had been depicted as fanatically anti-Semitic. Across France, there'd been riots outside cinemas showing the film – publicity, paradoxically, worth its weight in gold.

With *Normandie*, Hollywood had attempted to repeat the success of *Titanic* in the 1990s, but this time the liner was the most magnificent and expensive ever built – France's Art Deco wonder, the *Normandie*, the *Queen Mary*'s arch-rival. On the outbreak of war in 1939 – just four years after first entering service on the North Atlantic – the French government mothballed her in New York with a skeleton French crew to avoid her falling into German hands or being sunk. And then, when America finally entered the war following Japan's bombing of Pearl Harbour in December 1941, the U.S. government seized the liner and began converting her into a troop ship. Alas, a workman was careless with an oxyacetylene torch; within twenty-four hours she was a wreck, lying on her side at a Manhattan pier. Well, not according to Hollywood, which had succumbed to one of the many conspiracy theories. Consequently, Lionel plays a handsome young officer in De Gaulle's Free French Army helping to liaise between the liner's rabidly pro-Vichy skeleton crew and the Americans. And although Lionel uncovers the dastardly Nazi/Vichy sabotage plan, he and his U.S. Coastguard colleagues only manage to kill the sadistic German chief saboteur after he's gone berserk with the oxyacetylene torch. In France, the film's release had provoked more demonstrations; survivors and descendants of the crew had even instituted defamation proceedings.

Jane took a sip of her champagne and was momentarily transfixed by Moineau's staring eyes: they were just as big, dark and hypnotic as they appeared on the screen. And those pouting lips! And the cameras certainly hadn't misrepresented her boobs! Could that be what turned Lionel on? 'My husband and I have seen *all* your films,' she blurted. *Christ! There I go again! And now I sound like Queen Elizabeth.* 'We thought *Three Nuts And A Bolt – Trois Écrous Et Un Boulon –* was ... *un*believable.' *Stop gushing, idiot!*

'Did you understand it?' queried Lionel, grinning. 'All that necrophilia in the Soviet oil refinery! Jesus!'

'Of course she wouldn't have understood it – she's an Anglo-Saxon.'

'*I* didn't,' Lionel continued.

'I really ought to make a move,' Jane said. 'They'll be getting worried.'

'Oh yes,' sniggered Jeanne, rolling her large dark brown eyes. 'It's after seven! You know the Bosch – they'll be sitting down to dinner now – dumplings, *sauerkraut* and potatoes, with great *steins* of foaming beer. The Master Race! Ha!'

'I think dinner's at eight-thirty, actually, Madame Moineau, and–'

'"*Jeanne*" for Christ's sake, *chérie*! Don't "Madame" me! Have some more Krug. I don't normally drink this stuff, but dear, sweet Lionel's rich folks are paying for it, so what the hell?' Jane tried to put a hand over her glass, but she wasn't quick enough: champagne bubbled over the rim; Jeanne appeared oblivious. 'So, my little English rose, how come you speak such lovely French, and why in God's name are you staying at the *Eagle's Nest* with Hitler and his Eva Braun of a *hausfrau?*'

I'm really beginning to dislike you – you French cow. 'Actually, Frau Stumpf – Heidi – is the most wonderful cook, and her husband is one of Mike's – my husband's – clients. He's a lawyer – like me. They invited us for his birthday party. And my father's a diplomat, so he was always determined that I should speak French. When I was a child we often spoke French at home. Now I really must be going.'

'I'll take you,' said Lionel coming to stand beside her.

Jane thought of the spliff and the Krug. 'No thanks, I–'

He took her arm. 'I insist.'

'That Nazi,' sneered Jeanne, 'invited us to his lousy *Bierfest* – the cheek of the man! – he's never even spoken to us – except when he complained about the bonfires the old gardener used to light. Then he died and we now "share" that brooding, sultry Mateu.' Jeanne licked her lips. 'Not bad if you like local rough trade. He made Mateu put the invitation in our letterbox! You did tell Hitler what he could do with it, didn't you, Lionel?'

Sighing, Lionel nodded. 'Come on, Jane,' he said, putting an arm around her shoulders.

She relived holding onto his waist on the brief drive over and felt an odd tingle of expectation. 'It was a pleasure to meet you ... Jeanne.'

'*Pareillment, chérie*. It's been such fun playing doctors and nurses. We must get Lionel to run you over again. Better still, do come for dinner one evening – we could do with some light relief, couldn't we, Lionel? Bring your husband ... Mark – whatever. Lionel may not be able to act to save his life, but he's a treasure in the kitchen. So many well-hidden talents.'

The departing couple were almost at the end of the terrace, when Jeanne shouted: 'You could get one of the Filipinos to drive her back!'

Lionel ignored her.

They did not wear crash helmets: Lionel said it was too hot and that he'd drive slowly; he'd only worn his earlier because he'd been out on the main highway. His parents had a boat at Portopetro, and he'd gone down to mess around with the engine. Jane surprised herself by not insisting on one, and with the hot pine-scented wind in her hair, and Lionel's golden shoulder-length locks fluttering about her face, her embarrassed clutching of the star's waist quickly gave way to a feeling of total contentment. In truth, she couldn't remember being so alive for years. Back in London, she'd be able to dine out on this afternoon's experiences for months!

It took just a few minutes to get back to *Ca'n Pau*. Jane was standing by the Harley saying her farewells over its engine's throaty roar when a decrepit red Renault came bouncing along the *camino* from the opposite direction. As it pulled up in a cloud of dust, Werner and Mike stared at her incredulously through the filthy windscreen. Then Werner bounded out like a jack-in-the-box, followed by Mike.

'Monsieur de Tourny! *Quelle bonne surprise*! Let me introduce you to my *very* dear guests. This is Jane, the daughter of Sir Douglas Trench-Foot, the British Ambassador to Madrid. She has come for my little party. Such a terrible shame that, at the last minute, you cannot join us. I–'

'Footy, darling! What have you done to your legs? – ankles? – *arms*?' Mike was prostrate.

'Oh, this is Michael,' Werner began irritably.

'I'm all right, Mikey. I–'

'I am so sorry, Mike,' said Lionel, turning off the Harley's engine and holding out his hand. 'It was all my fault. I was driving just a bit too fast and–'

'You ran over my wife? Where? When? *Darling*–!'

'Mikey, I'm O – K. I was strolling in the middle of the road. I wasn't looking. Lionel has been so kind. He took me to his villa, and he – and Jeanne Moineau – washed the cuts and dressed them and–'

'You've met *already*?' croaked Werner. An expression of pure horror engulfed his bronzed angular face. 'You've been to the *Villa Tourny*? You've met Jeanne Moineau?'

'Do you need a doctor, Footy? – an injection? – tetanus? The travel insurance will–'

'Jesus! I only scraped myself against a stone wall! I'm *all – right*!'

There was a moment's silence.

'Well,' said Lionel looking at Jane with a warm smile, 'now *I'd* better get back before Jeanne thinks – *drinks* herself under the table.' Werner and Mike had furrowed brows. 'Just kidding, guys!'

The Harley burst into life.

'Goodbye, Monsieur de Tourny!' roared Werner, holding out a hand ravaged by gardening. 'An honour!'

Lionel flashed a boyish grin.

He looks so much younger than twenty-five, thought Jane.

Irresponsible androgynous playboy, fumed Mike.

Werner could not think.

'Oh, by the way, Herr Stumpf!' shouted Lionel. 'About your party. ... Look, that other engagement me and Jeanne had ... well, it's been cancelled. So, if the invitation still stands, we'd love to come. *When* is it?'

CHAPTER 4

Ca'n Xet, the home of Margalida Palmer Obrador and her son, Mateu, was a mere five hundred metres away from *Ca'n Pau* along the *camino* towards Alqueria Blanca. Like the Stumpfs' multi-million-euro residence, it was an old farmhouse built from the golden stone of the surrounding hills; even the colour of the roof tiles, like most things made traditionally from local materials, harmonized perfectly. But, unlike *Ca'n Pau*, apart from the installation of electricity and water pumped from Margalida's own well, no major refurbishments of the house or the adjoining outbuildings had occurred in living memory. Consequently, many of the 'foreigners' who passed this way – mostly visitors to the Stumpfs or to the *Villa Tourny* – found the Obradors' humble *finca* 'picturesque', despite the rusting agricultural machinery and piles of discarded glass and plastic containers in several corners of the cobbled courtyard. Some even stopped to take photographs: there were banks of colourful nasturtiums and geraniums cascading in profusion around the perimeter walls for much of the year; the former had seeded themselves; the latter had all grown from a single cutting given to Margalida years ago by someone whose identity had long been forgotten. Customarily, country folk in these parts did not indulge in ornamental gardening: there was neither the time nor the water.

The unwelcome photographers, however, were not so enamoured of the two large black dogs that were permanently chained at one end of the courtyard and which barked hysterically whenever anyone passed along the *camino*. Over the years, Werner had regularly made 'suggestions' to Margalida about both the dogs and 'the refuse'. Alas, having utterly failed to make any headway on either issue, he'd reluctantly concluded that making a denunciation to the authorities would be counterproductive. Margalida had reminded him that every Mallorcan *finca* had dogs, and they had to be secured to stop them running away or chasing the livestock; she herself still kept flocks of sheep and goats. They were *guard* dogs, not pets, and everyone knew that guard dogs had to be chained up. Margalida's current canine sentries had now been in situ for over five years, and as they'd never been unchained, the courtyard was the only world they knew; they'd never even been near a vet. If they needed shade from the burning summer sun, or shelter from the fierce winter storms, they had access to a former pigsty. Yet, despite this treatment, which the Stumpfs and most 'foreigners' regarded as monstrous, the beasts were affectionate towards their mistress and her son, even though they'd never demonstrated the least attachment towards them.

As for the piles of empty containers, Margalida and her parents' generation had grown up in a pre-tourist-prosperity age when nothing was thrown away; one never knew when the bottles could come in handy, a sceptical Werner had been repeatedly advised. They could be used for storing olive oil, petrol for the tractor or rotavator – even *hierbas*, the mind-blowing liqueurs Margalida concocted using brandy and her own herbs and fruits. And the large plastic containers were just as practical: she tied them together in bunches and hung them from her fruit trees to frighten birds away; with a tiny hole in the bottom and filled with precious water, they could be placed next to vegetable seedlings and operate as an ingenious irrigation system.

In view of his own avowed passion for the environment, it was difficult for Werner to argue with Margalida; he just wished that the stocks of prospective recycling materials could be kept out of sight and not offend both his and his visitors' aesthetic senses whenever they passed by. A couple of years ago he'd suggested the former donkey stable as a repository; Margalida said she'd look into it. After numerous reminders, she reported back some months later that it was really not feasible: the stable was already full of 'things'; it was also possible they might get another donkey. Shortly thereafter, empty tin cans began to accumulate in another corner of the courtyard; now there was quite an impressive rusting pile. Werner's dream was to buy *Ca'n Xet* and convert it into a holiday home for rent, but he knew Margalida would never sell. Mateu, on the other hand, was quite a different proposition, but although his mother looked older than her forty-eight years, she was as tough as nails; Werner feared she'd outlive both Mateu and himself.

This evening, as the Oakhearts tucked into their first Mallorcan dinner – frugal portions of Heidi's casseroled chicken served on one of *Ca'n Pau*'s terraces, the candlelight glinting in glasses of the local *rosat*, a wine which Werner claimed was 'rather expensive' – Margalida and Mateu were devouring steaming plates of *frito mallorquin* at *Ca'n Xet*. It looked as inelegant as their surroundings, but, as far as they were concerned, tasted heavenly – proof that a small amount of chopped liver quickly fried in olive oil with lashings of diced fresh vegetables seasoned with fennel and whole cloves of garlic, could knock the spots off 'foreign' food any day. Oddly enough, the Obradors were drinking the same *rosat* as their neighbours – albeit out of chipped tumblers and not Bohemian crystal goblets – but Margalida bought it at wholesale prices in five-litre plastic containers direct from the producer. He was a distant relative, a fact she'd been careful never to reveal to her employer.

Being summer, mother and son were also dining alfresco; they were sat at opposite ends of the white plastic garden table which Mateu had extricated from the local tip some months earlier. One of the legs had been missing, and there'd only been two matching chairs dumped with it – all cracked and badly stained – but one could not look a gift horse in the mouth. He'd found an old gatepost riddled with woodworm in one of their sheds and glued it on. Positioned just outside the front door, the table was illuminated by a bare 40-watt bulb that hung perilously from a socket at the apex of the door's stone arch; there was no bulb at *Ca'n Xet* with any higher wattage. There were, on the other hand, plenty of utilitarian white candles around the house, but these were only used when the power failed, a fairly common occurrence in the Mallorcan countryside. Dining by candlelight, however, when one possessed the miracle of electricity, would have struck the Obradors as no less ridiculous than turning one's back on the low-flush WC and resorting again to the prickly pear patch behind the pigsty.

'Have you met them then – that new lot?' asked Margalida, her mouth full of *frito*. 'What a carve up! That idiot, the *Caudillo* hadn't even told the *Esclava* that they were coming!'

The Obradors invariably referred to their employer and his wife using these terms, for they saw many similarities between Stumpf and '*El Caudillo*' – 'the Leader' – Generalissimo Franco, on the one hand, and Frau Stumpf and a slave on the other.

'You told me at lunchtime. ... Yes – well only the woman. ... I met her down in the olive grove this evening just as I was packing up. She was looking for the swimming pool, would you believe?'

'Never! She looked like the type that if you turned round twice would be lost. Looking for the swimming pool indeed! – after your body more like it.'

'*Mamá*! She was lost.'

They ate in silence for a while.

'*Mamá*, why didn't *you* remind the *Esclava* that these English people were coming?'

'None of my business. I'm a cleaner, not a secretary. They pay me little enough as it is.'

'Do you really believe that the *Caudillo* forgot to tell her, or is her mind going, just like he keeps saying?'

Margalida swirled the pink wine around in her tumbler. 'There's nothing wrong with *her* mind. Of course he forgot! I tell you, he's the one going senile. Anyhow, they had one hell of a row about it this morning.

Going at it like hammer and tongs, they were. I've picked up enough German in that house over the years to know some of the things he called her. She came down to the kitchen after the scene up in the guest room and had a swig of brandy – two, in fact, but who's counting?'

'So, they've come for his sixtieth birthday bash then – these English?'

'Now don't you go blabbing to a living soul that he's sixty, or he'll have our guts for garters.'

'I'm not some gossiping old woman, thank you very much. ... She was dead white – that English girl.'

'"*Girl*"?'

'They must never get any sun. Bet they're both as red as lobsters tomorrow.'

'Hmm. ... I told you that she's the daughter of the British ambassador, didn't I?'

'Yeah, I remember. ... And the man?'

'No idea – never mentioned. If you ask me, it's the woman that wears the pants. I only met them briefly, but I can tell. More *frito*?'

Mateu pushed his plate over. 'And Lionel is definitely not going to the party?'

'No.'

'I never thought he would. Not his scene – boring old German farts. Mind you, he never seems to go out much – except on that Harley and his parents' speedboat. ... So, it doesn't sound much of a party then – not without Lionel and that French tart of his.'

'Watch your language!'

'Well, she is. And a drunk.'

'Just be careful what you say, Mateu, down at the bar when you're boozing. There's always reporters sniffing around for dirt on them two. We can't afford to lose our jobs – not with things the way they are.'

'Meaning?'

'You know what I'm talking about.'

'I've told you before – I support their objectives but not their methods.'

'Oh, so you'll be happy when all the Germans pack up and leave – when your old mother no longer has her job down the road?'

'Don't start. We've been through all this before. So what if Stumpf sells up? Someone else will buy the place – English – French, like the Tournys – some bloody rich Mallorcans! Then I wouldn't have that fascist pig barking orders at me all day. I mean, what the hell does it matter if I weed around an almond clockwise or anti-clockwise, eh? This afternoon–'

'I'll tell you one thing – he's straight. The *Caudillo* pays our wages in full, in cash, on time – not like a lot of Mallorcans I could mention.

No deductions if I break one of their precious ornaments. The *Esclava* gives us cakes and–'

'Yeah, yeah. You still can't stand the sight of them though. They think they know *every*thing. They think they're so superior. The *Caudillo* even stands over you when you make your whitewash. "Add this! Stir slower! More chalk!" You've been doing it all your life, but just because he has a degree from some fancy university–'

'Yes, that does get my back up.'

'And *I* was almost born under a bloody olive! The git probably hadn't even seen one until he came here. Now it's "Prune *this* branch! Cut here! Spray with this! Fertilize with that!" Anyone would think I was a fucking child!'

'Mateu!'

'Sorry, *Mamá* ... sorry. It's just that sometimes when he's lecturing me with his stupid foreign accent and giving me the Latin names of bloody weeds and then testing me later, I feel I want to kill the *bas*– ... kill him.'

Margalida sighed. 'I know the feeling, *cariño*. ... There's a spoonful more *frito*, if you'd like it?'

After they'd finished eating, Mateu lit a cigarette. 'You still haven't told me who's *definitely* coming to the *Caudillo*'s do. They haven't asked you to help out, have they?'

'Of course not! That mean git's relying on the *Esclava* as usual, poor woman. Why are you so interested anyway?'

'No particular reason. I suppose if someone like Taylor Swift was going, I'd go down and take a peek.'

'Well, she's not. Mind you, she *was* invited – *and* Max Verstappen, who you seem to worship – *and* some ex-king – there were invitations lying all round his study at one stage. But from what I've heard, none of them famous lot's coming, thanks to ENABA and their little games. So, you've got no reason to be creeping around down there making a nuisance of yourself, OK?'

'I wouldn't be seen dead "down there", if I could help it.'

'Anyway, they've just got that toffee-nosed Professor Kommis–'

'Jesus!'

'–and his snooty bitch of a wife, and that Kraut conductor who lives over near S'Horta ... von Karpen – or whatever his name is – and his "friend" coming – just that lot.'

'Not another bloody queen! I'm beginning to think all Germans are queer. Sometimes I even catch the *Caudillo* giving me funny looks. It must be something in the water in Germany.'

'There's nothing bent about *him* – not with all them *chicas* he's got going on the side down in Palma.'

'So you keep saying. … Anyway, who's the "friend"?'

'Some dress designer.'

'Wouldn't you just know it!'

'Otto … um … Otto Pinsel.'

'Otto *Pinsel*! He's not a "*dress* designer"! He makes them posh underpants. Cousin Maria-Dolores gave me a pair last Christmas.'

'Well, both Stumpfs told me he was a dress designer … or fashion designer … something like that.'

'And that's it then – plus the English couple. Hardly seems worth the effort.'

'The *Caudillo* seems mighty pleased though. He says you can't pick up a German newspaper on any day of the week without reading about one or other of his guests. He said so this morning – *again*.'

'Oh … right.'

'Oddly enough – it may be a false impression, mind you – but I think he's most chuffed about having that English woman. Apparently, her dad's a real lord – hobnobs all the time with the British royals – *and* our king.'

'"*Our* king"? Ooh, I *am* impressed! The next time I find her wandering about the place, I'll curtsey and touch me forelock.'

Once the laughter had subsided, they began to clear the table, the dogs barking excitedly in anticipation of titbits.

'I'll do this,' Margalida said. 'You get yourself down to Calonge and meet your mates.'

Mateu and his friends preferred Calonge's Bar Camperol: it was so basic that no foreigner would go near it, whereas in Alqueria Blanca, with its impressive church towering over the square, it was impossible to get a drink without rubbing shoulders with outsiders.

'It's OK, *Mamá* – it's still early.'

Standing over the old stone sink in the kitchen, with its primitive gas cooker and diminutive fridge, Margalida said: 'You know, Mateu, I was just thinking – get a clean tea towel from the draw, *cariño*. … I was just thinking that if your father or his brother – God rest their souls! – could see *Ca'n Pau* now … all them fancy people in all their finery parading through the place like it was some palace …' She shook her head. 'Unbelievable.'

'Yeah. Even I can remember Uncle Bartomeu living down there on his tod with all them cats.'

'He had chickens in the big room – what them Germans made into "the Hall".'

'There were rats running everywhere. No wonder the cats were so big. The smell was awful.'

'Well, poor Tomeu only had the rainwater that collected in the *pozo* during the winter. Never could find a spring. Useless land, apart from some winter grazing. Almost impossible to scratch a living.'

'And then that scheming German cow turned up.'

'"Scheming" isn't the word!'

'Pretending to be a hippy! – them rags she had on! – that old banger of a Seat! I was only about nine, I think, but I remember it all so clearly.'

'Well, you didn't get many foreigners down the *camino* in them days. Of course, *I* knew there was something fishy about her from the start, but Tomeu wouldn't listen, oh no. She was around for weeks trying to get him to sell, plying him with booze and fags. He liked his brandy and Ducados – *and* pretty women, even though he'd never married. Well, no local girl would have been daft enough to take on *Ca'n Pau*.'

'I suppose fifty thousand euros was lot of money then.'

'Not really – for a place round here that foreigners could tart up – but for your Uncle Tomeu it sounded like a fortune – especially for a dump like *Ca'n Pau*. Still, we all thought he'd tell that "Sylvia" to sling her hook, but–'

'I bet you anything he was pissed when he signed the contract.'

'Of course! He was out cold when I got down there – reeking of brandy he was. … Never got it out of him what he did with the money … even when he came to live here … even on his death bed. … I still think he hid it somewhere at *Ca'n Pau*. … Old fool never had a bank account.'

'Still, Sylvia got her just deserts in the end, didn't she?'

The glass Margalida was rinsing under the cold tap almost slipped out of her hands. 'Don't speak ill of the dead,' she hissed.

Mateu dried the glass and checked the time on the fake Rolex he'd bought at the Felanitx Sunday morning market. 'What do you think it's worth now, *Mamá* – a million euros?'

'Hah! Don't make me laugh. Only the other day I heard the *Caudillo* on the phone to his accountants in Palma – them crooked ones that file the false returns to get him out of paying Spanish tax. He said that a German estate agent in Santanyí–'

'One of them that got burned down the other week?'

She nodded. 'Well, they'd valued it some months ago at' – she paused dramatically – '… two … *million* … five … hundred … *thousand*!'

'Jesus Christ!'

'Don't take the Lord's name in vain, *cariño*.'

'Sorry. … Why so much?'

'Well, with the extensions, the bloody gardens, the pool, the water they found after dynamiting half the neighbourhood ...'

'But they valued it before ENABA started their ... action?'

Margalida nodded. 'Yes, but that won't go on for ever, will it?'

Mother and son stared into each other's eyes for some seconds.

'Well, off you go to Calonge, and be careful on that scooter – especially on the way back. And don't drink too much – you don't want to end up like your Uncle Tomeu.'

'I won't!'

The machine-gun-like racket of Mateu's decrepit scooter subsided, and Margalida took up her traditional post-dinner position in front of the television. Restricted to Spanish terrestrial channels, she quickly discovered a choice of football, a game show, an Argentinean soap, or, on the Mallorcan station, a documentary about folk music. She chose the soap. After fifteen minutes, however, she was having difficulty concentrating: everyone was either a voluptuous heiress to a cattle ranch, or an unbelievably handsome polo player. Their South American accents got on her nerves, and the complexity of the numerous adulterous relationships was quite beyond her – certainly at this time of night and after a hard day's toil.

As her eyes began to glaze over, Mateu's judgment about Stumpf's second wife came to mind. She could see the wreck ... and all the blood. 'Yes,' she murmured, 'Sylvia certainly did get her just deserts.'

CHAPTER 5

It was a cold, wet and windy Monday morning in Berlin. In the Chancellery's Cabinet Room, Martin Klipper, Chancellor of the Federal Republic, was looking out of one the windows, thinking of his well-earned holiday in Turkey. Just another fortnight of German gloom and then he'd be off to the revitalizing sun of the Gallipoli Peninsula and the palatial villa of one of Turkey's most successful industrialists. By all accounts, in addition to an army of servants, there were three pools, a private beach, a yacht, tennis courts – in fact, plenty of space and opportunities to lose Heike and the children! Of course, the Turks were just trying to curry favour in order to get their very dusty application to join the EU off the backburner; currently, almost everyone with any political clout across Europe was being 'cultivated' by them. Indeed, it seemed that half of his own cabinet were vacationing in Turkey this summer; if there were a crisis, they could probably get a quorum out there – perish the thought! At least none of them was going to Gallipoli, thank God!

Naturally, the usual windbags had criticized the trip, but having weighed up the pros and cons, he'd not bowed to their pressure. In any event, he'd be very popular with Germany's large population of Turkish migrants – and they invariably voted for the Social Democrats. Indeed, vacationing in an Islamic country would make him look tolerant, broad-minded, progressive – an impression that would certainly appeal to the party's left wing. After all, the federal elections were less than a year away and his standing in the polls were ... well, frankly they were awful. Of course, that wasn't his fault: he'd inherited one hell of a mess from his lamentable predecessor – may she rest in peace!

On reflection, maybe he should give fresh consideration to seeking election next year as the first 'President of the European Union'. Of course, to start with, he wouldn't have much power under the EU's new constitution – greeting and entertaining foreign heads of state on visits to Brussels, formally opening the feeble 'parliament', dishing out the new EU 'honours' to deserving citizens – but, as with so much in Europe, the flesh would creep onto the bones later, almost imperceptibly, without anyone noticing. And then when they did, it was always too late. Hah! How many Europeans had got referenda expressly on the euro? Who'd been specifically asked if they wanted the citizens of ten backward nations in Eastern Europe to have the right to live and work without restriction in the EU? ... Exactly!

But as the Minister of Labour and Social Affairs continued to dissect the monthly unemployment figures in the background, Klipper was almost prepared to admit to himself that the expansion eastwards had been a bit of a two-edged sword. Still, his judgment would be proved right in the end: Spain, Portugal and Greece had been destitute dumps when they'd joined the EU all those years ago, and now look at them! And the East would prove to be a zone of unchallengeable German domination – wouldn't it ... eventually?

Anyway, delicious Turkey was only a fortnight away and this was the last cabinet meeting for quite a while, thank God! There were only so many depressing statistics he could cope with. In the meantime, as a Hamburg man he had to charm his local constituents and spend some rain-sodden days at his house overlooking the Elbe and pretend to enjoy fishing. Ghastly!

'That concludes my report, Chancellor,' said the minister sadly.

Klipper beamed. 'Good!'

'"Good"?' queried the Minister of Finance, her face a picture of incredulity. 'I'd say it was bloody disastrous. The last thing I need right now is another hike in unemployment – and in the summer months – cocking up all my calculations. The cost in extra benefits is frightening. We told the electorate that the economy would pick up two years ago. We've been repeating that ever since. But there's been virtually zero growth. The budget deficit is growing almost out of control, Chancellor.'

'"Out of control"?' Klipper rolled his eyes. 'I think you exaggerate, Renate. We're the world's third largest economy, and–'

'That's neither here nor there,' snapped Renate, waving her pen accusingly at Klipper. 'I have to try to balance the books. One can do something about unemployment figures – at least in theory – but short of euthanasia, what the hell can we do about a rapidly ageing population? We've got one of the highest percentages of people over sixty in the EU! Bluntly, we don't have the money to pay the generous pensions our predecessors promised in the good times. Add on to that the millions of Romanians, Bulgarians–'

'Peasants, the lot of them!' hissed Defence Minister Karl Stiefel. The Minister for the Environment, Nature Conservation and Reactor Safety tutted.

'To continue, Karl ... um ... the millions of Romanians, Bulgarians, Slovenians, Slovaks – et cetera, et cetera – who've come here "to work" but – surprise, surprise! – who've ended up on the dole with the right to be housed by the local authority, and yet another thumping great pile of expenditure has been dumped on my doorstep. We can't increase taxes because that would push the economy even further into recession, and every time I propose cutting expenditure, one of my dear colleagues tells me it's "a betrayal of our socialist values".'

'It's not just that,' whined the Minister of Labour and Social Affairs. 'Our last attempt to reduce benefits resulted in a national strike, an armed mob attacking the Bundestag, and a bomb under my official car. I warned you that–'

'Yes, yes, yes,' moaned Klipper. 'Let's not go over all that again.'

'We do have cheaper food – especially potatoes – *and* coal since Poland joined the EU,' chirped the Minister for Consumer Protection, Nutrition and Agriculture. 'In fact, lots and lots of ordinary household goods are so much cheaper now because of the lower costs of labour and – and ... *things* in the East. I just don't understand why all that hasn't reduced inflation and boosted the economy ... or something. That's what we were told would happen – and lots of exports the other way.'

Renate shook her head slowly and exhaled loudly; sometimes she wondered why she bothered with these halfwits in their ivory towers. They should have worked as a finance director in industry like she'd done, and not teaching in universities. 'The point is, Walter, all those potatoes you talk about have destroyed our own producers – agriculture is also one of your remits, remember? So, now I have to pay out wads of cash to bankrupt farmers. And our own mines have gone bust. And as for bloody exports, the average per capita GNP figure for those dumps in the East is about one *fifth* of Germany's – just a third of crappy Greece's, for God's sake! The market for our expensive luxury goods over there is peanuts compared to the rest of the EU – not to mention China – so don't kid yourself, mate.'

Klipper stared at his superbly manicured nails. 'Greece and Portugal *and* Spain were awfully poor too when they joined the EU, Renate. As soon as they got in, they boomed.'

Renate was losing her patience. 'That was bloody *years* ago! And anyway, they had tourist industries earning billions each year, thanks to sun, beaches, cheap booze *and* weak currencies. Now they're bust thanks to the euro – *our* currency – masking their years of gross extravagance and fraud. Anyway, I really don't see armies of package holidaymakers queuing up for sun-drenched weeks on the Costa del Latvia, do you?'

'I know where all this is leading,' wailed the Minister of Family, Pensioners, Women and Youth. 'You're going to demand massive cuts in public expenditure again, aren't you? Well, don't pick on me, love, because you'll have one hell of a fight on your hands. If anything should go it's bloody Defence. I've got the figures here as it so happens, and they are *outrageous*.' A file was flung open. 'Why the hell do we need two thousand five *hundred* tanks, two thousand *six* hundred armoured personnel carriers, two hundred and *four* attack helicopters, four hundred and *thirty-four* combat aircraft – not to mention *fourteen* submarines, twelve *frigates*–?'

'Christ Almighty!' exploded Stiefel. 'If we cut anything else, we'll be a laughing stock. We're a nation with over eighty *million* people, one of the richest in the world – economic crisis or no economic crisis – and yet we spend a pathetic percentage of our GDP on defence! The British and the French spend much, much more and–'

'Let them continue pretending to be great powers, if they want to,' interrupted the Family Minister. 'But let's be honest with ourselves – we haven't fired a bloody shot in anger since 1945! Hitler's dead! We don't need three hundred *thousand* military personnel and all them tanks, planes and guns. I mean, we don't have any fresh plans to invade Poland, do we? And now that the Ukraine mess has been resolved – well, sort of – who the hell is going to attack *us* – the RAF? And if there was any bleeding threat to an EU country, we'd all pull together, wouldn't we? Isn't that what the new European Army thing is for, Karl? – so we can share the burdens? – get the Danes and the Belgians and all the other sad minnows to start forking out for a change?'

Stiefel was about to respond, but the Foreign Minister, Ernst-Wilhelm von Höhenzug, got in first. 'Heinrich, old chap, you're forgetting we have *international* commitments, *treaty* obligations ... NATO.'

'Bugger NATO!' hissed an unidentifiable voice.

'Above all,' Höhenzug continued, 'we have *aspirations*.'

'"Aspirations"?' queried Klipper.

'Why yes, Chancellor – aspirations to take our seat ... as a *permanent* member ... of the UN Security Council.'

'Hear! Hear!' roared a couple of colleagues above the groans.

'Yes, yes,' snapped Klipper, '– the Security Council – absolutely! It's not right that the French and the British are on it, but not us.'

Renate sensed it was time to seize the moment. 'Right, you lot, listen – and listen good! For years our budget deficit has exceeded three per cent of GDP. That means we're in flagrant breach of the EU Stability and Growth Pact. As warned repeatedly by our "mates" in Brussels, we're now liable to a fine of up to half a per cent of our GDP. Have you any idea how much money we're talking about?'

The Cabinet were told; even Klipper was shocked.

'So,' continued Renate, 'I propose we cut the Defence budget by fifty per cent, spread over the next five years. Agreed?'

In the ensuing uproar, Stiefel offered his immediate resignation, but after Klipper had taken the prostrate man into a corner and given him a chance to calm down and wipe away his tears, the resignation was withdrawn: the last thing Klipper needed just before going on holiday was a cabinet reshuffle and all the attendant publicity.

In the end, it was agreed that there would be 'a very detailed enquiry' into Defence spending with a view to making 'significant' savings while not undermining the Armed Forces' ability to 'adequately defend' the Federal Republic and to meet its 'international commitments'.

Klipper was on the point of adjourning the meeting when the Minister of Justice said: 'I've got a villa in Mallorca.'

'Poor sod!' sniggered the Transport Minister.

'I'm supposed to be flying down there next week with my husband and the boys, and I was wondering whether we should go.'

'You should have grabbed one of them Turkish offers, love,' crowed the Family Minister, 'like what all us sensible lot did.'

Höhenzug smiled broadly at the Justice Minister. 'I'm so glad you've asked me that apposite question, Antje, for it gives me an opportunity to inform you all of the constructive discussions I had only yesterday, as it so happens, with the Spanish Ambassador, whom I had summoned to the Foreign Ministry to deal with this very issue of our citizens' security.' Eyes were already glazing over. 'Once again, I expressed our concerns about the inexcusable attacks on German property on the Balearic island of Mallorca, and requested firm assurances from him that his government was taking all practicable steps' – Klipper yawned – 'to guarantee the safety–'

'Speed it up, old man,' interjected the Interior Minister, 'I've got to catch a plane to Stuttgart in an hour's time.'

'Stuttgart? Oh, I'm *so* sorry. ... Anyway, I'm pleased to inform you all that the Duque de Lobotonto gave me the most categorical assurances that the days of the dastardly Balearic Nationalist Army – ENABA – are well and truly numbered. Madrid anticipates making some important arrests *imminently*. ... Actually, dear Antje, the outrages have only been perpetrated against *unoccupied* second homes and branches of Deutsche Bank. Frankly, I've never been able to understand what all the fuss was about. The ordinary German's "boycott" of Mallorca this year has caused havoc to the poor island's economy, and tourist numbers are down on mainland Spain too. Lobotonto was *most* upset, I can tell you. He suggested we'd not done enough here to reassure our people.'

'Well,' snorted the Interior Minister, 'if they'd pulled their fingers out and caught those few cranks in the first place, instead of having long boozy lunches and siestas, they wouldn't be in this bloody mess – and nor would we. We've taken a lot of flak in the press and social media over our alleged inability to put a rocket under those fat Spanish arses and get "our people" protected out there – one more blow to our standing in the polls. If there are any more of these outrages, the media will be egging us on to do something ourselves.'

Klipper was most displeased by this turn of events, just as the meeting had appeared to be winding up. In any event, he had an appointment with his manicurist in half an hour down in the Chancellery's Health and Leisure Centre, followed by his weekly session on the sun bed.

'Come, come,' he said, 'let's not start hypothesizing. Now that this nonsense has begun to seriously damage the precious Spanish tourist industry, I'm sure Madrid will stamp on it. And don't forget – that fop Azucena has got his sights on the EU Presidency, so he's desperate for my – *our* – support. He'll be bending over backwards and doing summersaults to crush those ENABA loonies.'

'I really can't imagine such a fat, ugly little man with a silly moustache presiding over *our* European Union,' wailed Antje. There were murmurs of agreement all around the table. 'And the oily runt can't even speak a word of German – or French. In fact, I understand his Spanish isn't too good either – appalling grammar by all accounts. All my Spanish friends think he's common.'

She's right, thought Klipper. *Maybe my advisers were wrong about the chances of a German being elected Euro President. I'd certainly be the youngest and best-looking candidate. And I speak four languages fluently!* He smiled broadly, pushed his chair back, and stood up. 'So, I hope you all have very enjoyable holidays. Barring a nuclear conflagration, I probably won't be seeing most of you for quite a few weeks!'

There was an end-of-term atmosphere in the Cabinet Room as Klipper made his way to the door, trying not to give the impression that he was anxious to get away. He was gliding regally down the corridor to his own office, when Stiefel caught up with him.

'You won't let them decimate my Armed Forces, will you, Martin,' he pleaded.

Christ! – is there no escape? 'Of course not, Karl! As usual, we'll make a few cosmetic adjustments to keep the doves happy. As I've said before, being the major power in Europe, we must have military clout. So don't worry! Go off on holiday and relax. Where are you and – and ... *Barbara* going this year?'

'An Arctic cruise ... on a Finnish ship.'

'Oh, how lovely!'

'I got an invite from one of those filthy rich Turks too – and from Werner Stumpf to go to his place in Mallorca–'

'Oh dear!'

'– but Barbara can't cope with hot climates ... she comes out in a vile rash all over.'

'How awful! Must dash! Give my love to ... um ... Barbara. And have a terrific time in Lapland!'

Klipper shot off down the corridor with his mind made up: the ridiculous flotilla of fourteen 'U-boats' – or whatever the number was – could be scrapped for a start.

CHAPTER 6

'It's not so bad with the fig jam,' Mike said unconvincingly as he attempted another nibble of the near-indestructible rye bread.

'We'll have to get a stock of proper stuff,' Jane replied. 'We can't go through this nonsense again.'

They were breakfasting alone on a shady terrace at *Ca'n Pau*, the one specifically 'recommended' by Werner, both in the Rules and at the end of dinner last night. It was just after nine and the Oakhearts had yet to see their hosts – not because they were slugabeds, but because Werner and Heidi were already hard at work in the garden somewhere, making the most of it before the July sun got too hot. None of this had come as a surprise, however, for the Stumpfs had forewarned their guests that they always breakfasted at Bar Pou Nou in Alqueria Blanca. It was, as Werner had stated at dinner, 'a special treat' for Heidi in order to give her a break from the kitchen. Heidi had glowed, adding that the Pou Nou made the most delicious coffee and the most wonderful ham and cheese *bocadillos*. And, of course, the shaded square with its tall trees was so peaceful early in the morning; one could almost imagine being in Provence. Werner had said it was better than Provence.

Eight o'clock certainly was 'early' for breakfast as far as the Oakhearts were concerned – at least if one was one holiday. They had, therefore, declined the somewhat hesitant invitation extended by their hosts to join them; it was only too obvious that the Stumpfs had a long-established tradition of taking breakfast *alone*. They very much enjoyed reading the local papers *in peace*, Werner had stated emphatically, provoking a brief conversation:

'Do you even sit outside in the winter?' asked Jane.

'Oh yes!' enthused Heidi, '– if it's sunny – and it often is.'

'From the end of October to the beginning of May we commence breakfast one hour later – at nine,' Werner said. 'So, as you will not be joining us tomorrow, Mike and Jane, let me remind you of a few things.'

He'd gone on to rehearse the whereabouts of everything – including the 'fantastic' rye bread which they purchased from a German baker in Cala d'Or who only used organically produced materials – and to emphasize that Margalida did not set or clear tables, or wash up: she had enough to do cleaning such a large house.

'If you ask me,' said Mike, abandoning his second piece of rye bread – Jane had stuck to fresh fruit – 'I think they're miffed that they haven't been invited out on that geezer Manilla's boat. There was a distinct drop in temperature when you came back from the phone last night.'

'"That geezer Manilla", Mikey, just happens to be Don Alfonso Pablo Juan Felipe de Santa Ponça y Paguera, the Conde de Manilla. The Manillas are one of Mallorca's oldest families. Perhaps Werner was just annoyed that he phoned during dinner – and, to boot, right in the middle of his erudite discourse on "The Problems With The World Today And How Everything Was So Much Better When I Was Your Age".'

'Maybe, but Werner jumped up quite chirpily from the table when the phone rang, saying something about his son always calling around that time. However, when he came back from the hall, didn't you think there was a sort of sneer on his face? And the way he said, "It's the Conde de Manilla for you, Jane," was just loaded with innuendo – as though he thought the title was fake, or the chap was an embezzler or a rapist – I don't know – and that just talking to him was going to suck you into some terrible, criminal conspiracy.'

'Good Lord! You certainly have a vivid imagination.'

'Well, *you* didn't hear him while you were out of the room, going on and on about how every Tom, Dick and Harry on this island claims to have some tatty title or other, and that most of them don't have two euros to rub together. He even said that before the Treaty of Versailles had "emasculated" Germany, with most of East Prussia and Silesia being "gifted" to Poland, his family's estates near Danzig had been almost as large as the whole of Mallorca!'

'Really? But Werner doesn't claim to have some title, does he?'

'I don't think so. When I drafted all those affidavits for the case against Piston-Jones, he never mentioned one.'

'Well, anyway, if we don't get a move on, the Conde de Manilla is going to sail without us.'

Twenty minutes later, Werner saw the Oakhearts drive away down the *camino* towards Alqueria Blanca. He was working on a rocky outcrop on the hillside above the house, clearing scrub around a clump of tenacious wild olives with a view to planting some Provençal lavender later in the year; Heidi, as was their custom, was working in a distant part of the garden. Werner's face was set hard.

'"The Conde de Manilla",' he sneered. 'I wouldn't have gone out on his pathetic boat even if he'd got down on his bended knees and begged me, the arrogant little fat bastard.' He struck an effeminate pose: '"Don

Alfonso and Daddy,"' he said mimicking Jane, '"got quite chummy when he was Spain's Ambassador to Prague some years back".'

Werner removed his thick leather gardening gloves, wiped his perspiring brow, and sat down on the hot bare rock. '"No room on the boat for all of us" – my arse!' he muttered. 'We're just not posh enough for those Spic snobs. If I'd been a bloody Hohenzollern, or Heidi had been a Bavarian Wittelsbach rather than a bloody factory worker's daughter, well ...

'He and his fat wife came here for dinner and drank my best wines – Château Lafite! – I only had the three bottles! – stuffed their faces, and babbled inane diplomatic niceties for hours. "You must come for dinner at *one* of our houses, or our pied-à-terre in town." *Pied-à-terre*! – sickening false modesty! – it's one of Palma's grandest palaces! "And you must join us on our boat. During the season we're always pottering about at the Portopetro Royal Yacht Club." *Royal*! The only thing "royal" about it are the sodding fees. If Heidi mentions one more time about getting a bloody boat, I'll–'

Werner could feel the anger dangerously bubbling up in him again: until last night, they'd not heard a word from the Manillas since they'd said goodbye to them after that bloody dinner more than three years ago. So much for breeding! But then, what could one expect from people who until thirty years ago thought a sceptic tank a luxury?

'I mean, what have this lot done since 1492 – apart from plundering gold and silver from a load of witless primitives in Latin America and then blowing it all on a load of over-the-top churches? Fuck all, that's what! A few painters, a couple of second-rate writers, and one or two guitar players. Oh yes – and they invented *paella*! Not much to write home about really, is it?'

He looked at the shade under the olive trees and thought of the cool interior of his Palma apartment. He needed to see the bank manager anyway, so perhaps he should go down to the house and phone Concha. She was only seventeen, but so experienced, and her breasts! ... He could feel himself getting hard. Yes, he'd tell Heidi he'd gone back to the house for the loo and the bank phoned – some problem about the new chequebooks. Spanish banks were hopelessly inefficient, especially Santander. She wouldn't suspect a thing! He'd be back well in time for tonight's concert. ... Now *that* would impress the Oakhearts! They'd meet some *real* class with *real* money – people who treated him with proper respect, not like that Mallorcan glorified peasant Manilla and his tub of lard of a wife!

Marching back down the hillside, Werner was feeling much happier than when he climbed up. '1492!' he sniggered as his Gothic entrance came into view. 'Jesus Christ! Even Columbus – the most famous "Spaniard" – was an Italian ... well, possibly – Jewish in any event! And the pillocks are *still* arguing about whether he's buried in Seville or Santo Domingo! God help us if that worm Azucena becomes European President next year!'

*

As the Oakhearts drove past *Ca'n Xet*, the black dogs charged across the courtyard towards the car, barking maniacally.

'So, we *were* right,' Jane said. 'That place we remembered passing yesterday is where the *Eminence Grise* hangs out.'

'It's outrageous! Those poor dogs! If this were England, those callous two would be prosecuted. I just can't understand the mentality.'

'Well, we're not in England, and Werner explained the mentality last night.'

'He obviously felt very strongly about it – he got quite animated.'

'Not enough to lay down the law to his bloody housekeeper though. I suppose Hitler was very fond of his Alsatian, Blondie, but he still tried out a cyanide tablet on it before taking one himself.'

'Footy! That's a horrid thing to say. What on earth–?'

'Sorry! I don't know why I said that. Quite out of order. Sorry. I suppose I just can't imagine those poor, poor dogs tied up like that, twenty-four hours a day for over five years. If she were my cleaner, I wouldn't hesitate to tell her what I thought. Actually, I don't think I could have someone so cruel working in my house.'

'Perhaps cleaners are hard to come by in these parts.'

'That's probably the very point I was trying to make in that awful, prejudiced way – that, for all his big talk, Werner's principles are malleable.'

Later, as they drove down through the olive groves between Alqueria Blanca and Portopetro, Mike said: 'So what do I call this Manilla bloke? – "Your Grace"? – "Count"? – "sir"? And what about his wife? – "Countess"? – "ma'am"? –'

'Don't be silly! Just shake his hand and say "I'm Michael" – or "Mike" if you want – and he'll probably say "I'm Alfonso," or something, "and this is my wife, Maria" – or whatever she's called. My God! – what *is* she called?'

'Why did Manilla call your father a few days ago before he and Betty left for England?'

'"A little business matter," he said, although I can't imagine what he meant. I mean, he's retired from the *corps diplomatique* now.'

'And his family are going to be on this outing too? I wonder how many there are.'

'Well, we'll soon find out.'

'And what time do we have to be back for this damned concert thing?'

'Don't be such a philistine!'

'I'm *not* a philistine. I'm just not that keen on cello sonatas.'

'Gudrun Schluck is one of the greatest cellists of our time.'

'I'm well aware of that, honey. She's one of the soloists on our CD of the Beethoven Triple Concerto.'

'Well, there you are then. We'd have to pay a small fortune to see her in London. Tonight, we get her for free, plus dinner and the privilege of being welcomed into the home of Herbert von Karpen. What an unexpected treat! I think it was awfully nice of Werner to get us invited.'

'*Aw*fully. ... But there's no such thing as a free dinner!'

'Oh, shut up!'

'So what time is the kick off?'

'Werner wants to leave the house at seven. He says it's a fifteen-minute drive to von Karpen's.'

'*Seven*! So much for a laid-back holiday!'

'Stop bloody moaning! We're going out on a boat! I'm sure that'll be "laid-back".'

The Oakhearts found Portopetro as enchanting as Alqueria Blanca, although Mike couldn't subscribe to Jane's initial reaction that it reminded her of Italy's Porto Fino. Apart from anything else, it was not much more than a fishing village with some waterside bars and restaurants. The grandly styled 'Royal Yacht Club', situated in a steeply incised inlet at the western end of the harbour, consisted of a single quay. There were thirty craft at most, and quite a few of them were no more than one- or two-man fishing boats. The Manillas' boat, the *Fleur de Lys*, was not, therefore, difficult to find. Contrary to the Oakhearts' expectations, however, it was neither a tall-masted sailing yacht nor a gleaming mass of white fibreglass resembling a paper dart, but a vessel resembling a traditional Cornish wooden fishing boat with an extended central cabin.

The bare-footed Conde and Condesa de Manilla were sitting on the rear deck, sheltered from the scorching sun by a wooden canopy that extended from the cockpit. They looked remarkably like twins, for both were around five-foot six and plump, with similar facial features and skin tones. Furthermore, they were kitted out in seemingly identical white shorts and short-sleeved shirts. With no evidence of anyone else aboard, they introduced themselves effusively in French, for some reason, and intimated that they should be addressed as 'Alfonso' and 'Beatriz'. After a few minutes, it began to dawn on the Manillas that, despite his valiant efforts, Mike would be happier speaking his native tongue. Effortlessly, they switched to English, which they spoke as though they'd received elocution lessons from Sir John Gielgud.

As Alfonso cast off, Jane said to Beatriz: 'I must have misunderstood, but I thought your children would be joining us. We'd been *so* looking forward to meeting them.'

Beatriz smiled sweetly. '*Quel dommage*, my dear! The children usually spend much of the summer with us here at the Portopetro house, but poor Jaime had to dash back to Palma this morning to deal with some tedious business. He's a notary, you know. And Elena has a bit of a stomach bug, and so Christina – Jaime's wife – has stayed behind to look after her and our grandchildren. Felipe, our son-in-law, is out sailing somewhere ... with the King. That's our place up there on the hill.' She pointed to a villa of palatial proportions nestling amidst pines and palms.

Mike and Jane exchanged glances.

'You must come over and meet everyone while you're here,' Beatriz added.

'So much nicer – just the four of us,' said Alfonso.

The *iot* – as the craft was known in Catalan – passed the outer breakwater and began to roll in the gentle swell as it turned to starboard and headed south.

'It's so very kind of you to invite us out,' said Mike to Alfonso, who was sitting on a tall seat in front of the helm, his short fat legs swinging childlike about a foot off the deck in rhythm to the boat's pitching and rolling. Mike glanced over his shoulder: Jane was sat at the stern with the Condesa, who appeared to be conducting some form of interrogation.

'Not at all, old boy, a pleasure,' intoned Alfonso. 'When I spoke with Douglas in Madrid the other day and learned you were coming to our neck of the woods – well, we couldn't believe our luck. We've heard so much about Jane over the years, but somehow our paths never seemed to cross. ... So, you're a lawyer too, er...?'

Mike cringed: he didn't want to talk about work. 'Yes, a solicitor.'

'Ah, the *junior* branch of the profession. Do you hope to become a barrister one day ... like Jane?'

Breathing deeply, Mike said: 'No, I don't think you ...' *Quick! Change the subject before you say something you'll regret!* 'You said your son' – he groped for the name – 'is a notary.'

'Yes – a very clever boy, Jaime. Damned difficult to join the club. Licence to print money, the notary racket.'

'Really? The notarial profession has almost died out in England. I must say, this is a lovely old boat. That's Cabrera on the horizon, is it?'

Without looking at Mike, Alfonso said: 'Yes, it *is* a lovely "*old*" boat. My father had her built in 1954–'

'Good heavens!'

'–and I love her dearly. Of course, the maintenance costs are rather steep – *and* the insurance, what with all the wood, but I really couldn't cope with that nasty fibreglass stuff. Still have the original English diesel engines. Can't make much more than ten knots, but I'm never in a hurry to get anywhere.'

'Why does it have a French name ... *Fleur de Lys?*'

'Hmm? ... Oh *that*! Beatriz's idea.'

'She likes lilies?'

'Not really. ... They're on the coat of arms.'

'Coat of arms?'

'Hers ... her family's. They're Borbóns.'

At the stern, Beatriz, having ascertained the precise reasons why the Oakhearts were staying with the Stumpfs, was now grilling Jane about Britain's king and his spouse, whom she insisted on calling 'Mrs Parker-Bowles'. To Jane's surprise, Beatriz had met them; Beatriz expressed surprise that Jane had not.

'But what I really want to know, Jane, is ... do they share a bed?'

Jane looked despairingly at Mike, but he appeared to be making a great effort to absorb Alfonso's every word.

'I must say,' Mike said, 'that until last night I'd never even heard of Cabrera. Werner Stumpf gave us a few details. Actually, he said it was a barren wilderness.'

Alfonso snorted and finally turned to face Mike; there was a smile on his round, chubby face. '"A barren wilderness"! Typical! I always thought the man talked through his arse – even when he was a journalist. Cabrera is a national park, Michael. In fact, it was Spain's first national maritime park. Thanks to being a military base for most of the twentieth century, it was completely untouched by any development. Now, apart from the park wardens, it's uninhabited. You can't land or even moor in the waters without a permit – and they're not easy to come by, believe me. I'm privileged to have one.'

'Oh! So, this is quite a special excursion?'

'Well, I suppose it is ... in a way. Although Cabrera proper is only seven kilometres long – it's the main island of an archipelago – it's home to a wonderful variety of wildlife, particularly birds – peregrines, cormorants, hawks – all sorts of seagulls, naturally. And there's also a unique species of lizard, *podarcis lifordi*.'

'Your enthusiasm indicates you're something of a naturalist or ornithologist, Alfonso.'

'I wouldn't say that. I hunt – not on Cabrera, naturally.'

'Naturally. ... Is there much to hunt on Mallorca?'

'Rabbits! No, I don't hunt *here*, my boy – Andalucia – the Sierra Nevada. One has everything there – well, plenty of game, that is, including boar.'

'Really?' Neither Mike nor Jane supported blood sports.

'Of course, for the big stuff one goes to Africa.'

'"Big stuff"?'

'Lions, elephants, rhino ... you know?'

Mike could feel his hackles rising. 'One can still shoot those animals? ... Where in Africa?'

'Botswana, Namibia – oh we Spanish are the most numerous big-game hunters out there now. You English are all too frightened to shoot anything with four legs these days in case some do-gooder puts a bomb through your letterbox. Do you shoot? Douglas does, doesn't he?'

'Well, personally–'

'*Darling*!' chirped Jane, stepping down into the cockpit and grabbing Mike's arm to steady herself, '– isn't this *wonderful*?' Beatriz was just behind her, clearly unwilling to be abandoned at the stern. 'The colour of the sea is just unbelievable! And Cabrera ahead looks like something out of an adventure film ... *The Land That Time Forgot* – that sort of thing. Oh, is that a ruined castle on the hilltop? Can we visit it?'

'No – unfortunately,' Mike said, concealing his relief. 'The whole island is a bird sanctuary – a national park. We can't land. Alfonso has just been telling me all about it.'

'Michael's right, my dear,' he confirmed. 'That's a fifteenth-century fortress, by the way. It's the only major structure on the entire island. If you'd really like to visit it, they do have "*organized* excursions" from Colònia de Sant Jordi ... occasionally.' It was clear from his tone that 'organized excursions' were not the sort of thing that he would expect the Oakhearts to indulge in.

'I'm afraid one would be in a party of *Germans*,' said Beatriz, '– or rather, but for these silly ENABA people, one might have been. Perhaps they've abandoned those tours now. I don't think many English were keen to leave the beaches and trek through hectares of sagebrush trying to find some rare species of damned lizard.'

'I do hope my wife has been entertaining you, Jane,' snapped Alfonso. 'What have you two been chatting about back there?'

'Never you mind!' snorted Beatriz.

'This and that,' said Jane, gripping Mike's arm even tighter as the boat road the swell of a speedboat that had crossed their path some minutes earlier. He looked into her eyes and smiled. 'Actually, Alfonso,' Jane continued, 'Beatriz has been telling me the most interesting things about your royal family.'

'Oh dear!'

'I'd no idea they were as bad as our lot.'

After a further forty minutes of gentle chugging, the Conde de Manilla steered his venerable *iot* to port and proceeded down Cabrera's rugged east coast, with the Oakhearts spellbound by the terrifying cliffs rising hundreds of feet sheer from the sea. Eventually, they rounded a headland and found themselves in a large arc-shaped bay with empty sandy beaches backed by pine woods.

Alfonso, having dropped the anchor into the crystal-clear water, returned from the bow saying, 'Well now, is this paradise or is it not? – a virgin, tourist-free Balearic island!'

There was a small ladder attached to the stern, and, after everyone had taken their turn to change in the cabin, Jane and the Manillas climbed down into the warm water; Mike dived in, having made a couple of jokes about his wife being a wimp. In truth, Jane disliked being out of her depth. Nevertheless, as the water was as calm as a mill pond, even she joined the others in their swim to the sandy shore, some hundred metres distant. Alas, the hosts' schedule only permitted a brief rest. When they'd all made it back, Beatriz decided it was time for 'a spot of lunch'. Leisurely, she and Alfonso laid out a banquet, including various salads, cured Serrano ham, cheeses, tortillas, olives, crusty white and wholemeal bread, smoked salmon, cold roasted vegetables, and red peppers stuffed with cod.

'My, my, *my*,' Mike gushed, 'you have been busy, Beatriz!'

'We have an excellent cook,' she replied, 'although she does complain about the kitchen in the Portopetro house being too small.'

'Ah,' said Mike nodding, as if he too had to cope with bolshie staff. Meanwhile, Alfonso was offering him the plate piled high with the ham. 'Oh, thank you. I love Spanish ham.' He was just about to remove some with his fork, when Alfonso shook his head with an expression of exaggerated horror.

'No, no, *no*, my boy, *never* with the *fork*!' Alfonso snatched some pieces off the plate and stuffed them into his little mouth. 'The fingers! The *fingers*! *Always* the fingers!'

Mike was groping for some kind of defensive – or even offensive – riposte over the public reprimand of his breach of Spanish table manners, when Alfonso added:

'I'm going to have a beer, Michael, while these soppy girls sip their *agua con gas*. Will you join me – or would you like some wine?'

Mike opted for beer and felt the animosity subside.

'We've been to all sorts of exotic places,' Jane purred, 'but I really can't think of a more beautiful location than this. Can you, Mikey?' He shook his head as he tucked into the mouth-watering ham with its extraordinary buttery taste. 'And we have it all to ourselves.'

'We're lucky, Jane,' said Beatriz. 'Occasionally, there are one or two foreign boats here – usually German. In fact, we've been here on some days over the last few years when there've been as many as half a dozen. Frightful!' She devoured an olive and spat the stone over the side. 'I suppose that's one good thing about all those firebombs and things. It's so awfully nice of you and all the other English to support us and keep coming. And I think the King and Queen are wonderful to holiday at *Marivent* as usual – so brave in view of all the assassination threats. Actually, we'll be at a reception at the Palace next week.'

'Us and several hundred others,' grunted Alfonso frowning. 'I really don't know how Their Majesties cope with those awful local politicos and functionaries, all jabbering away in their incomprehensible accents and acting like badly behaved children at a birthday party, the men sporting beards like a lot of clones, and the women looking like tarts. It really is laughable – the idea of such people trying to govern a sovereign state.'

'Frightening!' added Beatriz.

'You don't speak the local language, then?' asked Jane.

Alfonso pulled a face. '*Mallorquí*? – bastardized Catalan? Of *course* we speak it – we *are* Mallorcans – but only with trades people and petty officials in the town hall who refuse to speak anything else. Believe me, Jane, there's nothing worse than fanatical nationalism rearing its ugly head on an island only fifty miles across with just under a million inhabitants – most of them barely literate.'

'Oh, Alfonso,' scolded Beatriz, 'you *do* exaggerate so!'

'Do I, my dear? When we were young, all the lower orders were farmers, artisans, shopkeepers or servants – folk who are generally conservative by nature and know their place. Now, thanks to mass tourism, the bulk of the working class are unionised employees working in bars, restaurants, hotels and shops – people who drift from job to job, who have no loyalty to anyone or anything, and think only in terms of rights but never responsibilities – a right to a job, a right to a pension, a right to a home, a right to prosperity. They expect it all handed to them on a plate.'

'Now, now, don't get too serious, *cariño*. I'm sure Jane and – and–'

'I blame the schools,' Alfonso snapped. 'There's no discipline anymore.'

'Have some more tortilla, Jane ... Mark – *Mike*.'

'I'd love to,' said Jane. 'It's delicious. Well, everything's delicious, and I'm famished.'

'Me too!' said Mike.

'Aren't the Stumpfs feeding you?' asked Beatriz earnestly. She quickly learned about the portion control at dinner and the do-it-yourself breakfast. 'You poor, *poor* things! I remember our dinner there ... vaguely. It was rather minimalist – oodles of wine though ... a different colour with each course! Oh, and some frightfully sweet German thing with the pudding. Vile!'

'Typical Krauts!' barked Alfonso through a mouthful of smoked salmon. 'Always give you buckets of booze and morsels of food at dinner parties. Can't understand them. We try not to go if we can help it. Actually, a few weeks back – do you remember, Beatriz? – this German property developer chap ... wants to build a pile of little villas on some land we own near Cala d'Or ... well, he invited us out to dinner at Portals – the place west of Palma where all the millionaire parvenus have their tasteless yachts. He had rings all over his fingers like an American. Yuck!'

'And *she*,' sneered Beatriz, '– his "wife" – looked like a Christmas tree. There was enough Cartier jewellery on her to open a shop!'

The Oakhearts laughed politely.

'Well,' continued Alfonso, 'he asked us to choose the restaurant – quite difficult there because most of the eateries are foreign owned, a lot of them German. Anyway, we know a decent place – the owner used to be our chef in Palma – that does a damned good *paella*, so we took them there. Would you believe that when the *paella* came, old Fritzy told Tomeu to serve only *half* of it? – amongst *four* of us, mark you! – because he wanted to take the rest home for the bloody dog!'

This time the Oakhearts exploded, and now, well-oiled with his third beer, Alfonso also chuckled heartily.

As the laughter subsided, Jane's conscience could not help itself. 'To be fair,' she said, 'there might not have been a lot of food last night, but it was excellent. Heidi is a very good cook.'

'I'm sure,' said Beatriz. 'Well, she was a pastry cook in Germany, or something, wasn't she?'

Mike bristled. 'She had her own business – three or four *Konditorei* – very successful. That's what she told you, Footy, didn't she?'

'Yes.'

'I suppose she thought Stumpf was quite a catch,' said Beatriz eyeing the last piece of tortilla. 'A funny little woman, I seem to remember. Never said much – always darting about like a hyperactive servant, with that man giving her orders every ten seconds. Well, no doubt she has to put up with all that Prussian nonsense if she wants to get the house when he pops off. How old is he now? … sixty? … sixty-five?' She finally snatched the tortilla and took a bite.

'Surely not?' said Jane, staring hard at Mike, who was smiling at Alfonso as he poured more beer into his glass. 'He only looks about fifty-five to me. He's so fit!'

'It's his birthday in a few days,' said Mike. Jane kicked him under the table. 'No idea how old he is though. ... That's why we're here ... for the party.'

'So Jane was telling me,' said Beatriz. 'You did some sort of legal work for him in England, er ...?'

Mike nodded. *I'm not going to talk about work!*

Alfonso, who didn't seem to be listening, was humming something which sounded vaguely like Ravel's Bolero. 'If you ask me,' he broke off in mid-bar, 'it was old Stumpf who made the catch, tying the knot with Brunhilde – or whatever she's called.'

'*Heidi*,' said Jane.

'By all accounts, Stumpf was a bit short of the old readies at the time, and–'

'Alfonso! Don't be so indiscreet! That was told to you in confidence.'

'I just called in some favours owed to me by contacts in the German Foreign Ministry, that's all. It wasn't a state secret that journalism didn't pay that much at the time – doesn't now – and the royalties on historical biographies can't be that great either. It's not as though a book on Bismarck, for God's sake, makes the international best-seller list, is it? Stumpf isn't bloody Grisham!'

Jane didn't want to hear all this; nor, for that matter, did Mike; they both felt slightly disloyal.

'Lionel de Tourny and Jeanne Moineau are coming to Werner's birthday party,' said Jane brightly.

'Goodness!' exclaimed Beatriz wide-eyed. 'How exciting! I'd heard he was a bit of a recluse. We know his parents quite well, naturally. They have a mooring near ours, and–'

'The boy's a bloody nuisance,' snapped Alfonso, 'the way he drives that speedboat in and out of the harbour. Absolutely irresponsible! No respect for the Club's rules. Typical French! A law unto themselves, the lot of 'em.'

Sheepishly, Beatriz said: 'The parents, the Baron et Baronne de Tourny, are charming.'

'I blame Hollywood,' growled Alfonso. 'All this fame has gone completely to the lout's head. Can't act, of course – at least, so I've read in the papers.'

'He ran over my wife yesterday ... on his motorbike,' chuckled Mike.

'Oh, Mikey!' groaned Jane.

The Manillas were staring at Mike with such puzzled expressions that it made him chuckle even more.

'I thought he was very good in *Brittany* – and that Jewish thing,' opined Beatriz, believing that the motorbike remark had to be an example of dry English humour. 'I saw them in Palma with the children. Alfonso won't go to the cinema anymore.'

'What *are* you talking about, woman?'

Mike burst out laughing.

'Don't give him any more–' Jane yelped, but she was too late: Alfonso was already topping up the glasses with San Miguel. 'Um, you mean *Normandie* and *Dreyfus*, Beatriz,' she added, glaring at Mike.

'Oh yes! Silly me! I preferred the one about the boat, er ...'

'*Normandie*.'

'Yes. Oh, it must have been so wonderful travelling on such luxurious transatlantic liners in the Thirties. I thought *Dreyfus* was too long. And Lionel didn't look any older at the end of the film. And the years on Devil's Island were *too* horrid. I couldn't watch at times.'

'Dreyfus!' snorted Alfonso. '*L'Affaire*! *J'accuse*! The trouble generated in France for so many years by just one bloody Jew! It's no wonder the Middle East is in such a mess.'

The Oakhearts sat rigid.

'So,' Jane said as if addressing an irksome witness in court, 'is your government doing anything about these ENABA fanatics? I should think they must be pretty pissed off about the damage to the tourist industry.'

'A few communist cranks,' sneered Beatriz, waving a chubby hand dismissively. 'Imagine – they want secession from Spain! They want a republic! We'd never see the King and Queen here again. No more galas at the Auditorium, no more royal regattas – the *Copa del Rey* ... They'd nationalize *Marivent* – and the Almudaina Palace – and turn them into – into ... adult education centres, I shouldn't wonder, teaching folk dancing and basket weaving. Oh, it's just *too* awful!'

Alfonso leaned back, stretched, and yawned. 'Now, now, Beatriz, don't go getting yourself all upset. There isn't going to be any secession – or a republic – or any withdrawal from the European Union, or any other of the nonsensical claptrap preached by ENABA or their sidekick,

Jordi Adrover. Adrover, Jane, is the head of PANABA, ENABA's political wing. Ghastly little bearded four-eyed oik. He's an accountant.

'The point is that although the lower orders all detest the Kraut – who doesn't? – I mean they flock here in their thousands for the sun and to go native and let their hair down, and then start turning the place into a bloody colony! Oh, our lawyers, dentists, doctors, accountants, hairdressers, teachers, estate agents, electricians, plumbers, carpenters – you name it! – aren't good enough for your bloody Kraut. Oh no, they have to import their own.'

'I suppose that's what the EU is all about,' said Jane coldly, '– free movement of goods, capital, and people.'

'Well, they should stay in their own bloody country,' said Alfonso, 'and not turn our island into Hamburg-on-Sea where there's not enough room to swing a cat.'

'I mean,' said Beatriz, 'the English haven't brought all their own doctors and things with them. Our people seem quite good enough for *them – you*.'

'And, of course,' Alfonso continued, 'the German professionals and traders expect to get paid German rates, and then their local equivalents want the same. And they've completely cocked up the domestic service market.'

'I'll say!' agreed Beatriz. 'Some little cleaner asks a German for *thirty* euros an hour, believing they're a soft touch with more money than sense, which, of course most of them are, and the fool agrees immediately, thinking he's got a steal compared to what he's used to paying in Germany. No idea about bargaining! They think it's beneath their dignity.'

'And the next thing you know,' snarled Alfonso, 'every damned servant is demanding the same as their friend Maria is getting up the road at Fritzy's house. There's too much money sloshing about on this island, that's the crux of the problem. Well, there's not enough unemployment now, thanks to the Kraut. You see, Jane … and Michael, your average Mallorcan has forgotten what poverty is like and has become greedy. They think money grows on bloody trees – hence this independence nonsense. They've got this dotty idea that all this prosperity is *their* doing – the collective effort of a couple of hundred thousand Mallorcan plebeians working a few hours a day in a bar, or making hotel beds. So, now they've got too big for their boots and think they can run the show themselves. Pathetic! The very idea of leaving the EU! The entire inefficient agricultural production of the island would collapse without EU subsidies – and that's just for starters. Where did the money come from for all those new Mercedes buses in Palma, eh? – the restoration of the Cathedral? – the–?'

'And Madrid subsidises the cost of travel to the mainland,' interjected Beatriz fiercely. 'I do most of my shopping in Barcelona and Madrid. We don't even have Hermès here, would you believe?'

'My dear Jane,' Alfonso drawled, 'and er ... Michael, the Germans have to be taught that when in Rome bla, bla, bla. Anyway, the tide was already turning before ENABA started their antics. The flow of immigrants was slowing down thanks to economic woes in Germany, this island pricing itself out of the market, and lots of opportunities for Germans and other foreigners to buy dirt cheap holiday homes in places like Slovenia' – he sniggered – 'or one of the other "developing" nations in the East that's now sucking Europe dry.

'Actually, I can tell you that I have it on very good authority – from the top if you catch my drift – that ENABA's ringleaders will be apprehended imminently. So, Jane, don't you worry your pretty little head about them. Relax and enjoy our island! ... Now, I think we should clear up and have a nice siesta for an hour or two, hmm?'

Half an hour later, with everything packed away in the cool boxes and the washing up completed in the miniscule galley, the Manillas had retired to the single cabin. The Oakhearts were stretched out on the stern's shaded deck.

'I can't believe all those anti-Semitic remarks,' Jane whispered. 'We'll have to find an excuse not to go to dinner.'

The heat and alcohol were conspiring to frustrate Mike's attempts to respond meaningfully; the boat's gentle rocking was also wonderfully soporific. 'Um ... no.'

'I mean, in this day and age–'

There was a colossal roar of an engine, and Jane instantly had a vision of a motorbike speeding towards her. 'What the hell's that!' she cried, pushing herself up. A large white speedboat was entering the bay, its raked bows well out of the water with spray flying in all directions. 'Christ, Mikey, it's coming straight for us!'

With the sound of cursing and the patter of small flat feet, the Manillas waddled up the short companionway from the cabin and made for the rail.

'*Mierda*!' roared Alfonso, hopping up and down. 'I don't believe it! It's *him* – that damned Frog! – that lunatic Tourny! I'd recognise that sodding plastic torpedo anywhere!'

'Don't you dare open your big mouth!' barked Beatriz in *Mallorquí* so that their guests wouldn't understand. 'I've been trying to get the Tournys – including Lionel – and Moineau – to dinner for bloody ages!'

As Lionel throttled back the turbocharged motors and came to drop anchor just twenty metres away, both boats rocked violently in the backwash.

'Don't – say – a – bloody *word*, Alfonso!' hissed Beatriz, her eyes blazing. But with Jeanne Moineau terminating her sunbathing at the speedboat's stern, and rising to reveal her total nudity, Alfonso was, in any event, utterly lost for words.

A few minutes later, treading water beside the *Fleur de Lys*, a joyous Lionel cried: 'Hi, Jane! Hi, Mike! *Buenas tardes*, Doña Beatriz ... Don Alfonso!'

'What a pleasant surprise!' fizzed Jane, beaming.

'A very pleasant surprise,' agreed Beatriz.

'What a coincidence,' said Mike, looking at Jeanne, who was swimming languorously towards them – still topless, but at least she'd dived in wearing a pair of bikini bottoms.

Puffing himself up, Alfonso declaimed: 'I trust you have a permit to moor here, Tourny.'

'Sure! Papa bribed the right officials like everyone else. I thought I'd find you in this bay, Jane and Mike. Mateu said you'd come over to Cabrera with the Condes de Manilla when I saw him in the garden this morning. Come on in – the water's heaven!'

'We've only just finished lunch,' said Beatriz smiling; she was clearly open to persuasion.

Jeanne arrived and rolled over onto her back. '*Bonjour!*'

What gorgeous breasts! thought Alfonso; so, too, did Mike.

'You must be Mike,' said Jeanne, seemingly transfixed. 'You're so ... *white* ... so English. I hope Jane is putting plenty of cream on you. Come on – come and say hello. Dive! – or have you been sabotaged by Spanish "food"?'

'Come *on*!' added Lionel.

'Perhaps,' began Beatriz, 'you'd like to come aboard and–?'

'It's siesta time,' Alfonso thundered, 'and I absolutely forbid you to go swimming, Beatriz. You must digest your food.'

'Well, I'm roasting,' said Jane moving to the stern. 'Last one in's a sissy!' And with that she dived in with whoops of delight from the French.

For a moment, Mike couldn't believe his eyes: it was the first time he'd ever seen her dive. Then he was almost running to the stern.

When Mike came up, Jane and Lionel were already swimming side by side – and slowly making for the beach. Then Mike felt something touch his shoulder.

Jeanne was treading water behind him. '*Re-bonjour!*' she chirped in her sing-song voice. 'Now we can say hello properly.'

After they'd kissed cheeks under the bulging eyes of the Manillas, Mike said: 'I think we ought to catch the others up.'

'I suppose so, but don't swim too fast. My days as an athlete are long past, thanks to Gauloises. Anyway, you've probably eaten enough of their dreadful *tortilla* to sink an armada.'

As they approached Tourny's boat at Jeanne's snail's pace – the other two were now almost at the beach – Jeanne cried out and flailed her arms.

'What is it? What's the matter?'

'*Merde*! I think a *méduse* has stung me.'

'A what?'

'*Méduse* ... a jellyfish!'

Mike was first up the boat's stern ladder; to his surprise, he noticed it was called *Normandie*. He held out a hand to Jeanne behind him and helped her out of the water.

'Now, let's have a look. Where do you think it stung you?'

She pointed to a spot on her left thigh. '*Ici*.'

'Can't see anything.'

'It stings.'

'Hmm. ... What does one use for a jellyfish sting?'

She shrugged her shoulders. 'I think you have to pee on it.'

Mike looked up and tried not to focus on her breasts. 'Sorry?'

'You know ... pee ... piss.'

'Maybe vinegar would do.'

'Maybe. There's a bottle down in the galley ... in the cupboard beside the *four* – the cooker.'

'I'll look. You sit down and rest that leg.' As he entered the cockpit, Mike glanced towards the shore; Lionel and Jane were already sitting on the beach. They looked as though they were laughing, seemingly oblivious to the fate of their respective partners. Through the hatchway, he shouted over his shoulder: 'Can't see any vinegar! Are you sure it was in the cupboard by the cooker?'

'Maybe we've run out.'

Startled by the proximity of Jeanne's voice, Mike swung round on bended knees, only to find his eyes at the level of her shaved pubes. For an instant, his mind froze. Then he managed to croak 'Oh my God!' as she closed in.

*

'We were beginning to wonder what had happened to you,' Jane said as Mike ran panting up the narrow beach.

'That was an impressive piece of breaststroke,' said Lionel, grinning. 'You weren't an Olympic swimmer by any chance, were you?'

'Where's Jeanne?' asked Jane looking towards the *Normandie*.

'Stung – by a jellyfish – helped her on board – vinegar – she–'

The smile was wiped from Jane's face. 'Good God! She's all right, I hope?'

'I–'

'I should think any jellyfish making contact with Jeanne would die instantly of alcoholic poisoning,' said Lionel, still grinning.

'I – she's OK – she's ... resting.'

Lionel looked Mike in the eye and winked. 'Good ... rest ... best thing for her.'

They sat chatting for almost an hour – Mike made only the occasional remark – about London and Paris, hotels and restaurants, childhood pets, their experiences of the Stumpfs and Manillas – all uncontentious and light-hearted. There was no mention of the law or movies.

Finally, Mike spotted Alfonso, and then Beatriz, moving about on the *Fleur de Lys*. 'Looks like siesta time's over,' he said nodding in their direction. 'I wonder what the time is.'

Lionel looked at his Rolex. 'Er ... just after four-thirty.'

The Oakhearts stared at each other in horror.

'Christ, Mikey! We'll never get back in time for Gudrun Schluck now – not on that old tug. Werner'll blow a fuse!'

As Jane had a morbid fear of jellyfish, Mike did not swim ahead. Consequently, when they finally reached the *Fleur de Lys*, Lionel was already bringing the *Normandie* alongside.

'What the hell is that mad bugger doing now?' muttered Alfonso. 'If he scratches one millimetre of–'

'Please don't be offended,' panted Jane, 'but we've got Gudrun Schluck at seven-thirty, and if–'

'*Who? What?*'

'The cellist, *cariño*,' said Beatriz. 'Remember – we had her after dinner at the Marqueses de Arenal's golden wedding?'

'Yes, that's her,' Jane confirmed. 'We have to leave the house by seven. We need to shower, change – we won't have enough time if we–'

'Lionel has kindly offered to take us back,' Mike interjected. 'He can get us to Portopetro in just twenty minutes.'

'Who ever heard of a concert starting at seven-thirty?' scoffed Alfonso. 'In the summer, *nothing* starts in Spain before nine at the earliest – ten usually. Germans! As I said before, when in Rome–'

'We'll just grab our things,' said Jane.

After the Oakhearts had thrown their bags over to the *Normandie* and then swum the few metres across, Lionel accelerated out of the bay like a rocket.

'Well,' growled Alfonso as the *Fleur de Lys* rolled violently in the wash, 'what, may I ask, do you make of *that*? Gretchen Schmuck, my arse! They just preferred a couple of flash, talentless bloody film stars to a couple of pensioners. I bet they hatched the whole thing on the beach.'

'I think she did mention something about a concert this morning, *cariño*.'

'Typical French – and English! Always stab you in the back when you're not looking.'

'Every cloud has a silver lining, *cariño*. We might just be able to get Tourny and Moineau round for dinner if we also invite Jane and what's-his-name too. If you ask me, Lionel fancies her – and Moineau couldn't keep her hands off the other one.'

'Hah! From what I've heard, old Fifi probably fancies both of them.'

Aboard the speeding *Normandie*, the screaming of its mighty engines and roar of the wind made conversation almost impossible; the wind chill was such that Jane ended up wrapped in towels to keep warm. Mike stood in the cockpit beside Lionel, both of them clearly thrilled by the vessel's fifty knots. Jane thought they looked like a couple of schoolboys; the ice seemed to be melting between them. If things continued like this, then by the end of the holiday ... who knew? And it was all thanks to mad old Werner! They shouldn't forget that.

Mike's intoxication with the *Normandie* could not, however, blank out the ongoing sensations of shock and thrill over his attempted seduction. Frankly, nothing like that had happened to him since university. ... Well, there was that Solicitors' European Group visit to the Commission in Brussels a couple of years back, and the Law Society functionary who'd got blind drunk at the official reception. But she'd been at least fifty – with her hair in a bun!

*Jeanne Moineau! Christ! Me and her! She's still hiding down in the cabin, no doubt terrified of meeting Jane. She said I'd tell her. She's a foul-mouthed bitch though ... probably not used to being rejected. ... Tell Jane? Couldn't. No point. It would only upset her. She'd probably want to go home – our holiday ruined – Werner's party ruined. ... She'd never see another Moineau film. ... Now there's a thought! ... Be serious! A load of hassle for nothing. And then, perhaps there'd always be that nagging doubt that I'd lied – that I **had** given her what she wanted. Oh hell! What if Jeanne refuses to come to Werner's do, and Lionel won't come without her? Jesus!*

Mike was still fretting when they were about to disembark; true to his word, Lionel had got them back to Portopetro in twenty minutes.

They were shaking hands as the cabin door opened and Jeanne emerged dressed in a colourful *parea*. She was smoking.

'Oh, Jeanne, I do hope you're feeling better,' Jane gushed with what sounded like genuine concern.

Jeanne smiled. '*Formidable*, *chérie*! I think the toxin has been neutralized.' She embraced Jane, and then Mike; the odours of alcohol and nicotine were overwhelming. 'Oh, Mike, *chéri*, you're so … stiff. I think Lionel's driving has frightened you!'

'Not at all,' Mike said, unsmiling. 'For me, it was the most exciting part of the day.'

Jeanne burst out laughing. '*Vive* Noël Coward!'

'See you at the party, if not before,' said Lionel as the Oakhearts stepped down onto the quay.

Here it comes, thought Mike.

'Ah *oui* – the party!' shrieked Jeanne. 'I can't wait!'

Jane drove back to *Ca'n Pau* at speed, Mike telling her to slow down several times. It was just coming up to a quarter to six when they walked into the courtyard, congratulating themselves on having plenty of time to shower and change after all.

To their surprise, Heidi was sitting on one of the wrought iron garden seats that were arranged around the fountain. She was wearing an elegant black cocktail dress and a single string of pearls. They were almost as surprised to see her smoking a cigarette; it was the first time they'd seen her smoke.

After they'd exchanged greetings, Jane said: 'You're looking very elegant, Heidi. I hope we're not late. Werner did say we would be leaving at seven.'

'No, no! You are right. You have plenty of times. Werner is not coming back in the house yet. You have a nice day on the boat? You both look very red.'

There's something wrong, Jane thought. *I can see it in her eyes … a sadness.*

'Quite an extraordinary day,' said Mike. 'We–'

'Where's Werner?' asked Jane kindly.

'Werner? … He had to go Palma … to the bank … to see the … the top man. Problems with the new books of the cheques. There are always problems.'

'Oh!' said Mike brightly. 'So the concert's off?'

'No, no. Werner said–'

'Jane! Mike!' Stumpf's roar reverberated around the courtyard as he came striding through the Gothic arch, his arms outstretched and an expression of joy on his face. 'You have a wonderful day on the boat? Oh! The dear Manillas have turned you into lobsters!'

'Marvellous day!' said Mike beaming.

'Fantastic!' fizzed Jane. 'And you won't believe it, but–'

'*Ja, ja*! And I have a wonderful day too, making a Mallorcan bank manager work for once and do his job properly. So! Now we all get ready for the concert. It will be an experience to cherish!'

Heidi had stood up, and as Werner marched past her, he hissed in German: 'The pearls are OK, but you wore that dress the last time.'

CHAPTER 7

It was one of those steamy nights when the Mediterranean seems to be boiling like a volcanic hot spring. Luckily, Officers Llorenç Grimalt and Francesc Roig of the Palma City Police were in plain clothes – shorts, T-shirts and trainers. They had finally struck gold in the early evening while sipping ice-cold beers in one of the many seedy gay bars on Joan Miró, when they'd overheard two German youths trying to sell some ecstasy. The Germans, who unknown to their observers were not in fact gay, had given every impression of being high on something themselves, which probably explained their carelessness, but then as far as Grimalt and Roig were concerned, foreigners often behaved as if they were above the law. How many Germans drove motorcycles back home without crash helmets? Of course, most Mallorcans did – at least outside the towns – but that was beside the point.

    The amateur drug pushers were not very successful. Finally, the bar's proprietor told them they were annoying his customers and ordered them to leave. Grimalt and Roig followed. They caught up with them after a few minutes, and, using the German they'd learned as barmen and waiters during their college days and subsequently enhanced by the police language course, offered some friendly advice: don't waste time around Joan Miró; Palma was not Ibiza. After dark, they should go to the old city walls near the cathedral. The area was poorly illuminated, and if there were problems, it was easy to escape into the Old Town's maze of alleys. The Germans were grateful for the advice, saying they were touring the Balearics on a shoestring budget and didn't have enough to move on to Ibiza, where they hoped to get some bar work. Hence their need to realize some of their 'capital'.

    It was now after eleven, and Grimalt and Roig had had the Germans under observation for some time; they were attempting to do business in one of the dark corners of the broad walls where they zigzagged defensively around the cathedral, the massive floodlit building towering over them like a medieval airship hanger. They didn't appear to be doing good business here either, but then the tourists walking along the walls had come to admire the soaring Gothic architecture and the twinkling lights of the harbour, while the few local potential customers preferred to deal with their regular suppliers and not a couple of high Germans who could barely speak a word of Spanish – not to mention their ridiculous prices.

Finally, Grimalt and Roig made their move. They walked towards the Germans arm-in-arm, like a couple of lovers. As they passed them, Roig said:

'Hi, guys! How are things?'

'Hi,' said one of the Germans. 'It's shit.'

'We'll never have enough for the ferry tomorrow,' said the other.

'That's tough,' said Roig.

'*I know, cariño!*' said Grimalt, tousling his partner's hair. 'What about Jaume? He's *always* buying. He'll be in the Luna Amarilla now.'

'Oh yes,' said Roig. 'You guys could kill two birds with one stone – sell your stuff and pick up some trade. If you're into twinks, the Luna is *the* place.'

The Germans exchanged nods of approval. 'I'm Hans,' said the taller one, 'and this is Christian.' They all shook hands. 'But let's just get one thing clear,' added Hans as they set off, ' – me and Christian are straight, OK?'

They walked a short distance along the walls, descended some steps to ground level, and passed through one of the medieval city gates. Ahead of them, a dimly lit cobbled alley wound its way uphill. It was lined by tall narrow buildings that appeared as ancient as the adjacent cathedral, their windows shuttered and doors bolted. A dog barked somewhere; the Germans faltered.

'There doesn't seem to be much action around here,' said Hans.

Grimalt laughed. 'You'd be surprised! These back streets are full of clubs and bars. You just have to know your way about.'

They were rounding a corner when a door in a high stone wall to their left opened suddenly. Momentarily surprised, Hans and Christian stared through their bloodshot eyes into the gloom of an inner courtyard. Then they were flying through the doorway as voices shouted out in *Mallorquí*, the heavy door slamming shut behind them with a thunderous boom. The lads landed heavily on hard stone slabs, and were quickly pinned face down by Roig, Grimalt and two colleagues who'd rushed out of the shadows; they, too, were in plain clothes.

'Another sound, Krauts,' Grimalt hissed, 'and you're both dead!'

The struggling and protests stopped.

'That's better. OK, Doc, they're all yours.'

Dr Josep Ferrer, who'd been lurking behind a large potted palm, came forward cradling a briefcase close to his chest. He had no qualms about injecting the Germans with sufficient morphine to render them comatose for a couple of hours. On the contrary, believing them to be homosexual junkies, he thought they were such degenerate filth that they didn't really deserve to live at all. In any event, they were mere pawns in a much larger game, and to win it the end undoubtedly justified the means. For over fifty years he'd been closely associated with Mallorca's great cathedral – the *Seu* – as a choirboy, a teenage guide, and now as an honorary canon. He knew and loved every nook and cranny of the vast episcopal complex, including the labyrinthine bishop's palace and the cloisters – not to mention the corridors and passageways that linked them. But during recent years, he'd gradually come to look upon the *Seu* as a Korean father might have looked upon a beloved daughter who'd become a Japanese army sex slave in World War II. Day after day the Blessed Virgin Mary's church witnessed an endless parade of gawping bare-limbed tourists – the females almost topless, the males sporting baseball caps – all loud and coarse, with undisciplined children running riot and acting as if they were in a theme park. And there was nothing he could do about it. On the contrary, the liberal dean and bishop had remonstrated with him for daring to evict some of the worst miscreants. 'They're all God's children,' they'd said. 'The cathedral is not a tomb. It's a place of joy and celebration. There's nothing in the Gospels about churches only being open to those dressed in three-piece suits, or twinsets and pearls. We are not an elitist establishment, Canon. And don't forget, the tourists *pay* to get in – "The customer is always right".'

With torch in hand, Dr Ferrer led his four ENABA colleagues through the dark cloisters, Roig and Grimalt easily carrying the lean young Germans over their shoulders. Ferrer glanced at his watch: yes, Ramon the nightwatchman would now be safely ensconced in his cubbyhole, having his midnight snack and brandy. He opened a low Gothic door, led them through the chapter house, and then stopped before an ogee arch. He hesitated. 'Through there is the Chapel of Piety,' he whispered. Then he took a deep breath and opened the door.

Beyond the arch that separated the chapel from the nave, the diffused glow of the floodlights was streaming through the great rose window above the central aisle and the tall lancets of the clerestory. 'Follow me!' snapped Dr Ferrer. 'We've got about thirty minutes before Ramon makes his next round.'

But the police had no need to be shown the way: few true Mallorcans were unacquainted with the Chapel Royal, for their magnificent cathedral had originally been conceived as a mausoleum for the monarchs of the Kingdom of Mallorca, that most short-lived of medieval powers which had once encompassed not only the Balearic Islands, but also a great swathe of southern France and Sardinia. Hans and Christian were dumped in front of the sumptuous and almost identical carved stone sarcophagi of Jaume II and Jaume III, the monarchs' feet resting on lions and their heads supported by angels.

'Right, Martin,' said Roig to one of the other policemen, 'give us the hammers.'

As Jaume II lost his nose, and Jaume III the heads of his cherubic angels, Dr Ferrer turned away. 'I'll be back in a minute,' he hissed.

'Fucking coward!' muttered Roig.

Ferrer ran almost the full length of the nave until he came level with the Chapel of San Sebastian. Breathless, he shone his torch at the centre of the altarpiece. There in its niche was the revered eighteenth-century Italian statue of San Sebastian himself, the patron saint of Palma. Apart from a blue cloth around his midriff, he was naked. An arrow had pierced the left side of his abdomen and blood trickled from the wound. His left wrist was tied to a wooden stake, and, with the limp body sagging diagonally, the right hand almost touched the ground.

'Forgive me,' murmured Dr Ferrer as he reached into his briefcase, 'but it is for the best.'

It was the very first time he'd used aerosol paint; his attempt to write 'SCHEISSE' across San Sebastian's chest was a poor effort. He fared better, however, with the painting of St. Ignatius of Loyola, and was almost proficient by the time he reached the altar's frontal cloth. Embroidered in silk and gold on red velvet, it had, by coincidence, been made in 1550 by his namesake, Pere Ferrer.

When he returned to the Chapel Royal and flashed his torch about, the sarcophagi were devastated and all four policemen were weeping as they discussed how to position the hammers in proximity to the Germans.

'Where the hell have you been, Doc?' croaked Roig, wiping away his tears. 'For a minute we thought–'

Ferrer proffered the aerosol can. 'I've desecrated San Sebastian with German graffiti. I didn't want to be just a cowardly accomplice.'

*

'Oh, poor chap, Mrs. Babcock,' said Mike, speaking into his mobile as he rolled a peach around his plate. 'He'll buck up in a day or two. Is he being difficult about his pills? It's vital he has them – for his urinary tract problem. ... Oh good. Well, if he leaves them in the bowl, just open his mouth and ram them down his throat. Is he there? ... Oh, bless him! ... Is he really? Can I have a quick word with him? ... Thanks. ... Hello, Hugo! It's Daddy here. Are you being a good boy for Mrs. Babcock? Daddy loves you very much and it won't be long–'

'You won't believe this, Mike,' said Jane as she walked out onto the terrace holding a pot of coffee, but the *Eminence Grise*–'

'Hang on a sec', Footy, I'm just talking to Hugo. He's barely moved off Mrs. Babcock's sofa since we left.'

'Oh, poor thing.'

'Do you want to talk to him?'

'No, it's all right.'

'So, you be a good boy, Hugo, and do your poopsies when– Oh, it's you again Mrs. Babcock. ... Is he *really*? He's running round the house hysterically, Footy, barking – trying to find me! OK, Mrs. Babcock, I'll phone again tomorrow. Sorry about last night, but we were out at a concert until quite late. OK – bye for now and thanks again for everything.'

'I think you love Hugo more than you love me.'

'Don't be ridiculous – he's a dog!'

'She probably thinks you're quite mad, you know, talking to him like that.'

'Rubbish! *She* does. You took your time in the kitchen. Still no *real* bread then? Cornflakes?'

'Never mind about bread and cereals – we'll definitely do some shopping today – but I've just had the most bizarre experience – Margalida crying on my shoulder – not literally, but I heard this awful wailing and found her in a terrible state hunched over her mop bucket in the hall.'

Mike was pouring the coffee. 'Good Lord! Not Werner demanding more whitewash?'

'It's not a laughing matter.'

'Sorry.'

'Quite bloody serious actually – from what I could understand – she's got one hell of a weird accent. As soon as Werner and Heidi get back from their breakfast in Alqueria Blanca, I'll ask. ... Actually, they should be back by now and doing penance in the garden. Maybe I should check to see if–'

'Footy! What's the crisis, for God's sake?'

'Oh sorry! Well, it seems that last night two German kids – junkies according to Margalida – a friend in Palma phoned her early this morning and told her to switch on the telly. ... Anyway, these lads broke into the cathedral and went on the rampage desecrating some of the most precious relics and things.'

'Jesus Christ!'

'She mentioned a statue of Saint Sebastian and the tombs – I think she said tombs – of some kings.'

'Kings?'

'Kings of Mallorca presumably – I read about them in one of the guidebooks – thirteenth or fourteenth century ... whatever. Anyway, when the police arrived, they found them still there, unconscious – at least I think that's what she meant – not dead.'

'Bloody hell!'

'And the news must have spread quickly because Margalida mentioned big crowds in Palma overnight and German offices being attacked.'

'Great! That's just what we need.'

'Do you think I should phone Daddy and ask whether we should make a quick exit? He gave me the name of the Consul. ... I wrote it down somewhere.'

'Oh bugger! I just knew something like this would happen the minute Gudrun Schluck made that speech after her infernal recital and tempted fate – all that stuff about music spreading peace and goodwill, and the island's "inner self" having inspired that bloody trio of hers. I ask you – a cello, a cowbell–'

'They're worn by goats and sheep here.'

'–and an octave's worth of terracotta flowerpots hit with an olive branch!'

'I thought it was very kind of von Karpen to stand in for the indisposed campanologist.'

'You fell asleep!'

'So did you. Everybody fell asleep!'

'Werner didn't.'

'No, and he kept waking everyone up by clapping between movements. You'd think he'd know better.'

'Poor Heidi looked *so* embarrassed. ... Do you realize that we now invariably refer to her as "poor Heidi"?'

'Hmm, you're right. Actually, I have a nickname for Werner – "Ja-Ja".'

'Wicked girl!'

'He says it all the time!'

'I know. Anyway, this cathedral business ... surely we don't need to do anything precipitous? After all, they'll only be venting their anger against Germans. Perhaps we should just avoid going to Palma – at least until the dust settles.' He was thinking of how the shocking vandalism might save him from the torture of parading around historic monuments in the baking heat.

'We need to get more details from our hosts first. Talk of the devil!'

'Jane! Mike!' thundered Werner as he marched through the open French windows with Heidi in tow; smiling wanly, she had on the same salmon pink culottes and lemon-yellow T-shirt that she'd worn on their arrival two days ago. Werner was clad in tartan Bermudas, a green and orange striped polo shirt, and battered yellow loafers.

Under his breath, Mike hissed: 'Joseph and his multicoloured dream coat!'

Werner's broad smile was switched off like an electric light. 'Jane! Mike! Bad news!' He shook his head sadly as he sat down. Heidi remained standing and stared at the frugal spread of two peaches and coffee.

'You mean this cathedral business?' said Mike.

Werner jolted. 'You've heard? – already? – *how*?'

Jane began to recount her laboured conversation with Margalida, but was interrupted.

'*Ja, ja*, Jane, she is very upset.' Without looking up, he said in German: 'Get me a coffee cup, Heidi, if it's not too much trouble.' She shot away like a rocket. 'Heidi is very upset too. We heard all about it over breakfast at Alqueria Blanca. There were some nasty things – anti-German insults – I overheard from the locals at neighbouring tables. Heidi doesn't understand *Mallorquí*, thank God. Of course, everything is exaggerated by these peasants. I wouldn't be at all surprised if the whole incident wasn't fabricated by the nationalists to stir up anti-German feelings. Did Margalida tell you that a mob attacked the German Consulate last night and burned it down?'

'Never!' cried Mike.'

'How dreadful! Was anyone hurt, Werner?'

'I don't know. I'll phone the Consul shortly and find out. He's a good friend. He has a lovely house outside Palma ... beautiful paintings.'

Heidi scuttled out of the house with a cup and saucer and placed them in front of her husband. Mike stood up and pulled out a chair for her. For a moment she looked confused. 'Oh! Thank you, Mike!'

The coffee pot was a few inches from Werner's left hand. In English he said: 'Would you be kind enough to pour me a cup of coffee, Heidi, if it's not too much trouble?'

She looked at the pot, then at the cup; so, too, did the Oakhearts.

Mike beat her to it. 'Allow me,' he said. Werner scowled at Heidi, and Mike realized he'd made a big mistake. 'Well,' he added swiftly while pouring, 'this is an awful business. Presumably, Werner, you'd advise us to stay clear of Palma for a while, hmm?'

'*Ja, ja*, Mike – until these Mallorcan hotheads cool down. You'll see – in a few days the authorities will have to admit that these German boys are innocent. How could they break into Palma Cathedral? – it's like a fortress! A few years back, a local lunatic just walked in during the day and went crazy destroying things. Probably the same thing has happened again.

The lunatic hides behind an altar just before closing and then waits until dark before going on the rampage. Incompetent security – everything's incompetent here! And so, to cover up their own bloody shambles, they try to blame the whole thing on some innocent German kids. The police probably planted the drugs on them.'

'There was "*Scheisse*" sprayed all over San Sebastian,' Heidi said solemnly.

'Oh no!' cried Jane.

Werner glared at his wife. 'So?'

'Well, that doesn't sound like a Mallorcan lunatic.'

Werner grunted. 'The ENABA filth are always scrawling anti-German graffiti, Heidi – in *German*. Maybe ENABA is behind *all* of this.'

'And the German boys,' Heidi continued, 'were gay and had the sex in the Chapel of the Kings – there were condoms lying around. And it is clear to the police that they had–'

'Heidi!' barked Werner, thumping the table. 'Are you *mad*? Where did you hear such vile, preposterous things?'

'In the Bar Pou Nou – over breakfast. The TV was on and everyone–'

'*Ach*, you don't understand a word of Catalan … or *Mallorquí*. You–'

'I *do*. Mateu lent me a book. When we work together in the garden he gives me lessons.'

After a few moments' awkward silence, Werner said: 'Mike, today is market day in Santanyí, and Heidi always takes a few hours off from her gardening schedule to buy supplies of those fruits and vegetables which we do not grow ourselves. I should be grateful if you would accompany her in view of these disturbing developments.'

Mike shot a glance at Jane. 'Actually,' she said, 'we had planned to go and visit the monastery of San Salvador at Felanitx and then–'

'*Ja, ja*, Jane, but you can do that *any* time. I would suggest that Heidi's safety is–'

'That's exactly what I was about to say, Werner – that we can go to the monastery at *any* time and that we wouldn't dream of Heidi going on her own to the market. Presumably, Werner, you have a more *pressing* engagement?'

'I do not have the problems to go–' Heidi began.

'I have *vital* business in Palma,' said Werner gravely.

'Palma?' queried the Oakhearts incredulously.

'I need to check that our apartment is OK. I am a prominent German. And at the same time, I can check on my friend the Consul. On reflection, I think it is better than telephoning.' He jumped up from the table. '*Ja, ja*! I must depart *immediately*.'

Heidi stood up too. 'Maybe we could leave for the market at ten so that there are not the crowds?' She lowered her voice slightly. 'And we can buy the bread that you likes at the bakery.'

'Excellent!' said Mike.

'"*Like*", not "*likes*",' corrected Werner, scowling.

'I'm coming too,' said Jane. 'I love country markets, and I'm keen to see the baroque organ in the parish church.'

Heidi nodded. 'Good ... yes, the organ.'

'*Ja, ja*! – the organ is *magnificent*!' enthused Werner, the ear-to-ear smile back on his face. He hummed the first few bars of Bach's Toccata and Fugue in D Minor; he was flat. 'Marvellous! It always reminds me of the organ in the chapel of my boarding school.' His eyebrows momentarily furrowed. 'Jane! Mike! You enjoyed the recital last night? Gudrun is so gifted, and Herbert's house is a dream. ... Look,' – his eyes momentarily glared at Heidi – 'you must have thought it strange for me to applaud between the movements. Naturally, I know that is not the form, but I was ... I was not happy that Gudrun should see *all* the people sleeping. I had to wake you up. Do not think that I do not know how to behave in a concert hall!'

*

Plain double doors, a small rose window, and a token gesture of a Renaissance-style gable at its summit were all that relieved the severity of the cliff-like wall of local stone which constituted the west front of Santanyí's parish church. In all the circumstances, it was no wonder that so few tourists ever sought to gain access and thereby discover the exuberance of the baroque interior. But then, unless a service was taking place, the doors were usually locked. The church dominated the east end of the market place, while around the other three sides were six tourist-orientated cafés with umbrella-shaded pavement tables, a generous assortment of banks, and the offices of the two surviving German-owned estate agents; the other three, of course, had been gutted and were awaiting new tenants. Planning applications for two more cafés were currently under scrutiny at the neighbouring nineteenth-century *Ajuntament* – the town hall – its folly-like appearance invariably being enhanced by a profusion of Mallorcan, Balearic and Spanish flags – all red and yellow and looking remarkably similar to the casual observer.

This morning, despite being laid out with all the customary stalls, the market place was strangely quiet; groups of locals stood around talking gravely. The few tourists – predominantly British – who were milling about or sitting at the cafés, looked like partygoers who'd turned up on the wrong day; the events in Palma had yet to filter down to them. At her usual fruiterer, Heidi had watched in exasperation as three queue jumpers – all locals – had been served before her. Mike and Jane had told her to protest, but Heidi had said nothing: the Mallorcans were understandably outraged by what the German vandals had done in the *Seu*, and she'd no wish to exacerbate their animosity.

'I do hope the church opens before we leave,' Jane said, looking up the gentle hill as they moved to the next stall. 'I don't understand how they can stick up a sign asking for money to repair the organ and then not permit access to see the damned thing.'

Heidi was watching Maria – the stallholder from whom she'd bought most of her vegetables for the last five years – pick out the most bruised red peppers from the huge pile. She tossed them on the scales, and Heidi saw they were underweight.

'Six euros!' barked Maria.

Heidi hesitated, but then handed over a ten-euro note. '*Gracis*,' she said in *Mallorquí* with a smile. Maria muttered about the note and foreigners never having the right money. There was a lump in Heidi's throat: Maria had always been so polite and friendly. Surely, she didn't think that she or Werner could in any way be responsible for the terrible vandalism in Palma?

The change was slammed into Heidi's hand. '*Gracis*, Maria. I'm so sorry about–'

'Don't you "*gracis*" me!' snarled Maria in Spanish. 'You're not fit to speak *Mallorquí*, you filthy German. Why don't you and all the other stinking German pigs go back to your own country where you belong? You're not wanted here, understand? – you never were. And don't come to my stall again, you foreign bitch!'

Heidi began to cry.

'What the hell's going on, Footy?' asked Mike anxiously as Jane put an arm round Heidi's shoulders.

'Come on, let's get her back to the car and go home. I'll tell you later.'

'But–'

Jane was already moving Heidi away from the stall. 'Come *on*, Mike – *now*!' He shrugged and followed. After a few paces, Jane turned her head. Maria was pointing at them while talking to a couple of women. All three were nodding and looked as though they could smell something nasty.

'If there's any "bitch" around here,' Jane shouted in Spanish, 'it's *you*!'

The three women at the stall started shrieking; it sounded like a cat had got into the hen house. Now everyone in the square was staring. Bewildered and tense, Mike was startled by a tap on his shoulder, and spun round to find himself looking into black mirrored sunglasses on a strangely familiar bearded face.

'Hi, Mike! *C'est moi*! I'm in disguise – the fans! What the hell's going on?'

'Lionel?' Despite a false beard and the old, ripped and stained casual wear, Tourny looked as humble as a Fabergé egg in need of a good dust.

'Shush! No names!'

They were standing in front of one of the two remaining German estate agents, and out of the corner of his eye, Mike could see that '**NAZIS RAUS!**' had been sprayed right across its widow. Lionel was just about to greet Jane and Heidi, when a tall, elegantly dressed woman burst out of the door.

'*Scheisse*! – *mein Fenster*!' she cried, her eyes darting in all directions as if expecting to find the culprit. 'Heidi, look what these bastards have done to my window again!'

An unshaved man in his forties, smoking a cigar and with his shirt open to his beer belly, was walking by. In Spanish he bellowed: 'You can read, can't you, German whore? You'd better get out before we burn you down too!'

'That's right!' added a spotty youth, '– or maybe one night you might end up getting buggered like them two Nazi queers buggered each other in the *Seu* last night!'

'Don't talk to her like that!' boomed Lionel in Spanish, looking from one man to the other. 'You sound like a couple of Nazis yourselves.'

'What's it to you, Kraut?' said the fat man as a small crowd began to assemble.

'I don't like this at all,' whispered Jane in Mike's ear. 'We should get out of here now. Who's this bearded guy?'

'*Hombre*! I'm not "a Kraut" – I'm French!'

'It's Lionel – in disguise.'

'Lionel?'

'French!' snarled the youth. 'You're all *fucking* foreigners! Can't move for *fucking* foreigners! Me and the girlfriend can't afford a fucking one-bedroom fucking apartment because of fucking foreigners!'

'Me too!' someone shouted.

'I say we should throw *all* the foreign bastards out!' yelled the fat man.

'Up ENABA!'

'Germans out! Foreigners out!'

'Burn the Germans!'

'Death to the Germans!'

'In here – *quick*!' shrieked the estate agent in German as she grabbed Heidi, '– and your friends! I'll phone the police.'

In the scramble, the fat man made a grab for Lionel, but Mike punched him in the stomach. The cigar popped out of his mouth like a cork out of a champagne bottle as he fell to the pavement with a roar of pain. The crowd exploded and surged forward.

'Get the foreigners!'

'Kill the Germans!'

'Avenge the *Seu*'s desecration!'

Just as the estate agent bolted her steel door, the first seat from the adjoining cafe hit the German-made bulletproof plate glass; it bounced off and landed on the prostrate fat man. 'I'm Ulrike Braun,' she stated breathlessly, hearing the exchanges of shocked English around her. 'Thank God I had the doors and windows reinforced a few months back.' She grabbed the phone, began to dial, and then slammed it down, staring at Mike. 'That man you hit – if the police come, you'll end up being arrested for assault. They're probably all ENABA people.'

'Oh my God!' cried Jane. 'What the hell are we going to do now?'

There was a terrific banging at the front door as the spotty youth and two other men attempted to batter it down with a rubbish bin. There were cries of rage as it held firm.

'Never mind this tatty office!' someone shouted in *Mallorquí*. 'What's the biggest Kraut business in this town, citizens?'

'Heinrich Stern!' roared the mob with one voice.

'Come on then! To Heinrich Stern! Let's burn it!'

To the raucous chant of 'Burn it! Burn it!' the mob began to move off. One more chair, and then a table, ricocheted off the plate glass, followed by a barrage of red peppers.

'Jesus!' gasped Lionel. 'What in God's name is going on? I only came down here to ask you guys if you wanted to come out on the boat. I drove over to your place, Heidi, and Margalida told me–'

'Hang on, Lionel,' Mike interjected. 'Who's this Heinrich what's-it, Heidi?'

'It's a big shop for the furniture,' she said trembling. 'He is a famous design man – from Hamburg.'

'According to Jeanne,' added Lionel, 'it's full of real expensive repro antique stuff. Apparently, all the German houses around here are furnished with it – top to bottom – talk about déjà vu!'

'Werner won't have it in the house,' Heidi whimpered. 'He says it's for people with more money than sense.'

'Christ!' shrieked Ulrika. 'I should phone Stern to warn them!'

As she dialled, Jane said: 'I think we should make a run for it. Is there a back door?'

'No reply!' groaned Ulrike. '*Scheisse*!'

Mike wrinkled his nose. 'Do you smell burning? You don't really think that lot–?'

'Yes, there *is* a backdoor,' Ulrike snapped. 'Come on – *schnell*!' But after one step she hesitated and looked around her office. 'Well,' she sighed, 'that's it. I've had enough. Let the bastards burn my place down – it's only rented. It's Dubrovnik for me, Heidi – Germans snapping up property there like hot cakes. And if you ask me, you should persuade Werner to get out too.'

As they quickly made their way along a deserted back street in the opposite direction to the Stern store, Jane said: 'Hell! What if that Maria cow saw you hit the fat bloke, Mike? She saw us with Heidi and–'

'Maria, the fruit and vegetable woman?' asked Ulrike.

'Yes.'

'Don't worry about *her* – Jane, is it? She's a sort of collaborator. She had a German sugar daddy years ago before she got married. I sold him his house in Portopetro. She got pregnant. He took her to Germany to have the baby. It got adopted. I know *all* the details. If Maria threatens to make trouble, I'll fix her good and proper before I leave this island.'

CHAPTER 8

'I'm sorry,' moaned Otto Speck, Martin Klipper's Official Spokesperson, 'but you don't know how the ordinary bloke – or woman – in the street thinks – not a clue – neither of you.'

Klipper, who was sandwiched between Speck and the Director of Media Communications, Eva Heilbutt, nodded; she did too. On the other side of the table, the Foreign and Defence Ministers shifted uncomfortably in their seats.

'I think that's grossly unfair,' said the former, Ernst-Wilhelm von Höhenzug, who counted among his many titles Duke (Herzog) of Puttgarten, Count (Graf) of Delmenhorst-Cloppenburg, and Hereditary Bearer of the Royal Banner of Prussia. 'After all, I did command a battalion before I came into the hurly-burly world of politics, and, in consequence, got pretty damned close to many salt-of-the-earth types.'

Speck groaned; Eva shook her head slowly from side to side.

'My father worked in a steel works,' bleated Karl Stiefel, who, as Minister of Defence, wished that he'd served as an officer in the Bundeswehr like Höhenzug, and not merely as a miserable private doing his national service. In fact, at this particular moment he also wished that he was with Barbara on that damned Arctic cruise. Another few hours and the ship would have sailed; Barbara would never have allowed him to be winched off by helicopter!

'If my memory serves me correctly, Karl,' sneered Eva, 'your father was the finance director, wasn't he? Anyway, getting back to the matter in hand, Heinrich Stern is an icon – an interior design guru – a national symbol of German style, good taste *and* economic success. The burning down of his store in this San-Thingy–'

'Santanyí,' enunciated Höhenzug wearily. 'Jolly nice little town, actually – glorious Baroque organ in the parish church, and–'

'If you don't mind,' growled Eva, '... the burning down of Stern's store by that murderous mob of racist fanatics while the local police looked on, plus the near lynching of the staff–'

'Oh come, come, dear lady,' interrupted Höhenzug, 'no one was *seriously* hurt, and–'

'The manageress had to have a dozen stitches!' snapped Eva.

Höhenzug waived a hand dismissively. 'She tripped running away – a badly maintained pavement according to our Consul. She can probably sue the local council for compensation. Anyway, we have to put all this unpleasantness into context. Just hours earlier, one of the finest examples of Gothic architecture in all Europe was obscenely vandalized by a couple of German yobbos – nancy boys to boot.'

'For Christ's sake,' spluttered Speck, 'don't you dare say anything like that to the media!'

'Or I'll kill you,' added Eva.

'You'll lose us the next election at a stroke,' whined Klipper. 'We depend on the gay – *queer* vote, especially in Hamburg. Anyhow, what are we going to do about this damned mess? Mallorca isn't some distant trouble spot – in the Middle East or somewhere – with a German reporter getting shot once in a while. Your average Hamburger or Berliner doesn't give a toss about them – nor does anyone else, frankly. This is *Europe* – the European *Union* – our own backyard. No, this is an island – correct me if I'm wrong, Ernst-Wilhelm – that our lot have been busy colonising – *settling* – so to speak, for the last forty years or so … well, some niche zones anyway. Bloody *thousands* have settled there. How many, Eva?'

'Our chap in Palma,' interjected Höhenzug, flicking through a file, 'gave me the latest figures, um …'

'Twenty-five thousand,' Eva barked, '– approximately. I spoke directly to "our chap" this morning.'

Höhenzug's eyes bulged. 'Fräulein Heilbutt, I really must ask you to go through the proper–'

'We must have invested *billions* of euros there,' Klipper interrupted. 'Enterprising Germans have set up businesses – shops, hotels, restaurants, banks … craft workshops … manicurists – you name it! So, our voters see Mallorca as a very special case – it's *our* island in the sun. And if we had this sort of breakdown in public order here in Germany, we'd be doing something pretty damned serious about it.'

'Exactly, MK,' said Otto. 'And that's why the man – and woman – in the street is getting so bloody pissed off. Just look at social media. The Spics aren't doing a bleeding thing. The Mallorcan authorities are all anti-German anyway, and they openly support these terrorists – well, almost – while that burke Azucena and his cronies in Madrid don't want to get heavy for fear of adding fuel to the fire, attracting even worse publicity, and causing far greater damage to their lousy tourist industry.'

Höhenzug shook his head and sighed. 'Yes, I agree – it's a pretty pickle. But when all is said and done, Mallorca is an integral part of the

Kingdom of Spain – a sovereign state. Apart from issuing more diplomatic protests, I can't see there's much more that we can do.'

'Oh, *can't* you?' sneered Eva. 'Well, that's just not good enough, Foreign Minister. You and Karl here had better think of something pretty damn quick – and pretty impressive – or *all* of us around this table are going to be out of our jobs come the next general election, *comprende*?'

'Well,' snorted Stiefel, 'I can't for the life of me imagine what you expect the Ministry of Defence to do. Or did you have in mind the Bundeswehr launching a full-scale invasion? I don't exactly see them marching through the "liberated" streets of Palma with the locals sticking roses in their rifles, do you?'

'Don't be so bloody childish!' barked Eva.

Wide eyed, Höhenzug bleated: 'Any kind of German military interference in the internal affairs of another nation would be suicidal. The UN would have a fit. The *Americans* would have a *frightful* fit. And every peasant in Mallorca with a shotgun – and that's probably the vast majority – would be picking off our boys with relish before they even got off the beaches, or detached their parachutes. It would be like a turkey shoot.'

'And you know as well as I do, Chancellor,' added Stiefel, 'that after all these years of peace since 1945, the German people are not equipped psychologically to deal with the emotional stress that would arise should any member of the Armed Forces get injured – let alone killed – while on active service. We are now a nation of congenital pacifists.'

Otto was noisily tapping his pen on his notepad. 'What about this European Army thingy everyone keeps going on about, MK? Why can't we get that sent out to Mallorca – like UN peacekeepers – dressed in blue berets or something? I bet the French and the – the ... Who else have agreed to participate? ... Norway?'

'The Belgians and the *Luxemburgers*,' sighed Stiefel. 'Not exactly crack troops I would suggest. And to be honest, it's still only a paper army.'

Smugly, Höhenzug said: 'Norway, Herr Speck, is *not* a member state of the European Union.'

'Whatever. The point is that we could play the role of the great European peacemaker. We tell Azucena that as this is a *European* problem, there has to be a *European* solution. We invite him to a slap-up conference in Germany at some swanky hotel – plus France's President Chiffon and–'

'And the Belgians and the Luxemburgers?' queried Höhenzug.

'Er ... maybe. Anyway, at the conference we convince the lot of them that here is a heaven-sent opportunity to prove to the rest of the world – particularly the Yanks – how Europe can solve problems on its own. We propose that this Euro army of 'neutral' nationalities – the French and the other lot – go down to Mallorca and start strutting their stuff. Of course, we make sure that back at HQ us Germans are giving the orders, OK? So, there won't be any of our boys on the ground. I mean, I really don't see these ENABA nutters shooting French lads or Belgians, do you?'

'This is all most imaginative,' crowed Höhenzug languidly, 'but I think you're overlooking some pretty fundamental problems, the most obvious of which, if I may say so, is the French. Why on earth would they participate in this venture? And do you honestly see Chiffon or his generals accepting the principle of the Force being under ultimate German control? Frankly, the mind boggles. Most of the French top brass can't speak a word of German, and in my days in the Bundeswehr most of my colleagues hardly knew enough French to understand a decent menu.'

'Details, Ernst-Wilhelm,' snapped Klipper, '*details*. They all speak English anyway, don't they? – a sort of neutral language for these purposes. No, I think Otto's on to something here. The French love playing at soldiers – still trying to redeem themselves after their chronic humiliation in 1940 and that Maginot Line nonsense. I think Chiffon would be quite interested, as long as we sort of *pretended* they were in charge. But behind the scenes, we'd be pulling the strings.'

'And paying the bills?' queried Stiefel, thinking about his department's existing budget problems.

'Well, we'd have to pay quite a whack seeing how it's our citizens who need protecting down there. But as it would ostensibly be an EU show, maybe we could get *everyone* to chip in. Anyhow, don't worry, Karl, we'd make sure your department wouldn't be prejudiced.'

'And if anything went wrong on Mallorca,' Speck enthused, ' – some locals getting shot or something – the French would get all the stick.'

'Exactly!' chirped Eva.

Höhenzug's lips were pursed. 'Oh, this is *ridiculous*! Even if you got the French and the Belgians *and* little old Luxembourg to go along with this – and I very much doubt it – Azucena would be dead meat if he allowed "foreign" troops to set one foot on Spanish soil. Absolute political suicide!'

Shaking her head, Eva said: 'You're forgetting, Foreign Minister, that Azucena has set his heart on becoming the first EU so-called "president" next year, and he knows that he hasn't got much chance of that "honour" without our support – or the French, for that matter.'

Thinking aloud, Stiefel added: 'I suppose we could do a bit of flag waiving, by offering our warships and some planes to ferry the EU force over to Mallorca.'

'Well, I still think we're going to have one hell of a problem with the locals,' said Höhenzug. 'French, Belgian or otherwise, your average xenophobic Mallorcan is not going to take too kindly to a load of foreign squaddies roaring around the highways and byways demanding to see people's ID cards, looking for arms caches in haystacks, and waving automatic weapons at protesting nationalists shouting "Nazis 'raus!" in front of branches of Deutsche Bank.'

'Then we'll have to do something on the political and diplomatic fronts to soften them up, won't we, *Herr* Höhenzug?' Stiefel's wilful omission of 'von' made Höhenzug bristle.

'Like what, Otto?' asked Klipper hurriedly.

'Well, can't we fob them off with some talk of a thumping great EU committee of inquiry into the economic well-being of the Balearics – more subsidies – for the cost of fuel, energy, travel to the mainland – special tax status like the Canaries and VAT ... that sort of thing? An EU committee would take *ages* to report – years, maybe. Anyway, the more Mallorca's economy is dependent on EU subsidies, the more difficult it will be for the nationalists to pursue all this nonsense about independence and secession from Europe. Xenophobic or not, I don't see those canny islanders cutting off their noses to spite their faces.'

'Quite!' enthused Klipper, nodding vigorously. 'And lots more subsidies would also benefit our twenty-five thousand countrymen – and women – down there. Yes, I think we're on the right track. Well done, Otto and Eva! It's a pity my cabinet colleagues couldn't be so imaginative and constructive. ... Right! Well, I think we'd better move pronto. Ernst-Wilhelm, get hold of your counterpart in Paris immediately ... Baron Thingy and–'

'The Vicomte de Boulogne, Chancellor. Actually, I think Cyril will already have left for Scotland. We're both guests of the Duke of Cromarty at Inverbute Castle for a spot of fishing and shooting. I was due to fly to Edinburgh this morning, but–'

'Well *call* him! They do have telephones in Scotland, don't they? – and mobile cover? I'll talk to that peacock Chiffon, while Karl starts the ball rolling on the Euro Army front and mobilises the Navy et cetera. Get some ships steaming down to the Med, Karl – biggish ones – cruisers, or whatever they're called. Have we got any aircraft carriers?'

'Afraid not, Chancellor.'

'Damn!'

Höhenzug groaned. 'Sorry to be a pain, but I strongly suspect that Chiffon may already be en route to his villa in Martinique.'

'God almighty! Are we Germans the only people who ever do any work? Look! I want this Mallorca crap sorted by the end of the week, OK?

I'm due in Turkey, and you all know that my trip is *vital* to secure the Turkish migrant vote. Any postponement could be misinterpreted. You know how volatile these Orientals can be.'

'Too true, MK!' said Otto. 'Eva and I will start drafting some pretty powerful press releases immediately – and organise the summit venue. We need somewhere impressive yet informal ... somewhere that makes it clear we're in charge and yet not too German, if you get my drift. ... A five-star hotel near the French frontier?'

Höhenzug cleared his throat. 'Well, I'm quite happy to volunteer my hunting lodge in the Schwarzwälder Hochwald near Saarburg. It's only a few kilometres from the French frontier – pretty damn close to Luxembourg and Belgium too.'

'A "*hunting lodge*"?' queried Eva incredulously. 'We'll need something a bit bigger than–'

'It has twenty-three bedrooms,' bleated its owner.

'It *has*,' confirmed Klipper. 'I've stayed there. So did the last Kaiser.'

'And Hitler,' whispered Höhenzug, 'but we don't talk about that. Well, he invited himself, and Grandpapa could hardly have said "no", could he?'

CHAPTER 9

Contrary to Ernst-Wilhelm von Höhenzug's belief, the President of the French Republic had not yet departed Paris for his villa on Martinique. François Chiffon had a cold, and had been advised by his battery of doctors to rest up for a few days at the Elysée Palace: with blocked sinuses, air travel could play havoc with their patient's eardrums. Madame Chiffon, however, had gone on ahead with her two teenage daughters.

With both Prime Minister Patrick Agneau and most of his cabinet already on holiday, Chiffon was looking forward to a few peaceful days of 'sick leave'; indeed, his summer cold provided a heaven-sent opportunity to browse through the backlog of men's fashion and style magazines that had built up in his private study over the last hectic few months; once fully apprised of the latest trends, he could confidently instruct his tailors to get cracking with the Presidential autumn and winter suits.

And then came Martin Klipper's call from Berlin.

An Air Force helicopter collected Agneau from his rented beach house at Arcachon, and the British graciously permitted the RAF base at Lossiemouth near Inverness for the Vicomte de Boulogne to be ferried back from Inverbute Castle; he'd not even had time to unpack his fishing and hunting gear. With the Minister of Defence recklessly and inconsiderately canoeing up-country somewhere in Québec, and, therefore, out of contact for the time being, the Chief of the Defence Staff, Général Dominique Lamour, had been summoned to the Elysée to advise on what Chiffon was already calling tautologically 'a European crisis of international proportions'.

The four of them met in one of the Palace's magnificent eighteenth-century reception rooms. Around a coffee table comprising a heart-shaped sheet of plate glass resting on three roughly hewn sandstone pyramids, all the attendees were perched on solid concrete cubes softened only by minimalist cushions clad in slippery black hide. In truth, since Chiffon's election, almost all the furnishings of the staterooms – including objets d'art and paintings – had been replaced by works commissioned from contemporary French artists and 'craft persons'; the original treasures had been stored away, or loaned to museums. Chiffon had justified this apparent extravagance by proclaiming that he wanted his official residence to symbolise the French Republic of the twenty-first century – a dynamic nation at the cutting edge of all fields of human endeavour, and yet one steeped in history, style and breeding – in truth, the fountain of European Civilization's finest achievements, both past and present. There had been remarkably little public dissent.

'I think the Germans have taken leave of their senses,' moaned Agneau. 'I accept that the attacks on their citizens are outrageous, but what is fundamentally a Spanish *internal* law and order issue can't possibly justify the mobilisation of the European Defence Force – whether in a UN-style peacekeeping role or otherwise.'

'Is that what it's called then,' croaked Chiffon through a bunged-up nose, '"the European Defence *Force*"? I thought we were trying to get "Corps" substituted for "Force" on the grounds that it sounded less belligerent – and more French.'

'As I understand it, Monsieur Le Président,' said Général Lamour indifferently, 'the name – like most things – has still to be agreed. Actually, that's been put on one side for the moment while we try to decide where the "European High Command" should be located. Having had Brussels vetoed – we're not going to be cheek by jowl with the Americans at NATO – the last I heard was that the Belgians were proposing a compromise – separate HQs for the three services – army, air force and navy – in different countries.'

'So, we haven't got a damned Euro Army to deploy anyway!' growled Boulogne. 'If you ask me, Klipper's been on the old schnapps again – or too many hours on that sunbed of his. When I spoke on the phone to Höhenzug, I thought he sounded decidedly lukewarm about the whole thing.'

'Well,' snapped Agneau, 'army or no army – force – *corps*, Klipper's in a tizzy. The Boche are demanding action and Klipper knows that unless he does something jolly dramatic soon, he's up the Rhine without a paddle. The bastards have certainly pulled the rug from under us by going public on this proposed summit at Schloss Frankenstein – or whatever it's called.'

'Schloss *Wimpel*,' droned Boulogne wearily, 'a truly Wagnerian hunting lodge–'

'Yes, yes, Cyril,' Agneau interrupted. 'We all know that you and Höhenzug are the best of chums, but I trust you're not going to allow him to usurp your status as the premier European diplomat, are you? We can't have Höhenzug doing all the running in any intergovernmental effort to resolve this Mallorca crisis – an island, don't forget, that's only a couple of hundred kilometres from the mouth of the Rhône – in *our* backyard.'

'In that connection,' intoned Général Lamour, 'I should tell you that Naval Intelligence have intercepted signals ordering three German cruisers to the western Mediterranean forthwith.'

'Good Lord!' gasped the President. 'I didn't know we intercepted German signals, Général.'

'Naturally. In any event, one of the cruisers was on a 'goodwill' visit to Bordeaux. Without warning, it cast off about an hour ago to catch the tide and is now steaming down the Gironde.'

Chiffon's eyes narrowed. 'You don't think they're going to do anything ... *unilaterally*, do you?'

'I really wouldn't get alarmed,' said Boulogne. 'Ernst-Wilhelm told me about the naval stunt – slipped my mind. He said it would just be a bit of flag-waving to keep your average Fritz and Heidi happy.'

'That's probably what Ribbentrop said in 1938 when the Nazis lined up their tanks on the Czechoslovakian frontier, Cyril,' scoffed Agneau. 'This is how wars start.'

Boulogne rolled his eyes. 'I hardly think that Höhenzug can be compared to Ribbentrop, François. And the poor Germans have been at the receiving end of some pretty nasty pranks from those ENABA cretins in Mallorca, as you yourself have admitted. They're as bad as the bloody Corsicans – worse, picking on foreigners.'

'Now I'm glad you've mentioned Corsica, Cyril,' said Agneau, 'because if we're daft enough to start meddling in Spain's troublesome little island, we could provoke all sorts of dotty proposals from misguided do-gooders – the pot-smoking, same-sex-marriage Dutch, for example – to send EU "peacekeepers" to our *own* troublesome little island – Corsica – in place of French troops. And that, gentlemen, would be the first step on the ladder to independence.'

Lamour bristled. 'I served in Corsica. We should have imposed martial law when things first began to heat up over there – and shot the ringleaders.'

'Yes, well moving rapidly on,' said Agneau, 'presumably we're all agreed that we don't want to expose the non-existence of the "European Army", or get involved in any military adventure in the Balearics that could prove expensive, whether financially or politically. Yet again, France must be seen as the great *peacemaker* – the voice of sanity in an insane world, in stark contrast to the gun-happy Americans and British. So, we have to seize control of the diplomatic process immediately, and put it into overdrive. For a start, I'm sure our fellow Latins, the Spanish – including Mallorcans – would welcome a conference on *neutral* territory.'

'"Neutral territory"?' queried Chiffon, blowing his nose.

Boulogne sighed. 'I think Patrick means *France*, François.'

'Ah – of course! ... Are we neutral?'

'Indubitably!' spluttered Boulogne.

'Right.' Chiffon didn't sound wholly convinced. 'So,' he continued hesitantly, 'we invite the Germans ... the Spanish ... and some Mallorcans – not the terrorists, surely? – where? – to Paris?'

'Certainly not the terrorists!' snarled Agneau.

'Certainly not!' agreed Boulogne. 'No, they've got a "democratic" wing that runs the provincial government down there. Actually, an old chum of mine, the Conde de Manilla – we did masters' together at Harvard – he's the former Spanish ambassador to Prague – retired now – his wife's a Bourbon. ... Anyway, he's from one of the oldest Mallorcan families – stayed with him and Beatriz a few years ago at their beach place. I remember him spending a lot of time wittering on about these separatists – and his loathsome nouveau riche German neighbours, come to that. He could prove a pretty useful intelligence source, and–' With a deafening crack, Boulogne clapped his hands. 'I say! I've just remembered!'

'What?' croaked Chiffon.

'This could be a real diplomatic triumph!'

'What could, Cyril?'

'Well, Manilla used to spend hours lecturing me about the medieval kingdom of Mallorca, which included great chunks of the Midi. Its capital was Perpignan – now just a stone's throw from the Spanish frontier. So why don't we propose Perpignan as the venue for *our* summit conference? The former palace would be a first-rate venue! And so much better for Azucena's image than being "summoned" like an errant schoolboy to the headmaster's study at Schloss Wimpel.'

'We don't want to stoke up the expectations of these islanders,' said Agneau, '– or cause alarm in Languedoc-Rousillon that we're considering handing them over to some bloody Spic island.'

'Or look as though we're saying one thing to *Spanish* separatists, but quite another to our own lot in Corsica,' added Chiffon.

'Well then,' sighed Boulogne, 'we won't invite the Mallorcans – maybe just Manilla as an amicus curiae.'

Chiffon was about to ask what was an 'amicus curiae', but then thought of his image. 'What would be our agenda, Cyril?' he asked instead.

'Oooh, something vague – the Germans are suggesting a European Commission investigation – energy and transport subsidies, VAT rates – all that kind of stuff.'

'We could live with that,' said Agneau. 'Actually, if we proposed something similar for Corsica at the summit – maybe *all* EU Mediterranean islands – we could drag the thing out for *years*.'

'And what about these German warships steaming to the Balearics for "summer manoeuvres", Monsieur le Président?' asked Lamour.

'Well, Général,' replied Chiffon, 'we have to show Berlin who's in control of this neck of the woods. So, let's get some of our own warships out on "summer manoeuvres" – bigger ones, of course – an aircraft carrier or something.'

'The crews of most of the Mediterranean fleet, Monsieur le Président, are on summer leave at the moment. Toulon's a ghost town.'

Chiffon sighed and shook his head. 'I can't imagine de Gaulle was *ever* told such things.'

'We could order them back to their ships ... if you thought the gravity of the situation truly merited it, sir.'

Chiffon hesitated for just a moment: the honour of France was at stake; so were his chances of being re-elected for a second term.

'Issue the orders, Général!'

CHAPTER 10

It was a few minutes before eight-thirty on yet another cloudless morning, and in *Ca'n Pau*'s shady central courtyard, Werner Stumpf's annual 'Convertible Day' was already under way. Although the Oakhearts were still a little sleepy, they were both in excellent spirits: last night, the intensity of their sex had returned to premarital levels. Mike was even beginning to wonder whether he should broach the subject of a baby; it was almost a year since their last turbulent discussion about starting a family.

'Oh, isn't this wonderfully decadent, Jane?' twittered Mrs Brenda Enderby as Heidi refilled their silver beakers with buck's fizz. 'No, no, dear! Just half a glass – *beaker* – or you'll be getting me tiddly. And no more for Richard, or he'll never be able to drive. We're just not used to alcohol first thing in the morning, are we, Richard? ... *Richard*!'

A few paces away, Mr Enderby broke off his conversation with Mike, who was trying to stifle a yawn, and turned to face his wife. 'What's that, dear?'

'I was just telling Jane here that we're not used to drinking alcohol first thing in the morning.'

'Absolutely not! We've lived out here for ten years now, but–'

'Before his retirement, Jane, Richard was with Metal Box in Manchester – for more than thirty years in fact – and *very* happy years they were too. We had a lovely *detached* house in Wilmslow and–'

'As I was saying,' Mr Enderby continued, 'although we have siestas and know quite a few Mallorcans, we haven't gone completely native. Have you seen the local chaps in the village bars knocking back the double brandies at daybreak, even before they get cracking in the fields? Incredible! Of course, when we first came here for holidays, brandy was thirteen pesetas a glass and–'

'*Twelve*, dear.'

'Depended on the bar, love.'

Mike whistled. 'Twelve – *thirteen* pesetas! Bloody hell!'

'Extraordinary,' said Jane.

'Mind you,' said Mrs Enderby, 'you never see a drunk Mallorcan – well, I can't remember seeing one – well, hardly ever. We were at some Mallorcan friends' house only on Saturday having a barbecue – Bernardi and his wife, Catalina – Cati. Bernardi was the estate agent who sold us our house years ago. They have these big family dos all the time – Saturday was their wedding anniversary. Well, no one ever gets blotto or obstreperous – not like in England. And everyone has a role to play – doing the barbecue, looking after the kiddies, serving, washing up – men *and* women. *So* organized and with such good humour! The Mallorcans may be hopeless with anything technical – plumbing, electrics, and stuff – but when it comes to the old fiestas, they're in a league of their own.'

'Absolutely!' agreed Mr Enderby. 'And the kiddies are amazing too. Take Saturday – loads of them, as you can imagine, Jane and Mike, but you'd think they weren't there half the time. *So* well behaved! I never heard one of them cry – no fights. They could certainly teach us Brits a few things!'

'Well, it's all the love and attention they get, you see,' explained Mrs Enderby. 'I don't think I've ever seen such loving parents as the Mallorcans – and so tactile. Of course, the families here are *very* close. There's none of that nonsense you get in England – children packed off to boarding schools at one end of the social scale, or dumped on 'child minders' or left to roam the streets after school at the other – oh no! Here, there's always a granny or an auntie around to make sure the kiddies are all right if the mum goes out to work. Well, they don't dump the old folk in homes for a start.'

'No,' said Mr Enderby, nodding approvingly, 'from the cradle to the grave, Mallorcan families – the Spanish generally – are devoted. I take my hat off to them. All that's gone back in England now. No wonder the country's such a mess! Everyone's so bloody selfish and greedy. And the kids! Talk about indiscipline! A load of bloody, drunken yobbos! I mean, when we go back to Wilmslow, there are times when I can't bear the thought of having to put up with our own grandchildren. There's been many an occasion when I would have loved to put them across my knee and give them a bloody good–'

'And yet,' interrupted Mrs Enderby, 'although the Mallorcans can be very firm with their kiddies, you hardly ever see any smacking. It's the love and attention, you see.'

'And setting a good example.'

'Never being ignored or abandoned.'

'It's a pleasure to be invited to their family dos.'

The Oakhearts were nodding politely.

Suddenly, Mr Enderby pointed to an unusual yellowy-orange bougainvillea that almost engulfed one wall of the house. 'Smashing blooms, Heidi! You must use a pretty potent fertilizer – horse manure?'

Heidi had retreated to a table near the fountain, where she'd laid out plates of *coca* – a kind of Mallorcan pizza – that Werner had ordered her to cut into bite-sized squares. 'Horse ... man ... man–?'

'*Dünger*,' said Jane helpfully.

Heidi chuckled and offered her a plate of *coca*. 'Oh, **Dünger**! I think, Jane, you speak German much better than you pretend.'

'I say, Mike,' said Mr Enderby, 'what a clever wife you have! – not just a pretty face! "Doong-er" – I suppose that must be the derivation of "dung". Fascinating! Actually, it's only since we got to know Werner that we've learned just how much of our language comes from German.'

'Mmm,' Jane enthused, 'these little savouries are delicious. Try them, Mikey. Did you make them yourself, Heidi?'

'Oh no! They come from the bakery in Alqueria Blanca.' She offered the *coca* to Mrs Enderby; there was a choice of prawn or spinach.

Smiling sweetly, Mrs Enderby shook her head. 'No thank you, dear. My tummy can't cope with that sort of thing first thing in the morning – nor can Richard's. We'll wait until we get to the cafe in Algaida. I assume we're going to the same place we go to *every* year for breakfast – the one just out of the village that does a very nice plain *tortilla* and has Hornimans tea bags?'

As Heidi passed Mr Enderby, who looked as though he could have eaten the whole plate, she nodded and moved on to Mike. 'Yes, Brenda,' said Heidi, 'the same arrangements as *every* year. 'Oh, and the dung, Richard, is not from the horses, but from Margalida's donkey.'

'*Really*?' he gasped. 'You *do* surprise me. We've had some awful problems with donkey manure, I can tell you – almost killed a couple of our desert palms. We prefer goat's on the oranges and chicken's on the–'

'*Richard*!' cried Mrs Enderby, '– I'm sure Jane and Mike don't want to hear all about *manure* at this time of day.' Rapidly changing the subject, she continued: 'We used to go to that bakery, Heidi, in Alqueria Blanca until we worked out they were diddling us. I mean, they charge us foreigners more than the locals for the same stuff – quite a hefty whack. They're such cheats. Any road, Jane and Mike, I know you're going to love the Convertible Day. We look forward to it *so* much. This must be our sixth or seventh. Werner is *wonderful* at organising things, isn't he? – right down to the last detail. Everything's always perfect, just *perfect*. And although he devises different itineraries, we always have breakfast and lunch at the same two establishments, so any chance of the unpleasantly unexpected on the food front has been completely removed.'

'That's nice,' said Jane.

'Well, you have to be ever so careful out here, dear, what with the heat, garlic and ignorance of basic food handling techniques. Our housekeeper is forever putting raw meat next to cooked stuff in the fridge. It doesn't matter how many times I tell her, it goes in one ear and out the other. Well, it's not that long ago that they were still sleeping with the animals – I mean *living* with them – sharing the same farmhouse – the peasants – not the city slickers in Palma, of course.'

'Of course,' agreed the Oakhearts.

Adopting a serious expression, Mr Enderby said: 'Brenda and me were so afraid that this year's Convertible Day might be cancelled because of all this dreadful anti-German business. I just don't know what the world's coming to.'

'The Heinrich Stern shop in Santanyí,' gabbled Mrs Enderby excitedly, 'was burned down by a mob yesterday! Santanyí's a town just down the road, Jane and Mike, and Stern is this ever so posh – and expensive – German interior designer chap.'

'Yes, we heard all about it,' Mike said, shooting glances at both Heidi and Jane. 'So, you all have old convertibles – that's your common bond, is it?'

'Well, yes – amongst other things,' Mrs Enderby replied with just a hint of pique: the Stern Inferno was *the* topic of the moment, and as it was a store at which she'd never felt able to afford to shop, she was inclined to gloat over its destruction. 'We're all neighbours *too*,' she conceded, 'and about the same age.'

'Brenda!' yelped her husband. 'We've got two children back in Wilmslow who are lovely Heidi's age!'

The smile froze on Mrs Enderby's face. 'Sorry, I'd forgotten about "*lovely*" Heidi. Of course, I was *very* young when I had Daphne and Eric – we both were.'

'What sort of convertible do you have, Richard?' asked Mike brightly.

Mr Enderby grinned impishly. 'No less than a Morris Minor, Mike – 1963 model.'

'Terrific!'

'Oh, I love Morris Minors,' said Jane sweetly, '– they're so ... so' – she stared at Mike, willing him to suggest something complimentary – '... they're like something out of a cartoon – a children's book – like Noddy and, and ...'

'Our *proper* car is a Range Rover,' said Mrs Enderby defensively.

'A very old one,' Mr Enderby clarified. 'It's bloody difficult to get parts for the old banger out here now – almost as difficult as the Morris–'

'Professor Kommis,' snapped Mrs Enderby, 'has a ... um ... Have you met the Kommises yet?'

'Not yet,' replied Jane.

'They're coming too, aren't they?' queried Mike, trying to make conversation, as Heidi offered him the *coca* once more. 'Werner said last night they have an old Beetle. By the way, Heidi, where is Werner?'

'Yes, as I was about to say,' Mrs Enderby continued, 'the Professor has–'

'Werner is in the house doing again the schedules now that Lionel and Jeanne are coming. He started on the computer last night after you went to bed, but is accidentally deleting the programme. He was very cross. I better go and see how he goes.'

As Heidi sped away across the cobbles, Brenda Enderby hissed: 'We didn't know there were *other* people coming! Werner never mentioned it. I hope they're not Germans. I mean, Werner and Heidi are *won*derful, but just between ourselves, we've always felt a wee bit isolated as the only non-German speakers on the Convertible Day. And then when we heard you two were coming, it was such a relief. "At last," we said, "now the Stumpfs and the Kommises will *have* to speak English – *all* day."'

Jane nodded disingenuously. 'Well, it was only arranged last night,' she said. 'You'll probably know them – Lionel de Tourny and Jeanne Moineau – the film stars.'

Simultaneously, the Enderbys gasped and exchanged frowns.

'They're *French*!' groaned Richard.

Brenda gulped down the last mouthful of her buck's fizz. 'I fear we may be in for a bit of a shock,' she said. 'The Tourny boy is ... well, just that – a *boy* – a teenager – a tearaway. My God! – you don't think he'll come on that awful, noisy motorbike of his, do you, Richard?'

'I–'

With a straight face, Mike said: 'He ran over Jane the other day, but I've forgiven him.'

'So have I,' said Jane. smiling. 'Actually, Lionel is in his mid-twenties, I think, and Jeanne must be about ten years older. And they're not coming on the Harley, but in Lionel's parents' old Citroën.'

'It's a 1967 convertible DS – a Series 2 with the redesigned nose,' added Mike.

Momentarily, both Enderbys were lost in thought as they envisaged a white-knuckle drive along perilous mountain roads in a car driven by a juvenile delinquent – a *French* juvenile delinquent. What excuses could they make?

'Those old Citroëns all have that daft suspension system,' sneered Mr Enderby. 'Trust the Frogs to come up with something like that! We'll all get motion sickness. Brenda can't possibly–'

The bell at the front gate clanged, and heads turned as a diminutive yet extremely elegant couple in their sixties came regally through the archway.

'Stone the crows!' sniggered Mr Enderby. 'Anyone for tennis?'

'Their Majesties Professor and Mrs Kommis!' hissed Mrs Enderby. 'Don't ask us what their first names are, because they've never been uttered in our humble presence. Even Werner treats them like gods – well, the old prof anyway. And they both pretend not to speak a *word* of English. I mean, who's ever heard of a Nobel Prize winner who can't speak English, hmm?'

Solemnly, the new arrivals glided towards the four smiling English, Frau Kommis trailing a few steps behind her husband. There was a salvo of three 'Good mornings!' coupled with a '*Guten Morgen*!' from Jane.

'*Guten Morgen*,' said Professor Kommis coldly, looking at no one in particular. His wife managed a smile and a nod. Indeed, there was no obvious indication that either of them even recognized the Enderbys. Hands were about to be shaken, when, as if responding to a starting gun, Werner bolted out of his front door with Heidi in tow. He was dressed in orange trousers, an emerald green polo shirt, and bizarrely matching two-tone loafers. In one hand he gripped a clipboard as if his life depended on it. The grim expression on his face dissipated almost immediately.

'Professor Kommis!' he roared, making a beeline towards him without any acknowledgement of another living soul in the courtyard. '*Guten Morgen*! *Wie geht's?*' Instantly, Kommis came alive, and for a few moments the two men spoke animatedly, 'Tourny' being uttered several times with raised eyebrows and shaking heads. Heidi moved around them to kiss Frau Kommis on both cheeks, addressing her as 'Frau Kommis', and then began to introduce her to the Oakhearts.

In German, Werner barked: 'Drinks for Professor and Frau Kommis, Heidi!' Without attempting to complete the introductions, but after a cursory embrace of the star guest's wife, Werner finally faced the Britons. 'Typical unreliable French!' he blasted.

Jane held her breath. *Please, God, he must come – he must.*

'I make all the necessary rearrangements to the Schedule,' – he waved the clipboard violently – 'and then dilettante Lionel telephones a few moments ago to say that prima donna Moineau has had "a bad night" due to a spot of "food poisoning", and is still in bed, so that they will have to join us at Algaida. Food poisoning! – bah! More like *alcohol* poisoning, if you ask me.'

Jane grinned with relief. 'Oh, is *that* all?'

Mike laughed.

'*All*! *All*! Jane, now I must re-reschedule – who is to travel in which car from here to Algaida, and how that will affect our trip onward from there. You see, it is imperative to ensure that no passenger travels in the same car on two consecutive legs. And maybe our French friends won't even turn up for breakfast at Algaida, and all my efforts on the phone to get us a bigger table–' He turned to the illustrious professor, growling, '*Ach*! – young people today!'

Kommis nodded in apparent understanding of the English admonition.

Glancing at his watch, Werner said: 'We have fifteen minutes before departure,' – he repeated it in German – 'and maybe if I go back to the computer–' But then he realised that abandoning Professor Kommis was unthinkable. Almost immediately, a shock wave rippled through him. 'Dear Professor Kommis,' he said in German, glaring at Heidi as she distributed more silver beakers, 'have you been *properly* introduced to my houseguest, Jane Oakheart? She is the daughter of my dear old friend, Sir Douglas Trench-Foot, the British Ambassador in Madrid.'

Kommis exhibited no reaction, other than offering once more a very small hand for Jane to shake; for her part, she'd picked up Werner's assertion of friendship with her father, but had managed to stifle a laugh.

'Jane, my dear, it is my *very* great honour to present to you the eminent Professor Manfred Kommis,' – the Enderbys stared at each other wide-eyed, and silently mouthed 'Manfred!' – 'the winner of the Nobel Prize for Medicine for his discovery of certain growth-stimulating vitamins.'

Still smiling, Mike stepped forward. 'Your eminence, please allow me to introduce myself. I am the husband of the celebrated Mrs Jane Oakheart – Michael Oakheart – but you may call me "Mike".'

*

With the air temperature rising steadily, the convoy of three ageing soft-tops ambled its way north-westwards down the wooded slopes of the Serres de Llevant towards Felanitx, and then on across Mallorca's central plain. Naturally, Werner led the way at the wheel of his 1968 Mercedes 250 SL, with Professor Kommis in the front passenger seat. The Enderbys followed in their royal-blue Morris Minor, the Oakhearts comfortably ensconced in the back and holding hands. Bringing up the rear, Frau Kommis was hunched nervously over the wheel of a 1960 VW Beetle with Heidi for company. Back at their departure point, and to avoid potentially violent scenes with what he'd called 'the aborigines', Werner had 'requested' his fellow Germans to join him in wearing a hat of some description for the purpose of concealing their tell-tale blond hair. And, with profuse apologies to the Kommises, but to the all too obvious delight of the Enderbys, he'd also 'suggested' that speaking German in public should be avoided except in the case of 'an emergency'. It was a bitter pill to swallow, but these were difficult times.

Despite these strictures, however, everyone appeared to be enjoying themselves so far. Werner's months of patient research and reconnaissance had yet again resulted in an itinerary of little-known minor roads almost devoid of traffic that snaked their way through a landscape of unspoilt hamlets, picture-postcard stone farms ablaze with bougainvillea, and parched summer fields populated with herds of dark-tan goats enjoying the shade of olive and fig trees.

As the sedate convoy left the plain and began to climb into the wooded hills between Porreres and Algaida, a clearly ecstatic Brenda Enderby turned to the passengers and said: 'You have to laugh about all that Prussian clipboard malarkey, but I take my hat off to Werner. He goes to so much trouble to ensure we have a smashing day and see the *real* Mallorca. But for him, we wouldn't know half the places we take our friends and visitors to.'

'A *quarter*!' shouted Richard, keeping his eyes on the road ahead and Werner's cream Mercedes. 'He's so clever, so knowledgeable. He interviewed all the big Arab nobs during his journalist days, you know – Mubarak, King Hussein … um … Rabin. And his English is almost perfect, isn't it?'

When, just after ten, they pulled into the car park of the *restaurante* in Algaida – Brenda, with a rumbling stomach, was anticipating her customary plain *tortilla* and cup of Hornimans tea – everyone was surprised to see a gleaming black Citroën DS convertible. It was parked diagonally, taking up two spaces. Lionel and Jeanne were sat not far away at an umbrella-shaded table on the terrace, their clothes and demeanour indicating that they might have just come from an all-night beach party. With a baseball cap pulled low over his forehead and jet-black lenses in his sunglasses, Lionel was also endeavouring to conceal his star status. They both held a *café solo*; the ashtray evinced that Jeanne had already smoked two Gauloises Blonde; the third was hanging between her lips.

'Hi!' said Lionel cheerfully, rising from his seat. 'Great cars! What kept you guys?'

'ENABA?' suggested Jeanne with a curled lip.

It took more than half an hour for the staff to get their act together and serve breakfast – indoors. There were plate loads of local cheeses, cured ham, big juicy olives, tomatoes, thick slices of lightly toasted wholemeal bread, and bottles of the finest virgin olive oil.

'*Bon profit!*' shouted Werner from one end of the table.

'*Bon profit!*' everyone responded, albeit with varying degrees of enthusiasm.

'Well,' said Brenda, tucking into her omelette as the others concocted open sandwiches, 'you have to agree that this is better than sitting outside, even if' – she shot a withering glance at Jeanne sitting opposite – 'it *is* a bit smoky. I mean, why don't the owners enforce the law?'

Earlier, the four uninitiated under-forties had sought to convince the six regulars that, on such a lovely summer's morning, breakfast alfresco would be much more enjoyable than retreating to the *restaurante*'s air-conditioned interior. And then, even though it was a foregone conclusion after an enforced show of hands, Werner had insisted on organising a secret ballot. Lionel had pouted for a while; Jeanne had said some very rude things in French, which, it transpired, the mouse-like Frau Kommis had fully understood.

'There's never enough shade with those umbrellas,' Brenda continued, addressing the Anglo-French contingent at her end of the table, 'and the terrace is too near the road. And then there are the flies. Anyway, we *always* sit at this table – *always*, don't we, Richard?' With a mass of toast, cheese and ham in his mouth, he nodded vigorously. 'And it was very kind of the proprietors to put two tables together for the ten of us, don't you think?'

'*Très gentille*!' boomed Jeanne, who was now on her second glass of white wine – everyone else was on coffee and freshly squeezed orange juice – and feeling a lot better than when Lionel had dragged her out of bed two hours earlier. She even had to admit that the simple food was absolutely succulent.

So far, the staff had been pleasant, but then Werner had blasted greetings in *Mallorquí* when they entered after the plebiscite, and the German contingent had proceeded to place their orders in creditable Spanish. Now, they were continuing to talk to each other in the same tongue; with Heidi's regular autumnal chores only a few months away, Werner had chosen the uncontentious subject of preserving sun-dried tomatoes. Indeed, all of them seemed to be enjoying the linguistic experience, almost as if they were playing some kind of parlour game. Professor Kommis, it transpired, was now an expert on the subject of sun-dried tomatoes, having recently attended a course run by a Frau Glück who had set up an 'organic' market garden near S'Horta. As he rattled off technicalities, Werner converted them into Castilian of fewer syllables for Heidi's benefit.

'*Entiendes*, Heidi?' he kept repeating – and how skilled she was at concealing her irritation!

'Well now,' said Richard, glancing from Lionel to Jeanne, 'I understand that you two are in films.' It sounded like an accusation; in truth, he was rather put out by Tourny's failure to remove either his hat or sunglasses.

Lionel looked across the table at Jane and grinned. Then she felt a foot rub hers. Sandwiched between Jane and Mike, Jeanne cackled and squeezed Mike's knee. Involuntarily, he pulled it away and Jeanne cackled again.

'Did Richard say something funny, dear?' asked Brenda as she pushed the ashtray from the centre of the table towards Jeanne's plate.

Jeanne blew a cloud of smoke in Brenda's direction and knocked back her wine. 'Oh, you English are always so funny – *hilaire* – the masters of understatement!' A waitress bustled by. '*Otra copa de vino blanco, por favor*!' barked Jeanne, waving her empty glass.

'"Ee-lair"?' queried Brenda suspiciously. 'I think Richard was just trying to be polite, dear.'

'She means "hilarious",' explained Lionel.

Wagging a finger at Brenda, Jeanne said: 'So, you don't speak French or Spanish, but then I suppose Queen Victoria was on the throne when you–'

'What I think Jeanne is alluding to,' Jane interjected as if in court, 'but is too modest to say expressly, is that both she and Lionel are, to be frank, household names – worldwide.'

'Oh *là là*!' shrieked Jeanne. In French, she continued: 'Now you insult me! – putting me in the same category as *him*. I've never been in a "blockbuster". I–'

'I thought we were all going to speak *English*,' bleated Richard. 'It's really not fair. And as a matter of fact, Jan, Brenda and me are not too bad on the old Spanish.'

'I am saying, Mr Englishman,' Jeanne rasped – all discussion on sun-dried tomatoes had fizzled out in the German camp – 'that I am not "a household name across the world", because – unlike some so-called actors – I'm not prepared to prostitute my standards to appear in mind-numbing Anglo-Saxon Hollywood crap intended for brain-dead Anglo-Saxons with attention spans of fifteen minutes or less, and which are part of an Anglo-Saxon conspiracy to create a unipolar world led by the USA.'

From behind the defensive barrier of the bar, even the staff were silent and staring at Jeanne.

Out of the corner of her eye, Jane spotted a nodding head. She glanced up the table; it was Werner's. His eyes met hers and the nodding stopped.

Lionel sighed and finally removed his sunglasses. '*Merci*, Jeanne – *merci beaucoup*.'

'*Je t'en prie*.'

Richard cleared his throat. 'I'm not sure I really caught the drift of all that, Jan, love, but – of course, it's a very long time since I was at school – but I don't understand all this stuff about "Anglo-Saxons". Weren't they the lot raping and pillaging before your lot arrived – the Normans – William the Conqueror and Magna Carta?'

Brenda glowed with pride. 'That's right, Richard! And they definitely didn't go to America. That was the Vikings – the ones what got there before Columbus – via Iceland – or Greenland ... or somewhere.'

The removal of his sunglasses proved to be Lionel's undoing. Within minutes, an already suspicious waitress identified him, and the news spread like wildfire. While he signed autographs, Werner procured the bill, divided it equally among all ten of them – without a tip – and then proceeded to re-re-reamend the hallowed schedule on his omnipresent clipboard.

When everyone was finally on parade in the sweltering car park, travel warrants were issued. There were some shocks: Jane was to travel with Professor Kommis in the VW; Heidi would accompany Richard in the Morris; Frau Kommis, thanks to her admission of a knowledge of French, would have the pleasure of accompanying Lionel, Mike and Brenda in the Citroën; and Jeanne, with her breath reeking of cheap wine and French tobacco, would be Werner's sole passenger in the Mercedes.

Now four, the convoy crossed the western half of the central plain and made for the towering mass of the Serra de Tramuntana, its highest peak – Puig Major – at over 1,400 metres, dominating the horizon. Werner had promised cooler temperatures up in the mountains, and as midday approached, everyone longed for the ascent to begin. But this was not all that Jane longed for: after fifteen minutes with Professor Kommis, she'd reluctantly concluded that he had to be an Anglophobe. In her rusty German, she'd tried to make conversation on every topic that came into her head – his work, family, hobbies, experiences of Mallorca, the weather, the Beetle, the Stumpfs – all to no avail. Kommis could only manage a '*Ja*', a '*Nein*', a non-committal grunt, a nod, or a shake of the head. She gave up and enjoyed the scenery and recollections of last night's sex. Occasionally, she would turn round and wave to the occupants of the Citroën bringing up the rear immediately behind them. To her surprise, they all seemed to be getting on like a house on fire – even Frau Kommis was managing the occasional smile. How Jane envied them! And she hadn't seen Mike look so relaxed for years; today's adventure was clearly putting yesterday's horrible experiences in Santanyí firmly out of his mind, thank God. They both needed more holidays; they were working too hard, not seeing enough of each other. Their jobs were taking over, and when Mike got his partnership, there'd be even more demands on his time. The same would be true if and when she took silk.

Snaking up a switchback of hairpin bends, the convertibles were climbing higher and higher into the mountains, the pine forest closing in thickly around them. The Mercedes and Morris were now above Jane, running parallel but in the opposite direction – Werner and Jeanne, Richard and Heidi all looking down, laughing and waving. And she, in turn, could look down on the Citroën – Kommis kept his eyes on the road ahead and changed gear for the next hairpin – Mike now blowing kisses. She blew them back. Then she focused on Lionel.

He's just a boy.

While Richard and Heidi continued to debate the pros and cons of feeding Mediterranean and subtropical flora with different types of manure, Werner and Jeanne, up front in the Mercedes, were putting the world to right. Within minutes of leaving Algaida, Werner had succeeded in breeching the actress's formidable defences by proclaiming in French:

'You know, Jeanne, I shut my eyes listening to you back there in the restaurant, and I was transported to Cairo and the last time I interviewed Mubarak. Naturally, all his criticisms of the Americans and the British were off-the-record, but … well, you could have taken the words right out of his mouth. I do so agree with you about the Anglo-Saxons – my God, the Enderbys are such philistines! Sometimes I wonder whether the English study anything at school other than how to write their names and play football.'

The alcohol, heat and dramatic scenery were conspiring to generate a temporary mist of sereneness around Jeanne. 'Hmmmm? ... Right. ... Your French, *chéri*, is remarkably good. You weren't in France during the Occupation, were you? Does this seat recline?'

After Werner had reached over to point out the lever – in the process he managed to rub his arm against her breasts – he made it absolutely clear that his birth post-dated 1945. Later, as the cooler mountain air, spiced with the scent of pine resin, filled their lungs, he said:

'Jeanne, *chérie*, we have to be honest and admit that in recent years British diplomacy has been successful in its systematic endeavours to destroy Europe.'

'Mmmmm …' Jeanne thought of lunch and wine, and her escape from Werner's pernicious smoking ban in the Mercedes.

'Meanwhile, France's best efforts to make Europe an independent power have failed. Strengthening the Franco-German axis is the only way to save the ideal of a true European Union from U.S. neo-imperialism.'

'Mmmmmmm … neo-imperialism. You're *so* right. That's what we have to save Lionel from, before it's too late – Hollywood.'

'*Absolument*! – the dumbing down, lowest-common-denominator philistines – the Enderbys, Trumps and Corks of this world.'

'"Corks"?'

'*Mais oui* – Sandra Cork – the new British premier.'

Jeanne was not listening. 'Look at him!' she cried, '– in the Citroën! He's like a little boy – *my* little boy.' She started to sob. 'We have to save him! – for France!'

'For *Europe*!' roared Werner.

*

High up in the Serra de Tramuntana lies a valley which, being ringed by precipitous ridges, resembles the vast crater of an extinct volcano. Sheltered from all but the most violent of winds, it enjoys a microclimate of its own, and, in consequence, is planted with thousands of fruit trees, notwithstanding the winter frosts and snow. Tucked away at the valley's centre is the peaceful *pueblo* of Orient, which has nothing of particular interest to offer the visitor other than its charm and the *L'Hermitage* hotel.

'Well, Lionel,' said Brenda, descending from the Citroën and gripping the driver's proffered arm, 'may I compliment you on your driving? I would never have believed it, what with seeing you on that motorbike round S'Horta an' all. And I don't feel in the least sick! Richard *will* be surprised. And both you boys have been so charming. What fun we've had! – haven't we, Frau Kommis?'

'*Oui, oui*!' she agreed, flashing a smile at Lionel, but it dissipated immediately on spotting her husband. He was approaching from the far end of the car park, where he and Werner had, as always, managed to commandeer the only two shaded spaces, thanks to a large Peruvian pepper tree.

L'Hermitage, an old manor house which was converted into a hotel decades ago, has played host to most of the crowned heads of Europe – and quite a few others besides. The huge olive press now serves as the dining room, but during the summer months, tables are set in the large cobbled courtyard. In accordance with his usual procedures, Werner had reserved the best of them – the one providing not only the most shade, but also affording the finest views of the magnificent surrounding countryside. Late the previous evening, he'd engaged in frantic telephone discussions with the management to increase the covers from eight to ten; at dawn this morning, he'd emailed detailed instructions to ensure that name cards would be arranged in accordance with the seating plan he'd laboriously devised in the early hours, a plan that embodied his two fundamental requirements – that no two people of the same sex or nationality should sit next to each other.

Having left Jeanne to extricate herself from the Mercedes, Werner had rushed to find the *maître d'hotel* for confirmation that all his demands had been performed to the letter, and if so, to rearrange the name cards: Mademoiselle Moineau had been promoted from oblivion at the far end of the table to sit at his right hand in place of the superannuated Anglo-Saxon philistine, Brenda Enderby. Luckily for Werner, the Enderbys inadvertently allowed him to perform these vital tasks unobserved by organising 'group photographs' in front of the stone plaques that record the visits of all the former royal guests. And with Brenda constantly repeating that Richard had won the Metal Box Senior Staff Photography Prize for eleven years running, it took him several minutes to compose and take each snap. So, Werner's reappearance with instructions for everyone to take their seats and enjoy the cava he'd ordered, came as a welcome relief to Richard's victims.

'I would have arranged a *menu*,' Werner proclaimed apologetically, 'but certain people' – he shot a glance at Brenda – 'have the most unusual dietary requirements.'

In this halcyon setting, the Oakhearts simply wanted to eat good food, drink decent Mallorcan wine, and enjoy witty – or, at least, amusing – conversation. Werner, however, was determined to talk politics. It was not that the Oakhearts were disinterested in the subject; on the contrary, they took democracy very seriously. And although neither Jane nor Mike had ever belonged to any political party, they had voted in every general and local election since being entitled to do so. In this, however, they'd been motivated by a sense of public duty rather than any fervent political beliefs. Indeed, they prided themselves on voting for individual candidates rather than dogma; the election material that came through their letterbox was scrutinised with no less care than a document on which they might have been asked to advise a client. But fairness and reasonableness in all things were their guiding principles, not socialism or laissez-faire capitalism, or any other ism. In fact, quite a few of their friends – particularly the non-lawyers – found them maddeningly sensible: nothing was monocausal or black and white; gut instincts were particularly dangerous.

Now, as waiters hovered, the Oakhearts caught each other's attention, rolled their eyes, and inclined their heads enviously towards that half of the long rectangular table that seemed to be enjoying itself. It comprised the Enderbys, Heidi, Lionel, and Frau Kommis, who'd not only confessed to having been a French teacher in a Hamburg high school before succumbing to the charms of 'Manfred', but also an ardent fan of Lionel's two films. And notwithstanding her husband's scowls, she'd even begun to relieve Lionel of some of his translation duties by uttering the occasional sentence in English.

All this frivolity went unnoticed by Werner, who was sat at what everyone was clearly expected to assume was the head of the table. He was not interested in Lionel's riotous accounts of outtakes and blunders during the filming of *Normandie* and *Dreyfus*: he had more important things on his mind; he was building the New Europe, and in the process, sounding out ideas for *Mein Europa*, the magnum opus currently gestating within his

Ca'n Pau desktop. So far, there'd been a lot of Gallic hyperbole from Jeanne, and the occasional nod from Kommis; the Oakhearts were being polite and trying to change the subject.

Werner gulped down the last of his chilled gazpacho and let the spoon clatter onto the under plate. 'But, Jane,' he said, 'the problem with too much devolved power is that you end up with the sort of shitty mess you have on this damned island – a load of half-witted aborigines running the place for their own benefit, and – in practice – unaccountable to any higher authority. Whereas in a *federal* Europe, you get power vested in people who are under the constant glare of an entire continent's media. They wouldn't be able to sneeze or get involved in anything even faintly corrupt without it being reported on the front pages from Berlin to Barcelona.'

'"Aborigine",' said Jane coolly, 'seems to be your favourite word today. It's not very nice, is it? And I'd lower your voice if you don't want the waiters to hear.'

'Oh, I wouldn't worry about *them*. They can barely string a sentence together even in Castilian now, thanks to the miserable schools on this island. In fact, they don't even study Spanish literature any more, just the facile offerings in "Esperanto" of their own Balearic "race". And the kids, Jeanne, are so busy trekking around the islands on school trips trying to find their "roots", they don't have time to learn a word of French!'

'*Merde*!' hissed Jeanne, '– just like the English! That's why we had to adopt the new European Constitution, otherwise everyone will be bilingual, speaking some stupid little language in their village – like Breton or this vile-sounding *Mallorquí* crap – and English the rest of the time. Have you read the Constitution, Werner?'

He nodded vigorously. In truth, he had at some stage, but had only vague recollections of it.

'"The European Union,"' she intoned, '"shall promote territorial cohesion and solidarity amongst member states and shall ensure Europe's cultural heritage is safeguarded and enhanced." I had to learn it for my role in the play *La Tondeuse Suicide* … er … *The Suicidal Lawnmower* – a masterpiece about the inability of lawnmowers to circulate freely across the EU due to the failure to harmonise national regulations on noise emissions. … Anyway, nothing could be more at the heart of European culture than *La Langue Française*, could it?'

'*Naturellement*,' agreed Werner, desperately attempting to conceal his confusion about the play's title, '– *and* German, the language of its largest and richest nation.'

Despite similar confusion, Professor Kommis nodded sagely. '*Ja*,' he mumbled.

Mike sighed and looked at Jane. 'Bloody hell, this is jolly serious stuff! Anyway, all these references to "culture" in a legal document give me a creepy feeling. It sounds sort of elitist – racist even. The underlying principle seems to be that European culture – whatever that is – is superior to all others.'

'Well,' snapped Jeanne, 'you Anglo-Saxons don't take culture very seriously at all, do you? You never have done.'

Jane groaned. 'So much for Shakespeare, Turner–'

'They're all *dead*!' shrieked Jeanne. 'For the last two hundred years all you've been interested in is your bloody empire and *trade* – a nation of shopkeepers!'

The Oakhearts exploded with laughter.

'What bloody nonsense!' boomed Jane. 'You're beginning to sound like some fascist fanatic.'

'*Fascist*! *Moi*?'

'We're moving away from the point,' intervened Werner swiftly, as a waiter removed his soup dish. 'And anyway,' he said, placing a hand on an arm of each of his two female neighbours in an attempt to avoid an Anglo-French split, 'we Europeans must never fall out among ourselves – "United we stand," et cetera. No, my argument is that if we were a *federal* state – a truly united Europe – then the sort of civil disorder and criminality we are now experiencing on this island would never be tolerated – indeed, it would never have been allowed to get this far. Federal police, federal soldiers – a federal judicial system – would have intervened, cracked down on those responsible, and brought them to justice. Instead, we have a blatantly prejudiced and racist "government" in Palma that just sits back and allows those responsible to do what they like with impunity. It's a disgrace! Could you imagine Washington standing aside and allowing Californians to persecute Texans?'

As Werner tried to evaluate whether he'd shot himself in the foot by using an American example, Mike said: 'Well, I suppose Washington and the Supreme Court did stand by for decades and allow certain states to discriminate against black citizens with impunity. I must say my starter, the red peppers stuffed with cod, was absolutely delicious.'

'And my *frito mallorquin* – is that right? – was delicious too,' Jane enthused.

'So was my *fromage de chèvre en croûte*,' added Jeanne.

Kommis looked at his last piece of Serrano ham and managed a nod of apparent contentment.

But Werner was not going to be deflected from his mission by Anglo-French diversionary tactics. 'We are at a crossroads in history!' he suddenly declaimed. 'We can either allow this great continent to split up into ever smaller, inward-looking, narrow-minded regions – the Balearics, Cataluña, the Basque wilderness, Wales, Scotland, Brittany, Corsica – all with their mediocre devolved governments, vulgar languages and xenophobia, or we can unite and shape the world as *we* would wish it to be, rather than how the Americans – devoid of any real opposition – would like it to be – a MacDonald's on every corner, everyone "packing a gun", working every hour God sends us – a race that only understands the concept of the survival of the fittest. Frankly, I've often pondered how the Americans ever made the transition from walking on four legs to two. I can only think that someone told them that there was more money to be made walking that way. Indeed, my dear friends, I have concluded that the Americans have a natural ability to fall into decadence without the customary intervening and uplifting period of civilisation.'

Laughter erupted around him; even Kommis managed a titter.

Down at the other end of the table, the laughter was louder and more sustained, for nothing more serious than breaking wind was under discussion.

'Don't get me wrong,' said Lionel, 'Saul Wittgenstein is a great director, but–'

'He directed both your films, didn't he?' fizzed Frau Kommis, whose ability to speak English was growing in direct proportion to her consumption of the well-chilled Gran Viña Sol.

'He sure did, Frau Kommis.'

'Oh, *do* call me Anna, Lionel.'

The Enderbys gasped, stared at each other open-mouthed, and then exploded into another fit of giggles.

'Well, anyway,' continued Lionel licking his lips at the grilled *dorada* being placed before him, 'Saul's problem is that he's a vegetarian.'

'Beans!' shrieked Brenda.

'Exactly!' confirmed Lionel. 'I mean, on the set of *Normandie* when I was in bed screwing my co-star Monica Epsilon-Pitt, and Saul was just metres away doing his stuff, these awful farts just kept wafting over us. Well, we were like in hysterics for a while and then after about thirty takes, Monica fainted and they had to send out for this real powerful air-freshener.'

Richard exploded, thumping the table.

'No kidding! So, all the time you see us having sex in that scene, there's this guy going round and round the set spraying this stuff as Saul farts away in the background!'

The hysterical laughter made all further discussion of the new Euro superstate impossible. Werner abandoned his roast suckling pig and glared down the table with a forced smile. 'My, my,' he roared, 'you are all having fun, I'm pleased to see. Would you care to share the joke?'

'From what I've just overheard,' said Mike smiling broadly, 'it has a lot to do with wind, if you get my drift.'

'Wind!' sniggered Brenda.

'I was not aware,' Werner sneered, 'that meteorology could be such a source of entertainment.'

'"*Meteorology*"!' guffawed Richard.

'My husband,' said Frau Kommis with a straight face, 'has terrible problems with *pimientos verdes* – green peppers. All night long, he's–'

There was another explosion, and the sight of the professor's outraged face over his wife's use of the English language just compounded matters.

'Ah, now I understand,' said Jeanne grinning. 'Lionel is telling all his Hollywood farting stories.'

'Oh, they're brilliant,' tittered Brenda. 'And Lionel's English is *wonderful*. Your voice, dear, reminds me of Montgomery Clift.'

'"Montgomery *Clift*"!' sniggered Jeanne. 'Actually, sweet little Lionel farts a lot in his sleep.'

'So does Werner!' added Heidi.

'And Mike!'

'And Manfred!'

Over the shrieking, Kommis snarled something in German at his wife, and the smile was wiped from her face. After a moment's hesitation, she snarled something back.

'That's right, Anna,' chirped Brenda, poking Professor Kommis in the ribs, 'don't let the big bully push you around! We're all equal now – the European Human Rights laws and all that malarkey.'

Incandescent, Kommis turned to face his assailant. 'Do not touch me, please!'

'Just a bit of fun ... Manfred, love. Loosen up for Christ's sake, you old grouch.'

'Lionel!' boomed Werner, silencing everyone. All eyes turned towards him, just as he'd hoped. 'I was wondering when we might see you in a *European* production – a *French* film – even the theatre, perhaps.' Jeanne cackled. 'I mean, as a well-educated young man from such a privileged background – one of the oldest families of France – you will surely grow tired with the utter superficiality of America in general and Hollywood in particular – quite quickly, I should think.'

Lionel smiled, hunched his shoulders in Gallic fashion, and was about to respond, when Frau Kommis said: 'I really don't think there was anything "superficial" about *Dreyfus* – a film about one of the worst examples of institutionalised anti-Semitism in French history, or, for that matter, the tragic tale of the *Normandie*.'

In German, Kommis barked: 'My God, Anna! How many times do I have to tell you that I will not tolerate you speaking that language.'

Anna slammed her wine glass on the table and snapped the stem. 'For God's sake, Manfred,' she yelled in English, 'the bloody War ended in 1945! These people are not responsible for those air raids on Dresden, or your being orphaned, so give me a bloody break.'

'You tell him, love,' said Brenda.

'The *Normandie*!' scoffed Werner. 'It was just a ship – the *Titanic* but with only *three* funnels!'

'"Just a *ship*"!' screeched Jeanne. 'The *Normandie* was the most beautiful, the most luxurious, the most – the most ... It was the *chef d'œuvre de la techniqe et de l'art français* – the greatest ship ever built – a floating palace. The finest designers and artists of 1930s France worked on her, and you Germans sabotaged her to stop her being used by the Allies as a troop ship. You set fire to her in New York.'

'That's a damned lie!' growled Werner, '– a damned, stinking lie told by that Jew, Wittgenstein, in his anti-German propaganda film.'

'I say, old boy,' said Richard sternly, 'steady on. No need to get offensive.'

The Oakhearts were too stunned to say anything, and stared at their plates.

'It *was* a lie,' said Kommis quietly but firmly in English, 'as all the newspapers pointed out, Monsieur de Tourny, when your film was released. Even the official enquiry conducted by the Americans in 1942 concluded that the *Normandie* caught fire as a result of negligent American workers with oxyacetylene torches. There was no sabotage'

'Maybe Lionel doesn't read the critics,' said Werner. 'Or perhaps the American newspapers didn't carry those reports. Maybe Lionel didn't research his role – maybe American directors and producers don't want their stars to think too much.'

'Maybe you're anti-Semitic,' said Lionel.

'I'm sure Werner isn't,' said Jane, '– are you?'

Werner tried to laugh. 'Of course not, Jane – how ridiculous! That's the problem with our politically correct world today, one cannot criticise anything a particular race does without being labelled a racist. I'm sorry, everyone, if I did not make myself clear a few moments ago. All I meant was that this American film *Normandie* was not truthful. For dramatic effect, the producers decided that it would be better to have the great French liner destroyed by German secret agents than by a negligent welder from Brooklyn and the incompetent New York authorities who couldn't put out the fire properly.'

'To be honest,' said Mike hesitantly, 'I thought the film was more anti-French than anti-German. I mean, as soon as the War broke out in thirty-nine, the British converted their two super-liners, the *Queen Elizabeth* and the *Queen Mary*, into troopships and set them to work, notwithstanding the fears of U-boats and torpedoes. The French government, on the other hand, ordered the precious *Normandie* to be mothballed in New York for the duration.'

Groaning, Brenda said: 'Oh, *please*, let's not talk about the War. Anyway, Richard and me haven't seen the film, so we're a bit in the dark.'

'Quite,' said Werner. 'So, Lionel, as I was saying, when can we see you in a European film?'

'I don't think Europe can afford me at the moment.'

'*Putain*!' hissed Jeanne. 'You know Pierre Gambetta would love to direct you in *The Glass Eye of Brother Jacques*. We'd be able to work together – at last.'

'Now that sounds an interesting film,' said Werner with a hint of a conciliatory smile. 'Why don't you want to star in that, Lionel?'

Lionel sighed. 'Well, I'm not sure it's really me – a young one-eyed sadomasochistic priest trying to save prostitutes in Brest, while screwing his mother and twelve-year-old sister, and who finally castrates himself on the high alter of Quimper Cathedral. Anyway, Gambetta only offered me the part in the hope I'd let him touch me up.'

*

When the bill had been finally dissected, and Lionel had finished signing autographs for all the staff, Jane said: 'Do our contributions include a share of the tip – ten per cent, presumably – or is that extra?'

Werner tutted. 'Jane, one should never leave tips in Mallorca – the locals are very proud.'

Lionel said: 'But we can't have a meal like this – ten of us – and not leave a tip! They've worked their damned butts off.'

'We *never* leave tips,' Werner bleated. 'Now, if you could all just let me have your contributions of two hundred and forty euros and forty-six cents per couple–'

'I suppose,' interjected Richard hesitantly, 'we could round it up to two hundred and sixty-five euros per couple so as to include a decent tip.'

An indignant look gripped Werner's face. 'I suggest, Richard, that that would set a most dangerous precedent for future years.'

'Frankly,' said Mike, 'we *can't* leave without a proper tip – it would be a goddam insult!'

'It would,' agreed Jane.

Jeanne nodded. 'Any more wine in that bottle, *chérie?*'

Lionel pulled a fifty-euro note out of his trouser pocket. 'Well, I'm leaving this. If anyone wants to chip in, it's up to them, but not necessary.'

Mike pushed three ten-euro notes across the table. 'That's our share, Lionel.'

Brenda engaged in rapid sign language with Richard. He studied his wallet and, looking sheepishly up the table, matched the Oakhearts' tip. 'I'm sorry, Werner, but I'm with young Lionel on this one. I mean, we're such a big group this year, and the old *camareros* have been bloody first rate. Not a spot of bother, as we'd feared, even though they know you're German ... and all that hoo-hah in the Cathedral the other day. Mind you, they could have poisoned your food. You might drop dead in half an hour!'

'Richard!' scolded Brenda.

'Sorry! Bad taste! Too much *vino* – but I'm OK to drive. ... I hope we *all* are. I know young Lionel is, bless 'im, cos he's only had mineral water – apart from that glass of cava when we arrived.'

Werner rose and walked slowly around the table to Lionel. He picked up the entire tip and began handing the notes back to the donors.

'What the hell are you doing?' asked Mike.

In German, Heidi said: 'Werner, don't be silly. Let's just pay our share too.' As she opened her shoulder bag and extracted her purse, Anna Kommis quietly told her husband to go along with the majority.

'I really must insist that you don't tip these aborigines,' Werner said firmly.

'For Christ's sake,' snapped Jane, 'stop calling them that! You sound like an Australian bigot.'

Lionel refused to take the note proffered to him. 'I'm sorry, Werner, but I am not the sort of guy that can walk out of a restaurant without leaving something for the staff. It's not the act of a gentleman.'

'"*Gentleman*"!' scoffed Kommis.

Werner's face reddened. 'I think that I am not only a gentleman, Tourny, but, as someone who has lived on this island for many years – unlike you, young man – that *I* know these people. You insult their honour by leaving cash on the table.'

'Want a bet?' snapped Brenda.

Werner ignored the philistine and tried to push the fifty-euro note into Lionel's breast pocket.

Lionel jumped up. '*Non, non, s'il vous plait*! Please don't do that, Herr Stumpf. It is my right.'

'"Right"? "***Right***"? Everything is about "rights" with you people – never a mention of responsibilities. You don't know–'

'*Pour l'amour du ciel, putain!*' roared Jeanne as she flung a bread roll at Werner, scoring a direct hit on his temple. 'What the fuck's your problem, Adolf? Put that money back on the table or I'll cut your fucking balls off! Come on, Lionel, we're leaving. I'm sick of these shits – *all* of them!'

The party broke up rapidly. With Jeanne screaming anti-German abuse, Lionel marched her to the Citroën, and then drove off at speed. Fearing it was the end of an era, Brenda was still sobbing as her ashen-faced husband gently led her to the Morris; she just wanted to go home and lie down. Jane diplomatically succumbed to a spot of heat exhaustion, and the Enderbys offered to drive her and Mike back to *Ca'n Pau*. Kommis and Werner resolved to complete the itinerary; their volcanic spouses had no option but to join them – or walk home.

When he thought no one was looking, Werner pocketed the troublemakers' tip. Anna Kommis, however, spotted him.

'I'll return it to them later,' he said solemnly, '– when they've all calmed down. You know what these artistic types are like – especially French ones.'

When they reached the car park, the Mercedes and Volkswagen were still nicely shaded by the Peruvian pepper trees. But as the Stumpfs and Kommises approached their vehicles, bulging eyes were followed by gasps and howls of anger, for not only was 'NAZI' sprayed all over them, but they were also full of stinking, decomposing kitchen waste.

CHAPTER 11

Even most of Sandra Cork's supporters had doubted that their wiry and petite heroine with her boyish looks, bobbed hair and Mancunian accent, would succeed Gerry Briar as leader of the Labour Party when he made his shock announcement in mid-term to retire from politics and take up sheep farming in the Scottish Borders – along with a few non-executive directorships. But politics is a strange business, and Sandra, thanks to her neo-socialist passion for public services, coupled with a near-fanatical conviction that the British people were better qualified than anyone else to make the most important decisions affecting their daily lives, proved to be a winning combination at just the right moment – a leak from a 'Corkite' within No. 10 that Briar wanted the UK to rejoin the EU.

Her election to the leadership hit Westminster like a tsunami engulfing a Pacific island. Pro-Europeans in her party deserted to the Liberal Democrats, while many of the Briarite free-enterprisers joined the Conservative benches. Consequently, her majority was slashed to just six, and Parliament was dissolved. At the ensuing General Election, the Conservatives were almost decimated, while the Liberal Democrats, who won seats from both the Tories and Labour, emerged as the Official Opposition. Sandra, however, did not secure an overall majority. As a constitutional crisis loomed, a bizarre coalition between Labour and the forty-five remaining Conservatives was forged, the latter being prepared to do almost anything to preserve British sovereignty and keep the European tyranny at bay. Their price was one cabinet position – Secretary of State for Foreign and Commonwealth Affairs – and so it was that urbane Sir Peter Blithe-Blister, 15th Baronet, whose family had farmed great swathes of Northumberland for more than five hundred years, entered the Foreign Office.

Unsurprisingly, all the pundits were convinced that, being as different as chalk and cheese, the relationship between Sir Peter and Sandra would be a turbulent one; the coalition would soon collapse. After all, Sandra had been brought up on a council estate in Hulme; she'd taught maths in various Greater Manchester comprehensive schools before entering politics; and her husband, Craig, was a probation officer – now based in Brixton and commuting daily by bus from Downing Street. As for the Cork progeny – two boys and a girl – Sandra had given birth to all three between her eighteenth and twenty-fourth birthdays; she'd only married Craig after the second baby was born. So far, none of them had done much with their lives, but nor had they caused their mother any political embarrassment.

Now, after more than a year in office, and notwithstanding the social, educational and political gulfs between them, Sandra and Sir Peter were defying the pundits and getting on rather well together. Naturally, their common crusade against Brussels was a strong bond, but it was much more than that: they both shared a dry sense of humour; he loved her 'Northern' call-a-spade-a-spade style; she admired his exquisite manners. And, in truth, each of them found the other just a little attractive. The only thing that irritated Sir Peter was workaholic Sandra's penchant for meetings after dinner – or 'tea' as she endearingly called it – in the Corks' Downing Street flat.

'I do hope we're not keeping Craig from watching International Athletics,' said Sir Peter, glancing at the vast television screen which the Corks had had installed in one corner of the sitting room.

'Not at all,' said Sandra without looking up from the document she was studying. 'He's watching it on the set in the bedroom.'

'Oh good! I'd hate to think we were putting him out at all.'

Sir Peter and John Bitters, the Minister of Defence, exchanged knowing glances and kept straight faces.

'Actually,' said Peregrine Truetreat, the Joint Intelligence Committee's chairman, 'I think our boys are in with a pretty damned good chance of winning a few medals at this year's European Championships.'

'And the girls – thanks to us black kids,' added Monica Matthews, Sandra's Director of Communications.

'And the *girls – naturally!*' confirmed Peregrine. 'That's what I meant.'

'Thank God for a multiracial society!' said Sir Peter joyously. 'Most of Europe don't know what they're missing. I mean, it's no wonder these games things in Prague–'

'Ljubljana,' corrected Monica.

'–are a two-horse race between us and the French. What a blessing it was to have such whopping great empires after all. Poor old Germany!'

'Talking of "poor old Germany",' said Sandra, tapping the document on her lap, 'Klipper's clearly in a right tizzy over this Mallorca carve up – and that divvy Chiffon. And the way they're both reacting, they sound as though they're a few bricks short of a wagon load.'

'Absolutely!' chuckled Sir Peter.

'I'm sure you'll agree with me, Prime Minister,' said Truetreat, 'that our people down at GCHQ in Cheltenham have done a pretty damned good job monitoring all the careless radio and microwave chatter coming out of Berlin and Paris.'

'Can't complain,' said Sandra. 'More coffee anyone?'

'Oh yes *please*!' gushed Sir Peter. 'I really had no idea just how refreshing *instant* coffee could be until we started having these cosy chats up here.'

After the PM had topped up the mugs, Sandra said: 'Right, you lot, what are we going to do about these jokers?'

Sir Peter didn't hesitate. 'Well, clearly we have here a heaven-sent opportunity to let the French and the Germans make absolute chumps of themselves.'

'How so?'

'If I might be allowed just a couple of minutes to set the scene, Sandra?'

'No prob, Peter.'

'Most kind! ... Well, as you know, for the last few years the French and Germans have made such a big thing about this wonderful friendship of theirs – "the *entente cordiale par excellence*" – with Berlin and Paris seeing eye to eye on almost everything. Of course, *we* all know that they really can't stand each other, but they've had to pretend otherwise for three fundamental reasons. Firstly, their economies are up the spout, and so they're both failing dismally to live up to their own rules to keep the precious euro a strong currency – all that three per cent stuff, you know? So, they've had to put up a united front in their dealings with both the European Central Bank and the Commission to get the rules bent and then ignored.

'Secondly, they've got the Pandora's box of Eastern Europe and the new boys – and girls. The Germans thought they were going to be the leader of that gang, but when beastly Putin went bonkers in Ukraine, the poor Germans found that almost all those former communists out East were rather disposed towards Uncle Sam and ourselves, which was also a bit of a shock for the French. Consequently, fearful of the Easterners falling under our control as the Yanks' biggest European chum, Berlin and Paris had to work together to woo them over – you know, the usual promises – you support us in the Council of Ministers and we'll make sure you get loads of grants from Brussels to rebuild Warsaw's sewers and Prague's crumbling monuments, and to subsidise Romania's mediaeval farming practices.

'Well, as I said, we know that the entente is all a facade. The Germans are not only convinced that the French are on the way out as they slip ever lower in the economic league tables, but that with the ongoing expansion of the so-called "European Union" eastwards – I mean, it has nowhere else to go – Berlin will, at least geographically, become ever more central, with poor old France out on the western margins. Hence Chiffon's – and France's – ever growing paranoia. On one side, us and the Americans – the world's only super power – "the Anglo-Saxons" – with our omnipotent language that completely dominates international trade and modern culture, and on the other, the Germans – the economic engine of Europe – even with their current tribulations – dominating the new Europe from Berlin at its heart.

'And now they're alarmed about their precious plans for a European Army, er ... Defence Force – whatever it's called. What a joke! I mean, we're the only Europeans with any real experience of conflict post-1945. It was the French who went overboard with all those requirements in the newfangled European Constitution thingy for common foreign and "security" policies. The goons believed they'd be top dog in the Euro Army, bossing everyone else around – including the battle-shy Germans – maybe even giving orders in French!

'Well now, I've prattled on long enough, but I'm just trying to explain why I believe that if we give the French and Germans enough rope over this spot of bother down in the Balearics, they might just hang themselves.'

'How do you mean, Peter?' asked Sandra. 'Another Chips Ahoy! by the way?'

'Oh yes *please* – such yummy biscuits! – so moreish! I'll have to get my man to get a stock in. Where do you get them? ... Fortnums?'

'Any supermarket.'

'Oh, right. ... Where was I? ... Well, we know that Klipper is in one hell of a mess – particularly on the economic front. As things stand at the moment, his chances of being re-elected at next year's federal elections are pretty remote. This nasty anti-German terrorism in sunny Majorca' – he pronounced it 'Mar-jaw-car' – 'is the final straw. Madrid seems unwilling to take control, and that in turn makes Klipper look impotent. From our reading of the GCHQ intercepts, the French are terrified that the Germans will do something dynamic for once on the diplomatic front, thereby cementing Berlin's ambitions to claim the "Leadership of Europe".'

'And I suppose,' added Bitters, 'that if they did get to the point of some kind of mobilisation of this embryonic EU Army farce, the French might look even further marginalized.'

'Exactly. They're obviously having kittens about those three German gunboats chugging down to the Med!'

'But from the intercepts, Peter,' said Truetreat, 'it seems pretty clear that the Germans haven't the slightest desire to do *anything* on the military front. They want the French and the Belgians, as "neutrals", to do the dirty work – God help them! – while they pull the strings'

'Correct, but *we* know that Chiffon has no intention whatsoever of getting embroiled in a UN-style peacekeeping operation in damned

Majorca. I mean, he and Klipper both want a diplomatic solution, and clearly hope they can bribe that dimwit Azucena to wheel out the riot police and lay down the law, while they bribe the Majorcans with a load of Euro-taxpayers' money – "Stop burning down German villas in order to drum up support for your daft secessionist ambitions, and you'll all get half-price fares to Barcelona." That kind of thing.'

'If you're suggesting, Sir Peter,' said Martha, 'that we just sit back and let the Franco-Germans try and sort this mess out on their own in the hope that they'll make a cock up, you're overlooking our own problem. The UK media – particularly the tabloids – are obsessed with the fate of scores of thousands of British holidaymakers out in Mallorca – ditto social media. At any moment they could be caught up in a terrorist outrage. Travel agents are being inundated with cancellations. The airlines are banging on our door wanting to know whether it's safe to fly to Palma. And I just happen to know that in tomorrow's tabloids there'll be plenty of headlines about the action apparently being taken by the French and Germans – Berlin lost no time releasing the news about those ships going down there. And tonight's Channel 4 News even made a speculative reference to a possible evacuation of German holidaymakers. So, while our continental partners are arranging summit conferences with the Spanish and organising an armada, we're doing *nothing*. And yet, there are more British tourists on the island than any other foreign nationality!'

'Yes, Peter,' said Sandra, 'Martha's right. We have to do *some*thing.'

'Oh absolutely! I didn't intend to suggest that we should just sit back and allow our NATO allies to dig themselves into a very deep hole. Naturally, the Foreign Office has a responsibility to look after British subjects, wherever they may be – even Majorca. However, we have to bear in mind that, so far, these terrorist chappies have only been targeting *Germans*. Incidentally, I got up to speed on this one today thanks to a long and most useful discussion with our man in Madrid – Doug Trench-Foot. As chance would have it, he's currently on leave at his place in Derbyshire. Doug is quite convinced that Britons are in no danger at all. In fact, his daughter and son-in-law are out there at the moment on holiday.'

'Good Lord!' gasped Bitters theatrically, '– presumably, not Magaluf.'

'Magaluf?'

'It's a dead naff resort,' explained Martha.

'Me and Craig used to go there when we first got together,' cooed Sandra dreamily.

After a moment's silence, Sir Peter said: 'I understand from Doug that they're the guests of that German writer, Stumpf – the one that sued

Professor Piston-Jones for defamation a little while back – at his rather grand *finca* in the country.'

'Bloody hell!' snorted Truetreat. 'He's some kind of Nazi, isn't he?'

'Certainly not!' declaimed Sir Peter. 'I've read *all* his books. They're paragons of objectivity. It's no wonder he won his action against Piston-Jones.'

'Anyway, Peter,' said Sandra, 'whatever "our man in Madrid" says, we have to be seen to be doing *something* about Mallorca – if only to give us some good headlines in the papers – and stop all the slagging-off we're getting on social media.'

'I was just coming to that, Sandra. For a start, I think we could really set the cat among the pigeons by calling for an *all*-Europe summit, including us – excluding Russia and Belarus, of course – not just EU states, thereby making it clear that the summits proposed by the French and Germans are *exclusionary*. If Berlin and Paris object, they'll shoot themselves in the foot. And we'll flatter the Spanish by saying that the Majorca palaver is fundamentally a Spanish internal matter, and that we have complete confidence in their ability to sort it out. We'll represent that the sole purpose of our proposed summit is to see what help, if any, Europe *as a whole* can provide, bearing in mind "the global threat of terrorism". Doug, by the way, mentioned some stories being "leaked" by Azucena that these ENABA nutters are getting weapons from Iran.'

'Are they, Perry?' asked Sandra.

'Not according to *our* intelligence, Prime Minister.'

'I don't think that just summoning an "all-Europe" summit will satisfy the tabloids here,' sniffed Martha.

'Probably not,' agreed Bitters, 'which is why Sir Douglas and I will place ourselves in front of the cameras and tell Jo Public just how safe Mallorca is for us British, thanks to "the deep bonds of friendship between our two great nations" – bla, bla, bla.'

'And what about these French and German warships whizzing around the Med, John?' asked Sandra.

'I've had a quick word with the Chief of the Naval Staff, Admiral Sir Stephen Itchingneck, and he advised that at the moment we have a few ships returning from a tour of duty in the Gulf, including the carrier *HMS Impenetrable* and the destroyers *Impertinent*, *Imperious* and *Impudent*. Currently, they're just off Sicily, and, if you like, PM, they could put in at Gibraltar for a convenient spot of "minor maintenance" … or something.'

'That might upset Azucena,' said Sandra. 'You know how bloody sensitive he is about Gib.'

'I dare say,' said Sir Peter, 'that he's also pretty sensitive about French and German warships circling the Balearics, the damned Euro Army marching into Palma, and being summoned to Perpignan – and-stroke-or the Black Forest – for a dressing down by Headmaster Klipper and Head Prefect Chiffon.'

'On the other hand,' said Bitters, 'we all know that the clot is convinced that, as the sad compromise candidate, he's in with a good chance of being elected EU "President" next year – what a joke! So, he's got to try and keep *everyone* happy.'

'A thankless task indeed!' hissed Sandra.

'Quite!' agreed Sir Peter. 'Anyway, that's why I think he'll jump at our proposal for a thumping great powwow in … well, let's propose Geneva in "neutral" Switzerland. And in the process, we'll get to look like the good Europeans – the good Europeans who believe in a Europe of *sovereign* states sorting out their own bloodthirsty citizens. … Any more of those Chips Ahoy!, Sandra?'

CHAPTER 12

In the event, Werner Stumpf did not keep the gratuity of a hundred and ten euros that he'd pocketed at L'Hermitage: it was the fee demanded by the staff 'volunteered' by the manager to remove the refuse from the Mercedes and Volkswagen convertibles. Furthermore, when handing over the cash, Werner excused the behaviour of his French and English 'acquaintances' for their refusal to sanction his proposal for the leaving of a ten per cent tip. There was really nothing that could be done, however, about the graffiti, and so, once the cleansing operation had been completed – by which time it was past five o'clock – Werner decided that the Convertible Day should be abandoned and that the survivors of the experience should return home by the most minor of minor roads. En route, he ruminated on the day's events, while Heidi sat rigid in silent protest over his behaviour. Reluctantly, he concluded that he'd made one or two minor errors of judgment. Of course, in principle, his stand over tipping was unquestionable. Nevertheless, this was one of those very rare occasions when some form of compromise was imperative. After all, Tourny and Moineau were world-famous celebrities, and the ability to claim them as good friends would greatly impress his circle, both on and off the island, particularly the people that mattered – his publishers for a start, and the Great and Good of Berlin, including those snooty bastards who'd declined his invitations to celebrate his birthday with him in Mallorca.

Moreover, if *Mein Europa* was going to receive the international attention it deserved when published, contacts such as Jane Oakheart were vital: her father was a conduit into the very heart of EU-sceptic Whitehall, and if he played his cards right, then, within the next few months, there'd be every chance of getting Trench-Foot over from Madrid and sowing the necessary seeds. The British had to be made to see that an Anglo-German alliance of the kind proposed in *Mein Europa* would be an unstoppable combination.

But there was also a more pressing reason to butter up the disruptive elements at the L'Hermitage lunch: without the culprits, Sunday's party would be a most embarrassing flop. To be honest, he wasn't bothered about the Enderbys: they'd passed their use-by date; after several years' acquaintance, it was now crystal clear that they knew no one of any importance – anywhere – and, with their bourgeois clothes and gardening chit-chat, they certainly didn't impress any of his German friends.

And so it was, that when the Stumpfs finally made it back to *Ca'n Pau*, Werner profusely apologised to the Oakhearts for his unusual behaviour over lunch: he'd only been trying to avoid a potentially explosive situation with Professor Kommis, who, on more than one occasion in his presence, had manifested an almost pathological hatred of tipping, which would probably explain the rumours commonplace in certain scientific circles in Germany that Kommis had been undergoing 'therapy' for some years. He then telephoned the *Villa Tourny* and recounted the same story to Lionel, who, to Werner's intense relief, confirmed there were no hard feelings. The communication of all this misinformation occurred while Heidi was preparing a supper of cold cuts and cheeses. Consequently, she retired to bed believing that good relations had been universally restored thanks to her husband's exceptional – indeed, unique – decision to apologise for his behaviour.

The next morning, Mike awoke to find Jane already dressed and sitting in front of the window reading a guidebook. She smiled at him sweetly.

'We'd better make an early start,' she chirped, 'if we're going to have time to see *every*thing in Palma, especially as we're also having lunch with the Consul.'

Mike rubbed his eyes. '*Are* we?'

'Of course we are! Come on – chop-chop!'

As they crossed the courtyard for breakfast, Mike sniffed the air and furrowed his brow. 'Maybe I'm imagining it, but I'm sure I can smell bacon and eggs.'

'My God, so can I. It must be some lucky English neighbours – the Enderbys perhaps, consoling themselves after yesterday's debacle.'

But when they reached their customary breakfast venue, they were stunned to find Werner sitting at the table reading a newspaper.

'Good morning!' chorused the Oakhearts.

'Jane! Mike! Good morning!'

'Back from Alqueria Blanca so soon?' queried Mike.

'Today I decide that we should have breakfast with our delightful guests.' Before they could overcome their shock, Werner swiftly added: 'And so I have arranged for Heidi to prepare us a traditional English spread. Sit, and I shall inform her of your arrival.'

After he'd marched off, Mike said: 'Well, what do you make of that? Clearly, he's still trying to make amends.'

'Possibly, but if you ask me, after that riot in Santanyí the other day, he's probably frightened of being poisoned down at the bar – or lynched!'

Almost immediately, Werner was back. He held a silver teapot; behind him Heidi struggled with a large silver tray laden with dishes of fried food. Mike jumped up to assist, and Werner momentarily scowled.

After everyone had helped themselves, Werner pointed to the newspaper and said: 'Well, we're all in the same boat now, it seems. I really wonder whether it's sensible for you to go into Palma today, Jane and Mike.'

Expectantly, Mike looked up from his heavenly treat. 'Oh? How do you mean?'

'Although your prime minister says that British tourists here are in no danger from the wicked terrorism of ENABA, she's sending an armada to Gibraltar.'

'"*Armada*"?' sniggered Jane. 'I very much doubt the Royal Navy have enough ships these days to put together an armada. Sounds ridiculous to me.'

'Well,' retorted Werner defensively, 'although the official line from London is that a carrier and some destroyers returning from the Gulf are just putting in for some minor maintenance, *El Mundo* and the *Diario De Mallorca* are convinced it's a ruse. You know how worked up the Spaniards can get over Gibraltar. Of course, it's pure hypocrisy, seeing how they've got their own two "Gibraltars" just across the water on the North African coast.'

'Oh yes,' said Mike, 'Melilla and Ceuta – however you pronounce them – that they pinched from Morocco.'

'Exactly! How well informed you are, Mike. And they've no intention of ever handing *them* back, but then, unsurprisingly, the highly subsidised inhabitants say they want to remain Spanish. Anyway, the media here are rife with speculation that your navy is building up its presence in the Western Mediterranean just in case the situation here deteriorates so much that it becomes necessary to evacuate the tourists.'

'Good Lord!' cried Jane, just managing to stifle a giggle.

Heidi sighed. 'Margalida is not happy. Already this morning she has broken two cups. She says the British are imperialist pigs and must be forced out of Gibraltar. She also makes bad words about the German and French ships.'

'German and French ships?' queried Jane.

Werner shrugged his shoulders. 'Oh, she hears such nonsense on the local radio. The German and French navies are just on summer manoeuvres. Nobody's going to be evacuated.'

'Hah!' snapped Heidi. 'I think it is not chance the ships come to Mallorca on the day Chiffon and Klipper order the Spanish to meetings in the Schwartzwald.'

The Oakhearts exchanged puzzled glances, while Werner's fork, laden with a mass of fried egg, froze in mid-air. 'Pah!' he scoffed. 'Where did *you* learn such things?'

'In the *Frankfurter Allgemeine* this morning.'

'When do you have time to read the paper?'

'As I squeeze the oranges.'

Werner seemed incapable of envisaging the possibility of his wife reading a serious newspaper. 'Anyway,' he finally snorted, 'you have it all wrong. We have proposed a summit with the Spanish in the Schwartzwald to tell them to end the violence here, but that buffoon Chiffon has tried to interfere and get the parties around a table in Perpignan on the Franco-Spanish frontier – of all places!'

'Perpignan?' pondered Jane. 'Oh yes! – how very clever of the French! – such tact! Perpignan was once the capital of the Kingdom of Mallorca.'

'No, you cannot be right,' said Werner confidently.

'Yes, I read it in one of my guide books this very morning. Which reminds me, Mike. As gorgeous as this breakfast may be, unless we make a move very soon, it won't be worth going to Palma.'

'Maybe Werner's right, Footy. Maybe we should mooch around here today – by the pool, down at the beach ... go and see that nunnery place.'

'*Ja, ja!*' agreed Werner. 'There are bound to be anti-British demonstrations in Palma over Gibraltar. And tonight we have our annual moonlight picnic at the Portopetro lighthouse with Professor Kommis and von Karpen. Heidi is making all sorts of wonderful dishes, and there are the hampers to prepare. I have a schedule. Some assistance would be most helpful.'

Jane dabbed at her lips with a napkin. 'Oh, it all sounds *so* wonderful! We're really looking forward to it. And we would have loved to help with the preparations, Werner, but unfortunately Daddy has been such a bore and arranged for us to have lunch with the British Consul.'

Momentarily, Werner seemed to be on the point of exploding. Then, with an exaggerated smile, he boomed: '*Ja, ja!* Of course you must go! And I should be delighted to invite him and his lady wife to my party.' Jumping up, he added: 'I shall fetch a formal invitation from my study. What are their names?'

*

Prime Minister Jesús Azucena – *el Presidente del Gobierno* to give him his proper title – was never at his best first thing in the morning: he was a night owl. Last night was no exception: in common with many Madrileños, he'd sat down for dinner at around ten-thirty in one of his favourite Madrid restaurants; he departed some two hours later. After a nightcap or two with some very pretty young Russian 'models' at a leading banker's apartment, he'd finally got to bed at his official residence shortly before four – alone: his wife and children were already avoiding Madrid's suffocating heat at the Azucenas' summer house on the Galician coast. Now, at the unusually early hour of ten-thirty, and fortified solely by three cups of very strong coffee and a large Cuban cigar, Jesús had to cope with power politics and a deepening international crisis. Alas, the foppish Duque de Lobotonto, who'd just arrived by air from the Berlin embassy, was not helping to put him in a good frame of mind.

'It's a monstrous insult to our national honour to be presented with this German ultimatum,' fumed Azucena. 'The very idea of foreign "peacekeepers" in Mallorca–'

'*European*, Prime Minister, to be precise,' interrupted Lobotonto.

'Bollocks! That's "foreign" in my book. Anyway, we're more than capable of dealing with a few lousy terrorists. We certainly don't need a load of Belgians, French, Germans–'

'No, no, Prime Minister! Höhenzug was quite clear about that. There'd be no Germans on the ground in Mallorca.'

'Bloody hell, Ambassador,' snarled Minister of the Interior Eduardo Zangamanga, 'you sound as though you're in favour of this outrageous plan!'

'Well, getting someone else to do our dirty work could cool things down on the island, *and* help us to salvage something of the summer tourist season. I mean, if *we* get tough, we'll just make things worse, won't we? – like in the Basque Region and Cataluña – and look where that got us.'

Azucena grabbed the coffee pot and poured himself yet another cup of the treacly brew. 'I just don't believe I'm hearing this! I'm *not* going to see this great nation disintegrate like, um ... Yugoslavia or ... Russia. If we'd been tougher with the upstarts in Cataluña in the first place, the bandwagon for independence would never have gathered momentum. And if we give in to these damned islanders, Galicia will be next, then Andalucia – the whole country will end up as a tatty confederation of little states, all blathering away in their own ghastly uncouth tongues. No, we have to stamp out this nonsense *now* – and I mean *us* – the Spanish. The Germans and the French can stick their bloody summits up their arses!'

Lobotonto bristled. 'Do you think that's wise, Prime Minister, bearing in mind your ... your *ambitions* with respect to the European presidency? I should have thought that their support would be rather important.'

'Oh, I wouldn't get too worked up about that. I'm the only credible candidate anyway.'

'Hmm,' murmured Lobotonto. 'Still, Klipper has to do something about Mallorca or he and his Social Democrats will be dead meat at their general election next year. So, they're pretty determined to get these peacekeepers in. Höhenzug certainly didn't give me the impression they were bluffing.'

'Bluff or not, I know that windbag Chiffon, and there's no way the French are going to do the *Germans'* dirty work. Why do you think they're so desperate to have this bloody Perpignan summit? No, on the old European front, we'll go along with Señora Cork's nice suggestion of a slap up do in Geneva – in the autumn – when everyone's had their holidays – but only if Gibraltar's put on the agenda.'

'Talking of Gibraltar,' said Zangamanga, 'I wonder what sexy Sandra is up to with all this carrier business.'

'That's just bloody flag waving,' snarled Azucena, '– to keep the British gutter press happy – and their fat, tattoo-riddled, naff tourists – and to make it clear to the Frogs and Krauts that their navies are tat compared to theirs. The Brits love rubbing salt in the wound – you know, that the "European Defence Force" crap just isn't viable without them.'

Lobotonto sighed. 'Be that as it may, and bearing in mind my firm advice, Prime Minister, that Klipper is deadly serious about getting this anti-German terrorism stopped – and stopped *now* – what are we going to do that will satisfy him?'

'I say we send in a few thousand troops, arrest every possible ENABA suspect, and order the King and the rest of the bleeding "Royal Family" back to Madrid – and make it clear to all the local bigwigs in sodding Palma that unless and until they put an end to all this independence nonsense, "His Majesty" won't be spending any more holidays on Mallorca. Quite frankly, I never could understand what he and his brood ever saw in that dump *Marivent*. Once outside the gates, you've got some dead tacky package-holiday resort, the docks, and the delicious odours of the oil storage tanks.'

'It was a gift from the City of Palma,' sniggered Lobotonto, rolling his eyes.

'Very clever marketing for the tourist trade! What with every European royal turning up in their yachts for a free stay, handing out silver cups at regattas, appearing at local restaurants, waving from boxes at the theatre – Christ! – without all them lot, Mallorca would be no more bloody exclusive than what Benidorm is.'

'But can we stop His Majesty from going?' asked Lobotonto incredulously, thinking about his own invitation to spend the last week of August at *Marivent*.

'Of course!' thundered Azucena. 'If we say it's not safe, he has to abide by our advice. He's a constitutional monarch, isn't he?'

'I did express doubts about him going this year,' whined Zangamanga defensively. 'Anyway, can't we wait and get tough after September, when the holiday season has peaked?'

'The Germans won't hang around wringing their hands until then,' muttered Lobotonto sadly. 'The hounds are baying across the Fatherland, and I would suggest that, if anything, ENABA are going to step up their activities over the forthcoming weeks as the holiday season reaches its zenith – to maximize our discomfort and international publicity.'

'Tricky,' said the Interior Minister, 'a sort of catch-22, really.'

There were a few moments' silence as Azucena twiddled the ends of his moustache and puffed on his cigar. 'You know, he said finally, 'it occurs to me that this Gibraltar business might be turned to our advantage. I mean, all these daft regional differences go out the window whenever there's a perceived external threat to our "national" honour – be it a football match, an attack on bullfighting, or British colonialism rearing its ugly and arrogant head again at Gibraltar.'

'Ah ha!' crowed Zangamanga, thumping the table. 'I get your drift.' Azucena was relieved, for he really had no clear idea how Gibraltar could be used to his advantage. 'What I suppose you have in mind, Jesús, is that we leak a story to the press – perhaps through our London embassy – that we've been given assurances that the British warships putting in at Gibraltar are not intended to be provocative, or an undermining of our bilateral efforts to achieve some recognition of Spanish claims to sovereignty, but are merely part of a contingency plan to evacuate British citizens from Mallorca in the event of a serious escalation of the terrorism. We'll then publicly deny the report, claim the leak has come from Whitehall itself, and express outrage on the grounds that the manoeuvre can only be interpreted as a plan to revitalize Gibraltar's status as an outpost of British naval power. After all, talk of evacuating anyone from Mallorca is clearly ludicrous.'

'Brilliant!' roared Azucena, '– I mean, you're a veritable mind-reader, Eduardo! And, of course, the Brits will be in a dilemma, because they won't want to deny that they've no such contingency plans, because then the Germans would look more caring about *their* citizens, what with them three frigging cruisers steaming towards the island – not to mention the sodding French gunboats that have put out from Toulon.'

Lobotonto was shaking his head. 'This all sounds too Machiavellian for words. Don't you think we're more likely to exacerbate the situation?'

'No, I don't, as a matter of fact,' said Azucena chuckling. 'And I can't wait to tell that bumpkin Jordi Adrover and his lousy "Balearic Nationalist Party" that the King's coming home and *our* fleet's on the way with reinforcements!'

*

Mike didn't dislike museums, art galleries, churches, palaces or other historic monuments: on the contrary, he'd voluntarily and happily visited a great number over the years – even before meeting his wife – but there was a limit to just how many he could digest in one long, hot morning in the heart of Palma. Certainly, he'd been impressed by the quantity and quality of the city's architecture, from the thousand-year-old Arab baths to the most bizarre Gaudiesque art nouveau extravaganzas. But now, as one o'clock approached, never had lunch with a British consul seemed such an attractive proposition. There was only one problem: their rendezvous with Crispin Blackstump was down in the old port at the Restaurante Lubina, and the Oakhearts were still up at the cathedral; Jane was finding it impossible to drag herself away. Having braved the chanting demonstrators – without police hindrance, they were interrogating all visitors as to their nationalities in order to intimidate foolhardy Germans – Mike and Jane had explored the cavernous interior, albeit the desecrated Royal Chapel had been screened off. Now, with gay abandon, Jane was snapping photos of the exterior from every angle.

'I really think we should get down to the harbour, Footy,' pleaded Mike for the third time. 'It's quite a trek, and it's almost one.'

'Oh, Blackstump can wait,' Jane said, continuing to stare rapturously at the cathedral. 'I must get some more pictures of the flying buttresses – they're just unbelievable!' Such was her passion, she spent a further five minutes finding the perfect perspective from the city walls before relenting to her husband's pleas.

As they passed the Almudaina Palace – the military governor's residence – Jane stopped a young soldier trotting out of the main gate as he came off duty. In Spanish, she asked him if he could direct them to the Lubina. Without returning her smile, he fired off something in *Mallorquí*.

Jane, continuing in Spanish, said: 'I'm sorry but I don't understand. I'm English.'

'Oh,' replied the soldier, 'I thought you were German.' Then, still unsmiling, he gave them directions. After Jane had thanked him, and Mike had also added a '*gracias*', the soldier snarled: 'Gibraltar is ours! We'll have you British out very soon, mark my words!'

Crispin Blackstump was already at the Lubina when the Oakhearts arrived. Dressed in a cream linen suit, blue-and-white striped shirt, and a tie that was undoubtedly a souvenir of his old school or college, he was sat at a table on the terrace, which bordered the adjoining fish quay. True to his word on the phone last night, he was reading a copy of the *Financial Times*. In any event, he was the only client.

He looked up as they approached, put down the paper, and smiled. 'Jane and Michael Oakheart, I assume?'

'Mr Blackstump?' asked Jane.

'Oh *Crispin*, please! How do you do?'

After Mike had been introduced, Blackstump said: 'What's your poison? I'm on *fino*. I asked for La Ina but I think they've given me Tio Pepe. I think they're cross that I arrived at five to one. They were still setting tables. Of course, no local has lunch before two.' He proceeded to advise his guests on the house specialities; after an unfriendly waiter had taken their orders, he finally got down to business. 'So, how are things down Santanyí-way at present? No hordes of barbarians battering down Stumpf's front door yet? I suppose you know all about the riot in Santanyí the other day and that German shop being burned down? Who would have thought that a spot of arson in some piddling little Mallorcan town could have such international repercussions? So much for a quiet life dealing with lager louts who fall off Magaluf hotel balconies, and OAPs who slip on those lethal marble tiles at the airport and fracture their damned hips.'

Mike said: 'Yes, we heard all about the Stern shop from our hosts, Werner and Heidi. It really is dreadful that people can be so bigoted, prejudiced and narrow-minded in this day and age. I thought we'd put all that behind us.'

'*Really?*'

'Well, yes – with the EU – "an ever-closer union" – you know?'

'Ah yes, Mike, the EU ... of *course*. You seem to be overlooking Brexit. ... I suppose you've been keeping abreast of the latest developments – Berlin, Paris, London ... Gibraltar?'

'Werner was telling us over breakfast this morning.'

'Hmm, hardly the most objective source of information, I should imagine.'

'Oh, I don't know,' said Jane.

'Well, he's pretty right wing by all accounts – even my German counterpart here, Anton Zimnt, thinks so. And then there was all that hoo-hah in England – the Piston-Jones defamation case. Well, Mike, *you* know all about that.'

'We did *win*!' riposted Mike, glancing at Jane, albeit also recollecting Stumpf's attack at L'Hermitage on Jewish Hollywood moguls.

'Well, I hear from Sir Douglas that you're a very clever lawyer.'

'He *is*,' said Jane.

Within minutes, plates of *tapas* were being thumped on the table.

'These fresh sardines are heavenly,' Jane fizzed, '– and the whitebait – and the prawns in garlic. I love *tapas*!'

'I hope we'll be able to eat our main courses,' added Mike.

'Anyway,' said Jane, 'those warships lurking at Gib – London's not really expecting to have to evacuate us, are they, Crispin?'

'Of course not! Just Downing Street sucking up to the media as usual, what with the French and Germans playing silly buggers. Us British are as safe as houses.'

Unable to attract the attention of the wine waiter, Blackstump topped up the glasses of his guests. 'Not bad this white wine from Galicia. I had toyed with the idea of ordering some of the local vino – when in Rome and all that – but although Mallorcan red is passable, the white is pretty ropey.' He paused, tapping his chin. 'Look,' he continued, 'I know he's a client of yours, Mike, so you have to be careful what you say, but are you both *enjoying* your stay at Stumpf's place down at Santanyí? The reason I ask is because one hears such odd things – it's a small island. Anton, the German Consul, has a *very* low opinion of him, I must say.'

'Oh?' queried Jane. 'We got the impression they're the best of friends.'

'Good Lord no! One doesn't want to tell tales out of school, but even by Prussian Junker standards, Stumpf's a martinet, as you've no doubt discovered. Not that he *is* a Junker. Apparently, all this stuff about him coming from some great landowning family in East Prussia is a load of cod's wallop.'

'What's your evidence?' quizzed Mike judicially.

'Well, East Prussia, of course, was given to the Poles after the War – the Russians in other words – so it was all a bit tricky, I admit, to check up on these things. Records were destroyed, people disappeared – you know how it was. But I have it on very good authority that although Stumpf's father was raised on some thumping great estate near Danzig, as claimed, Stumpf's grandfather was *not* the owner – only the estate manager. Not a bad job running thousands of acres – don't get me wrong – I'm not being snobbish. I'm just making the point that the chap has made himself out to be something he isn't.'

'I see,' said Mike.

'And then there's his wife, Helga.'

'*Heidi*,' corrected Jane.

'Exactly.'

Blackstump was beginning to irritate Jane. Leaning back in her chair, she said: 'Well, Heidi's been completely open with me about *her* "humble" origins.'

'Oh, I'm not alluding to her background. No, it's her husband's philandering. As far as I can work out, he's had just about every pretty young girl on this island – well, at least those who are easily impressed by big talk and who are prepared to let an old man touch them up.'

Jane put down her knife and fork. 'You really don't like him very much, do you?'

'Stumpf? Never met the fellow, to be honest.'

Later, after they'd finished their main courses, and as another unsmiling waiter was removing the plates, Blackstump said: 'I don't suppose you know anything about some chef-d'œuvre that Stumpf's writing at the moment, some political track advocating a "federal" Europe? Anton was chatting about it the other day at a reception at the French Consulate – smashing food and wine, as usual – such bloody show-offs. ... I think it's called *Mein Europa*.'

Mike shook his head.' I don't think he's mentioned writing anything at the moment.'

'Oh ... right. Well, if you do hear something, I'm sure the FO would be jolly interested. You could let Sir Douglas know. Always pays for us chaps to be up to speed on what our continental brethren are thinking on the federal Europe front.'

Gloomily, the headwaiter was handing out dessert menus while bleating '*Postre?*' Blackstump shook his head, '*No, no gracias,*' he snapped. Turning to the Oakhearts he added: 'Few races can cook fish as well as the Spanish, but the poor buggers can't make puddings to save they're bloody lives.'

After coffee, Blackstump paid the bill and walked with the Oakhearts as far as the park in front of the Almudaina Palace. It was just after three – siesta time – and apart from the tourists braving the burning sun, the city was dead.

'Well, it's been *delightful*,' said Blackstump. 'And don't forget, if you *do* get any gen on *Mein Kampf* – sorry! – Freudian slip! – *Mein Europa*, well, London would be jolly grateful. I go this way' – he pointed up a broad, tree-lined street – 'back to the old labour camp and the herds of half-witted Tracys and Kevins who've lost all their money and expect HMG to bail them out. Sometimes, I almost wish I were back in Mogadishu! Cheerio!'

When he was a safe distance off, Mike said: 'Well, if you ask me, your dad has probably put old Crispin up to recruiting us as spies. I'm surprised he didn't ask us to creep into Werner's study with a camera and photograph the bloody manuscript.'

'Don't be ridiculous!'

'Well, you heard what he said.'

'I can't imagine the Foreign Office being in the least interested in some political essay written by Werner Stumpf. I mean, he's not a politician or anything, is he?'

'Perhaps he has ambitions.' Mike looked at his watch. 'Well, we might as well head back to *Ca'n Pau*, seeing how everything's shut until half-four or five – *and* there's that bloody picnic with the old gang tonight.'

Jane groaned. 'God! I wish we could get out of it and just go out on our own for a nice meal.'

'No doubt poor Heidi's worked herself like a slave preparing for it.'

'You're right, bless her. ... Fancy Werner being a Don Juan!'

'That's if you believe that gossiping old woman, Blackstump. I bet he was just trying to prejudice us against Werner in order to recruit us.'

'Oh, don't start that again!'

With no particular destination in mind, the Oakhearts had ambled up a narrow alley, only to find themselves back in the Old Town.

'I suppose we'd better find that underground car park near the Plaza Mayor,' said Mike. 'It's been a long day.'

With obvious reluctance, Jane nodded, but just a few minutes later, as they rounded a corner, the exuberant facade of a grand baroque church caused her to gasp. 'Oh, what luck!' she shrieked, already flicking through her guidebook. 'It must be San Whatsit's – the one we tried to find this morning.'

Mike forced a smile. 'Extraordinary luck indeed, but I fear it'll be closed, Footy.' The words were barely out of his mouth, when a door creaked open and a little old lady dressed in black from head to toe stepped out, shading her eyes against the blinding sunlight.

There were a great many monuments in the church; Jane studied all of them – and translated the inscriptions for Mike's benefit. Then they moved on to the numerous side chapels, all of which could be dramatically illuminated by inserting a one-euro coin in a slot. In the event, they ran out of coins, but a helpful Swedish tourist pointed out the change machine in the north aisle. At ten minutes to five, when the Oakhearts found themselves back in the square, shops and bars were opening and preparing for the brisk evening local trade. And there were certainly many people about; indeed, there was almost something of a festive air. As the alleys and lanes broadened into the streets and avenues of the city's commercial heart, the crowds became larger and more boisterous. Police klaxons grew in intensity, and somewhere in the distance chanting was discernible. Just a hundred metres from the car park's entrance, adjacent to the *Teatro Municipal*, the Oakhearts found their way blocked by a huge crowd at the foot of the massive flight of steps that ascend grandly to the Plaza Mayor; earlier in the day, Jane had likened them to Rome's Spanish Steps. Halfway up, papers and files were being flung out of the windows of an elegant eighteenth-century terraced building, the crowd roaring with delight. Then, half a dozen young men trooped out of the building's double doors dragging a terrified middle-aged gentleman. Apart from a tie around his neck, the prisoner was completely naked.

The crowd erupted. '*Viva Gibraltar Español*!' they roared.

'Jesus Christ!' shrieked Jane.

'God Almighty!' hissed Mike. 'It's Blackstump!'

*

Still reeling from their experiences in Palma, it was after eight when the Oakhearts finally drew up in front of *C'an Pau* and parked in their allotted space. On the drive back, anxious to ascertain Blackstump's fate, they'd listened continuously to the local radio, but had only been able to glean that he was 'in protective custody in a secure location'. Jane had even called her father on the mobile, but the Foreign Office in London, he advised, had no further information. Mike had phoned the Stumpfs to let them know of the delay, and now, as he and Jane hurried through the archway, they were anticipating an irritated host clutching his clipboard and watching the seconds tick away to the planned time of departure to the Portopetro lighthouse at eight-thirty. But to their surprise, Werner was sat at the wrought iron table at the centre of his courtyard, sipping a glass of cava, and looking cool and relaxed. Around him on the cobbles, and lined up in neat order, were several cool boxes, two wicker picnic baskets, a folding table, and four folding chairs.

He jumped up, smiling with almost childlike joy. 'Jane! Mike! Thank the Lord you are both safe! I have been watching the TV and listening to the radio – alternating at five-minute intervals.'

'We're *so* sorry to be late–' Mike began.

'Not at all! No problem! All our friends have been informed of these extraordinary developments, and our picnic has been postponed – by half an hour. So, you have plenty of time to get ready.'

'Actually,' said Jane, 'we're both absolutely bushed. Would you mind terribly if we didn't come? We–'

'Everyone is *so* looking forward to seeing you. Now, just sit down here for a moment and have a glass of cava. I bet you could do with one! Then you can have a nice shower. And anyway, Herbert von Karpen and Otto Pinsel are bringing Gudrun Schluck with them this evening, seeing how her planned recital in Palma has had to be cancelled in view of the riots. And in your honour, she's going to bring her cello and perform some traditional English sea shanties – you call them "shanties", *ja*?'

*

Down at the Portopetro lighthouse, which, in fact, transpired to be no more than a navigation beacon atop a concrete plinth, it soon became evident to Mike and Jane that the reason for the general air of excitement and jollity of the assembled Germans had nothing to do with the dramatic beauty of the cliff-top location, the stunning vista of the setting sun, or the expectations of feasting on the huge and magnificent stock of food that had been laid out on the folding tables. And nor was the rapid and copious quaffing of well-chilled cava the primary cause of the unexpected bonhomie, although it was undoubtedly contributing to the dilution of inhibitions. No, everyone was electrified by the news that Germany was fighting back at last – on the march – taking the struggle against the racist ENABA into the lion's den. And they were convinced that they had an ally – the British!

Of course, it was true that the oiky upstart Azucena had been rude to both Berlin and Paris, telling them what they could do with their summits and peacekeeping forces, but on the other hand, he had laid down the law to the Mallorcan 'peasants', and soon there would be mainland troops everywhere – thousands of them! Yes, it would be like the good old days under Franco, Kommis reminisced nostalgically. So, thanks to Azucena, the 'aborigines' were now attacking their 'fellow Spanish'! Indeed, the Oakhearts were able to confirm that when they left Palma, the main Post Office – a symbol of Madrid's hated rule – was burning furiously.

But the icing on the cake was definitely the involvement of the British. It was not that the Germans were glad to see Britain's Consulate devastated or its consul debagged and publicly humiliated: the so-called provocation caused by the Royal Navy's reinforcement of the British military presence at Gibraltar – which Britain had every right to do – evinced that, despite their official coolness towards the European Union and the planned Defence Force, good old Britain had promptly and generously responded to the mobilization of the Franco-German navies – 'Three cheers for our boys in the *Kriegsmarine*!' – with nothing less than a bloody great aircraft carrier and its escorts. No wonder Azucena had been scared shitless and had finally pulled his thumb out!

Fräulein Schluck was coping bravely with *Bobby Shafto* – albeit her cello was not too happy with the marine humidity – when Sir Douglas called Jane on her mobile with the news that Blackstump was on a plane heading for Gatwick.

'Excellent!' boomed Werner when Jane reported the conversation once the over-enthusiastic applause for *What Shall We Do With The Drunken Sailor* finally died down. 'You know,' he added, 'I think this "crisis" could be the long-awaited catalyst to bring about the great Anglo-German alliance which I – and many others – have been praying for. I mean, I love the French dearly – such style, savoir-faire ... and the wines! – but they're so excitable, unpredictable ... unreliable. Well, Mike and Jane, you British know all about *that*! They certainly let you down in the spring of 1940!'

Professor Kommis slapped his thighs, and von Karpen and Pinsel shrieked and hugged each other.

'It's really what my new book, *Mein Europa*, is all about,' Werner continued, emboldened by the cava. 'My publishers are *very* excited, I can tell you – and a few top politicians in Berlin. It's simple really. In a nutshell, there are only two countries in Europe with any real credibility on the world stage ... *us*, the nationalities gathered here tonight.'

'More paprika chicken anyone?' asked Heidi, first in German and then English.

To everyone's surprise, Werner didn't explode. Instead, he looked at her with an expression that could almost have passed for fondness. 'And very good it is too!' he cried. 'A toast to Germany and Great Britain!'

Glasses clinked. 'Germany and Great Britain!'

'In both area and population,' Werner pushed on excitedly, 'Germany is Europe's biggest country and it has its largest economy – the third largest in the world! – and Great Britain has the most dynamic, thanks to its laissez-faire entrepreneurialism. Add on to that the City of London's colossal financial power, your Commonwealth, military excellence, special relationship with the USA, the birthplace of the English language – what a powerful combination! – unstoppable! Now, don't misunderstand me. I do not hate any nation, people or race – and certainly not the United States – unlike the French, but we cannot go on any longer allowing the world to be led and dominated by a nation of mongrel philistines. It's time to make a stand for civilisation and tradition.

'And what is holding Europe back, my friends? What is the cause of all the suspicion and rivalry? Well, I'll tell you – language. There can be no European unity without a common language. Look at the madness in Brussels today, a ludicrous number of official languages! – a special Directorate for Interpretation! – with over nine *hundred* staff! – *nine hundred*! How can we Europeans ever be a superpower if Brussels is just a Tower of Babel? Madness!'

'Madness!' shrieked Otto, blowing a kiss towards Mike.

'So, in *Mein Europa* I propose that at the national level, all member states must adopt one of only five official languages – German, English, French, Spanish or Italian. All the other languages will be consigned to village gossip for old women. But at the European Union level – in the Parliament, the Commission, the Council, and all official publications – there should be one, and *only* one, language – English!'

For a moment, all that could be heard was the swell gurgling and whooshing around the base of the cliffs.

'*Englisch?*' spluttered Professor Kommis finally. '***Englisch!***'

'Come on, Manfred,' Werner said soothingly in English, 'we all know that it's the only language that matters internationally and which all young people will be keen to learn. The teaching of French in German schools has been declining for years – and vice versa – despite all the fake friendship between idiots like Chiffon and Klipper and their awful predecessors.'

'But your proposal will *hasten* the decline,' bemoaned Anna Kommis, '– will pamper the Americans. We'll fall into the trap they've set for us.'

Werner was shaking his head. 'Oh no! I've thought of that. This huge concession on our part – Germany's part – would be in return for the EU's headquarters being moved from Brussels – now on the periphery of the Union – to its heart, Berlin, and for the study of the five "foundation languages", as I like to call them – German, English, French, Spanish and Italian – to be compulsory for all EU citizens from the age of five. So, we'll all be polyglots at home and masters of English on the world stage. My plan is bound to reverse Brexit! Dear old Britain will rejoin our Greater Europe! We'll make the Americans look like village idiots – even more so!'

Gudrun Schluck knocked back her glass of cava, wildly rotated the cello between her firm pink legs, and, with a whoop of light-headed enthusiasm, launched herself into the *Ode to Joy* theme from Beethoven's Ninth Symphony, the 'European Anthem'. Singing in a booming tenor voice, von Karpen promptly jumped onto a rock and began conducting a scratch chorus. To his surprise, everyone knew the German words – everyone, that is, except Werner, who, with a swaying head and an exaggerated grin, resorted to rhythmless tum-tee-tahs.

Behind a fixed smile, Mike groaned inwardly: he hated the *Ode To Joy*; it was one of the most tedious tunes ever written. And played on a solo cello tortured by intense humidity, it sounded even worse – quite tragic in truth, a situation compounded by the discordant voices bellowing around him.

CHAPTER 13

Jordi Adrover, the leader of the Balearic Nationalist Party – PANABA – and the head of the provincial government, had done rather well for himself since leaving school at the age of sixteen and joining his father's carpentry business. Thirty years on, Adrover, together with various members of his extensive family, now controlled one of Mallorca's largest construction companies. And thanks to his political connections and high office, it was getting bigger and more profitable all the time. A labyrinthine network of nominee companies seemingly controlled by spouses and in-laws of his four brothers and three sisters, ensured that a great number of government contracts ended up somewhere inside the Adrover empire. Most recently, the Balearic Department of Transport had embarked on a massive programme of road widening, roundabout construction, and the installation of crash barriers. All very commendable, except that the bulk of the work had been carried out on lightly used rural byways. There had been some queries raised in the local media, but nothing too critical: journalists and their editors tend to enjoy hospitality, and the government – in some form or other – hosted most of the islands' grander social events.

So, Señor Adrover was a very wealthy man. He had a vast thousand-square-metre apartment in Palma's most fashionable street, an eighteenth-century country house with fifteen bedrooms in the hills near Valldemosa – of Chopin and Georges Sand fame – and a palatial beach house with its feet in the sea at Portopetro. It was situated just a stone's throw, in fact, from the slightly less grand villa of the Condes de Manilla, who, despite branding the Adrovers as hideously nouveau riche, never declined an invitation to any of the numerous fiestas they threw during the summer season.

Jordi Adrover also had a yacht, that is to say, a twenty-metre-long motor cruiser with deluxe air-conditioned accommodation for ten passengers. Indeed, it was the largest craft birthed at the Royal Portopetro Yacht Club, and, therefore, the object of constant scorn from the likes of the Manillas and other 'old' families. Moreover, it was the custom of the parvenu Adrovers to commute between their villa and the yacht club by means of the six-seater speedboat moored at the jetty at the bottom of their garden, rather than driving around the highly indented inlet; it only saved them five minutes, but it made much more of an impression.

This evening, with the Anglo-German festivities in full swing up at the 'lighthouse', it was unusually quiet at the Adrovers', but then they'd had four successive nights of dinners and parties, and Señora Adrover had wanted a rest. After dinner, therefore, she'd said goodnight to the brothers-in-law and their wives who were staying with them, and turned in. Jordi said he was popping over to the Caracola bar in Portopetro to have a quick drink with a German property developer who was hoping to build a new golf-hotel complex near Andratx; he'd just phoned to say he was in the neighbourhood with his wife and family.

'I'll have to put in an appearance,' Jordi moaned. 'Just one drink – an hour at most. I mean, the fat Kraut will gladly pay a small fortune for a little help to get those bloody planning consents.'

But after casting off from his jetty and motoring out into mid-channel, Adrover turned his speedboat hard to starboard and headed for the open sea. Some ten minutes later, he came alongside a small fishing boat.

'Evening, Jordi,' said Tomeu Grimalt.

'Good evening, Tomeu,' whispered Adrover. 'I don't have to call you "Jaume", I assume? We *are* alone, aren't we? … Give us a hand, mate.'

Grimalt held out a muscular arm. 'Correct.'

'Thanks. It's just that those other boats a way off–'

'Stop whispering, you prat. They're my district commanders keeping watch. One can never be too careful, especially now.'

'Yes. Madrid have gone absolutely crazy! Fantastic news, eh?'

'Fantastic. A beer?'

'Got any whiskey?'

'Sorry. I don't touch foreign alcohol.'

'I'll pass then.'

'So, Madrid are sending three thousand crack troops – "battle trained" somewhere overseas, apparently. We haven't half sucked up to the sodding Yanks!'

'Quite. Anyway, just as we predicted, the populace have erupted. Mind you, ordering the King back to Madrid surprised us in the Balearic Government. My phone's been red hot with businessmen calling about the damage that'll do to the local economy. A smart move by Azucena, though, I have to admit.'

'You think so?'

'Definitely. I never anticipated–'

'*We* did – ENABA that is.'

'Oh? You have a contingency plan for that too, I suppose?'

'Yes.'

Adrover snorted. 'And what might that be, Tomeu?'

'I'll come to that in just a minute, if you don't mind. First things first. Presumably you agree that we have to act before all these soldiers and marines arrive from the mainland and attempt to impose martial law.'

'Well, I'm not sure Azucena's called it "martial law", or even sought to invoke any emergency powers–'

'You know it amounts to the same thing.'

'Yes, that's what I was about to say. So, yes, I agree that we have to–'

'Accordingly, you will give the orders tonight to implement Operation Resist and arrest the Military Governor and his staff.'

'*What*! Tonight! So soon? I was thinking that we could–'

'We can't delay. The reinforcements could start arriving as early as tomorrow. And now that the British Consulate has been attacked, Azucena has got more credibility about using Gibraltar as his justification for the strong-arm tactics. Anyway, the fake documents indicating that Madrid is planning to assassinate the King at *Marivent* and pin it on us have already been planted in the Governor's office.'

'Christ! I'd no idea we were so well organised that we could implement Operation Resist at such short notice. I need to consult–'

'You don't need to consult *anyone*, Jordi. We've run through these plans a hundred times. All our people in the Army, Navy and Air Force, plus the *Guardia Civil* – they're almost exclusively islanders – and the *Policía* are ready to go – likewise our guys in Menorca and Ibiza ... even Formentera! We seize the Almudaina Palace and the Governor tonight, surround *Marivent* and take the King into "protective custody". Simultaneously, we secure the airport and the docks. All you have to do now is give the order as head of the Government. You've brought your mobile, I assume?'

'I – I ... No, I left it at home. I didn't think. I–'

'No matter. You can use mine.'

After half an hour's frantic phoning, Adrover looked drained. 'God,' he croaked, 'I could do with a drink. I wish you had some whiskey.'

'Well, you'll be home soon and–'

'I'd better get into Palma – go to my office. Get ready for the fireworks. I'll have to make a broadcast on local television tomorrow. Do you think I should make the Declaration of Independence then? Christ! This is all happening so quickly – *too* quickly maybe. I–'

'Just go back to Portopetro and wait until we tell you that we've got the Governor safely under lock and key. We don't want you acting as though you know about the Madrid "plot" until we've "found" the incriminating evidence – you know, when the *Guardia Civil* stop a speeding car and find faked orders and–'

'Yes, yes – I know! ... Right, I'll stay here – very wise, Tomeu.' Adrover rose unsteadily and moved to the rail, saying, 'Give us a hand.'

When Adrover was safely back in his speedboat, he said: 'Well, good luck, Tomeu. When all this is over and we've got independence and ... everything, there's going to be an important position for you in my government – Minister of Defence ... or something. No more undercover nonsense as the owner of a tatty little restaurant dishing up grotty *paellas* to dim tourists.'

'Thanks.'

'It's the least PANABA can do.'

'Too kind!'

After Adrover had roared away, Grimalt tapped out a number on his mobile. It was answered almost immediately. 'He's just left,' he said.

'Yes,' replied Ricart, the Santanyí District Commander, from his boat.

'Did you plant it? I never heard anything.'

'You weren't supposed to, boss. Yes, it's under his seat.'

'Well done! And Antoni?'

'Slight hitch. He couldn't take up position at the lighthouse.'

'Jesus! Why not?'

'Don't worry. It's OK. He's in the old fort just along the cliffs. Some fucking foreigners were having a picnic – drunk – singing their heads off – like half a dozen cats on heat. They've just packed up. Anyway, Antoni will still be able to see the boat enter the harbour from the fort.'

'Thank God! Let's make tracks. And good luck, Ricart!'

CHAPTER 14

Jane and Mike were replete with sex. Last night they'd been so exhausted after their long and extraordinary day that they'd fallen asleep as soon as their heads hit the pillows. This morning, however, they'd more than made up for their abstinence. Now they lay naked on the bed, glistening with perspiration.

'Is it the sex,' asked Mike, 'or is it even hotter this morning?'

'It's certainly more humid. It's like being in the tropics.'

'The sky isn't as blue either,' said Mike, looking out of the windows; they'd remained open and shutterless all night to get some air. 'It's a sort of bleached colour. Maybe the weather's changing. Maybe there'll be a storm.'

'Maybe. ... Mikey?'

'Yes.'

'I love you more than words can possibly describe.'

Mike turned to face Jane. 'And I *worship* you.'

They kissed long and passionately until they heard agitated voices in the courtyard below.

'I wonder what that's all about,' said Mike. 'Heidi slacking again?' He sighed. 'I suppose we ought to get up.'

'I suppose so. What time is it?'

Mike glanced at the travel alarm clock. 'Twenty to nine.'

'God! I suppose we had. Do you think we've got the Stumpfs for breakfast again? I'm not sure I can face another instalment of *Mein Europa* so early in the day.'

'How much did you drink last night? Of course we have! – don't you remember? Werner said we were going to have "a real German breakfast" this morning.'

'Oh, Christ – not that pumpernickel again!'

Mike got off the bed and stretched sensually. Jane licked her lips and he laughed, saying, 'Do you think there's something wrong with us?'

'Wrong? – sexually?'

'No, of course not! I mean politically and emotionally. I mean, how come Werner and his gang can get so worked up about this vision of "The Great European Superpower"? We're not wholly committed to any political party, we don't demonstrate against global capitalism or abuses of human rights in China – or anywhere else – and we don't see the Americans as a greater threat to civilisation than Al Qaeda. In fact, the only things we really take seriously are our beloved careers. Perhaps we're just horribly shallow.'

'Bloody hell, Mikey, what on earth has brought all this on? I bet it was that damn Gudrun and her "energy fields". She kept cornering you all evening – well, once she'd put that wretched cello back in its case.'

'I–'

'Come on! Let's shower. I think we're both suffering from Werneritis. Straight after breakfast, we're going out on our own. It's *your* day, Mikey. We'll go to the beach. I've done a bit of research, and just down the coast there's this peninsula – completely untouched – miles and miles of forest and wonderful empty beaches. How about that?'

Mike beamed ecstatically. '*Really*? Terrific! You can shower first.'

'No. We'll shower together.'

When the Oakhearts finally appeared on the terrace, there was no sign of breakfast – German, English, or otherwise. Instead, there was the strange sight of Werner embracing a sobbing young man beside a half-set table. The Oakhearts froze in their tracks.

'Jesus!' hissed Mike. 'Don't tell me he chases after boys too.'

'That's Mateu, the gardener, you pillock – the *Eminence Grise*'s son.'

'So? ... Bloody hell! Maybe she's snuffed it or had an accident.'

Werner looked up, saw the Oakhearts, and, without any sign of embarrassment, beckoned them to approach. As he greeted them solemnly, Mateu broke away; still sobbing, he ran down the steps and disappeared into the garden.

'Poor lad,' said Werner shaking his head. 'He needs to be on his own for a while. It's been a bit of shock for him – well, for *all* of us.'

'It's not his mother, is it?' asked Jane.

Werner continued to shake his head. 'His mother? Well, she's in a terrible state too – Heidi's with her – in the kitchen. I'm afraid breakfast will be a little delayed. Look, you'd both better sit down. My God! When I think how close we all were last night to being blown to bits ... shocking!'

As Werner recounted all that he'd gleaned from his 'staff', together with the wild speculation being broadcast by the media, it transpired that Jordi Adrover had been 'assassinated'. Some reports had blamed the Deutsche Mallorca Bund: Señora Adrover was asserting that her beloved husband had been lured to a bogus meeting with a German businessman at a bar in Portopetro. Then there were the 'sources' who claimed that Adrover's death was part of a fantastic conspiracy by the Spanish Secret Service which involved assassinating the King at *Marivent* and blaming it on ENABA. Evidence would then have been adduced purporting to show that as regicide was too much even for Adrover, he'd been on the point of tipping off Madrid. So, ENABA had had to liquidate him. But, somehow last night, Madrid's plan had been discovered, and Adrover had managed to give the orders to arrest the conspirators just minutes before his boat blew up. The hero had been unable to save himself, but at least the efficient island authorities had managed to arrest the King's would-be assassins and their co-conspirators – including the Military Governor – before they could implement their dastardly plan. *Marivent* was now ringed by island troops; the airport and all ports were sealed; and an emergency session of the Balearic Parliament had been summoned amid calls for an immediate declaration of independence.

While Werner put the stunned Oakhearts in the picture, Heidi trooped to and fro from the kitchen, bringing dishes of 'German' food to the table – smoked salmon, cream cheese, an assortment of hams, the inevitable pumpernickel – and tea, coffee and hot chocolate. Apparently, Margalida was still distraught and incapable of work; she was on her third tumbler of brandy.

'It is my view,' said Heidi when she'd finally finished her shuttle service from the distant kitchen, 'that Adrover was probably killed by ENABA. I tell Margalida this, and she is very cross. But at least she stopped the crying. She should go home and cry.'

'Are you *mad*?' snorted Werner. 'Why should ENABA kill one of their own, you fool?'

'To make him a ... a ... I do not know the word in English – like a saint.'

'A martyr?' suggested Mike

Heidi nodded. '*Ja*, a martyr. I think it is the same with this stupid story about the King, and Madrid wanting to kill him. It's the work of ENABA also.'

'*Mein Gott*!' snarled Werner. 'Just shut up! This murder is bad enough without all your insane ravings.'

Heidi shrugged her shoulders. 'I do not know why you are so upset. You hated Adrover. You always say you wish someone would burn down *his* house – *all* of his houses.'

'I did not!'

'You did. Anyway, he despised us Germans. He led the party that wanted us to leave.'

'I do hope the airport will be open by Monday,' said Mike. 'We've got a plane to catch, and Mrs Babcock is going up to Scotland to stay with her sister, so she won't be able to look after Hugo. He can't be left on his own.'

Jane looked horrified. 'Christ! I hadn't thought of that.'

The Stumpfs stared at each other across the table. 'Hugo?' they queried.

'Our dog,' replied Jane.

'He's the most beautiful Dalmatian in the world,' added Mike mistily. 'I better phone Mrs B. She'll be up by now. If she's been listening to Radio 4 as usual, she'll be having kittens. God only knows what the Today programme is reporting. And then I better phone my parents in Cardiff.'

'And then I'll phone Derbyshire,' said Jane.

Heidi was nodding. 'And I suppose I must phone my family in Germany and tell them we are all right.'

As Mike got up from the table to return to the bedroom for the mobile, Werner said: 'Pah! This is crazy – all this telephoning. Now we are having breakfast. Surely your damned dog can wait?'

Mike hesitated for only an instant. 'No, Hugo is *very* sensitive.'

As he marched away, Jane said: 'You have to understand, Werner, that he loves that dog … *intensely*.'

Werner exhaled noisily and thumped the table. 'I have absolutely no doubt that this whole assassination thing is a complete tissue of lies. I bet you anything, this has got *nothing* to do with ENABA, Madrid, the King, or any other such nonsense. It will be a gangland murder. That crook Adrover was Mallorca's nearest thing to a mafia boss, with his finger in every lucrative pie. He was so corrupt – he and his family.' His eyes narrowed. 'It could even be a squabble between the Adrover brothers for control of the business. Yes, I bet that's it, and all this talk of royal assassinations, the Deutsche Mallorca Bund, and Madrid's secret agents is just a typical peasant smokescreen. The King in protective custody! *Marivent* surrounded! What rubbish! If Adrover ever coughed during a session of Parliament, five minutes later the local TV station would be reporting he'd been rushed to hospital with typhoid.'

After recounting many more examples of the mediocrity of the island's 'journalists', Werner pushed back his chair and proclaimed: 'I don't believe the airport *is* closed. Absolute crap! In fact, I'm going to phone my good friend the German Consul and get to the bottom of this. Anton will know exactly what's going–'

'Hugo's fine,' shouted Mike as he trotted out of the French windows. 'Mrs B had been worried, thanks to some pretty wild reports on Sky – and Hugo wouldn't touch his breakfast.'

'Oh, poor thing!' said Jane as Mike resumed his seat.

'And as I was crossing the courtyard, your dad phoned. Apparently, all that stuff about the airport is spot on. Nothing's landing or taking off. The tour operators have gone ballistic. Douglas will be on a RAF plane to Madrid within the hour to present a formal protest to Azucena.'

'God! Mummy must be livid. That'll upset all her plans – especially next week's garden party.'

Werner was rubbing his right temple furiously. 'I think you should phone Sir Douglas, Jane. He must not be fooled by PANABA propaganda. But maybe if the airport is *really* closed, Mrs Cork may order his plane to fly on here to negotiate a deal with these piratical aborigines to release the English tourists. Maybe he could join us for the party after all. Yes, he should have first-hand knowledge of the true position on the island. He is bound to come. Phone him – *now*!'

But when Jane finally got hold of her father at RAF Brize Norton, he made it quite clear that he had no intention of provoking a diplomatic row with the Spanish by demanding a 'site inspection' on Mallorca. In any event, it was inconceivable that Madrid could not land a few thousand troops on the island and regain control of the airport. The 'whole shooting match' was nothing more than 'a stunt' by the secessionists to gain attention at the height of the holiday season. Everything would be back to normal within twenty-four hours.

'And anyway, darling,' he said just before ringing off, 'I've got to be home by this evening as Mummy's got the Cavendish-Woodhouses coming for dinner.'

During the call, Mike had eaten the last slice of smoked salmon, Heidi had removed the savouries and replaced them with plates of waffles and bowls of maple syrup and whipped cream, and Werner had disappeared, only to return with a shotgun and his faithful clipboard.

'Well,' said Jane putting down the mobile while eying the shotgun, 'you've probably gathered that Daddy has no plans to come to Mallorca.'

'A big mistake if you don't mind me saying so,' said Werner.

'What's the gun for?' asked Mike with obvious amusement. Jane kicked him under the table.

'Maybe there are deer in the woods,' said Heidi, 'and tomorrow at the party we have the deer meat.'

The Oakhearts laughed heartily.

'May I remind you,' intoned Werner coldly, 'that last night, only five kilometres from here, the prime minister of the Balearics was blown up by a bomb on his boat. One of the ludicrous rumours spreading like wildfire amongst the aborigines is that he was assassinated by the Deutsche Mallorca Bund led by that vile neo-Nazi, Haber-Bosch. We are in danger from reprisals. Already I have barred the main gates and told Mateu to fetch his gun from home. Naturally, he doesn't believe the anti-German rumours at all. Now I am about to plan twenty-four-hour armed patrols around the perimeter of *Ca'n Pau*.'

'Good Lord!' said Jane, wide-eyed. 'Are you serious?'

'Most certainly! Mike, you can shoot, yes?'

Mike could not. In truth, he'd never held a gun in his life and had no intention of starting now; his stance on blood sports had been a bone of contention with the Trench-Foots ever since he'd first met his then prospective in-laws. He'd even managed to exacerbate the situation by converting Jane to his way of thinking. As Werner viciously struck out his name from the first draft of the patrol schedule, Jane said:

'Well, Heidi, thank you again for *the* most wonderful breakfast. We'll just help you to clear up and then we'll be off and out of your hair for the rest of the day. We thought we'd got to the beach – at last! Apparently, there's this wonderful unspoilt peninsula beyond Santanyí that–'

'*Ja, ja,*' said Heidi enthusiastically, '– around the lighthouse of Ses Salines.'

'That's it!'

'Such lovely beaches – no people – like Es Caragoll.'

'Yes, that's the one I've read about.'

'It is *wunderschön*. I remember when I first come to the island and Werner took me–'

'The *beach*?' snapped Werner, removing two sheets from his clipboard. 'You intend to go to the *beach*? But tomorrow is my party.'

Despite her protests, Mike was helping Heidi to load her tray. 'Yes,' he said, 'the party's tomorrow. So?'

'Is there a problem, Werner? asked Jane wearily.

Werner handed the sheets to his guests. 'Well, I am sure you can imagine the amount of work *we* two have to perform in order to organise tomorrow's grand event, especially as we are to dine on the *Olive Terrace*.' The words 'Olive Terrace' were emphasised with almost religious reverence.

Heidi sighed, shook her head, and looked across the garden to the precipitous rockery on the far side, where a flight of stone steps ascended into carefully manicured shrubbery.

'"The Olive Terrace"?' queried Mike, with a sinking feeling.

'Up there,' Werner pointed proudly, 'we have a splendid belvedere with views right across *Ca'n Pau*. Everything will look so magical, with all the hundreds of candles twinkling along the paths, in the trees and beside the pool. And the central feature of the Olive Terrace is – as you may have surmised – my magnificent olive tree. It's at least two hundred years old. Lanterns will hang from its branches and we shall dine under them.'

'It sounds a long way from the house,' said Mike.

'From the kitchen,' added Jane.

Heidi nodded.

Seemingly oblivious to these observations, Werner declared: 'It will be an experience you will *never* forget. But we need to carry up the tables and chairs, the copper serving dishes with their oil burners, hang up the lanterns, arrange the hundreds of candles in the garden and–'

'Can't we do all that tomorrow?' asked Mike.

'Can't Mateu and Margalida–?'

'No!' boomed Werner. 'Tomorrow there are so many *other* things to do! – taking up the porcelain, all the glasses, the ice buckets, the wine, the flower arrangements, setting the table, preparing the hors d'oeuvres, collecting things from the bakery – there's a *huge* list!' He turned over a page on his clipboard and tapped it. 'And Margalida can't be expected to lift tables. And Mateu has his patrol – and last-minute gardening chores.'

The Oakhearts were trapped.

*

In Berlin, Chancellor Martin Klipper felt trapped too. The way things were going, it looked less and less likely that he'd get his Turkish vacation. He and Minister of Defence Karl Stiefel were alone in the Cabinet Room. Stiefel had just arrived after a lengthy early morning meeting with the Chiefs of the Defence Staff. As he came in, Foreign Minister von Höhenzug dashed out, saying: 'Off to Madrid! Well, if Mohammed won't come to the mountain ... It's a bitter pill to swallow, but with Lobotonto reporting to Azucena, there's no Spaniard of any importance in Berlin to summon to the Foreign Ministry for a dressing down.'

The Chancellor sighed. 'Höhenzug's report was dismal, Karl. Yesterday's anti-British riots in Palma and elsewhere across Spain have fizzled out, thanks to this Jordi Adrover's violent demise overnight. Gibraltar has been well and truly eclipsed, at least for the time being. Now, to shift suspicion away from himself, even Azucena is hinting that there might be some truth in the vile allegations that Haber-Bosch and his gang of right-wing vigilantes were behind the assassination. In the last six hours, scores of German-owned businesses have been looted and burned. The thousands of Germans who've been brave enough to holiday on the island are under siege in their hotels, and they, together with the thousands of German residents, are bloody marooned, thanks to the suspension of flights and ferry services.'

'I don't rate Höhenzug's chances in Madrid, Chancellor,' said Stiefel.

'Frankly, nor do I.'

'Especially as the British have been let off the hook. Our military attaché in Madrid thinks they're going to do a separate deal with the

Mallorcans – allowing British planes to resume flights. Azucena's desperate, now that his "get-tough" plan has backfired. He hasn't a clue what to do – a complete heap of snivelling blubber by all accounts. I think he'll be prepared to accept the Mallorcans' demands that no German will be allowed to leave the island without satisfying the local police that they were not involved in this Adrover's death. Pure victimisation!'

Klipper sighed once more and shook his head.

Stiefel knew that this was the moment to lay his cards on the table; he might never have another chance. Only a few days ago, he'd been near resignation, thanks to that bitch Renate demanding the near annihilation of his armed forces. And with their respective empires about to be emasculated, the Defence Chiefs had been alarmed too; so much for their chances of controlling the new European Defence Force! Hence the extraordinary plan which they and the head of the Secret Service had put to him just before he came over to the Chancellery.

'Martin,' said Stiefel, 'these are desperate times, and, therefore, desperate measures are required. I've got the three Defence Chiefs waiting outside with Josef Brotrinde, the Secret Service's big cheese. They've got a very interesting idea you might like to hear.'

Half an hour later, Brotrinde – a man with no distinguishing features, dressed in a grey suit – said softly: 'The way I see it is that we need a death of our own – a *German* martyr.' The Admiral, Air Marshal and General all nodded their heads.

'Do we?' queried Klipper nervously. 'Why?'

'Because, Chancellor, we will then have the perfect excuse to send in our armed forces – in the name of the European Union, naturally – to restore order, round up the terrorists, and install an interim administration. Our problem at the moment is that, despite all the bombs and intimidation, no German has yet been killed – or even seriously injured.'

'Yes,' said Klipper, 'you're right. That *is* a bit awkward.'

'In fact, no damned foreigners have been killed or injured,' said the Admiral.

'Which is one of the reasons why it's so bloody difficult to get our EU partners off their butts to help us,' whined Stiefel. 'Of course, once we've got the situation under control and the ringleaders under arrest, they'll be queuing up to send peacekeepers, just as they always do. Then we pack up and go home. So, it should be an in-and-out operation really.'

Klipper still looked puzzled. 'I see … I think. But someone has to be bumped off first – this martyr chap.'

'Exactly. Someone well known, admired, respected – loved, if possible.'

'"*Loved*"?'

'Yes.'

'A German?'

'Yes.'

'Is there anyone remotely like that? – not that I'm sanctioning this mad idea for one second – I mean, we're not Americans, for God's sake, are we?' And anyway, how could we "take out" someone like that? – and at short notice? – the bloody airport's shut!'

The Admiral and Air Marshal fidgeted in their seats.

'We have aircraft of our own.'

'We have *ships*, Chancellor, including submarines. In fact, *Albrecht Dürer* is just west of Sardinia as we speak.'

'And who's this "Albrecht Dürer"?' asked Klipper wearily.

'It's a sub, Martin,' muttered Stiefel, '– one of the fourteen my cabinet colleagues wanted to scrap.'

'Look, Chancellor,' said Brotrinde, 'I won't beat about the bush. We could fly down some of our top guys in the Special Forces and drop them near the *Dürer*. Then, under cover of darkness, the sub takes them in close to the Mallorcan coast. Our boys go ashore by dingy near the target's location. They yomp the few kilometres inland, do the business, and they're back on the sub before daybreak. We make it look like the work of these ENABA bastards, of course, and then there'll be such international outrage, we'll have carte blanche to go in there with a full-scale task force with the German flag flying high. The electorate here will go wild – you'll be a national hero – and we'll make the French and British – and Spanish, *naturally* – look like lily-livered wind bags. You'll then have all the credentials to be the economic, diplomatic *and* military leader of Europe.'

Klipper had a fleeting vision of himself driving in a huge open-topped Mercedes along the great thoroughfares of Berlin, all lined by cheering and flag-waving crowds. Somewhere in the background was the orchestral might of the Berlin Philharmonic blasting out the triumphant chorale finale of Bruckner's colossal Fifth Symphony ... the Eighth? ... whatever.

'Um,' said Klipper as his moist eyes met Brotrinde's glassy stare, 'I really can't sanction state terrorism. To be honest, Director, I'm shocked.' He studied his divinely manicured hands. 'Shocked,' he repeated. 'But, just out of interest, who was your ... "target"?' He shivered.

'Well, tar*gets*, to be honest,' said Brotrinde. 'Werner Stumpf – patriotic biographer of German national heroes, young Herbert von Karpen – our greatest conductor and world ambassador of musical superiority, Otto Pinsel – our only significant contribution to world fashion since the War, and loveable, *cuddly* little Professor Kommis – Nobel Prize winner and the darling of all those folk across the globe who, but for his discovery, would be midgets like him.'

Scratching his head, Klipper finally said: 'Those names ring a bell – I mean in combination.'

'And well they might,' said Stiefel. 'You received an invitation to Stumpf's birthday party, didn't you? The entire cabinet did.'

'Oh, God, yes! Stumpf's frightful party! Now I remember. Karpen and that lot were recited in the covering letter – as if *I* would be impressed – someone who meets bloody heads of state all day long!'

'Indeed,' said Stiefel. 'But can you imagine the reaction of your average voter turning on his telly only to discover that "that lot" had been brutally murdered by Mallorcan terrorists – *and* at a birthday party – TV pictures of blood all over the cake and stuff?'

Klipper felt quite queasy: he could see the grisly scene in glorious Technicolor.

'Apparently,' said Brotrinde, almost in a whisper, 'ENABA have weapons supplied by Iran. We still have quite a cache of guns taken off those Bin Laden supporters we picked up in Hamburg years back. I had in mind we might put them to good use.'

'Ahh,' Klipper murmured. 'And ... and when is this ... party?'

'Tomorrow night at Stumpf's house.'

'Jesus! That doesn't give us – *wouldn't* give us – *you* – any time at all. We–'

'No problem,' snapped Brotrinde. 'We've had a contingency plan for ... quite a while. And, as a not infrequent visitor to the homes of some very rich acquaintances in the neighbourhood – did you know it's called "Hamburg Hill"? – I know Stumpf's place fairly well. Actually, I had dinner there once. ... Anyway, if you give us the green light, Chancellor, those voters of yours could be turning on their tellies on Monday morning to see that gore-covered birthday cake ... and your broadcast to the nation.'

'If it went wrong,' whispered Klipper, 'I – *we*–'

'We'd say, Martin, that we'd learned of an ENABA plot to assassinate Stumpf – and Azucena would back you up – we *all* would. He'd lick your arsehole to be Euro President.'

Klipper nodded. 'Yes ... I suppose he would.'

CHAPTER 15

Events were conspiring to destroy the Oakhearts' seemingly unshakeable British phlegm. They were paragons of all the virtues that contemporary democracies professed to hold dear – above all, an abhorrence of prejudice and discrimination. And yet, on this Saturday morning as the electronic thermometer and hygrometer of Werner's state-of-the-art weather station crept inexorably upwards, cracks began to appear in their stoic facades. Bearing loads of party paraphernalia like Himalayan sherpas setting up an elevated base camp, anti-Stumpf sentiments trickled out. No longer was their host eccentric 'Ja-Ja', but 'the Führer'; Jane's initial discomfort over uttering such a politically incorrect blasphemy soon evaporated.

Later, as she descended from the Olive Terrace with a pile of empty cardboard boxes, she passed a bare-chested Mike ascending with a precarious load of chairs.

'*Arbeit macht frei*!' he muttered. 'So much for the bloody beach! The Führer's wondering what's happened to you. He says the round trip from the storeroom shouldn't take more than six and a half minutes – for a female, that is – five for a male.'

'You must be kidding!'

Mike shook his head and resumed the ascent. 'Forget *Ca'n Pau* – this is bloody *Ca'n **Dachau***. Vee have vays of making you verk!'

Jane snorted. 'Roll on the next break.'

'The heat!'

'The humidity!'

But despite these stereotypical allusions to the Third Reich, and notwithstanding indications to the contrary, Werner was no neo-Nazi. In fact, he was – and always had been – an ardent supporter of liberal democracy. Nor was he inherently anti-Semitic; indeed, he felt as much revulsion for the Holocaust as most Germans. Yet, although he had no time for ludicrous theories of racial superiority or wild talk of Jewish bankers conspiring to control the global economy, Werner, nevertheless, bore a grudge. And from his long years of experience, he knew that the overwhelming majority of the German-speaking peoples bore it too, even if only subconsciously. Moreover, it was a grudge that was now compounding what he feared was the seemingly incurable Teutonic weakness, the Achilles heel that had always made them fall at the last fence in the race for world power, and that had predestined them to be one of history's also-rans.

The grudge was that Jewish influence – particularly in America – ensured that the media and entertainment industries continuously bombarded the world's population with reminders of Nazism and the Third Reich. It was not that Werner or his fellow Germans disagreed in principle with the objective of ensuring that the Holocaust should never be forgotten – far from it. But it was the sheer scale of the undertaking: it was beyond reason; it was a vendetta. And now, with most of Germany's population having been born long after the end of the War, the propaganda machine was harder at work than ever before, perpetuating the view that Germans remained racist brutes hiding behind the thinnest of civilized veneers – that a congenital moral defect afflicted them all, and that in consequence the world must be permanently on its guard.

With his usual thoroughness, Werner had conducted surveys to test his theory. When travelling, he'd watch television in his hotel room and flick through all the ghastly channels And it didn't matter whether he was in New York, Singapore, Cairo or Bogotá, there'd always be at least one channel at some time during any twenty-four-hour period churning out something about the Third Reich; if there were scores of channels, there could be at least four documentaries and movies running simultaneously: *Hitler's Women*; *Stalingrad*; *Sink the Bismarck!*; *Schindler's List*. Werner was prone to conjecture how an 'average American' would react to a daily bombardment of European programmes about the wickedness of the Vietnam War, or the institutionalised and legalised racism that had prevailed throughout the States until only recently.

Once the anger provoked by these subjective surveys had died down, Werner would invariably be afflicted with the sort of depression he'd regularly suffered since his early teens, even though he'd been blessed with a fine body, good looks, an excellent brain, and devoted parents. Although his grandparents had lost everything in 1945 and had spent the first seven post-War years with their children sharing an old villa with five other 'refugee' families in Winkelbaden – a sleepy spa devoid of targets worthy of allied bombing – they'd worked miracles to rebuild their lives. Consequently, by the time Werner was twelve his parents could afford to send him to Germany's most prestigious boarding school, Schloss Sämling. And it was there, surrounded by so many boys with a 'von' in their name, that Werner began inventing the Stumpfs' antecedents as country gentry in East Prussia, now so conveniently behind the Iron Curtain.

Like generations of Germans before him, Werner received a formidable education: he could speak English and French fluently – as well as Latin and Ancient Greek; instruction in the sciences and mathematics reached a level that might have taxed a first-year undergraduate at a British university; he possessed a creditable knowledge of the history and geography of every part of the world; despite lacking any practical aptitude, he could read music and knew the names of all J. S. Bach's sons; he could distinguish a Gainsborough from a Reynolds, and critically analyse the architecture of Frank Lloyd Wright. Nevertheless, by the age of eighteen he was exhibiting most of the complexes that would play such important roles in shaping his adult life; perhaps an 'Anglo-Saxon' headmaster would have concluded that Werner, like his schoolmates, had spent too much time gorging on knowledge in the classroom and perfecting acts of individual athleticism in the gymnasium, and not enough time outdoors playing team games. On the other hand, Werner's predicament could simply have been the product of his immediate adolescent surroundings: the unsettling black hole of the years 1933 to 1945 – a taboo subject both at home and school; the omnipresent indicia of national failure and humiliation as evidenced by the thousands of American servicemen still based in Germany, and the dreary reconstructed city centres. Above all, there were the Russians – the partition of the Fatherland, the fake East German 'nation', and tragic divided Berlin.

In any event, during his last few terms at Sämling, Werner would lie awake in his Spartan dormitory repeatedly analysing the fear that he'd inherited some genetic defect – a terrible self-destruct mechanism, like a child with a set of building bricks who studiously constructs an impressive edifice, only to succumb to an irresistible urge to destroy it. And then, wracked by guilt, he starts the whole process all over again. How else could one begin to explain German history? Why had they lost the First World War despite having the best soldiers, the best equipment and the best organisation? After all, the British had barely been able to defeat a few thousand Boers just ten years earlier in South Africa! The French hadn't won a battle on their own since Napoleon! On the Eastern Front, the Russians were a joke! And the late arrivals, the damned Americans, had no battle experience at all! As for the replay, while Hitler should never have come to power in the first place – that was all the fault of the excessively vindictive victors at Versailles anyway – why hadn't the blitzkrieg knocked out Britain in 1940? And with its medieval agriculture and unsophisticated technology, why had the Soviet Union managed to turn the tide at Stalingrad? Why? *Why?*

Hour after hour, Werner would ponder these questions. He would pore over history books, both German and foreign, searching for clues. There'd be earnest debates with his most trusted friends as they took long walks through the forests around Sämling. There were so many persuasive arguments: an incompetent general here; bad weather there; a treacherous ally; Hitler – a certifiable Austrian; bad luck. But alone with his thoughts in the small hours, Werner would slowly but surely discard all these excuses for his nation's military disasters and return to the invidious suspicion that failure was in the Teutonic blood. Or was it some diabolical curse?

Now, after decades of peace and liberal democracy – perhaps too liberal – and with one of the highest standards of living in the world, the reunification of East and West, and the government back in Berlin, where was Werner's nation and its people? Where indeed! – in the wings of the world stage, self-effacing, terrified of doing or saying anything that might provoke an iota of criticism. And even though very few foreigners ever made any direct references to his face about Nazism or the War, whenever Werner was in the presence of a non-German – whether young or old, and whatever the nationality – he knew what they were all thinking:

I wonder what his grandfather did in the War.
For all I know, his grandmother could have been a camp guard at Auschwitz.
I bet his father was in the Hitler Youth.

Was it any wonder, therefore, that Werner never felt truly relaxed in the presence of any foreigner? – that since the War, Germans had manifested such a passion for holidaying abroad in protective groups and creating ghetto resorts? – that the German settlers in Mallorca had imported all their own professionals, craftsmen and tradesmen? If only subconsciously, was it not the case that Werner and his countrymen were constantly endeavouring to minimise contact with the brainwashed victims of the 'Jewish propaganda machine'? Was this the explanation for fewer and fewer foreigners learning German? Even reasonably educated French and British now had no idea who Goethe and Schiller were; nor could they name even a single contemporary German novelist, composer or artist. And at the level of popular culture – rock music, movies, TV – Germany was a pathetic wilderness. The wretched truth was that the world today just thought of Germans as people who made Mercedes, VW, Audi and BMW cars somewhere in Europe – a race of lager-swilling, sausage-eating autoworkers.

Thus it was that Werner had been converted to the school of thought that Europe had to unite and become a great power. Then it could take on the USA and its 'Zionist-controlled' entertainment and media industries. It would be Germany's last chance to redeem itself: by reason of its geography, size and economic power, there was every chance it could become the dominant and guiding force. 'European Culture' would have to be promoted – by law – in schools, on television, at the cinema. The tide of anti-German propaganda would be slowed, halted, and then ebb away for ever.

*

When, with her load of empty cardboard boxes, Jane reached the storeroom beneath 'the Breakfast Terrace', she felt totally drained; perspiration was trickling down her arms and legs. She craved to sit in the shade and slowly sip a long cold drink. Werner, however, had different ideas. He came marching out of the door, clipboard in hand, smiling broadly, his gold fillings flashing.

'Ah! At last! I was beginning to think you'd succumbed to heat stroke.' He laughed almost hysterically.

'Actually, Werner–'

'*Ja, ja*! You need a minute's rest. Sit down here' – he pointed to a wooden bench to one side of the door, while ticking something on his clipboard – 'and have a glass of this fresh home-made lemonade that Heidi has just prepared.'

'Oh ... right ... thanks.'

Werner looked at his watch. 'And then you can start the candle installation programme. I've produced a plan showing *exactly* where each one must be positioned in order to get the optimum effect when viewed from the Olive Terrace after dark. If you start' – he glanced again at his watch – 'at eleven forty-five, you should finish Zones One and Two before lunch. These are the areas shaded red and green respectively – here and *here*. See?'

Jane sighed and shook her head. 'Yes, I see. And what have you got lined up for Mike?'

'Mike? Well, initially he'll be hanging lanterns in the olive tree. I've already got the stepladders out for him.'

'How thoughtful. And what will *you* be doing?'

'I have to go into Palma.'

'*Palma*? What on earth for? I mean, I thought it was too dangerous.'

'It's probably *very* dangerous, Jane. But that's the point. I need to check on my apartment – make sure ENABA haven't ransacked it. And I'm concerned about Concha. She works at the airport. God only knows what's going on there. She's a cleaner.'

'Concha?'

Werner flashed his smile again and winked. My girlfriend – *chica* – mistress – well, one of them. She's eighteen.'

For a few moments, Werner continued relaying instructions about the candle arrangements, but not a word registered with Jane as she tried to digest the import of what he'd just told her.

Finally, he said: 'Well, I suppose we'd better get back to work, Jane. I've told Heidi to serve you and Mike with a salad at one o'clock. Now, I've put all the candles–'

'You *were* joking about ... about this Concha, weren't you?'

'Joking? Sorry? What? – about her being a cleaner? I'm not a bloody snob, Jane!'

'No for Christ's sake! – about her being–?'

'"My bit on the side"? – as I think you English say. Of course I wasn't joking!'

'But – but Heidi–?'

'Oh, Heidi doesn't mind!'

'She knows about it? – *her*?'

'Naturally!'

'But–'

'We have a very *open* relationship, Jane. I made it clear to Heidi right from the beginning that I could not possibly restrict myself to just one woman. Frankly, I don't think it's natural for men to be monogamous. We got married on that clear understanding. I do not love these other women – at least not in the way I love Heidi. She is *very* special. And my ability to screw other women ensures that my sex with Heidi does not become stale.'

Over Werner's shoulders, an open-mouthed Jane spotted her husband recrossing the garden and making for the storeroom. Mike put a hand on either side of his face, wiggled his fingers and stuck out his tongue.

'Believe me, Jane,' Werner continued, 'if you want to ensure the long-term success of your marriage, don't make the mistake of forcing Mike into a straitjacket and–'

Jane's mobile began bleating its distinctive ringing tone – Beethoven's *Für Elise*. Making a mental note to change it, she said sharply: 'Excuse me.'

'Pah! Bloody telephones! Anyway, I must–'

'Lionel! *Bonjour*! *Ça va*?'

'Thank God!' groaned Mike as he reached the storeroom. 'Is that lemonade or something, Werner?'

'What? Oh, Mike! Yes. Heidi–'

'Out on the boat? Now? Well, we're all–'

Werner, whose hand had jolted as he began to pour the lemonade – it flowed across the table – bellowed: 'No, no, Jane! *Impossible*! Tell him we cannot go. There is too much work. Tell him–'

'Who's she talking to, Werner?'

'Down the coast, Lionel ... Es Caragoll! I don't believe it! What a coincidence! That's exactly where we'd planned to go this morning–'

'The *candles*, Jane!'

'Who's she talking–?'

'Well, I ... Werner? He ... well–'

'*Jane*! Now I must go to Palma. The *candles*–'

'We'd love to, Lionel! Fine! OK – see you in about thirty minutes. *A toute à l'heure*!'

'Footy, what's going–?'

'Jane, my dear, I hope you have *not* agreed to go out with Tourny.'

'For Christ's sake, Werner! I'm not a bloody servant. I'm hot, tired and bloody bored, OK? We *are* on bloody holiday, in case you've forgotten. And if you're too bloody mean to hire some staff to organise your bloody party, that's your bloody problem.' She turned to her stunned husband. 'Mike, we're going out on Lionel's boat for lunch – down the coast to Es Caragoll. Come on, let's have a quick shower.'

Mike shot an anxious glance at their host. 'But – but – the party? The–?'

'Oh, stuff the sodding party!'

Mike was about to respond when Werner said: 'Come on, Jane, you're just not used to the heat. All you need is–'

'What I need is a break from *you* – and so does your long-suffering wife.' She turned on her heels and marched away.

'I'm sorry, Werner,' Mike bleated. 'I don't understand. What's been going on? I–'

'She's–'

Jane spun round as she reached the steps that ascended to the terrace above. 'And if you think you're "happily married", Werner,' she shouted, 'you must be stupid as well as a slave driver. Mike! Come on! We're about to be bloody liberated by our French allies. I'll see you in the room. I'm just going to ask Heidi if she'd like to be liberated too.'

*

Es Caragoll was a wide, gently curving bay of fine golden sand. Backed by dunes and dense woods of stunted pines, it was about a quarter of a mile long. Even on this blisteringly hot Saturday afternoon in July, there were no more than two dozen people dotted along the beach: in addition to the complete absence of 'facilities', vehicles could only get as far as the Ses Salines lighthouse, half a mile away eastwards along the coast.

Mike looked beyond the small rubber dinghy that had ferried the party ashore and focused on the *Normandie* lying at anchor in the gentle swell about a hundred metres away. He kept picturing the scene below decks when Jeanne had attempted to seduce him; it was only a few days ago and yet it could have been a lifetime. And now she was sitting within touching distance on a huge orange Hermès beach towel, topless and spreading Provençal tapenade – 'there's this wonderful little place in Aix that sends me a regular supply to Paris!' – on thick chunks of crusty local bread. But it was neither the sight of Jeanne's voluptuous breasts nor the recollections of attempted seduction that were putting Mike off the magnificent spread that she and Lionel had prepared – and, no doubt, one or two servants back at the *Villa Tourny* – but the implications of the *Ca'n Pau* bust-up. Even now, Jane was still in shock; she, too, had barely eaten a thing. On the other hand, she was on her third glass of chilled Chablis; if she wasn't careful, she'd succumb to dehydration and heatstroke – thank God Lionel had the sense to bring a big umbrella and plenty of water. But, in all the circumstances, Mike didn't have the heart to tell her to slow down; later, he'd get her to drink litres of water.

'Mike, *chéri*,' rasped Jeanne, 'have some of this *magret de canard fumé* with the green salad. These are roasted *pignons* – how do you say that in English–?'

'Pine nuts,' mumbled Lionel through a mouth full of Serrano ham.

'Ah *oui*, pine nuts, and the dressing is made with roasted peanut oil – *un délice*!'

Mike was trying to concentrate on the Tupperware box being proffered by Jeanne as she leaned towards him – not on her nipples. *Christ! I'm getting an erection. Sit cross-legged. Quick!* 'No – no thanks, Jeanne. I'm still on the lobster. In a minute maybe.' *There's that funny grin of hers again. She knows! She's doing it deliberately!*

'Jane, *chérie*?'

Jane shook her head. 'It's all *so* wonderful, but that business with Werner has destroyed my appetite.'

'You don't want to let Stumpf get you down,' advised Lionel, smiling. 'He's just a bully. You have to stand up to bullies, and then they treat you properly.'

'*Bien sûr*,' Jeanne purred. 'And I am betting that when you get back, he's as sweet as anything.'

'A real ass-kisser!' sniggered Lionel

'Oh, God! I dread going back. I just don't know what came over me. I mean, I could have been firm about coming out with you, but polite. And his sexual adventures are really none of my business. But after *all* Heidi told me the other day – her blind devotion, the unrelenting drudgery of her daily existence – well, he was so bloody pompous, so selfish, so – so …

'I just can't stop picturing Heidi's face when I went into that inferno of a kitchen and told her we we're downing tools and coming out with you two. She was crying. We've got on so well together. ... I feel so mean. I feel like a traitor. I do hope that tyrant doesn't take it out on her. Maybe he's got her doing the candles now, as well as all her other chores. I said we'd do them first thing in the morning and–'

'Honey,' Mike said tenderly, stroking Jane's arm, 'don't cry, *please*. It'll be all right – just like Lionel said. I mean, we had all that bloody nonsense over the tip – remember? – and–'

'The tip!' snorted Jeanne as she poured out more Chablis. '*Il est fou, cet homme*! He's crazy!'

'And when we got back,' Mike continued, 'he was as nice as anything.'

Lionel put down his plate and lay on his side, facing the Oakhearts. 'That's what's wrong with the Germans – no give and take, no compromise, no pragmatism. I had a German director once. He was like that. It was one of those joint venture things between three or four TV companies – French, German and Italian ... I think. ... No matter. Germans believe that you can *plan* everything. It's this obsession with "order" they have. And then when something unexpected happens – something that's not in the script – they go to pieces and blame it on some goddam conspiracy. It wouldn't stop raining in Prague and the script said it was a hot sunny day, and–'

'*Alors*,' Jeanne interrupted, 'you must remember, Jane, that Stumpf wants to impress all his sad little German friends by parading Lionel at his precious party tomorrow night because he is so famous.'

'I still feel awful about Heidi,' whimpered Jane.

'Oh, I wouldn't worry too much about her,' Jeanne sneered. 'She's not such a timid creature as you think. And maybe she likes a bit of rough treatment – many women do – especially German women.'

Both Jane and Mike stopped picking at their lobster.

'*Do* they?' queried Jane.

'Of course! You only have to watch some German TV. I can't think of a nation more obsessed with sexual perversions. And then there's that Mateu. It's obvious he's screwing her. He drops enough hints.'

'Does he?' asked Lionel, looking surprised.

'Oh yes. I think she must pay him. He's always saying things like, "Don't think I'm just a gardener, Señora Jeanne. I do *special services* in the *casa*. I have very good *equipment*. Señora Stumpf is always very satisfied. She pays me well." And then he rubs his groin! *Merde*! Such a *short* boy!' *Quelle horreur*! ... *Alors*, are you English ready for the *magret* now?'

*

After the remains of the picnic had been placed in the cool boxes, and Lionel had treated himself to a spliff, Jeanne rose unsteadily to her feet. Removing her bikini briefs, she said: 'Well, I need to cool off in the sea before my siesta. I cannot lie in wet clothes.'

'Nor me,' said Lionel pulling off his shorts.

The Oakhearts were staring at the horizon with exaggerated interest as Jeanne planted herself firmly in front of them. 'Aren't you two hot?'

Jeanne's knees now appeared to be as fascinating as the horizon.

'We need to digest our food,' mumbled Jane without looking up. Mike managed a nod.

'Suit yourself.'

'It's all right, guys,' said Lionel as he followed Jeanne to the water's edge. 'Haven't you noticed? Most people are naked.'

By the time the French returned from their refreshing dip, the Oakhearts were pretending to be asleep. And then, after all sounds of bodies being dried and suntan cream being replenished died away, they succumbed to the wine and really did fall into a deep sleep. An hour or so later, Jane was on the threshold of consciousness. She was in bed; Mike was snoring just inches away. And yet it was so hot, and the bright light ... *so* bright? One of them must have left the bedside lamp on ... *and* the central heating. But the rhythmic beating? ... no ... whooshing ... like waves ... the dishwasher? But the dishwasher wasn't in the bedroom. Oh, the light and the heat! She'd have to get up and–

As Jane placed a hand over her eyes to shield them from the intense glare, she detected a bizarre and yet all too familiar groaning. The realisation of where she was hit her like an explosion, and as she turned her head to the right and squinted, she saw two intertwined naked bodies on the Hermès towel. Lionel's shapely buttocks were rising and falling in sequence to the groans emanating from Jeanne beneath him. Jane gasped, and he turned his head, flashing that boyish grin of his. She froze for a few seconds. Then she turned her head to the other side; Mike was still snoring.

It was some time after a raucous climax that Jane heard Lionel and Jeanne agreeing on the need to cool off in the sea.

'You're not really asleep, are you, Jane?' asked Lionel. 'Fancy a dip?'

Jeanne cackled her smoker's cackle.

'Jane?'

But Jane remained firmly immobile.

Shortly after, Mike awoke. He was desperate for water. As he drank from the bottle, he spotted the French frolicking like baby seals in the water. 'Christ! They haven't been in the sea all this time, have they?'

'No. They certainly have *not*.'

'Oh, Footy, don't be so down. It'll be all right. Werner–'

'Mike, you remember this morning when you wondered whether there was something wrong with us, and I thought you were talking about sex, and you meant politically – idealistically. Well, perhaps there is something wrong – sexually. I mean, first Werner with his mistresses, Heidi being bonked by the gardener – if one believes that crazy Jeanne – and now – God! – I don't believe what those two – so brazen! – here! – on the beach! – in *broad* daylight! – just feet from us! Jesus *Christ*! Maybe they're trying to lure us into an orgy!'

Jane had barely recounted the scene of alfresco intercourse, when Lionel and Jeanne ran out of the sea. Mike, who'd been forced back into a lotus position as Jane recounted her tale of beach lust, resorted to a fixed grin.

'Aren't you two ever going to get off your butts?' asked Lionel, clearly in excellent spirits.

'Yes,' said Jane. 'We're just about to. Come on, Mike – last one in the water's a sissy.'

Mike shifted uncomfortably. 'Oh – sure.' *Maybe I could make a dash for it before anyone has time–*

'Actually,' said Jeanne, 'we've just had a wonderful idea. Why don't you tell Stumpf to go to hell, and spend the rest of your *vacances* with us at the *very* relaxed *Villa Tourny*? We'd love to have you.'

*

It was just after seven when the Oakhearts were dropped off before *Ca'n Pau*'s Gothic gateway.

'Well, thank you again for a most *memorable* afternoon,' said Jane. 'And we'll phone later with news on the Werner front. But unless he's evicting us – which seems pretty unlikely – I think we really must stick it out here. It would be awfully bad manners and–'

'"*Awfully*",' mimicked Jeanne sourly.

'His car's here,' said Mike pointing to the battered Renault, 'so he must be back from Palma.'

'Maybe he'll have news about the airport,' said Lionel. 'I have to fly to the States next week.'

The smirk disappeared from Jeanne's face. 'So soon? I thought it was the week after next.'

They were still arguing about the dates when the convertible Citroën drove off down the dusty track.

The Oakhearts sighed and held hands.

'Well, we'd better face the music,' said Mike.

In the event, Werner was, as predicted, both charming and profusely apologetic. The morning's debacle had been entirely his fault. He'd been a monstrous host. He was deeply ashamed of his presumption and insensitivity. He begged forgiveness. He'd forgotten how folk from northern latitudes found the heat and humidity such an ordeal, whereas he positively thrived on it. There would be no more 'chores'.

'But tomorrow we'll be more than delighted to help out with the last-minute arrangements,' Jane earnestly asserted.

'Absolutely *any*thing!' added Mike.

Werner was adamant. Almost everything had been done during their absence – there'd been no trip to Palma – including the distribution of the candles; he cheerfully specified the precise number – three hundred and seventy-five. How ashamed the Oakhearts felt, especially as Heidi looked so exhausted as she sat sipping her glass of chilled cava in the courtyard, where she and Werner, dressed as if for a cocktail party, had regally awaited the return of the mutineers.

Finally, when diplomatic relations appeared to have been fully restored – notwithstanding Heidi's virtual silence – Mike said: 'Well, seeing how you're already all dressed up, maybe Jane and I could take you out to dinner at your favourite local restaurant. Just give us half an hour or so to shower and change.'

'Oh yes, why not?' enthused Jane. 'It's the least we can do. You haven't prepared anything, have you, Heidi?'

Heidi smiled sheepishly and shook her head.

'That is a *most* kind offer indeed,' said Werner rising from his seat and glancing at his watch. 'However, we have already accepted an invitation from Professor Kommis to dine with him and his dear wife. We are due at *Valhalla* in … fifteen minutes. So, now we must make a move. Well, I hope you have a lovely evening. I can recommend Port Petit if you want to eat *à la française,* or La Scala if you prefer Italian. And although Spanish, Botavara is excellent for fish. They are all at the marina in Cala d'Or. It is predominantly British tourists down there these days, so I doubt there'll be any trouble from ENABA. Come, Heidi. Oh – and be sure to lock up if you go out, Mike … Jane.'

The miscreants were lost for words as Heidi passed them. 'Goodbye,' she said.

Frankly, the Oakhearts were too exhausted to get dressed up for a restaurant. Instead, they raided the fridge and drank two bottles of Werner's cheap *rosado*, rehearsing all the events of the day and eventually convincing themselves with alcohol induced fervour that in their very different ways, both the French and the Germans were morally defective;

they could do with a bit of good old British backbone. And then, as the evening seemed to get hotter rather than cooler, they both agreed that a swim in the Stumpfs' pool was in order.

'So, who has to trudge up to the room to get our gear?' asked Mike with exaggerated exhaustion.

'No one,' Jane giggled. 'And there are plenty of towels in the pool house.'

When the Oakhearts finally found the switch for the pool lights, the effect was positively Hollywoodian. From her vantage point on the Olive Terrace, Margalida could be in no doubt as to what the entwined naked bodies were doing at the shallow end, thanks to the submarine illumination.

'Sick,' she muttered, 'absolutely sick! No shame at all. They're worse than animals. And they're not even German. They're all the same – them dirty, filthy foreigners!'

CHAPTER 16

There was no known photograph, or, for that matter, any other pictorial record, of Sir Richard Shaddock, the Chief of the Secret Intelligence Service – commonly known as 'MI6' – since his schooldays, when, shortly after his eighteenth birthday, he'd allowed himself to be photographed as Eton College Philatelic Society's secretary. Then he went up to Cambridge to read History of Art and became invisible. This evening, he'd entered 10 Downing Street expertly disguised as a bearded Metropolitan Police sergeant, and, accordingly, without the least display of interest by the media circus camped outside. Now, some fifteen minutes into the conference, Sir Richard was becoming just a little prickly.

'I assure you, Prime Minister,' he said, 'that the intelligence comes from the most trustworthy of sources, and – my profound apologies for labouring the point – it's backed up by all the electronic chatter monitored by GCHQ down at Cheltenham, as already reported by my colleague Mr Truetreat.'

As Peregrine Truetreat nodded, Sandra Cork shrugged her shoulders. 'Yes, well you'll have to excuse my scepticism, Sir Richard, but–'

'*Orange*,' snapped Sir Richard.

'"Orange"?'

'I prefer to be called "Orange", Prime Minister, as I've pointed out previously, on more than one occasion.'

'Oh yes. Sorry.'

'As I was saying, we at SIS–'

'Why "Orange"?'

'I beg your pardon?'

'Why is your codename "Orange"?'

'It's a citrus fruit, of course.'

'Yes?'

'Well, it's a little joke – about my name – Shaddock ... a citrus fruit ... yes?'

As on so many occasions, Sir Peter Blithe-Blister came to the rescue. '*You* know, Sandra! – it's a thumping great *fruit* with *thick* yellow skin and a very *bitter* pith' – he glared at the SIS Chief – 'named after a Captain Shaddock, I believe, who is thought to have introduced it to the Caribbean in the eighteenth century. Any relation of yours, Orange, old boy?'

Orange glared back. 'Quite probably, Peter.'

'What fame!'

'The point is,' said Sandra, 'that in view of all those "extremely reliable sources" who assured one of *your* predecessors, er ... Orange, that there were mountains of "weapons of mass destruction" in Iraq, and the resulting "dodgy dossiers"–'

'I take your point, Prime Minister,' Orange interrupted, 'but, with respect, that was *years* ago. This is quite a different kettle of fish. These sources are *European* chaps – in Paris and Berlin – not Iraqis.'

'Be that as it may, I do have some difficulty believing that Martin Klipper – of all people – could possibly sanction the assassination of a whole cast of German bigwigs just to find an excuse for a show of strength by the German army, and, if that wasn't daft enough, to persuade Chiffon to do the bloody same. I think those two are trying to make monkeys out of us.'

Orange made a feeble attempt to smile. 'I'm *so* sorry, Prime Minister, if I failed to explain myself with *absolute* clarity, but I had thought that I'd stated that, to the best of our knowledge and belief, the French and Germans are acting quite independently of each other, and that, therefore, there is no question of Klipper having "persuaded"–'

'But then, Sir – *Orange* ... that makes the whole dog's dinner even dafter. Am I expected to believe it's a bloody coincidence that Klipper and Chiffon–?'

'No, no, PM,' interjected Truetreat. 'The eavesdroppers are saying that Berlin came up with their plan *first*, the French got wind of it–'

'Through *their* agents in Berlin,' snapped Orange.

'– and Chiffon went ballistic. You know what a crushing inferiority complex the poor chap has.'

'Indeed,' agreed Sir Peter. 'He can't possibly allow Klipper to be perceived as the captain of the S.S. *Euroland*. So, Sandra, if our hush-hush chaps here are right, by this time tomorrow night we could have the French bumping off some Grade A Frenchy up here' – he tapped the large-scale map of Mallorca spread out on the coffee table – 'around Pollença, while old Martin's gang are down here around Santanyí pumping lead into some heroes of the *Vaterland*. And then the balloon goes up, the French land in the north of the island, the *Bundeswehr* land in the south, and, pretending, no doubt, that it's a carefully planned combined operation, there's a race to see who can get to Palma and the airport first.'

'You mean to tell me that you believe that the Spanish haven't got a clue what's going on? – that *their* spies in Berlin and Paris–?'

'The old Iberians, PM,' sniggered Truetreat, 'are not too good on the intelligence front – at least not from *our* experience.'

'And you're convinced that the French and Germans haven't liaised with each other at all, or that French intelligence don't know – I mean that *German* intelligence don't know that French intelligence have got wind of what Berlin has in mind, or that they – neither of them, that is, won't know that we know–?'

'Maybe I could save us all a lot of time, Prime Minister,' Orange said drily, 'by short-circuiting this speculation and giving you the *facts*.'

Sir Peter and Sandra exchanged theatrical glances. 'Please *do*, Orange,' said Sandra. 'But first, would you like some more coffee? Oh! You haven't touched it!'

'I'm currently endeavouring to reduce my consumption of caffeine, Prime Minister.'

'It's *instant*,' said Sir Peter, grinning, '– less caffeine. And try a Chips Ahoy!. They're *scrump*tious!'

Orange shook his head. 'If we could get back to the matter in hand? ... Madrid – *naturally* – know that there are French and German warships in the vicinity of this island, Mallorca, but otherwise they're completely in the dark. And we are convinced that the Germans haven't a clue that the French have discovered their stratagem. I mean, when it comes to intelligence, Paris are *almost* on our level – to give credit where credit is due.'

'So, they'll know that we know what they're up to?'

'I said "almost" on our level, Prime Minister. Of course, *they* don't have anything like GCHQ, or our access to U.S. intelligence. Accordingly, although they may *suspect* we might have an inkling, they won't be *certain*. Anyway, the French are a law unto themselves – they probably couldn't give a fig whether we know or not.'

Sandra was staring intently at the plate of Chips Ahoy! as if willing herself not to succumb to another. 'I must say I find all this absolutely sickening. I can't believe that people like Chiffon and Klipper could be so callous, so mercenary, so unscrupulous – that they'd be prepared to kill their own citizens in cold blood just to further their own squalid political careers. It's beyond my comprehension.'

Orange, Truetreat and the Foreign Secretary kept their thoughts to themselves.

'Anyway,' said Sandra, 'if our spies are so much better than theirs, how come we don't know who this "famous actor" is that the French are planning to bump off – or the identities of all these German "national heroes" Klipper has in his sights?'

'We're working on that, Prime Minister,' said Orange. 'We're pulling out all the stops.'

'Any ideas?'

'Well, there are an awful lot of "top Germans" on Mallorca, or so I'm led to believe.'

'And "top French actors"?' queried Sandra. 'Surely there can't be that many, even in France itself?'

'The "actor" could be male or female. And it could be someone who's only there on holiday, so our trawling of the local electoral registers, et cetera, could be a waste of time.'

'Wouldn't our consul know, Peter?'

'I'm afraid, Sandra, Blackstump's still under sedation in the psychiatric unit at a secluded military hospital. I doubt we'll get any sense out of him for some days – weeks even.'

'So, what do you think we ought to do? Surely we can't stand by and allow these bastards to do their evil deeds and plunge Mallorca into some kind of bloodbath, assuming – and I still think it's a pretty big "if" – our intelligence is correct? We'd be accessories!'

Orange emitted an almost inaudible groan. 'We can't possibly let them know that we know. It would wreck my entire Continental network.'

'And as I said the other day, Sandra,' added Sir Peter, 'the Franco-German rumpus over Mallorca could be regarded as a wonderful spectator sport. They could be digging themselves into such a jolly big hole that they'll never be able to get out of it!'

'Good God! You're a heartless bunch. Is that what they taught you two at Eton? And if this German-cum-French escapade goes horribly wrong and these ENABA folk put up a fight, we're going to have one hell of a lot of British tourists caught in the crossfire. And then we'll have no option but to send our boys in and sort the mess out – as usual.'

'Precisely!' chirped Sir Peter. 'One long, thick nail in the coffin of the United States of Europe, and one jolly big feather in our – *your* electoral cap, Sandra. But if we're lucky, it won't quite come to that. The French and Germans won't even get off the beaches. They'll withdraw ignominiously and Chiffon and Klipper will be the black sheep of Europe, while we British can play the role of honest broker, summoning all the little squabbling Euro-brats to London for a jolly good telling off.'

'Well, Peter, *I* don't want assassinations, invasions, or "ignominious withdrawals". I want these wankers to see sense and to understand beyond any shadow of a doubt that if they're daft enough to start playing silly buggers down in Mallorca, they're going to have *us* to account to. I want every available bloody warship we've got steaming flat out round that island by this time tomorrow – we've the perfect excuse in view of the do at our consulate, *and* the assassination of that local politician geezer – Thingy–'

'Adrover,' assisted Sir Peter.

'Him too. If that doesn't act as a deterrent, then at least if "the balloon" does go up we'll have some guys on hand with *real* experience of civil unrest, terrorism and belligerent local fanatics.'

'Fair enough, Sandra,' said Sir Peter rubbing his hands.

With the hint of a sneer, and staring at his untouched coffee, Orange said: 'I suppose it's fortuitous, Prime Minister, that we have lots of "guys" with that sort of experience after all.'

CHAPTER 17

Even though it was his sixtieth birthday, Werner had been up since the crack of dawn; as on every other day of his meticulously planned life, a lie-in was not on the itinerary. Heidi, nursing a slight hangover after imbibing just a little too much wine at the Kommises' dinner party, finally crawled out of bed shortly before seven and crept down to the subterranean laundry room where the two huge cardboard boxes she'd brought back by car from Germany some months ago had been secreted. In truth, both this precaution against discovery and her impressive wrapping paper were rather pointless: earlier in the year, and after having exhaustively scrutinized the websites of several German auction houses, Werner had told Heidi precisely what he wanted as a gift for this very special, albeit clandestine, anniversary.

And so, while the Birthday Boy was enjoying his customary alfresco cold shower in a rocky glade just below the house, Heidi struggled to transfer the huge packages to *Ca'n Pau's* hall. She was still sitting there, with her head between her legs and dripping in perspiration, when Werner strode in. Save for a pair of decrepit espadrilles on his feet and a towel over his shoulder, he was naked. His eyes rested on the boxes and his face lit up.

'Happy Birthday, Werner,' Heidi wheezed.

'Thank you. I wondered when you were finally going to make an appearance.' He ripped off the paper without commenting on either the decoration of hearts and arrows, or the sprigs of bougainvillea taped to the red silk ribbons.

'I do hope you'll like them when you see them in the flesh.'

'Oh, I'm sure I will!'

Minutes later, after the matching pair of eight-branch candelabra had been carefully extricated from their boxes and all the layers of protective bubble wrap, Werner beamed with almost childlike delight. The photographs on the website had not done them justice: at almost a metre high, and bristling with a mass of high-Victorian, neo-baroque detail, they were precisely the sort of antique decor that Werner adored – the theatrically spectacular.

Heidi thought they were hideous: they reminded her of Wagner and Baron von Frankenstein. 'They're not *solid* silver,' she said apologetically, 'but only silver plate. The man said they were made around 1870 by WMF, the Württembergische Metallwarenfabrik–'

'For God's sake, Heidi, don't tell anyone they're silver *plate*! That's just between you and me. After all, no one's going to lift up these monsters to look for any bloody hallmarks, are they?'

'Um ... no, I suppose not.'

'They'll look wonderful on the table tonight.'

'Table? What table?'

'*Which* table. ... Which table do you think? – the bloody *dining* table, of course, *Dumnkofp* – on the Olive Terrace.'

Heidi stared glumly at the two towering fussy masses of silver-plated Corinthian columns, with their tree-like branches, foliage and cherubs. 'Do you think there'll be enough ... space? And if there's the slightest breeze, candle wax could drip–'

'I've pictured these chefs-d'oeuvre on the table ever since I first saw them on the Internet. I've even included them on the table plan – the one that's been hanging on your notice board in the kitchen, Heidi, for the last *fortnight* – as "Illumination Generators". So that's that. Now, you'd better go and make some coffee. Then you can give my candelabras another polish, seeing how it's Sunday and Margalida's day off. Mind you, I wouldn't trust that clumsy aborigine to lay one finger on these masterpieces. I'll be in my study updating today's schedule. Quite a few points occurred to me overnight while you were snoring your damned head off. Oh, and don't forget what I told you last night – be nice to the Oakhearts when you see them. I don't want any repetition of that frostiness you displayed when they got back from their jaunt with those French bastards yesterday.'

'You were the one who said they had to be taught a lesson. You were the one who sucked up to Professor Kommis to invite us–'

'I was still *polite* to them. Anyway, that was yesterday. And I'm sure they've learned their lesson. They'd just better help out today as promised or–'

'Do I have to make them a special breakfast this morning?'

'No! You've got more than enough to do. Just toast and marmalade. The English love that.'

As Werner sat in front of his desktop, running through the voluminous Birthday Schedule, his mind kept drifting back to the thorny issue of the Oakhearts. Over and over, he kept picturing that precocious child with his building bricks, the great tower rising up towards the nursery ceiling. Then, glowing with admiration, he stands back to survey the fruits of his genius. But even as he does so, the urge begins to manifest itself. Behind his back, fidgeting hands curl into fists; his right foot starts to tremble. Before he knows what's happening, he's lashing out, hitting and kicking, wooden bricks flying into every corner of the room.

Werner sighed. Yet again, he'd behaved like a fool. How could he have walked out on the Oakhearts? What on earth had possessed him? He hadn't been able to relax for one minute at Kommis's awful dinner, complete as usual with his hideously ostentatious wines – Château Pétrus indeed! Who the hell did that parvenu academic – albeit with his grotesquely profitable 'growth' clinics in Hamburg, Berlin and Munich for fellow dwarfs – think he was impressing?

Tutting, Werner scrolled down the Birthday Schedule's second page. What other duties could he transfer from the English, notwithstanding all their assurances to help out today? Anyway, in view of the two empty bottles of *vino rosado* he'd spotted in the kitchen rubbish bin when he and embarrassingly tipsy Heidi got back from dinner last night, the guests would probably be suffering from hangovers even when they did finally get out of bed.

'I blame that Mike,' Werner muttered. 'He's a bad influence on Jane, with all his bourgeois ways. If he'd gone to boarding school too, there'd be none of this lolling around in bed until all hours. Jesus – and he's so *dull*!'

Meanwhile in the background, the television set that Werner professed rarely, if ever, to watch was tuned to one of the local stations with the sound turned down low. Cameras were panning over scenes of tourist chaos at both Palma's airport and the *estación marítima* after another night of thousands bedding down on very hard ubiquitous marble floors. Members of the armed forces loyal to the regional government were serving breakfast in shifts; German passport holders were last in the queue and only entitled to one stale bun – not two like all the other victims of the transport crisis. And talking like a machine gun, a seemingly ecstatic reporter was informing viewers that passenger services to the mainland by air and sea were still severely restricted as the hunt for Jordi Adrover's assassins continued.

*

Mike awoke with a start and pulled his hand away from an erect penis. He turned his head; Jane was still fast asleep. And lying naked and uncovered, how beautiful she looked! He sighed and shook his head. All night – or so it seemed – he'd been dreaming about that bloody Jeanne and her breasts! There really was nothing else about her that he found in the least attractive, physically or otherwise, but those breasts ... and the nipples! He looked back at Jane. She was so beautiful, but if only she had breasts that were just a little bigger – like the ones he'd always fancied since ... well, since that holiday in Brittany with Mum and Dad when he was fifteen and that local girl–

Think of something else! – Hugo – and Mrs Babcock. Mike smiled as he pictured Mr Dog – his wagging tale, his lovely black spots, his unique Dalmatian smile, his fragrance – so reassuring, so comforting ... almost intoxicating.

God! I love that dog. I miss him so much.

To his surprise, Mike felt tears begin to form. Gently, so as not to disturb Jane, he reached for his wallet on the bedside table. He opened it and stared at the photograph. Then he kissed it. 'I hope you're being good for Mrs B,' he whispered. 'Papa'll be home tomorrow and–'

The airport!

Within five minutes, Mike was making his way into the house, searching for either of his hosts and news of the political situation. In the hall, the shock of being confronted by a matching pair of gigantic and horrific candelabra stopped him dead in his tracks with a blast of 'Jesus bloody Christ!' Then the aroma of fresh coffee led him to the diminutive kitchen. It took some arm-twisting to persuade Heidi to leave her inferno and join him on the terrace for a cup of coffee and a well-earned break from filling scores of vol-au-vents. As far as Mike was concerned – and notwithstanding Werner's strictures – she still hadn't returned to normal.

'Werner should be down from his study soon,' she said coolly. 'I hope the news will be good. It is impossible for all the tourists to be imprisoned. I don't think your government – or mine – will accept it much longer – or Madrid. Things will happen soon – very soon. I am sure of it.'

'I hope so. We *must* get back tomorrow.'

'Yes. Your work. I know it is very important.'

'"*Work*"? Oh no, I'm not too bothered about *that*. I've plenty of colleagues who can cover for me – do my job, that is. No, it's Hugo.'

At last, Heidi managed a genuine smile. 'The dog! *Mein Gott*, you are loving him a lot!'

Mike pretended to be embarrassed. 'Yes,' he laughed, 'Hugo's like my son – a baby.'

Heidi laughed too. 'I understand. When my daughter grew up and left home, I only had the dog – you know my husband died many years ago – my *first* husband – not Werner – he is not a monster returned from the death – like Igor and Boris Karloff in the old movies! ... Oh, I don't know?'

'Heidi, behave – it's his *birthday*!'

'Am I ever to forget it? Anyway, I only had the dog, a Weimaraner – Ludo was his name – well, Ludwig really. He was bought for Anna and I was always complaining about him, but when there were only the two of us in the house, he is becoming my best friend. And then when he died, well ...' She shook her head. 'So, I understand why you want to go home and see your Hugo.'

'Perhaps you should get another dog. It could be great company for you.'

Heidi snorted. 'Oh no! Werner does not want a dog in the house.'

'Why not?'

'The hair.'

'He's allergic? The hair makes him ill?'

'No. He just thinks it is dirty. He says dogs should stay outside.'

'Ah, I see.' Mike looked across the garden to the steps that ascended to the Olive Terrace. 'Look, Heidi, I'm very sorry about what happened yesterday – we both are. It's so unlike Jane to lose her temper. I think that the heat–'

'There is no need to say anything. It is forgotten.'

'And to be honest, Jane was very upset when Werner started talking about his ... his *relationships*, and that it was good for a successful marriage, and that she shouldn't force me to be faithful otherwise our marriage would fail, and ... Heidi, the fact is that Jane and I believe very strongly that fidelity is of the essence – I mean, that–'

'Werner told you about his ... his *girls*?'

'Well, yes – Jane that is – and she told me. ... Didn't Werner mention it?'

'No.'

'Ah.'

'I am so sorry. It must have been very embarrassing. But then he tells almost everyone. I think it makes him feel young – younger than he is. I can't really complain. He is making it clear when we first started to see each other that he could not be with only one woman. I just thought that after we got married he would change.' She stared into her empty coffee cup for some moments.

'Anyway, Mike, you do not want to hear these things. Werner does talk much nonsense, I think, about marriage. But then at least he is honest. There are no nasty surprises for me. And now I must return to the kitchen. There is so much on the schedule that Werner has put above the cooker.'

'Don't worry! Today, Jane and I are *definitely* going to help you as much as we can.'

'Thank you, but I think Werner wants to give you as little as possible to do.' She looked up into the sky. 'And it looks like it will be a very, *very* hot day – worse than yesterday. I think we are going to have a storm, but Werner says no. He tells me many technical things – by the phone he speaks to the weather people in Madrid, and they swear that the bad weather will go to the north.'

Mike carried the coffee things to the kitchen. As he put the cups in the sink he said: 'A few moments ago you said that you thought Werner talked a lot of nonsense. Do you think his political views are nonsense too – *Mein Europa* and all that?'

Heidi laughed oddly. 'Oh, I do not have "political views". I am not clever enough.'

'Heidi! Don't be silly. In the last few days I've heard you talk very knowledgably – wisely – about so many things. Frankly – please don't tell him I said so – but you often seem to know an awful lot more about what's going on than Werner.'

'*Mein Gott*! Don't let him hear you say that. I think he would never use your law firm again! No – leave the cups, Mike. I can wash them.'

'No problem. I told you we were going to help out today!'

'Thank you.'

'Well?'

'Yes?'

'What do you think about *Mein Europa*?'

Heidi groaned. 'I think Werner is all wrong. I don't like big things – I mean big companies and big shops and big countries. Of course, we should all try and work together to solve common problems – like pollution and crime. And I like being able to travel around Europe without all the passport controls, and to use the same money – the euro – even if the notes and coins are so boring. But I also like the old Europe – many little countries where the people can see what their governments are doing – you know – feel close to them. I don't think the Americans feel close to their government, do you, Mike?'

'No … no I don't think they do.'

'I like variety, the variety you get when people are allowed to decide things for themselves and not be told all the time what to do by people far away who think they know better. I like the Europe of my youth. … You could travel a few hundred kilometres, cross so many borders, and experience so much – so many different kinds of the living, yes? – all the different languages, customs, food, wine, architecture, films, fashions. You travel from one side of America to the other and it is all the same – the same supermarkets, the same fast food, the same "malls" – even the people look all the same with their jeans and T-shirts and trainers. Dull, dull, dull! That is not what I want to see in Europe, but I am thinking that is what we are getting.

'And that, Mike, is what Werner seems to want with his "United States of Europe" – whatever he calls it. I think it is a nightmare. I think maybe we had it almost right about thirty years ago. We were "the Community" then – yes? – not "a union". We had the free trade – a "common market" – but we had our independence too and decided our own ways. Now I think our governments spend all their time and *our* money sitting in big meetings trying to get so many different peoples to agree on things most of us don't give the damn about – the size of cucumbers, whether to send soldiers to Côte d'Ivoire, what can be called "chocolate". I think they want to be seen to be speaking with one voice just to make it look as though Europe is as important as America – that Europe is also a superpower.'

Nodding slowly, Mike was visibly wilting in the heat.

'Now I think you ought to go outside,' Heidi said. 'I am used to it – Hell's Kitchen! Go and have a swim in the pool before breakfast.'

'Yeah, good idea. I'll just pop up to the room for my Speedos. Maybe Jane–'

'Oh, I wouldn't bother. It's very private down at the pool.'

After a few seconds, Mike said: 'Right, well I'll go and have that swim. Thanks for the coffee – and for your thoughts. I think you've talked a lot of sense – as usual. In fact, to be honest, Heidi, I think you've convinced me that *Mein Europa* is not my cup of tea at all.'

Ca'n Pau, the House of Peace, lived up to its name for the rest of the day as the Stumfps and Oakhearts worked together in remarkable harmony – and notwithstanding the heat and humidity, with Werner's electronic weather station flashing new records; even the barometric pressure reached an all-time low for July, indicating inclement weather was imminent. Nevertheless, the preparations for dinner on the Olive Terrace went ahead; it was in The Plan. The newly inserted additional refreshment breaks were even supplemented by enforced fifteen-minute dips in the pool every two hours. And to Werner's delight, the Oakhearts volunteered to undertake extra duties. He also genuinely appreciated their birthday present – three bottles of claret purchased in a German wine merchant's on the Campos ring road while driving back in shock from Palma after Crispin Blackstump's very public debagging.

When Werner opened the wooden case and read the labels, his first thought was: *Hah! These will put Kommis in his place with his nouveau riche and predictable Pétrus crap.* 'Château Léoville Las Cases!' he boomed, '– of Saint-Julien – the magnificent 2005 vintage! *Three* bottles! You spoil me! Thank you, Jane ... and Mike.' *You can rely on breeding. This will be all Jane's idea. I bet Léoville is what the Trench-Foots have been drinking for generations in Derbyshire with their roast beef – a real gentleman's claret!*

Mike said: 'The German chap in the shop said it was ready for drinking. Personally, I think you could wait another few years.'

183

Werner tried to keep smiling: would Kommis live another few years. 'Oh? Really? What do *you* think, Jane?'

Jane shrugged her shoulders. 'No idea! Don't know a bloody thing about wine. Mike's the expert. Apparently, this Léoville stuff is supposed to be OK. Mike was gobsmacked to find it in that place in Campos. Of course, if we'd known it was your birthday before we came out, we would have got you something a bit more original than *vino*.'

An almost equally satisfying birthday treat occurred later in the morning, when Lionel phoned and invited the Oakhearts round for lunch; the harbour master at Portopetro was warning of *tormentas*, so Lionel's preferred option of a high-speed trip to Cabrera to cool off on this suffocating, windless day had had to be abandoned.

Jane declined the invitation. 'We'll see you both tonight,' she said into her mobile while carefully removing crystal glasses from a cardboard box on the Olive Terrace under Werner's supervision. 'I'm sure it will be spectacular.'

At the *Villa Tourny*, Jeanne lay prostrate on one of the art nouveau sun loungers in the shade of the terrace; even lifting her wine glass in this heat and humidity was an effort. 'Well, I've always told you that you can't trust the English. They're so perfidious – *Perfide Albion*! And pragmatic – to the point of having no real principles at all.'

'If they don't want to come round for lunch, what's the big deal?' drawled Lionel. 'They're just being polite – helping out some old German and his slave of a wife in this God-awful heat so that we can have a good time tonight.'

'"*Good time*"! I can't think of anything more pissing awful. Anyway, yesterday those two were cursing that Boche pig, wishing they'd never accepted his poisoned chalice of an invitation. So mixed up! I'm telling you, all these Anglo-Saxons are schizophrenic. On the one hand they're desperate to do the right thing – stiff upper lip – political correctness – "no sex please we're British!" – "God save the King!" – "God Bless America!". And on the other, when they think nobody's listening or watching, they let their voyeuristic hair down – or try to – a quick grope on the back row of the cinema – yelling obscenities in the safety of a football crowd – revealing all their prejudices against blacks, Arabs, "Japs", "Chinks", "Krauts", "Frogs". And then when the urge subsides and the guilt overwhelms them again, they put their clothes back on, zip up their flies, zip up their mouths and–'

'Give me a break, for *Christ's* sake! You could be describing my parents – my uncle and his xenophobic, racist family in Bordeaux.'

'The Bordelais are *special*. You haven't exactly chosen a typical French city, have you?'

'It's French.'

'The Anglo-Saxons–'

'I'm going for a swim in the pool.'

'You always run away when you lose an argument. You–'

'You always talk crap when you're pissed. Instead of constantly analysing all the faults of your goddam Anglo-Saxons, Jeanne, maybe you should spend a bit more time trying to figure out why you drink so much – what *you're* trying to run away from.'

'I'm not trying to run away from anything. I–'

'Sure!'

As Lionel walked languidly across the terrace, Jeanne screamed: 'You're like all the others! You just use me! You just want a bit of class at your side and not another one of the brainless Barbie doll whores that everyone else in your precious Hollywood has clinging to their arms whenever they show their designer faces in public. Well, I'm sick of you – bored out of my bloody mind! And I'm not going to that fucking party! I've already had that wet fish of an Englishman – on the *Normandie* – at Cabrera. And that stuck-up bitch of his is never going to part her legs for your joke of a prick, so it's a waste of time you going. Do you hear me?'

But Lionel just kept on walking across the manicured lawn.

CHAPTER 18

At his ten-bedroom 'cottage' perched dramatically on a cliff top near the fishing hamlet of Ballygally, Maine, President Patrick O'Connell should have been having pre-Sunday-lunch aperitifs with the First Lady, Caronia, and their weekend houseguests, including the Roman Catholic Archbishop of Boston, the Mexican Ambassador, the CEO of Appalachian Aluminum, and twenty-one-year-old movie starlet Pine Stein. Alas, due to a 'non-anticipated-event situation', Caronia O'Connell had been temporarily abandoned and was now using her very best endeavours to keep the motley assembly amused out in the 'back yard' – an easily defendable peninsula comprising several acres of almost treeless and flowerless grassland, thanks to the salt-laden Atlantic gales that frequently blasted the terrain. Her husband, the nation's youngest President since Kennedy, was closeted in his den with half a dozen visibly troubled advisers, including the Head of the CIA, Denzil – pronounced 'Denzeel' – Splint, Secretary of State Dralon Schwartz-Rodriguez, and Defense Secretary Buck Goosepepper.

'The British,' said Splint, 'first told us yesterday – almost straight away, Mr President, to be fair – of Chiffon's and Klipper's screwy plans, but it was only a couple of hours ago that we – and they – learned of the U.S. angle.'

'And Chiffon was speaking to Premier Agneau on an *ordinary* cell phone?'

'Yeah, that's to say, the official one he normally uses.'

'Incredible!'

'Well, it's a French model, so the encoding technology's fairly basic.'

O'Connell scanned the transcript once more and shook his head slowly. 'Is Sandra lined up for my call?' he asked without looking up.

'Sure,' said Dralon. 'She's waiting by the phone at Number Ten.'

'OK. And do we know what her view is?'

'In a word – disgust.'

'Well, naturally – Tourny's got great talent! What I meant is, do the British have any plans to try and stop the French taking him out? Do we know where the bastards plan to do it, by the way? – or who the Krauts are aiming to take out? – Jesus! – what the hell is going on over there in Europe?'

'First, Mr President,' Splint replied, 'all we know is that the Germans are concentrating their forces – a couple of lousy cruisers and a sub – down here, off the south-eastern coast of the island.' He circled an area on a metre-square satellite photograph of exceptional clarity that had had to be spread out on the den floor. 'At this moment in time we are informationless with respect to *their* target – apparently, this Mallorca place is liberally populated with German big noises. The Krauts have kinda colonised it, which is why the natives are revolting.'

'Yeah, I read Dralon's reports.'

'By coincidence, sir, this zone is also where Tourny is vacationing. He's at his folks' place. It's this structure ... *here*. That's the pool. Actually, this could be him swimming. The geeks say it's a male Caucasian, and that he's ... naked. Anyway, he's staying there alone – well, with a girlfriend – some has-been French actress.'

'How do we know?'

'His Hollywood agent is proving *very* cooperative.'

Dralon was beginning to feel sidelined. 'I think Sandra is scared shitless, Patrick,' she said. 'She's got thousands of English vacationers stuck on this dump and has a nightmare of them being liberated by a load of French and German marines, with the old UK looking weak and sidelined on the European stage, as usual. So far, she's only ordered the Royal Navy to sail around the island waving the Union Jack.'

'A carrier and some teeny-weeny destroyers,' snapped Buck, anxious to make a contribution.

'Christ, their entire fleet!' retorted O'Connell.

Everyone laughed.

'Maybe,' opined Dralon, 'we should just let the French and Germans make goddam fools of themselves, Patrick. Knowing them, they'll probably end up shooting each other. And the Spaniards are going to go ballistic once they discover they've been violated. Another nail in "the United States of Europe" coffin, perhaps?'

'Hey!' boomed Buck. 'What about stirring things up by tipping off Madrid? We owe them a favour or two. And I've heard that guy Azucar–'

'Azu*cena*,' Dralon drawled.

'Whatever – is in with a good chance of becoming "President of Europe" – whatever that fricking means – next year, and he could be a useful guy to have on our side at the head of things over there, don't you think?'

'Stick to Defense business, buddy,' Dralon snarled.

O'Connell glanced at his watch. 'We're running out of time. You're all missing two very important points. First, we owe the Brits a hell of a lot more than the Spics, OK? And secondly, Tourny is currently one of Hollywood's hottest properties. The media giants have a lot riding on him – he could earn them *billions* over the next ten to twenty years – another Gere, Pitt, Cruise, Depp ... Thingy. They're going to be pretty pissed off if and when they learn that we stood by and allowed their prime asset to be liquidated just to be nice to some greasy politician in Madrid. Bill Klamp of Cyclopean was one of the biggest individual donors to my campaign fund last time round, and he's promised to help out with my re-election. And I know for a fact that Cyclopean are negotiating with Tourny to star in *Betsy*, a movie about Betsy Ross and the War of Independence – with him playing that French general who defeated the English at Yorktown ... er–'

'Lafayette?' suggested Splint. 'His agent didn't mention that, sir. How do you know?'

O'Connor lowered his head and pretended to reread the transcript of Chiffon's indiscreet mobile call to Patrick Agneau. 'Miss Stein told me last night – over ... over dinner. She'd had quite a lot of Chardonnay. They want Pine to play Betsy Ross. Lafayette gets to knock her up when she personally delivers a consignment of her new U.S. flag to his camp. The project's still under wraps, by the way. She made me promise not to tell anyone.'

A few minutes later, the President was speaking with the Prime Minister.

'Of course we've tried phoning him, Sandra, honey – well, his agent has – he's with the CIA people now in Los Angeles – but the phone lines down that way must be bust, what with the revolution an' all, and Lionel's cell phone seems switched off. ... No, we haven't got the French lady's number. ... Oh, you've heard of her? ... No, no, I can't say I've ever seen *Three Nuts and a Bolt*. I'll look out for it. ...

'Well, naturally we can't stand by and let these murderers ... Me too! I always said that Chiffon was a shifty sonofabitch. When he came here last time, this silver ashtray – Roosevelt's favourite – went missing from the Oval Office! ... Absolutely! We have to uphold the rule of law, justice and – and liberty – above all *liberty*, Sandra. ... Yes, we *are* partners, and that's why we don't expect you to shoulder the entire burden. ...

'We've got the *Herbert Hoover* in the neighbourhood with some of our best guys being briefed as we speak, Sandra, and we can have them securing Lionel's place within an hour – *two* hours, Denzil's signalling to me. We'll back you up all the way, Sandra – logistics, satellite surveillance – you name it. ... We have *every* confidence you can take the airport. ... Sure, it'll look like a British show – heck, there may not even be any reason for our involvement to be revealed. ... Well, I accept that your SAS folks could protect Lionel, but your guys have told ours that they're on a training mission in Scotland or some place, Sandra, whereas the *Herbert Hoover* is on site. ...

'OK, Sandra, we'll talk again in a couple of hours. ... Not at all, a pleasure as usual. ... Sorry? ... Oh great! I'm thrilled you can get them in England. ... They sure are very "moreish". Yeah, Caronia has to hide them from me, but I've got a secret cache in my desk – here and at the White House. ... Really? – Sir Peter's an *addict*? Hah! I knew you'd find his weakness sooner or later. You're a dangerous woman, Sandra. *Ciao!*'

President O'Connell put down the receiver, and, beaming broadly, scanned his colleagues' expectant faces. 'Well, that's all sorted! The British are going to do the Mass Parachute Drop, the Beach Landings, and the Liberation of the Airport scenes – and expose themselves to the wrath of the local Latins and international opinion, while our boys do a *Where Eagles Dare* routine and slip behind enemy lines and rescue the Big Name.'

Splint said: 'We should have him safely on the *Hoover*, sir, before he knows what's happening.'

'Did I hear you say that the English Foreign Secretary's on drugs?' asked Dralon incredulously.

'What?'

'I gathered that Cork told you he's hooked on something.'

'"Hooked"? ... Oh, for Christ's sake, honey, just cookies – Chips Ahoy!'

CHAPTER 19

Surrounded by his guests in *C'an Pau*'s charming courtyard, Werner was glowing with pride as he commenced the ten-second countdown to his welcome speech. The party, which he'd so carefully planned for all these months, had now been steaming on its precisely plotted course for some forty minutes, as if on a millpond. There hadn't been the slightest hint of a ripple of turbulence – proof positive of the benefits of careful planning. Even the French had arrived within five minutes of the time specified for casting off – 20:30 hours – and although the Moineau woman had initially given every indication that her attendance was no more enjoyable than a trip to the dentist, within minutes she'd been mollified by the champagne and the gushing attention of both Otto Pinsel and his partner, Herbert von Karpfen. Pinsel, sporting one of his own creations – baggy black silk trousers cut six inches above the ankles and a décolleté white silk shirt, an ensemble that suggested a piratical waiter – proved to be a movie buff who could not only name every film in which Jeanne had ever appeared, but also their directors and supporting casts. He also won favour with enthusiastic fizzing over Jeanne's outfit, which, it transpired, had been created in Paris by one of his many youthful protégés. Karpfen was almost as enthusiastic, gushing that he admired *Three Nuts and a Bolt* so much, he was seriously thinking of 'transforming' it into an opera.

Werner, earwigging a few metres away as he endeavoured to maintain some semblance of a conversation in German with Kommis and Jane Oakheart – on her father's diplomatic efforts to 'liberate' the island – had spun round ecstatically when Jeanne, grabbing a bottle from Heidi's hands as she topped up glasses, squealed:

'Oh *là là*! I knew this wasn't cava – Spanish cat's piss! ... Champagne de *Jacques Selosse*! – le **Grand Cru Substance**! Werner, *chéri, quelle extravagance*! You spoil us! I thought only a few select *amateurs* around Reims and in Paris knew about this *très*, *très* exclusive producer.'

Helping to serve the vol-au-vents, Mike proffered a large and highly ornate silver-plated salver towards Jeanne. 'Yes,' he agreed, 'I was pretty impressed when I helped Werner bring up the bottles from the cellar this afternoon. If my memory serves me correctly, Selosse produce only about forty-seven thousand bottles a year, from just six hectares of vines.'

Kommis stared at Mike as if he'd just thrown off a cunning disguise. Then he moved forward and seized the bottle, just as Heidi was about to resume her waitering. 'I have never heard of it,' he sneered in English, while scowling at the label. 'We always drink Bollinger, do we not, Anna?'

Frau Kommis broke off her conversation with Lionel and smiled, but before she could respond, Jeanne said: 'Oh *you* would! *Every*one drinks Bollinger.'

'Well, they do produce almost two million bottles a year,' added Mike. 'A vol-au-vent, Herr Kommis?'

Werner tingled with joy. *Bravo, Mike! This is getting better by the minute!*

Glaring at her husband but stifling a giggle, Jane said: 'Mike is a mine of useless information, Manfred.'

Handing the bottle back to Heidi as if it was something that had been blocking the drains, Kommis retorted: '*Ja, Herr* Oakheart, but then they are some of the most *expensive* bottles in the world. The *Vieilles Vignes Françaises* brand I am buying for *my* special invitements costs over *three hundred euros* a *bottle*!'

Anna Kommis sighed audibly and looked deeply into Lionel's sympathetic eyes.

Smiling at Werner, Kommis asked: 'How much is this ... *stuff* costing?'

Anna groaned.

'*Quel crétin*!' cackled Jeanne as she lit up a Gauloise.

'I've absolutely no idea, Manfred,' Werner said triumphantly. 'In appreciation of a series of articles I wrote for *The New York Times* some years ago about my extensive travels in Jordan, His Majesty the late King Hussein most graciously sent me several cases of "this stuff".' He let the import of the remark sink in before adding: 'And now, *meine Damen und Herren*, if I may have your attention ...?'

And with this introduction, Werner began his speech of welcome.

Over the years it had become yet another Stumpf tradition on the occasion of a major reception at *C'an Pau* to present a labyrinthine masterpiece of puns and double entendres into which he managed to insert the surname of each and every one of his guests. This evening, as usual, his party piece was performed in German, with just the occasional sentence in English or French when he came to weave in the words 'oak', 'heart', and '*moineau*' (sparrow); Tourny had defeated him. The German guests found it all riotously amusing, including Professor Kommis. After almost thirty minutes, and by extraordinary feats of mental dexterity and allusions to music, fashion, medicine, the law, acting, flower arranging, and paperweight collecting – the latter two being Anna Kommis's presumed passions – Werner finally built up to an apparently serious conclusion. In so far as any of them could understand it – even the Germans were unsure whether he was still attempting to amuse – the hypothesis seemed to be that the three pre-eminent European nationalities – the Germans, French and British – who, for the last thousand years had dominated every field of human endeavour, and who, in consequence, had civilised the globe, were finally putting petty differences aside and working together in harmony – more musical allusions to flatter Karpfen – and, indeed, within the European Union's true spirit, in order to bring political, moral and military pressure to bear on the fractious, self-interested and back-stabbing Hispanic rabble in this outback of the continent who were maliciously undermining all the Triple Alliance's noble efforts to build a European Superpower – the Superpower of Superpowers that would finally put the American barbarians in their subservient place. True, the British had yet to rejoin the EU, but it was 'just a matter of time'.

Meanwhile, as Jane mercifully slipped away to help Heidi in the kitchen, and the sun began to set behind the shroud of dense cloud that had enveloped it all day, Mateu suspended his patrol of *C'an Pau*'s perimeter of stone walls. With his old shotgun hanging on a leather strap over one shoulder, he began lighting the hundreds of candles in accordance with his own very detailed schedule. Cursing with ever-filthier obscenities as the Teutonic laughter drifted through the trees, Mateu thanked God that he could go home for supper in another fifteen minutes or so: he was allowed a two-hour break, after which he was due to return for the 'night patrol'. How easy it had been to convince the *Caudillo* that no self-respecting Mallorcan terrorist would launch an attack between nine-thirty and eleven-thirty, when, because of the summer heat, the island's entire indigenous population would finally sit down for their evening meal, as had been the practice for as long as anyone could remember! But then, Stumpf was attracted to any suggestion that appeared wholly logical.

'I hope you didn't mind my few words of welcome being spoken mainly in German, Jeanne,' chirped Werner in French as he gallantly escorted the tipsy actress up the precipitous flight of steps to the Olive Terrace, 'but it's a tradition that I have–'

'*Pas de tout, chéri*. I thought it was so – so ... witty – as only you Germans know how to be.'

'*Merci beaucoup! Vous êtes si gentille.*'

'Tut, tut! "*Tu*", *chéri* – "*tu*"!'

A few paces behind, Otto Pinsel, who was escorting Jane, lamented: 'It does not matter what Herbert or me to that dragon of a housekeeper say – you probably see her when you came over for that concert the other evening – God, I hate cellos! – she will not the plastic stuff put – what do you call it again?'

'Clingfilm'

'*Ja*, she is not putting the clinging film on *anything* – *nada*. I go into the fridge and all the time there are the plates and bowls of food not covered. So, the chocolate cake is smelling of the onion, and the cold chicken is smelling of– *Ach*, it makes me so mad, Jane! These people are primitives! We might as well be in Africa – or even India!'

Struggling with the ascent – abetted by his notoriously minimalist style of conducting – an unfit Karpfen wheezed: 'Jesus, Mike, I am glad I bring a change of clothes in the car. I am sweating like a pig. It is as bad as when I conducted *Zauberflöte* in that hellhole Manaus on the goddam Amazon. You have heard of it?'

'Actually, it's on the Rio Negro, a few miles from its confluence with the Amazon. I spent some time there between school and university.'

'Working in a bar to earn some money, I suppose?'

'No, I was a volunteer on a UNESCO project – conservation of the rain forest. For several months, I paddled three German botanists around in a canoe up and down tributaries of the Amazon. Unfortunately, I never got to visit the *Teatro Amazonas*.'

Bringing up the rear, and without any indication of discomfort, were Anna Kommis and Lionel. 'Well, if *I* could go back in time,' said Anna in French, 'and be one of the *Normandie*'s celebrated passengers, I'd choose Marlene Dietrich.'

Lionel laughed. 'She was a lesbian.'

'I know.'

As if by magic, Heidi was already on the Olive Terrace, awaiting the other diners. She stood to attention beside the serving table that bore the great copper dishes warmed from below by methylated spirit burners. Only her husband and the Oakhearts had any comprehension of the Herculean efforts that had been involved in the production and transportation of the feast. In truth, the others gave the logistics no thought at all, but then to be fair, the sight of the colossal candelabra dominating Werner's truly theatrical set even managed to silence Jeanne for a few seconds. Then, exclamations in national tongues erupted. There were allusions to State Banquets, Versailles, and Mad King Ludwig of Bavaria and his fantastic Schloss Neuschwanstein. Just managing to keep a straight face, Otto said: 'I bet you can get satellite TV with them.'

Lionel said: 'This reminds me of a wild party at Ted Tickle's place in Las Vegas I went to a few months back. *You* know, Ted Tickle? – the twenty-nine-year-old computer genius? Well, he's just built this "ranch" out in the desert that's an exact reproduction of the Château de Chenonceau.'

Staring covetously at the candelabra, Kommis said: 'I am presuming these are new, Werner. I have not seen them before. They are *solid* silver, I presume? How much do they weigh?'

'"*New*", Manfred! *Mein Gott*, they have been in my family for several generations. In fact, they were a gift to my great-great grandfather from Kaiser Wilhelm I in 1875 after one of his visits to our estates in East Prussia – he often came to hunt, you know. But they disappeared during the ... er ... the War. And then last year, I tracked them down to the president's palace in Warsaw. It took quite a lot of tough negotiation, I can tell you – and even a threat of legal proceedings to get those thieving Polaks to give them back. As for the weight, Manfred, well, I'm not in the habit of weighing my silver.'

Heidi turned away and looked at the reflection of the sixteen flickering candles in the gleaming copper covers. They were polished to perfection, just like the generous gift to her husband's ancestors from 'the Kaiser'. She brushed the tears from her eyes, took a deep breath, and glanced at her watch: 9:33. Three minutes behind schedule! Time to start serving the vichyssoise.

Jane watched Heidi serve Anna and Jeanne, who each managed a cursory 'thank you' in their own languages before returning to their conversation. Then, unwittingly, Jane set a time bomb ticking. Tapping one of her wine glasses, she said: 'Look, everybody, it's been a very, very hot day. I know that Heidi's been toiling since early this morning to prepare this magnificent meal, so I think the least we can do is to help out by serving ourselves.'

'No sweat!' said Lionel. 'Come and sit down, Heidi.'

'*Absolument*!' cried Jeanne.

'Hear, hear!' agreed Mike. 'I just don't know where this wonderful woman gets all the energy.'

Momentarily, Werner and the other Germans – all of whom had dined regularly at the Stumpfs for many years – seemed to lose all understanding of English. Then Anna said: 'But of course! Oh, Heidi, *Liebling*, how thoughtless of us. Oh dear, oh dear. I feel terrible.'

Werner was about to tell Jane to keep her most unwelcome and revolutionary thoughts to herself, when he suddenly had another vision of the little boy in a sailor suit, hurling and kicking wooden bricks around his nursery. He inhaled deeply. '*Ja, ja*! Teamwork! English, French and Germans all together. Like I said in my little speech! And I shall be the sommelier!'

But offering to serve the wine was no concession at all, for Werner always did so at his dinner parties: it was only he who could impress the guests with seemingly knowledgeable comments about vintages and grape varieties.

*

'They're having champagne,' sneered Margalida as she served Mateu with another piece of chicken from the barbecue – one half of an old oil barrel standing lopsidedly on four welded iron rods just a few metres from the farmyard table. 'Champagne! Ha! Cava's not good enough for that load of posers. If you ask me, that there foreign muck tastes like cat's piss. Mind you, I've never been a great fan of fizzy wines – not even cava.'

'I know. Smashing chicken, *Mamá*!'

'Just how you like it, *chico*, with rosemary and garlic.'

'Yeah. Thanks.'

'In fact, all them wines he's serving tonight are foreign.'

'No! Really?'

'Oh yes. It's always the same when he has a posh do. Only French and German stuff are good enough. The French ones don't have any taste at all – thin as water – more cat's piss – both the red and the white. As for the German, well, talk about *sweet* – like alcoholic honey! One mouthful and you're gagging.'

'How would you know anyway?'

'How do you think? There's always half-empty bottles lying around the next day that have to be sealed up with that bloody vacuum pump thing he's got, not to mention all the glasses with dregs that I have to put in old jam jars for the *Esclava* to use in her sauces. Nothing gets thrown away in that house, I'll say that for them – well, *him*. They don't chuck out stuff like most of them Germans do. More money than bleeding sense.'

Then they talked about the political situation, and what they believed was the mounting pressure on Madrid from those European powers whose navies were now circling the island to make some significant movement down the road to granting independence. They were still debating who was really behind the killing of Jordi Adrover when Margalida began clearing the table.

'I bet that German, Haber-Whatsit, gets some rough treatment down in the cells of Palma police station tonight,' she said. 'Are you sure you don't want another piece of chicken, *chico*?'

'Couldn't eat another thing. ... Haber-*Bosch*, *Mamá*. Fancy him hiding out in that German *hotel rural* up around Arta! Mind you, I still don't think it was him and his Nazi friends who killed Adrover – they're a bunch of amateurs.'

'He looked as guilty as hell when I saw him on the eight o'clock news being dragged out of that hotel cellar. Big fat pink thing he was. Horrible – like one of them crappy German sausages.'

Mateu followed his mother into the kitchen. 'Let me do the washing up, *Mamá*. You've been slaving over a hot barbecue–'

'No, no! You get yourself down to the bar in Calonge and have a nice ice-cold beer or two with your mates.'

'You kidding? I'm on bleeding guard again at half-eleven – until the *Caudillo* relieves me at six – if he remembers, what with all the booze he'll be knocking back tonight. Mind you, I've never seen him pissed – *ever*.'

Margalida dropped the sponge in the bowl and turned to face her son. 'Guard duty! Like hell you are, *chico*. You're not spending the night out in the open trudging around *C'an* bloody *Pau*.'

'*Mamá*, we've been through all this–'

'Look, have ENABA ever attacked an *occupied* home?'

'No, but–'

'Have ENABA ever killed anyone – or even tried to?'

'No – well, Madrid says they might have assassinated Jordi–'

'Madrid my arse!'

'*Mamá*!'

'Whatever ENABA are, *chico*, they're not murderers. The *Caudillo* is bloody showing off as usual, telling his German fogies that he's got an armed guard! It's all for show. Everything's for show in that bloody house. So don't waste your time going back tonight.'

'He'll check up.'

'He *won't*! He's got a load of nobs to impress. He's not going to dump them to go traipsing around the boundaries of *C'an Pau* in the dark just to make sure you're carrying out the orders on your bloody schedule.'

'And what about at six tomorrow morning then – when he comes to relieve me?'

'He's not going to – you just said so yourself.'

Mateu looked at his watch and thought of his mates playing pool down in the bar. 'It's dishonest.'

'Don't talk daft! But if you're going to have some bloody guilt thing about it, set your alarm and nip down there just before six. He won't be none the wiser.'

*

Von Karpfen, who'd taken something of a shine to Mike following his revelations of adolescent globetrotting and an in-depth knowledge of the champagne industry, refilled his mouth with Heidi's delicious roast baby lamb in a red wine and shallot sauce, and continued chattering. 'As I was saying, Mike, Stockhausen's music is the essence of sublimity. His concept of serialism is quite amazing, don't you think? I mean, the way he deploys instrumentation, pitch register and intensity, melodic form, duration ... well, it all assumes an almost geometric level of organization, doesn't it?'

Mike stared at his plate as he cut another slice off his chunk of lamb, and wondered how Karpfen could ever have got it into his head that he had the slightest liking for Stockhausen's ghastly and unlistenable music. 'Hmm,' he managed, nodding.

'I conducted a performance of his *Gruppen* in Cologne Cathedral some years ago – three orchestras, no less! Well, my dear Mike, you can imagine the drama! Those fanfares and passages of varying speeds flung from one orchestra to another. Such an impression of movement in space!'

'*Wunderschön*!' enthused Werner from the head of the table as he juggled with several conversations simultaneously. 'I think I was at that concert,' he lied; he had heard of Stockhausen, but hadn't the slightest knowledge of his music. At the other end of the table, Heidi giggled into her wine glass; Karpfen shot her a withering glance.

'You don't like contemporary music then, Heidi?' he accused, still masticating his lamb; some sauce trickled down his chin. 'Like my little Otto here, I suppose you're more into' – he cringed – '"Elton John" and "Robbie Williams" – and the talentless "Taylor Swift"?' He pretended to vomit.

Heidi smiled sweetly. 'I certainly prefer them to Stockhausen. I like something with a bit of a tune in it – something you can sing, hum or whistle.'

Karpfen spluttered, desecrating the white linen tablecloth around him. '"A bit of a tune"!' he screeched. Werner laughed too as he broke off yet again from lecturing Jeanne on the secrets of olive-tree pruning and the superiority of German botanical science over local 'aboriginal lore'. '"A bit of a *tune*",' Karpfen repeated. 'Did you hear that, Mike?'

Mike looked up from his plate and smiled at Karpfen across the table. 'Well, to be honest, Herbert,' he said, 'I prefer music with a bit of a tune too.'

'Oh, was that a flash of lightning over there?' asked Anna Kommis in German to no one in particular.

Karpfen waved his fork at Mike like a baton. 'Ah, I *see*. You prefer somewhat more *conventional* twentieth-century composers – Messiaen, Shostakovich – the bleakness of his Fifth is breathtaking! – Bartok, Stravinsky, Poulenc?'

'No, I meant ... well, these days I seem to spend most of my time listening to Haydn – in the car, in the train–'

'He's Haydn bloody mad!' giggled Jane. 'Mike must have every CD–'

'Anna and I,' intoned Professor Kommis, helping himself to more lamb from the side table, 'always go to the New Year's Day concert in Vienna. The tickets are costing a *fortune* and are *so* difficult to get. Full of foreigners these days ... the audience. Once upon the time they are being Japanese. Now you cannot be moving for fat Chinamens and their ugly womens. All millionaire businessmen – criminals, of course – who couldn't make a distinguishment of a Strauss waltz from a ... from a ...' Words failed him; in truth, he'd been tone deaf all his life and hadn't the slightest interest in 'classical' music.

'I'd love to go the New Year's Day concert,' pined Otto dreamily, 'but my friend here says it's only for tourists and the common people. I think Herbert is just angry because they never ask him to conduct it.'

'Oh look!' chirped Anna. 'It *is* lightning. I am sure of it.'

'Yes,' said Lionel. 'I saw it too.'

'Pah! Far to the north!' snapped Werner, trying to laugh as he spotted Kommis's glare of abject loathing directed at Pinsel. 'Nothing to worry about, I assure you. I have spoken to the Meteorological Office in Madrid – this morning – *personally*.'

'"Personally"!' mimicked Jeanne, refilling her glass with red wine; it had been her own revolutionary suggestion that the bottles should be placed on the table in order to relieve the hosts of yet another task.

Karpfen was still shaking his head. He looked as though he'd been stabbed in the back. 'Haydn,' he muttered. '*Haydn!*'

'A great composer,' said Werner, misjudging the mood.

'Hah!' snorted Karpfen fixing Mike a stare. 'It has always amused me how the English like Haydn so much. They always have done – even when the old boy was alive. The *London* Symphony – the *Oxford* Symphony! Maybe there's a *Cambridge* Symphony too – one named after *every* English town. After all, he wrote so many – one a day, I think. Nothing too demanding, too revolutionary, or too dramatic. "Cosy", I think would be the word in English ... "quaint" maybe – a sort of musical country cottage with rambling roses around the door – music that doesn't tax the brain too much – music that doesn't cause any distress or discomfort. In brief, music that reassures, that pretends everything is all right with the world, that there is no unpleasantness anywhere. Haydn's music, my dear, *dear* Mike, is like wallpaper. Thus, it accords perfectly with your English cosy and quaint musical world – Gilbert and Sullivan, Elgar, Vaughan Williams, Britten – all so ... so *charming*, so–'

Jeanne began clucking like a hen about to lay half a dozen eggs simultaneously, into which she tried to weave some kind of theme. Werner stared at her open mouthed; Lionel burst out laughing.

In German, Kommis asked: 'Now what is that mad French tart doing?'

'*La Poule!*' chuckled Mike.

'Of course!' said Jane. '*Tum*-tee-tum-tee-tum-tee-tum-tee-*tum*-tee-tum–' Harmonising, Heidi joined in. '*Tum*-tee-tum-tee-tum-tee–'

'Spare us this mind-numbing idiocy!' groaned Karpfen, putting his hands over his ears.

'Heidi!' admonished her husband, leaning to one side to peer around the vast candelabra blocking his view.

After a few bars of musical clucking, the quartet broke off with shrieks of laughter.

'One of your best performances, *chérie*,' said Lionel, smiling impishly at Jeanne. 'I had no idea you liked Haydn – at least I assume that was Haydn, judging by Herbert's face and groans.'

'Symphony number eighty-three,' said Mike, 'in G minor.'

'*En sol mineur*,' added Jeanne grandly. 'Actually, I don't really know anything about Haydn except these *Symphonies Parisiennes*–'

'Numbers eight-two to eighty-seven,' said Mike.

'*Mein Gott*, he's like a computer,' Karpfen groaned, 'but then Haydn produced so much wallpaper, one probably needs a computer to keep track of it all.'

'Don't take no notice of my friend,' said Otto. 'He's a rude bitch – always has been.'

'*Any* notice, Otto,' Karpfen corrected.

'You sound like Werner,' said Heidi. 'I am feeling sorry for you, Otto.'

'I know all about *La Poule*,' Jeanne continued enthusiastically, 'because I was in a film made by Antenne Deux – the TV channel – called *La Poule Schizophrénique* – both Lionel and Jane exploded – 'which was all about these six symphonies that Haydn wrote for the most important orchestra in Paris at the time. It was just three or four years before the Revolution – the 1789 one – and–'

'You've had so many,' Karpfen sneered.

'– and Marie-Antoinette, who was Austrian, of course – I played her – loved one of the symphonies, er–'

'Number eighty-five,' said Mike, somewhat tipsy. 'Hence the nickname *La Reine*.'

'Oh, for God's sake, Mikey, stop bloody showing off!'

'*En si bémol majeur*, if you must know, Footy, my sweet.'

'*Ah, tu parles français très bien, chéri*,' Jeanne said, licking her lips. '*Alors*, in history, Haydn did not come to Paris to conduct the symphonies, but in the film he does, and Marie-Antoinette, who is a lesbian, *naturellement*, loves this *La Reine*, which includes a number of variations on the *air français*, *La Gentille et Jeune Lisette*, because at the time she is in love with this servant girl, Lisette, at Versailles. Haydn knows this, you see, so he is trying to get the favour. But to avoid a scandal, the King allows his wife to dress Lisette as a boy and pass him off as a Russian prince who can't speak any French. But Lisette is, in fact, not a lesbian but a girl from Provence whose family is noble but has fallen on bad times and so she came to Paris to make money. Now she sees how her class treat the workers, so she is planning to help the Republicans by working as a spy in the palace. Well, she goes to the Haydn concerts with Marie-Antoinette and hears the number eighty-three symphony, which has this strangely schizophrenic first movement with the rapid changes from the menacing first theme in the minor key, to the almost comical second theme with the oboe clucking away like a hen. Lisette, who sees Haydn as a man from a humble background toiling away for years for his aristocratic patrons, believes he is making a revolutionary statement. The first theme represents the oppressing aristocrats, and the second – *la poule* – the proletariat. Of course, at the end of the movement it is the second theme that triumphs over the first, and the hen reigns supreme.'

'So profound!' enthused Werner.

'What utter crap!' blasted Karpfen through his last mouthful of lamb.

'Why are French plots always so bizarre?' asked Mike.

'So, Lisette falls in love with Haydn,' Jeanne continued, 'and tries to win him over to her cause, but he thinks she is a boy, and is both disgusted by "his" advances and the suggestion that *La Poule* is a revolutionary work. Well, he is being a reactionary at heart and very happy with his aristocratic patrons back in Austria. So, he denounces Aliette to me – Marie Antoinette – and I have her thrown in the Bastille and tortured. She's locked in a cell with hundreds of chickens – hens and cocks–'

'Cocks!' shrieked Otto. 'At last, it gets interesting!'

'– which peck out her eyes and nipples and–'

'Jeanne!' shouted Lionel. '*Ça suffit*! Herbert's turning green.'

A few minutes later, after the diners had returned to less dramatic conversations with their immediate neighbours, a flash of lightning lit up the entire western sky and silenced everyone.

'I think we *are* going to have a storm, Werner,' said Anna. 'Perhaps we should start moving things indoors.'

Werner sighed: he was getting rather fed up with this merchant of doom and gloom. 'My dear Anna, I have told you that the people in Madrid have assured me–'

'Ha!' barked Jeanne. 'I've never known a Spanish weather forecast to be correct. I mean, how can one take seriously those people on TV when they only tell you the weather for *Spain*, with Portugal and France just shown as grey bits of land beyond the frontier? So much for your "United Europe", Werner, your *Mein Europa*! Spaniards! – *so* nationalistic! – *so* insular! You live in San Sebastian, yes? Tomorrow you want to go to Biarritz for the day – a forty-minute drive across a line on a map. Can you find out the weather from your Spanish TV? Like hell you can! Pathetic!'

'There will be *no* storm,' said Werner magisterially. 'And now, Heidi, you may clear away the plates and prepare for the next course.'

'We can *all* help,' said Jane, 'can't we, every–?'

'No! Heidi must–'

'I bet you a hundred euros, Werner,' said Lionel, 'that it will be raining within ten minutes.'

'This is not Las Vegas,' Werner snapped ambiguously.

But the first raindrops were detected on Karpfen's sensitive bald head even before Heidi had finished clearing away the plates.

*

Margalida had no more faith in the TV forecasters than Jeanne Moineau, for she'd lived on Mallorca long enough to know that the island made up its own mind when it came to weather. In any event, it could be pouring with rain up in the mountains far to the west, while the skies were cloudless over Santanyí. And when it got this hot and humid in July with the wind coming up from the south, you could almost guarantee there would be a *tormenta*. Which was why she'd been nervous all day, for the plans she'd made for the *Caudillo*'s party to be a truly spectacular occasion would come to nothing if the weather broke before eleven o'clock, when, in accordance with the sacred timetable, the *Esclava* would be serving the birthday cake – with its diplomatic ten candles. At that precise moment, the powerful bomb made by her ENABA colleagues in the South-East Division, and which she'd dutifully secreted in a large clump of plumbago just metres from the *Caudillo*'s chair, would explode and send him and all his vile foreign guests to kingdom come.

But now, barely ten minutes after she'd managed to get Mateu safely out of the way, she sat at the table in her airless yard wafting herself with an old battered fan watching the spectacular lightning illuminating the whole sky and detecting the first rumbles of thunder. Her fanning became frenetic as the dogs began to bark and pull on their chains.

'Shut up!' she cried. 'It's only bloody thunder. ... "*Only*"!' She shook her head. To fail in this mission was unthinkable. So much was hanging on it. If the party moved indoors, then she'd have no choice but to go down there and move the bomb too. But she knew the *Caudillo* like the back of her hand – well, she'd scrubbed and polished for the son of a bitch for more miserable years than she cared to remember – and there was no way he would budge one millimetre from that Birthday Schedule of his unless and until a *tormenta* was actually raging around him.

Perhaps she should creep down there now – not too close, of course – Ricart had said it would be a huge blast, but–

Madre de Dios! What if they had to make a dash for the house just before eleven? How could she get the bomb down to the terrace adjacent to the dining room without being seen, what with all those bleeding people moving about with chairs and silver and food and glasses and–?

Oh, but summer storms had threatened so often – lightning and thunder – flooding in Felanitx just a few kilometres away – roads washed away at Ca's Concos – but not a drop of rain at Alqueria Blanca. And then the centre of the *tormenta* would move off northwards, or out to sea, and the summer would continue, scorching and rainless until the real storm season began in the autumn.

The fan fell from Margalida's hand as a drop of water plopped into the cracked tumbler of her cousin's *rosat*.

*

Mateu, with his crash helmet over the handlebars, had almost reached the end of the *camino* and its junction with the main highway, when his scooter died. For some minutes, he tried everything he could think of to restart it, and then resorted to shouting obscenities and a few well-aimed kicks. Consequently, he took little notice of the gathering storm until the rain started. It took him some fifteen minutes to push his thoroughly cursed machine back home, by which time the rain was torrential and the dogs had retreated to the relative protection of the former pigsty. To his surprise, the door to the house was locked and the lights were off.

'*Mamá*! ... *Mamá*! ... Where the hell is she? ... *Mamá*!' Perhaps she'd decided to have an early night. But upstairs, her room was empty, and he began to panic. He was soaking and needed to change into some dry clothes, but all he could think about was his mother. Where could she be? Why should she go out in a storm?

Back downstairs, he scanned every room for clues. Her old bag was on the kitchen table, her purse was in it, and–

'The Stumpfs, you stupid bastard!' he hissed. 'She'll have gone down to *C'an Pau*, the old hypocrite!' She never stopped whingeing about them, day after day, week after week – for bloody years, but she had a heart of gold, of course, as only he knew – and as soon as the *tormenta* broke she'd have rushed down there to help out and move all that sodding clobber indoors. 'Christ, she'll be getting soaked!'

He was fetching a lightweight waterproof jacket, when he realised that, by now, Stumpf might well have discovered his dereliction of duty by skiving off down to Calonge. Maybe he'd got so mad shouting himself hoarse while trying to attract his attention that he'd smelt a rat and come storming up here to interrogate *Mamá*. He'd have spotted the gun by the door and blown his top. She'd have taken the blame, and in order to butter him up, would have volunteered to go back with him and help in the removal job from the Olive Terrace.

'I'd better get down there and put in an appearance,' he muttered, grabbing his shotgun. Water was now trickling under the front door, just as it had always done for as long as anyone could remember whenever there was heavy rain and a southerly wind. 'Shit! I must get that fixed.'

*

In *C'an Pau*'s dining room, Werner was once more seated at the head of a table. With his lips placed firmly together, he was trying very hard to maintain a smile. He'd said little for some minutes, making a pretence of listening to the buzz of conversation going on around him. But within him, a firestorm of anger burned. All his meticulous planning had come to nought. Moreover, he'd been made to look a fool over the meteorological predictions and his blind faith in them. And yet, in a sense he knew that he should feel jubilant, for a potentially disastrous situation had, in fact, been transformed by the most extraordinary teamwork on the part of his disparate guests. Indeed, they'd regarded the whole escapade of transferring the venue of the birthday festivities as some kind of party game – like musical chairs! In less than fifteen minutes, and before the deluge began in earnest, they were comfortably ensconced here in the dining room – albeit soaked in perspiration – as though the Olive Terrace had never existed. It had been a most pertinent example of what the Triple Alliance could achieve. However, he – Werner Stumpf, the Great Organiser – had been humiliated.

Oh, would he ever be able to live with the shame of Heidi taking charge when his own nerve momentarily failed him? Well, it never rained in July – hardly ever. So, it hadn't been catered for in the Schedule – nothing unreasonable about that – and if only Heidi and the others had just given him a few minutes to think, well, he would have got teams organised – the *right* people for the *right* jobs – and certainly not that tick Kommis and his thick wife carrying the candelabra down to the house! *Scheisse*! He was bound to have spotted the maker's marks; he certainly looked hard enough, the bastard!

For Christ's sake, Werner, old boy, get a grip! Look! Everyone's enjoying themselves. This is living proof of the underlying wisdom of Mein Europa. *English, French and Germans getting on famously – stimulating highbrow conversations over the dinner table, the sort of conversations one dreams about, that one prays for when one selects one's guests and arranges the seating plans – indeed, the sort of conversations one reads about in books, sees in films and on the stage.*

Take Karpfen and Oakheart – and what a pleasant surprise he's turned out to be! – still rabbiting on about bloody Haydn and his influence on the modern symphony, or whatever. You know, I've always suspected that the English have long had a penchant for pretending to be thick, especially on the arts side of things. Which reminds me – I'll have to get some CDs of this Stockhausen fellow so that the next time I see Karpfen, I can make just the right impression.

And just listen to Moineau and timid little Anna! They're getting on like a house on fire with all this lesbo talk about Marie-Antoinette. The things one learns! I'll have to borrow that DVD of La Poule Schizophrénique *that Moineau's promised to send her. Typical French, of course – sexual perversions masquerading as incomprehensible pseudo-intellectual crap, but I suppose one gets to see Moineau starkers and doing God only knows what with this Aliette character. I bet they're both lesbians – Jeanne and Anna. ... So, what does that make Lionel?*

Talk of the devil! There's the pièce de résistance, Kommis and the French lad – chatting! – in English! – about ships! Manfred really is a scheming bastard. All these years he's never let on to me about this 'passion'. Oh, we know all about his yacht – and the speedboat, and how much they cost, and how fast they go, and the speedboat's horsepower. But an encyclopaedic knowledge of transatlantic liners? Why did he keep that quiet? What's his game? Normandie *this,* Normandie *that. ... Turbo-electric engines? Now he's trying to blind the boy with science ... the formula for calculating a ship's gross tonnage? What an actor – better than Tourny! Christ, if Anna's a lesbo – as we've always suspected – maybe Manfred's queer too. All that scorn directed at Karpfen and his little seamstress over the years, well, I always thought it was a case of 'The lady doth protest too much, me thinks.' And now he's chatting up Tourny! Oh, what's he saying? Do Otto and Heidi have to shriek like that? Hell! Lionel's correcting the old fag's gross tonnage equation! He'll burst a blood vessel. He'll–*

He's laughing! – giving the boy a playful punch on the shoulder! Oh, I don't believe this! It's my sodding birthday and no one's taking a blind bit of notice of **me**. *Everything was so much better up on the Olive Terrace.*

No! Stop sulking! Get a grip! Say something witty! Impress them with another story about a VIP interview – that one with the King of Saudi when he–

Shit! If I hear those two halfwits giggle again–

'Heidi!' roared Werner. 'I think everyone has had enough cheese and salad.' He tapped pointedly at his watch. 'Perhaps you might like to consider procuring our humble offering of pudding while I serve the next wine, hmm? – if it's not *too* much trouble? Now, I think you're all going to enjoy my *eiswein*. It's–'

Heidi shot up from her seat, bellowing, '*Jawohl, mein Führer*!'. As she goose-stepped away, Otto squealed hysterically; Werner's eyes burned into her back.

'While you're up, *Liebling*,' Otto yelled, 'put some music on. It's like a bloody university debating society in here. Anything'll do – except Haydn or sodding what's-his-name.'

Heidi was passing the grand piano in the adjoining living room and making for the almost life-expired mid-nineties music centre, when Karpfen, raising his voice, said: 'Perhaps Heidi could play us a "tune" on the piano-forte.' Then he giggled, adding: 'Oops! Silly me! I almost forgot that no one at *C'an Pau* can actually play that giant dust collector.'

'I wouldn't be too sure about that,' said Jane under her breath, as Heidi sat down at the piano and raised the lid. There was a tremendous flash of lightning, followed immediately by a deafening roar of thunder.

Incandescent, Werner hovered over his monumental silver-plated ice bucket; he'd completely lost his thread about the intensely luscious Austrian *eiswein* and its individually selected grapes, complete with 'noble rot'.

'What about *Raindrops Keep Falling On My Head*?' suggested Otto.

'No, no, no!' shouted Karpfen across the room. '*The Thunder and Lightning Polka* – by Strauss. He wrote a few "good tunes" – or so people say, eh, Mike?'

Werner roared: 'Heidi, I'm afraid, 'does *not* play–!'

And then the *tormenta* received some powerful competition as Heidi's nimble fingers flew across the keyboard.

*

In the pelting rain, secreted in the lush undergrowth which Stumpf had created from a barren, rocky hillside over many years, and now nurtured by his computer-designed irrigation system and home-produced fertiliser, Margalida had to admit to herself that the evacuation from the Olive Terrace had been an impressive exercise – albeit a pointless one. Confident that everyone was finally indoors, she crept out of her hiding place and, with less than twenty minutes before it was due to explode, began searching for the bomb in the mass of plumbago with its profusion of blue flowers. With all the candles having been extinguished, she had to await the flashes of lightning to illuminate her search, but just as she located the device, sounds of movement through the dense shrubbery some metres away made her instinctively throw herself flat on the wet ground. And then, with more bolts of lightning, she saw several legs clad in camouflage fatigues and muddy black boots.

After a few seconds, she heard the boots reach the hard stone of the Olive Terrace. She crawled slowly to the edge of the plumbago and peered out. Six men, each one armed with an automatic weapon of some kind, were looking down towards the house. Then one of them indicated with his arms as if the group should fan out. Was it possible that, in view of the 'crisis', Tourny – or one of the German guests – had hired a private army? Well, whatever the truth, judging by their kit and discipline, they certainly weren't locals! Which meant, on reflection, that they couldn't be ENABA reinforcements either.

Unfortunately, only five of the men moved off, with one remaining as if to guard their rear. Clearly, her chances now of getting to the house unobserved were remote, especially as the terraces were all lit up like Christmas trees. In any event, there just wasn't enough time to get the bomb down to the house now; she'd have to make a circuitous route just to avoid this one sentry. On the other hand, if she left the bomb where it was, it would be obvious to everyone that, but for the *tormenta*, Werner and his cronies would have been blown to smithereens, and the international outrage, particularly in Germany, would be almost as vitriolic as if they'd actually been killed.

So, during a mighty boom of thunder to mask any sound of her movements, Margalida crawled back into the soaking plumbago and made her way in the opposite direction, down the steep rocky slope to the swimming pool. From there, she'd be able to slip into the pinewoods and make for home. But as she crept closer to the pool house, the lightning picked out several figures moving along the path that led up from the olive groves. *Déu meu*! How many guards were there? Panicking, she dived into the changing room. Within seconds, they filed silently past the open but shuttered window, casting shadows on the slats.

Minutes passed. Gingerly, she opened the door and looked out. Nothing. The pool lights, which had meant to impress the diners up on the Olive Terrace, were still burning. Just as she peered at her watch – it was a few minutes before eleven – there was a shout from the direction of the house. Two shots followed in quick succession. What on earth could be happing? Then there was a cry of '*Mamá*!' and she was running as fast as she could.

As Margalida pounded up the steps that led into the magically illuminated courtyard, her eyes focused on the wrought iron table: it still bore several gleaming silver-plated ice buckets; underneath, her son was lying on his stomach, frantically reloading his shotgun.

'Get him!' roared someone in German.

'Fire!' yelled a French voice.

'Mateu!' screamed Margalida.

CHAPTER 20

Out of the corner of his eye, Mike spotted Heidi enter the adjoining living room; she was carrying a large cake with some burning candles. He broke off from his recitation to von Karpfen of Haydn's numerous admirers, including Mozart, Beethoven and Wagner, and burst into song with 'Happy Birthday to you'. With alcohol induced gusto, the other guests followed in German, English and French; Werner continued to maintain the fixed grin that he'd adopted five minutes earlier when rapturous applause had greeted his wife's accomplished performance of *The Flight of The Bumblebee*, *The Minute Waltz* and a Scott Joplin rag in rapid succession. In fact, in his burning fury he was convinced that the singing, which competed with the sound of the electrical storm and torrential rain so visible through the open French windows, was, in reality, an anthem for Heidi's benefit – *Hail The Conquering Hero*. And as she approached, singing more vociferously than any of them – or so it seemed to him – and with such a smug expression on her face, his eyes focused on the ten non-committal candles. Immediately, he experienced a terrifying vision of The Dinner Parties To Come: the 'star' would be humble Heidi, being begged to tinkle the ivories; flattering admirers armed with cognacs and coffees would encircle her at the grand piano, showering her with praise after a performance of another one of her showy little numbers. Jesus! – in due course, she might even move on to the heavy stuff – Beethoven sonatas and–

'– Happy Birthday, dear *Wer* ... ***ner***–'

As Heidi lowered the cake onto the table with great ceremony, Werner and his guests could finally see the spontaneous addition to the decoration which she'd just made in her claustrophobic kitchen – the kitchen Werner had been promising to have extended ever since she'd first set foot in *C'an Pau*, a project which, however, always ended up at the bottom of his annual Priority Improvements Schedule.

Several voices faltered.

Otto Pinsel screamed girlishly.

'Oh my God!' gasped Jane.

Almost in a whisper, Mike just managed to sing, 'Happy Birthday ... to ... *you*.'

Crudely arranged on the cake's pink icing was the figure '60', crafted with plump fresh strawberries.

As Werner began to hyperventilate and emit odd gurgling noises, Jane said brightly: 'Good grief! This must be a joke! You can't be sixty, Werner! Impossible! Not with your fantastic skin and muscular body!' Otto and Herbert shrieked mockingly. 'Not with your – your ... your *gorgeous* hair!' she added. More shrieking from the Karpfen-Pinsels. 'To be honest, we thought you weren't a day over fifty-five – at *most*, didn't we, Mikey? ... *Mikey*!'

But before Mike could respond, a strange cry came through the French windows, followed almost immediately by the unmistakable reports of a double-barrelled shotgun.

Otto screamed; Jeanne raised her glass with a bark of '*Vive la révolution*!'

'*Was ist dass*, Werner?' demanded Kommis.

Werner's and Heidi's eyes finally met, the mutual loathing replaced by fear; they seemed to read each other's thoughts.

'Mateu!' shrieked Heidi, the colour draining from her face.

Werner bolted from the table, yelling in German, 'Get my gun, Heidi!' As he began running towards the French windows, more shouts could be heard somewhere in the garden. Then there was a tremendous burst of light followed by a deafening roar and a blast of hot air. Everything and everyone in the room was in motion, as if *C'an Pau* had been picked up by a giant and shaken. And as the screaming continued, bursts of automatic gunfire opened up.

*

All electric power had been lost – whether as a result of the storm or the ENABA guerrillas who were presumed to be attacking the house was still a matter for speculation – and so, the pair of gaudy candelabra now provided the only illumination in the beleaguered L-shaped dining-cum-sitting room. As stray bullets and their associated shrapnel-like debris ricocheted above them, the hosts and their guests were huddled under the long table, the floor-length cloth creating the impression of being inside a tent – a very hot and humid tent. At one end, Werner was holding court with the Kommises and the Karpfen-Pinsels. They all sounded hysterical: despite posting an armed guard, a violent attack by ENABA had not been catered for in the Birthday Schedule – and certainly not one by what sounded like an entire battalion of the 'foul aboriginal militants'. Manfred Kommis was accusatorial; he'd already made nasty references to 'occupiers' liability' and his high-powered lawyers with offices across three continents, who would most certainly be instructed if he or, for that matter, Anna, left the house with a single scratch – not to mention his brand-new Mercedes coupé parked out in the *camino*.

Meanwhile, at the other end of the table, Heidi, the Oakhearts, Lionel and Jeanne had almost convinced themselves, above all, Lionel – 'I'm too young to die!' he'd initially wailed incessantly – that no one would be hurt, least of all Mateu: as a fellow Mallorcan, he was probably being held captive until the 'fireworks' – as Jane called them – were over.

'He's probably in on the whole thing,' Jeanne sneered. '*Franchement*, I never trusted him – never, the little piece of *merde*, with his constant lecherous grin and filthy suggestions. We'll never see him again. He'll be living in a cave up in the mountains for years to come, bearded – like Bin Laden.'

'You are a crazy woman,' Heidi said coolly. 'Mateu is a good boy.'

'We'll see,' Jeanne replied, offering her the bottle of red Rioja that she'd grabbed from the table just before descending to the floor for cover.

After they'd all taken a swig, Mike said: 'Oh dear, I've finished it. Do you think we should have offered it to the others?'

'No,' said Heidi.

'I'll get another,' Jeanne said.

'No, Jeanne, don't–!' But before Mike could grab her, she'd scuttled under the tablecloth.

'Oh shit,' Lionel moaned. 'I'm not going after her, not with all that flying glass and stuff. I've got a screen test in Los Angeles in a few days – with Pine Stein. I can't risk any facial scars.'

Mike shook his head. 'My God, you're pathetic! Well, I'll go then.'

'Mikey – *no*–!'

'*Voilà*!' crowed Jeanne as she scrambled back with her fresh supplies, narrowly missing a head-on collision with her would-be protector.

Meanwhile, seemingly oblivious to the multinationals' antics, Werner's camp continued to bicker, with Karpfen lecturing everyone on the phenomenal loss of earnings he'd suffer if his conducting arm were to be injured.

'*Je suis désolée*,' Jeanne sighed, 'but I could only find this *merde*.' In each hand she held a bottle of *eiswein*.

'Oh, I love that,' said Heidi, 'but you have to have it with the cake.'

Despite the Oakhearts' strictures, now the hostess disappeared into the battle zone. Then, after a brief debate, Jane and Mike followed her.

'Did you see the candelabra?' asked Jane when the foragers were safely back under the table with both the cake and dessert plates, '– the one at Werner's end of the table? Something seems to have hit it. One of the branches has completely snapped off.'

'Shall I pass these around?' asked Mike.

'Oh, that would be kind,' Heidi chirped.

'I'm so sorry,' said Jane, tutting, 'but I think I only grabbed nine cake forks.'

'That's all right,' said Mike. 'I'll use my fingers.'

'No, no,' Heidi protested, 'I will.'

'Jesus Christ!' groaned Lionel. 'What the fuck's wrong with you people? Here we are, trapped in this hellhole – maybe with only minutes to live – and you geeks are arguing over who's gonna eat the fucking cake with their fingers!'

'Steady on,' said Mike. 'Don't frighten the ladies with that kind of talk.'

'Screw you!'

'Charming!'

'Shut up and drink this,' ordered Jeanne. 'It's disgusting – so sweet – but has quite a kick.'

'There is much alcohol in the *eiswein*,' said Heidi, nodding. 'And I tell you, Lionel, that ENABA do not kill *people*. If they had wanted to kill us, they could have just walked into the dining room and shot us all, yes? They are just shooting the house to make a mess. And the big bang we heard at the beginning was a firework, I think – like the very big ones they have in Palma on the fiesta of San Sebastian.'

'Some firework!' scoffed Lionel.

'Cake, Anna?' asked Mike as he crawled down towards the other end. 'Cake, Manfred?'

Kommis slammed his mobile on the marble floor and the back fell off. 'The Consul is not answering!' he screeched in German. 'What do I pay all these taxes for? I'll make sure he is back in Berlin making coffee–!'

'Where are you getting this cake?' spluttered Werner, his eyes bulging, '– and the wine?'

'I'll give you three guesses,' said Mike.

'But – but – *but*–!'

'So brave–' Anna began.

'*Ach so!*' barked her husband. 'You see, Stumpf! If Oakheart here has the guts to go and fetch *cake* ... and *plates* ... and *wine*! ... well, it is quite clear that it is more than safe for *you* to go and telephone the authorities, and, moreover, to fetch the gun you have always made such a song and dance about. By all accounts, you kill enough rabbits, although I have always suspected that your treacherous gardener – your *part-time* gardener – shot them for you. These miserable little Spanish bastards are cowards, you mark my words. They always have been cowards, the Spanish. The least sign of trouble and they run screaming like frightened women and children – just like Franco and his bunch of bullies during the War. All that help we gave him to get rid of the communists, and as soon as *we* needed help, suddenly they're bloody neutral!

'Well, Stumpf, you got us all into this mess, thanks to your peasant Mateu – or whatever he's called – failing in his duties – or worse – leading these terrorists here – and don't forget, as far as I'm concerned, you, as his employer, are vicariously liable for his – his ... his *crimes* – so you can bloody well get us out of it. I demand that you go and get your damned gun this instant, and give these ignorant thugs a taste of their own medicine. Believe you me, they'll be out of here with their tails between their legs before you can–'

'Shut up, you stupid little man!' screamed Anna, slapping her husband fiercely across the face.

'Bravo!' shouted Jeanne. 'Encore!'

'That does it!' roared Werner. 'I'll get my gun all right, and show *you* – you nouveau riche dwarf – *all* of you – how a Prussian gentleman behaves.'

Still proffering the plate of birthday cake, Mike said: 'Come on, Werner, don't do anything rash. I'm sure no one doubts your honour. Heidi's absolutely right, as usual. If these ENABA nutters meant us any real harm, they could have stormed the house ages ago and bumped off the lot of us. It's just a stunt – a frightener. Give them a few more minutes and they'll probably knock off and toddle back to their farms.'

Above their heads, a bullet whizzed across the room, hit something hard and metallic, and a mighty thud resounded on the tabletop.

'Oh *là, là*!' giggled Jeanne. 'I think that was another piece of the Kaiser's candelabra.'

'Oh yes,' sneered Kommis, who was still in shock and rubbing his cheek, 'the silver-*plated* candelabras made by WMF – the Württembergische Metallwarenfabrik. I saw the marks when I helped carry the bloody monstrosities back from the Eagle's Nest. "Prussian gentleman",' he sniggered, '– Prussian gentleman, my arse! I've heard some pretty rum rumours about, you, Stumpf–'

Anna slapped him across the face again. 'Maybe they'd like to know about the Bangkok police arresting you for gross indecency with little boys, Manfred, and how you bribed your way–'

Kommis lunged towards his wife, but Pinsel grabbed him, shouting in a remarkably deep and loud voice, 'Oh no you don't, you two-faced bastard.'

'This is the best party I've been to in *years*!' rasped Jeanne, beaming. She took another swig of the *eiswein*. 'Anyone want a cigarette? You know, I blame the Americans for all this. Turn on the local TV and what do you get all day long – apart from football and bullfighting, that is? ... American *merde* – dubbed films, dubbed soaps, dubbed documentaries courtesy of *National Geographic* and the like – all peddling the Anglo-Saxon diseases of greed and self-interest. To hell with anything and everything that doesn't make a profit – worse! – anything that doesn't make a fifteen per cent return on your investment within three years. So, *no* public transport, *no*–'

'Shut the fuck up, Jeanne!' snapped Lionel.

'– *no* public health service, *no* subsidised theatre or ballet or opera – or films – that poor people can afford to see, just–'

'Werner!' cried Heidi, but before she could disentangle herself, he'd dashed out and was zigzagging across the room in the direction of the hall. As he flew past the grand piano, a bullet hit it and splinters flew in all directions. He yelped, stumbled – Heidi screamed – and fell to the floor. Then he rubbed his left cheek, and, at the sight of the blood on his hand, promptly fainted.

Without hesitation, Heidi and the Oakhearts scrambled over and dragged him back to the relative safety under the table, where Jeanne insisted on bathing his superficial cuts with what was left of the sticky *eiswein*, while Lionel pointed out that they were precisely the sort of injuries he himself had anticipated. A few minutes later, Werner was not only conscious, but also savouring the attention and universal praise for his heroism – universal, that is, with the exception of Kommis, who was now the only occupant of the former German enclave. He sat there, head bowed, with his little legs pulled up to his chin, sobbing and muttering to himself.

*

'It's gone awfully quiet,' Jane whispered. 'Even the storm seems to be moving away.'

'Oh yes,' Mike murmured. 'Maybe the *Guardia Civil* have arrived.'

'Pah!' Werner snorted. 'That would be typical. They usually turn up when all the trouble is over.'

'Or maybe the guerrillas are moving in for the kill,' Jeanne rasped, '– after they have raped us all!' Then she exploded with hysterical laughter.

'*Salope!*' hissed Lionel.

After the reprimands had died down, Mike said: 'I think we ought to pop out for a recky and see how the land lies. It's a pretty dead cert that those bastards have all pissed off. I bet your garden's a bit of a mess though, Werner.'

Werner groaned.

'Well, you can count me out,' said Lionel.

'*Quelle surprise!*'

'You really are a selfish git, aren't you?'

Lionel stared at Jane, like a little boy ordered to bed without any supper by his beloved mother. 'You don't understand, Jane. My face is insured for millions, and–'

'Well, I'm going out to investigate,' Mike snapped, pushing up the tablecloth; a branch of one of the mighty candelabra lay just inches away, amidst a mass of broken glass and porcelain. 'Anyone coming?' he asked, crawling out gingerly. 'For all we know, Mateu could be lying out there – dying.'

Heidi gasped; Jeanne sniggered.

'I *would*,' said Werner making a show of trying to sit up, 'but I still feel rather ... dizzy.'

Karpfen waved his conducting arm and smiled wanly.

Otto said: 'Well, if they are not here already, I am sure the TV people will arrive very soon. They can't possibly see me like this – not the fashion guru of all Germany. ... Do not stare at me like that, everyone. I mean, *look* at me! I have to clean myself. This is being my priority!'

'I'll come with you, Mike,' said Anna.

'Me too,' said Jane.

Just as Heidi started to disentangle herself from her recumbent husband, several figures threw themselves through the French windows and darted in all directions around the room. Jeanne's cry of '*Viva la revolución*!' soared over the hysterical screams as one of the presumed terrorists rushed the table brandishing a weapon that looked more than capable of destroying a tank. Then Jane grabbed the inebriated actress and pushed a hand over her mouth.

The revolutionary certainly looked as lethal and unpredictable as a loose cannon. With a blacked-up face and combat fatigues, he stood with his legs wide apart, his murderous weapon panning the terrified faces of the group huddled under the table. Behind him, his colleagues approached in a wide arc. Slowly, a disconcerting smile appeared on his face, revealing an expanse of perfect teeth that appeared quite dazzling against his camouflaged skin in the flickering light cast by what remained of the candelabra.

'One of you guys better be this Lee-o-nel dee Turn-ee,' he drawled in a Texan accent, 'or the President's gonna bust my ass!'

CHAPTER 21

Wave after wave of helicopters were flying in reinforcements from the *Herbert Hoover* to set up cordons sanitaires around both *C'an Pau* and the *Villa Tourny*, where, due to the vast expanse of lawns, the landing site had been set up. Hum-Vees, brought in by huge transport choppers, were ferrying men and materials over to *C'an Pau*; the Americans seemed disinclined to walk over or commandeer Lionel's old Citroën – or, for that matter, Werner's Renault or Kommis's Mercedes, albeit the latter had lost all its windows.

For their own security, the Stumpfs and their invited guests had been confined to the house, but then none of them wanted to witness the aftermath of the bloodbath. Their initial barrage of questions had been almost ignored by the tight-lipped soldiers, but as the excessively thorough medical examinations got underway, they finally learned from a young and talkative paramedic from South Dakota that the British were in the process of 'liberating' the island. He also admitted that he and his colleagues had parachuted in to protect Tourny from a terrorist plot to assassinate him. To their consternation, however, the *Villa Tourny* had been deserted. Then all hell had broken loose nearby with what sounded like a bomb and sporadic gunfire. Assuming a terrorist attack on a neighbouring property, they'd dashed over – even without waiting for orders. Well, whoever's house it was, they couldn't just sit on the sidelines! And maybe Lionel had come round for some chow. And how right they'd been!

'Clearly, the terrorists must have known all about your party, Mr Stump, sir, and that Mr de Tourny was the star guest.' He shook his head. 'Your security personnel, Mr Stump, sir,' he continued solemnly, 'must have put up one hell of a fight. It's a goddam shame none of them appear to have survived. The young guy we found out in the courtyard, there by that table, was full of holes. All he had was some rusty ol' shotgun. You ought to invest in some new hardware, sir, if you don't mind me saying.'

With the exception of Professor Kommis, who sat alone in a corner, everyone thought of lone Mateu and shed a tear; Heidi sobbed. Eventually, Kommis, the Oakhearts and the Karpfen-Pinsels fell asleep in camp beds set up in Werner's study; it was one of the few rooms which had not been affected by broken windows and flying glass. Anna and Jeanne, however, remained on a high, reliving the excitement and drama, marvelling at their cool, and vilifying their respective male partners. Heidi retreated to the kitchen, making endless pots of coffee and baking fresh bread for the remarkably good-looking American forces.

Meanwhile in the entrance hall, the Americans set up what they called 'a Central Administration Module', where identification badges – complete with photographs – were produced for all the civilians, and where, in the early hours, after a direct call to the President himself, a paranoid Lionel was finally persuaded to abandon his demand to be flown out to the *Herbert Hoover* immediately: the terrorists could still be in the vicinity, armed with air-to-ground heat-seeking missiles. So, his camp bed was put in a windowless storeroom, with two armed sentries outside the door.

Throughout the night, Werner wandered in a daze through his house, clipboard in hand, noting every item of damage, and trying to keep a watchful eye on the occupying forces: convinced that the Americans would be unable to distinguish solid silver from silver plate, he assumed they'd be pocketing every piece of shiny metal they could get their thieving hands on. He also fretted about the cost of the clean-up and the many extra hours Margalida would have to work – well, provided she hadn't been killed herself. After all, it was highly likely that on hearing the commotion, she would have dashed down from *C'an Xet* to check on Mateu, and then been caught in the crossfire. Otherwise, she'd surely have been wailing out in the garden somewhere, and the Americans would have found her. If she hadn't been such a mean, stubborn old misery who'd always rejected the need for a telephone, he could have tried to call her, if, that is, the phone lines had been working. At least Mateu had rebelled a year ago and got his own mobile.

But as Werner fought against exhaustion, a puzzle kept returning to haunt him: why in God's name would ENABA have gone to such extraordinarily violent lengths to kill a Franco-American Hollywood matinée idol? And why choose *Ca'n Pau* for the place of execution? They could have bumped off the little runt at the *Villa Tourny* much more easily – or when he terrified the neighbourhood on his damned motorcycle. It made no sense at all. And, furthermore, how would ENABA have known that Tourny would be attending his birthday party?

At first light, and having ascertained that all the corpses – none of them apparently female – had been removed and deposited in his pool house, where even a mobile refrigeration unit had been installed, Werner finally plucked up the courage to survey the devastation to his garden. Initially, the sentries posted at his front door refused to let him out, even after he agreed to wear the identification badge issued to him. The officer in command was summoned and talked about snipers and live ammunition, but Werner cut him short.

'This is my damned house and I'll do whatever I bloody want. Technically, you're all trespassers, and if you hold me here against my will, you'll also be guilty of unlawful imprisonment. I'll have you know that the daughter and son-in-law of Sir Douglas Trench-Foot – the British Ambassador – are upstairs–'

'I know.'

'– and that they're two of the finest lawyers in Europe – lawyers who have already sued some of the Continent's biggest names on my behalf and earned me some very handsome damages.'

Within minutes, Werner was signing a disclaimer hastily drafted by a paralegal in the Central Administration Module absolving the United States of any and all liability in the event that anything untoward should happen to him outside.

By the time Werner reached the Olive Terrace, his voice was hoarse from ordering gum-chewing U.S. servicemen – and a few formidable yet sexy women – not to trample on what was left of his exotic and expensive botanical specimens as they combed the ground for abandoned 'terrorist weaponry'. Where the first two courses of last night's dinner had been consumed, there was now an enormous crater; apart from a shattered stump, the olive tree had disappeared. He slumped to the ground and wept: it would take a small fortune to reinstate his belvedere. But then, suddenly stunned by his staggering sang-froid, he realised how close he himself had come to being blown to smithereens. This had been no attempt to assassinate an adolescent ham actor, but a carefully planned conspiracy to kill one of Germany's greatest contemporary literary figures!

When Werner finally managed to regain his composure, he decided to pay his last respects to Mateu, who, despite his ignorance and unwillingness to learn, had been a pretty hard worker. There was no one on guard at the pool house, and, after taking a deep breath, he plucked up enough courage to enter. Shivering, he surveyed thirteen corpses laid out on the floor, all packaged in U.S. body bags. Not for the first time, he marvelled at the Americans' extraordinary efficiency, and, as he did so, the thought occurred to him whether, in view of their 'taking-out' of the ENABA assassins, and, therefore, of having fired a considerable quantity of ammunition, a claim for compensation could be made against the Americans for some – or even all – of the damage to his house and grounds. Indeed, it stood to reason that they must have known about ENABA's dastardly plan for some time – if only to get the *Hoover* and their forces into the vicinity. In consequence, was there not a powerful prima facie case for arguing that they'd been grossly negligent in not warning both Lionel and himself – a neighbour within spitting distance – of the imminent threat? And what about the paramedic's admission that protecting Tourny had been their mission's sole purpose?

While these thoughts occupied him, Werner went down the line looking for Mateu, unzipping each bag and peering in disgust at the gruesome remains of the degenerate filth who'd come so close to killing himself and destroying the fruits of so many years of hard labour. Finally, he came to the thirteenth corpse, which he now noticed had been placed a little distance from the others – a symbolic gesture by the Americans, no doubt; frankly, he was surprised they hadn't covered Mateu in the Stars and Stripes. Perhaps one was on its way from the *Hoover*.

For some minutes, Werner stared at Mateu's face. He thought of all the hours he'd spent teaching the lad how to prune olives ... and almonds – figs, too, come to that. What a waste! Now he'd have to find a replacement and start all over again. But how? There weren't many youngsters around Alqueria Blanca these days who were prepared to work on the land – and certainly not for the sort of money Mateu had accepted. In all probability, he'd end up with some old codger – a know-all, set in his ways and wilfully refusing to learn anything. And without Mateu regularly servicing her, Heidi would become ever more cantankerous, especially as the worm had now appeared to turn.

He was still staring at Mateu's face when his own voice startled him. 'They're not Mallorcans,' he said nonchalantly. His brow furrowed and his head tilted to one side. 'They're ... *not* Mallorcans?'

As he re-examined the other corpses, Werner moved faster and faster, a strange sense of excitement building within him. Naturally, he couldn't be completely sure, but six of the bloodstained and mangled bodies looked decidedly Teutonic, while at least another five, although embodying some Latin features, just didn't resemble locals; for a start not one of them sported a beard.

Then, as he stood shaking his head from side to side in bewilderment, his teeth chattering in a temperature he'd not experienced since an unusually cold morning in late April, he spotted a pile of clear plastic pouches laid out in a row on the bench beside the shower cubicle; normally, it was piled with fluffy white bath towels. The folders were all numbered and clearly contained the belongings found on each of the deceased. Within seconds, Werner was rummaging through them as if his life depended on it. There were no identity papers of any description – nothing bearing a name, not even a credit card, but there were packs of Gauloises and Gitanes cigarettes, a bar of Ritter chocolate, a photograph of a teenage girl who could have easily passed for a Rhinemaiden, a crucifix stamped 'Lebois, Dijon', and a German-Spanish phrase book stamped – in English! – on the inside front cover: 'Property of the German Ministry of Defence. Please return if found.'

Was it really possible that the Americans could be so stupid?

'Hey, buddy, what the hell are you doing in here?' A GI stood in the doorway, pointing a formidable weapon at Werner. 'This is out of bounds to civilians, *comprende*?' He motioned menacingly with his weapon. 'You – vamoose – pronto!'

As Werner was propelled protesting along the path that led up to the house – noting on the way a crushed pink trumpet vine here, a mangled oleander there – his mind was in overdrive, endeavouring to assemble the pieces of a truly bizarre jigsaw. And yet, the more he thought about it, the more convinced he became that the Americans, notwithstanding all their state-of-the-art equipment and technology and their apparent efficiency, had, in fact, made one hell of a balls up. After all, it wouldn't be the first time: immediately before their invasion of Iraq in spring 2003, they'd been convinced that Saddam Hussein had enough chemical and biological weapons to kill half of humanity; Colin Powell had even given an audio-visual presentation to the UN Security Council to prove it! Well, if the grisly evidence in the pool house was anything to go by, the Yanks' intelligence about smarmy, lily-livered Tourny and ENABA had been just as reliable.

Leading his armed guard up the final few steps into *Ca'n Pau*'s courtyard, a thin smile broke out on Werner's tired face. Immediately the Oakheart slugabeds roused themselves, he'd start probing about possible compensation claims. In all probability, Jane and Mike would advise him to instruct lawyers in the States, but at least they'd be able to point him in the right direction. This train of thought evaporated, however, just as his feet hit the courtyard's cobbles. His eyes widened in disbelief at the sight before him. '*Mein Gott!*' he boomed, grinding to a halt.

'What the–?' but the escort was lost for words as his gun slammed into Werner's back, provoking a roar of exaggerated pain.

'Jesus!' someone yelled. 'A terrorist! They got one of the bastards!'

In the centre of the courtyard were half a dozen media types in their twenties, all – bar one – casually dressed in jeans, T-shirts, baseball caps and trainers. Two of the males were holding large video cameras; another was tinkering with a battery of electronic equipment clustered around a huge satellite dish sporting a CNN logo; a bearded youth, whose jeans had been shredded to just above the knees, was arranging portable spotlights; a frenetic stylist was endeavouring to comply with the barked instructions of a capless prima donna with a mass of ultra curly hair that cascaded around her shoulders.

Fifteen minute later, and after a quick dab of CNN makeup, Werner was standing in front of one of his smashed windows with a pile of devastated terracotta pots that had been dumped at his feet by one of the technicians: back in Atlanta at CNN Center, people were getting desperate for some real-time reports; replaying footage of Limeys liberating Palma's airport was even provoking protests from Ballygally, Maine. So, until the star they'd come to interview awoke from his beauty sleep, the old German would have to do.

'Well, Mr Stump,' said Kitty Hawk – she with the curly hair – 'how did it feel to be rescued by the U.S. military just as you and Lionel de Tourny – and all your other world-famous celebrity guests here at your palatial and historical villa on the Mediterranean coast of Southern Europe – just as you thought the terrorists – according to the latest Pentagon briefing they appear to have been equipped with Russian-made weaponry of the type used by the Taleban – just as you were running out of ammunition? You were injured, I believe. Is Lionel OK?' She turned to the camera. 'Our latest information is that Mr de Tourny is still in the Trauma Unit after his terrifying ordeal.'

Werner sighed. 'Yes, Kitty, I *was* injured – shrapnel as I tried to provide much-needed cover for my bodyguard, the fine local lad who last night was fighting alongside the French and German Special Forces sent secretly to protect me and my illustrious guests from the racist troglodytes who wanted to–'

'Troglo-*whats*? Are they another Fundamentalist Islamic–?'

'– who wanted to kill me and destroy *Mein Europa* – my grand vision of the glorious European Union. While our British friends were securing the airport and restoring order in the capital, these *European* Special Forces, Kitty, were clearly on top of the situation here – ENABA are peasants who can barely shoot rabbits – when your American gung-ho interlopers arrived on the scene – unwanted and uninvited – having first gone erroneously to Tourny's neighbouring villa, I should add – and then mistook *our* brave boys for the terrorists, slaughtering them in cold blood. Frankly, Kitty, it's obvious from even the most *cursory* examination of the corpses in the pool house, and–'

'Pool house? I–'

'My lawyers, Kitty, the celebrated Trench-Foot-Oakheart team, are already in situ, and you can expect my claim against your government to run into *billions*.'

CHAPTER 22

President Chiffon had got his Perpignan conference after all. However, as Europe awoke to the stunning news that Mallorca had been the scene of intense Anglo-American military action overnight, it was not exactly the grand affair that the French head of state had had in mind. For a start, the venue was not the former palace of the kings of Mallorca, but a dreary small hotel surrounded by discount warehouse stores on the city's southern outskirts. On the other hand, at least the meeting with Azucena and Klipper was taking place on *French* soil, albeit not in the Elysée Palace as he'd originally suggested at around three in the morning when the extent of the disaster was becoming apparent and he'd finally been persuaded to eat humble pie and phone both Madrid and Berlin.

The formal recriminations in the presence of officials having concluded, Chiffon, Klipper and Azucena were alone in the hotel's claustrophobic conference room. To Chiffon's dismay, English was the lingua franca.

'It's not fair, Jesús,' whined Martin Klipper petulantly, 'to talk about François and me having egg on our faces. With due respect, we've *all* got egg on our faces – above all *you*, Jesús. We – François and me – can at least say that our boys were on your island to foil a terrorist attack against our nationals. And everyone will believe that the reason we didn't tell you was because we had absolutely no confidence in your people on the ground in Mallorca. By all accounts, most of them are supporters of these ENABA thugs. And damn it – you'd completely lost control of the situation. And now *you* have the miserable spectacle of the British and Americans controlling the place.'

'British and Americans!' cursed Azucena. 'May they rot in hell! Mallorca will be their graveyard. This Stump–'

'*Stumpf*!' corrected Klipper.

'– has already sown the seeds with his spectacular live interview on CNN.'

'Exactly!' enthused Chiffon. 'And that is what we must build upon, *mes chers confrères*. Now is our chance to make both of them the object of total hatred – not just across Spain, but across the whole of Europe – the *world*!'

Klipper and Azucena stared at Chiffon expectantly.

'And how are we going to do that, François?' asked Klipper. 'Our Special Forces – yours and mine – are dead. We've been made to look complete amateurs, whether by ENABA or by the Americans, we do not yet know for sure. The Union Jack flies over Palma airport, where our citizens are being "liberated". And the English are trying to get the support of the locals – at least for the moment – with treacherous Sandra–'

'I spit on her!'

'– and that snobbish ambassador, Trench-Foot, broadcasting messages on local TV and radio that the UK supports "regional self-determination" and will raise Balearic independence at the earliest opportunity at the Security Council – with O'Connell's support, apparently.'

Azucena started crying again. '*Mierda*!' he wailed. 'I'm finished – *finished*!'

I hope so, thought Klipper. *And then I'm home and dry – on my way to the European Presidency – at least if Chiffon can get me out of this heap of shit. My God, Azucena is so short! And his teeth! Well, smoking all those filthy cigars, it's no wonder.*

'*Courage*, Jesús!' urged Chiffon. 'The officials out in the corridor will hear you, and you know how they all leak to the press. Try one of these croissants. They're quite good. You ought to eat *something*.'

'I never have breakfast – certainly not at this time of day.'

'It's nine-thirty.'

'*Exacto*! *Madre de Dios*, I'd murder for a cognac with this coffee.'

Coughing theatrically, Klipper tried to waft away the smoke from Azucena's fat cigar. 'So, François,' he said, 'do you have a ... a plan?'

'Oh, *naturellement*! I think we are in a very strong position.' The President cast a sideways glance at the notes prepared for him by Patrick Agneau. 'In fact, I think we are in a better position this morning than if *either* of our little strategies for justifying French, or, for that matter, *German* military intervention in Mallorca had succeeded last night.'

'How so?'

'Invading my island behind my back, you bastards!'

'*Scheisse*! Don't start all that again, Jesús.'

'*Hombre*, "better position"! Are you mad? The British are in control of *my* Mallorca!'

'*Exactement*! With the Americans "rescuing" de Tourny, don't you see, Jesús? This is perfect! For years now, every opinion poll in Europe has shown that the overwhelming majority of Europeans can't stomach the Americans, whom they see as imperialist barbarians intent on destroying every value that we Europeans hold dear. And as for the British, well they're regarded as the Americans' poodle. So, from the outset, most

Europeans are going to view what those two have been up to in Mallorca with extreme suspicion. They'll see it as Anglo-Saxon mischief-making designed to divide Europe and weaken our efforts to stand up to that arrogant so-called superpower.

'On the other hand, Jesús, for the time being they've got all of us off the hook over this ENABA nonsense and the use of our tourists as pawns in their game with you over independence. The airport and ferries will now get back to normal, but we all know how these things go. In a matter of weeks, at most, the islanders will loathe these British troops patrolling their streets and see them as colonial occupiers.'

Azucena managed a hint of a smile. 'Hmm ... yes, you're right, François.'

'We three, on the other hand, can say that last night's action by our heroic Special Forces was planned and agreed in advance as an urgent *European* response to the crisis resulting from this Jordi Adrover's assassination – perhaps we could even hint at a CIA involvement in all that – and the subsequent intelligence we intercepted about a massive bomb attack on a gathering of distinguished French and German citizens.

'Trench-Foot's daughter was there too.'

'Yes, Martin, and wasn't *that* an amazing "coincidence"? I'm sure the press will pick up our signals that there was something rather strange about that. They love conspiracy theories. Anyway, our dead compatriots, Martin, will now be seen as martyrs – martyrs in the cause of a Greater Europe battling against a unilateralist, neo-imperialist Anglo-Saxon conspiracy to divide and rule Europe.'

'I see.'

'Oh, that's fine for you two,' grumbled Azucena, 'but how does it help me ... or Spain?'

'I was just coming to that, Jesús. For a start, if you confirm that the Franco-German operation was being conducted with your *full* knowledge and support – due to fears of ENABA infiltration, you understandably didn't want to use any local contingents of the Spanish Armed Forces – we could confirm that you tipped us off, thanks to the *brilliant* endeavours of your intelligence services. *And* we could throw in some support over ... over Gibraltar, for example. Couldn't we, Martin?'

'What sort of support?'

'Ooh ... well, we could give Jesús our *unconditional* support for Spain's claims to sovereignty.'

'Oh ... right.'

'And this unilateral British action in Mallorca,' Chiffon continued, 'cannot go unpunished, can it? Technically, it was an act of war against an

EU nation – aided and abetted by their American friends. I think we should impose sanctions ... for a while.'

Klipper's eyes bulged. 'Oh, come on! The UK is a very important market for a hell of a lot of German – and French – companies. Big business would slaughter us.'

Chiffon sniggered. 'We wouldn't impose *real* trade sanctions, Martin! They'd be more ... symbolic. ... We could impose a small duty on marmalade imports ... withdraw our ambassadors from London ... for a weekend ... ban Britain from the Eurovision Song Contest – that sort of thing.'

'I see.'

Jesús was nodding. '*Sí, sí*! I am liking the sounds of this. Your support over Gibraltar would even win me support in the lousy Balearics! And maybe you could get Brussels to issue a warning that if the bastards secede from Spain, they'd have to pay back all the money they got for the new buses in Palma, and the restoration of the old buildings, and–'

'Yes, yes,' Chiffon snapped. 'No problem. Those little nationalists will be staring bankruptcy in the face. The voters will soon tell them to go to hell. They'll be licking your butt, Jesús, before you can say ... um –'

'Julio Iglesias?' suggested Klipper.

'*Hombre*! He's my favourite singer!' Twiddling his moustache, Azucena added coyly: 'But there is just one little thing – *muy, muy pequeño*.'

'Yes?'

'I'll tell everyone you were not wanting to murder this *chico*, Tourny, and Señor Stump–'

'*Stumpf*!'

'– on the conditioning that you don't try to be Mr President of Europe – *boths* of you – but support *my* election next year.'

For some minutes, Chiffon and Klipper played hard to get. Then, in accordance with their pre-arranged plan, they gave Azucena the assurance he so ardently desired.

The trio were about to invite their ministerial colleagues and officials to squeeze back into the conference room in order to agree the wording of the mandatory communiqué, when Klipper said sheepishly: 'Oh, there's just one other little matter that needs to be resolved. ... These weapons that the Americans are saying could have something to do with Islamic extremists, well, it would be a great service to me and the Federal Republic of Germany if we could all agree that the story is a scandalous American lie. They must have planted them. After all, they seized enough in Afghanistan.'

Azucena puffed on his cigar. 'Agreed – provided *you* support Spain's bid for the new EU Directorate for the Harmonisation of Television Advertising Standards to be sited in my home city of Córdoba.'

Chiffon groaned. 'Nantes has a very strong bid too ... but – oh, ça *ne fait rien*. Agreed!'

Azucena popped out of his chair like a jack-in-the-box, and Klipper was comforted by the fact that he appeared barely any taller than when he was seated. The chances of North Europeans electing such a tiny man as their President – one, moreover, who smoked such politically-incorrect monstrosities in public – were so remote that he could safely discount them.

President of Europe here I come!

CHAPTER 23

Mike put down the copy of that morning's *Herald Tribune* given to him by one of the American officers. Across the pool, the same two guards were still standing in front of the door to the temporary mortuary. 'They must think we're weird sunning ourselves like this – here – of all places.'

Without opening her eyes, Jane said: 'I wish you'd stop saying that. After all, we *are* on holiday.'

Mike glanced at his recumbent wife lying at his side in the shade of a large umbrella; it was just after two o'clock, when the sun was at its strongest, and she was not going to take any unnecessary risks. 'It's turned into a lovely day,' he said finally. 'That storm certainly cleared the air. Humidity's way down, and the temperature must be around a pleasant twenty-six Celsius, I should think. Must be a ridge of high pressure building. ... That was probably a weak cold front passing over us last night. ... Wind's moved round to the north, so the low-pressure system must have moved off down the Med ... probably over Sardinia now.'

The meteorology report provoked no response from Jane. He changed the subject. 'I bet those squaddies over there are laying bets on how long it'll be before you take your kit off. They've probably been told that all Europeans are nudists.'

Jane groaned. 'Please, Mike. There *are* bodies in the pool house. Have a little respect.'

'Sorry.' Mike glanced at his watch. 'Werner will be linked up by satellite now – doing that interview with CNN's big cheese, Tulip Rouge – his boilers refuelled after watching Chiffon, Klipper and Azucena at their Perpignan press conference. It was almost a declaration of war against Uncle Sam! Werner was positively smug, glowing with vindication. What a hypocrite!'

'Tulip Rouge?' murmured Jane.

'No, Werner. All that anti-American, neo-imperialist stuff in front of the cameras, but sucking up to the officers here.'

'Well, he does want the place spruced up – and all that talk of booby traps and mines and things certainly scared him.'

'They've even had blokes in the pool with some kind of detector.'

'He insisted.'

'I know. I might have a dip in a minute – cool off ... once I've digested lunch.'

'Good.'

Mike renewed his efforts to read the *Herald Tribune* but after a few minutes he abandoned the effort. However hard he tried, his eyes kept flicking back to the pool house. 'I suppose we *are* doing the right thing – staying on for Mateu's funeral. I mean, Hugo–'

'Stop worrying about Hugo! I'm sure the Foreign Office chap Daddy's sent to collect him from Mrs B will do a smashing job.'

'But Hugo doesn't know him and–'

'The funeral's on Wednesday evening – we'll be home by midday Thursday. It's not the end of the world.'

'I know, but–'

'Anyway, Daddy said our attendance was important politically, bearing in mind the UK's current position as the occupying power. Surely you can see that? And he should be flying over tomorrow, so then you can seek reassurance that all's well in person.'

'I suppose so,' Mike said, without conviction. He sighed: Jane, for once, seemed maddeningly relaxed about everything, which was particularly puzzling in view of all that had happened overnight. 'Mrs Babcock,' he continued, 'sounded pretty pissed off about all the reporters and TV people outside her door demanding interviews and stuff. The last time I spoke to her she said there was even a Sky refreshment van in the street.'

Jane tutted and realised there was no chance of peace, let alone a much-needed snooze. She turned onto her side and propped herself up on one elbow. 'Believe you me, Mrs B will be lapping up the attention after her hitherto mind-numbingly dull sixty-odd years on this planet. So, I wouldn't worry about her. And talking of the media, we'll have to put our heads together and formulate a strategy for dealing with them ourselves. Actually, I intended talking to you about that later – after my little siesta. I mean, we don't want to fall into the same trap that Werner's fallen into.'

Mike's brow furrowed. 'Sorry? ... "formulate an agreed strategy"? What on earth do you mean? I thought we did pretty damn well this morning when Kitty Hawk interviewed us, and that wasn't the result of an "agreed strategy".'

'Yes, well, we were lucky. No, I take that back. We're both lawyers – and we're English. So instead of a spontaneous tirade of hysterical allegations, we calmly and wisely said that we regretted the tragic deaths – whoever the victims might be – and, pending an independent investigation, were prepared to give the Americans the benefit of the doubt that they'd acted in good faith.'

'Well, you "calmly and wisely" said that. I hardly managed to get a word in.'

'Daddy was *very* pleased – about our performance.'

'So you said. Any bright ideas yet as to why he thinks Werner's going "to look a right Charlie" in the very near future?'

'I can't imagine, but reading between the lines I think we and the Americans have got something up our sleeves. "*Sic transit gloria*," he said at the end of his call. Which is why we have to keep our powder dry, Mikey, OK? I mean, we've got the world's media focused on us at present. Just think how that's going to affect our careers – our names being intimately associated with two film stars – one of them a megastar. I bet you'll get your partnership the minute we get back to London – provided you don't say anything bloody stupid to the media – like lambasting the Americans or Cork or the French or the Germans or the Spanish – or anyone. OK? And that's why we have to distance ourselves from the Stumpfs. I mean, at this very moment Werner's probably prattling on to Tulip Rouge about "aborigines".'

After a few seconds, Mike said: 'Right. ... I see.' He glanced again at the pool house. 'Poor Werner! I wonder how much of a Charlie he's going to look.'

'"Poor Werner"! The man's *barking*! It's Heidi I pity.'

'She's certainly cut up over Mateu's death. She's hardly left that kitchen since our "liberation". God only knows how many cakes she's baked. I suppose it's some kind of therapy.'

'Well, now that her source of extramarital fun has been liquidated, she would be cut up, wouldn't she? Anyway, that's not what I meant. She put all her eggs in one basket setting up home here with Werner and burned her bridges, and now she's trapped. The gloves came off last night and she humiliated him – publicly – in front of his beloved friends, not that he'll ever see Prof Kommis again. He'll make her life hell for that – and in the cold light of day she knows it. If you ask me, she's toiling in the kitchen just to keep out of the ogre's way.'

'Oh, come on! It was so obvious last night that she cares for him – *loves* him. She was beside herself when he got injured by the piano.'

'I've no doubt she *worships* him. That's her pathetic weakness. That's why I pity her – she's a sadomasochist.'

Taken aback by the force of her criticism, Mike closed his eyes. Without opening them, he said softly: 'She was so funny last night – getting that cake, oblivious to the danger.'

'We were *all* bloody reckless, Mikey. We'd had too much to drink.'

'Oh ... right.'

'And for God's sake don't say *that* to the media – to anyone!'

'Of course not! *Jesus*!'

'At least CNN had the good sense not to interview Anna and Moineau this morning. Talk about pissed!'

'They couldn't have broadcast Jeanne's obscene outbursts anyway.'

'And Kommis has flipped his lid, so that's him muzzled.'

'Well, for the time being. Anna wants to get him into some clinic in Vienna.'

'She also wants to divorce him.'

'Oh! When did she tell you that?'

'Just before the Americans took her and the loony home. And we've got nothing to fear from Herbert and Otto telling tales out of school either. The sales of Otto's designer-label knickers across the USA keep those two in the lap of luxury.'

'And Lionel?'

Jane hesitated. 'Well, you saw Lionel's CNN interview – pure maple syrup – clearly well-rehearsed by his Hollywood agent. I'm surprised he didn't burst into *Born in the USA*. I liked all that stuff about us keeping cool and praying to the Good Lord! And marvellous PR to convey his condolences over the airwaves to Margalida.'

'Actually, I thought that was the one bit that sounded genuine – from the heart.'

'Don't be so naive!'

'God, you're in a cynical mood today – mercenary.'

'*Really*? Well, let me just remind you that so far on our "holiday" we've been almost lynched by a murderous anti-British mob, subjected to forced labour by a paranoid martinet, almost killed by bombs and bullets, and seen our chances of cultivating a megastar nearly wrecked. Well, *darling*, as I've already made clear, I'm determined to salvage something from this God-awful, bloody mess.'

Shocked, Mike tried to think of some soothing words, but none materialised. Finally, he said: 'Frankly, I can't imagine why the *Guardia Civil* have got Margalida's house surrounded.'

'Oh, that's obvious! It's to avoid another international incident – her storming down here with a shotgun and shooting any Yank she can get in her sights – Brits too, if she believes we're in league with them.'

'Hmm ... possibly. Maybe we should have volunteered to go up and speak to her – to tell her just what the Americans told us – that the gunfight was over even before they arrived on the scene – that they never even fired a shot.'

As her mobile began to ring, Jane snapped: 'Don't be bloody stupid!' She snatched it from under the sun lounger and glared at the number on the screen. 'Oh hell! It's that bloody fascist Manilla *again*. Talk about persistent! The idea of staying with *them*! Too ghastly!'

'Ignore it.'

'I will.'

When the ringing stopped, Mike said: 'I noticed that Lionel didn't make any fresh offers to stay at the *Villa Tourny*. I suppose we were quite abrupt with him last night.'

Jane rolled onto her back. 'He's got to leave for the States – for that screen test with Pine Stein. He was nice enough when he left in that armoured car thing.'

'I was amazed Anglo-Saxon-hating Jeanne agreed to get in it. It was a Hum-Vee by the way.'

'Whatever. And don't say a word to anyone about him ... er–'

'Being a miserable, selfish little coward in the heat of battle? Don't worry, honey, I'll add it to my ever-growing list of taboo subjects.'

Mike reached over to the table at the side of his sun lounger and extracted one of the two bottles of Vichy Catalan from the ice bucket. 'Top up?' Jane shook her head. 'Maybe I should offer those poor lads some. They must be roasting in those uniforms.'

Jane sighed. 'Don't be wet. They're Americans. They probably only drink Coke.'

Mike inhaled deeply as he screwed the top back on the bottle with unnecessary force. 'Well, I think I'll ask them anyway. It's only fair.'

*

The Oakhearts didn't have long to wait to discover how Werner would be transmogrified into 'a right Charlie'. Later that Monday in Balygally, Maine, President O'Connell was so outraged by Europe's vitriolic outbursts against himself and his nation – thanks to both Werner's live diatribes on CNN and the joint press conference given by Chiffon, Klipper and Azucena in Perpignan – that he decided to risk an entire break with the Continental powers. And so, he authorised the release of a recording of Chiffon's reckless mobile telephone conversation with premier Patrick Agneau, together with a succinct but damning summary of the intelligence which Sir Richard Shaddock and his subordinates at MI6 had collected in respect of both the French and German assassination plots. Indeed, such was O'Connell's fit of pique that he neglected to inform Sandra Cork of his decision until the representatives of the world's media camped out for the summer at Ballygally were already assembled on his windswept backyard for the press conference.

Sandra's incandescence, however, only lasted a few minutes, thanks to Sir Peter Blithe-Blister's soothing words of wisdom. And, as he predicted, by Tuesday morning, with violent demonstrations breaking out in Madrid, Paris and Berlin, heads were rolling across Europe. While Azucena took refuge with his family at his Galician holiday retreat, Klipper fled to soggy Hamburg, the invitation to vacation in Turkey having been unceremoniously withdrawn. Chiffon, however, stayed put in the Elysée Palace and denied everything in a live televised interview with two of the nation's top political journalists, claiming that both France and himself were the victims of an Anglo-Saxon smear campaign. It was a performance worthy of the Comédie Française, and most of the French nation wanted to believe it.

Nevertheless, the Continental media promptly toned down their anti-British hysteria. And luckily for Whitehall, the Conde de Manilla had emerged from his summer residence at Portopetro on Monday evening, and, with breath-taking initiative, had promptly revealed to the summoned Mallorcan press scrum his ideal qualities to negotiate with the British and their 'Provisional Civil Administrator', none other than his 'dear old friend' Sir Douglas Trench-Foot. Furthermore, by the time a Royal Navy helicopter had transported Manilla to Palma, he'd smoothly propelled himself into the power vacuum left by Adrover's assassination.

At midday on Tuesday when Manilla and Sir Douglas shook hands on the tarmac at Palma airport before the cameras, the Briton – at well over six foot – towered literally and symbolically over the diminutive Mallorcan. But the islanders, sitting glued to their television sets, felt nothing but pride whenever the local reporters repeated the mantra that Manilla – one of their own race, no less, who could trace his ancestry back to Jaume III and beyond – had not only represented the entire Spanish nation in some of the world's most important capitals during the course of his distinguished career in the Diplomatic Service, but could also hold his head high – at least metaphorically – with the supremo of their temporary occupier: as a count, Manilla outranked Trench-Foot – a mere knight.

After an excellent lunch at Manilla's 'town house' in Palma's historic quarter, the two men commenced negotiations in 'the State Drawing Room' with the overawed representatives of the Balearic Nationalist Party. Indeed, there were only a few grumbles when Trench-Foot 'suggested' working through the traditional siesta hours. By contrast, the USA's ambassador to Madrid, Gary Streisand Junior – he belatedly materialised after receiving orders from Ballygally to abandon his Wyoming hunting vacation – provoked a PANABA walk-out by insisting on decaffeinated coffee and a smoking ban for the benefit of both himself and his team of sixteen 'advisors'.

By the time an overdressed Beatriz popped her head around the double doors and asked whether everyone was staying for dinner and who would like a cocktail, the bones of a deal had been negotiated. Normal service would resume immediately at the ports and airport. All British and American military personnel would withdraw by the end of the following week. The 'house arrest' of the King and other members of the Royal Family at *Marivent* would terminate forthwith. PANABA also undertook to renounce violence, condemn ENABA, and work within the current constitution to negotiate independence from Spain. In return, both the UK and the USA would champion the islanders' right to self-determination, including implementation of the promise already made by the British to procure an appropriate resolution at the UN. And, most importantly, in the event of the Balearics achieving independence, the United States would be granted a ninety-nine-year lease of the former naval base at Pollença. Initially, this had proved a bit of a sticking point, for it was disclosed that the Adrover Group had already reached a secret deal with the Mallorcan authorities to redevelop the site as a luxury hotel and villa complex. After hushed conversations in the corners of the vast room, Mr Streisand offered to give the Adrover Group 'a covert option of first refusal' to undertake all reconstruction work at the base, which, he assured everyone, would be 'considerable'.

'That's all very well,' said Manilla petulantly, 'but I don't have any shares in the Adrover Group. On the other hand, my family's Palma-based merchant bank, Banca Manilla, controls a development company that's been trying to build an ice hockey stadium near the university for years. It's a sport that's becoming increasingly popular across Spain, you know ... er, Gary. Ice hockey matches would be a great boon for U.S. personnel at the anticipated Pollença base. I suspect they'd probably get a bit bored with just soccer and the occasional bullfight, hmm?'

Streisand sighed. 'I'm sure something can be arranged, Alfonso,' he wheezed through the thick smoke generated by the PANABA contingent.

Sir Douglas, who was not commercially minded, found all this talk of property development both boring and distasteful. In consequence, no financial benefits for the United Kingdom were either requested or offered. In any event, he thought the chances of Madrid granting independence in the foreseeable future were remote – even if a UN resolution were procured – and that the Americans' talk was all bluff: having rescued their precious film star, they probably didn't give a fig about the Balearics. But over cocktails, Streisand, who sipped a Diet Coke, surprised him by asserting he was quite wrong.

'O'Connell's pretty steamed up, Doug, and keen to milk the situation for all it's worth as an adjunct to his election promise to maintain the War on Terror. And seeing how the CIA has enough dirt on most members of the Spanish government – and on several big noises in the House of

Borbón – everything from mistresses and gay lovers to massive tax evasion and fraud – Washington has the power to convert Madrid into Ground Zero at the flick of a switch. They'll give these rednecks their independence all right, Dougie boy, just you wait and see.'

Sir Douglas finished his La Ina *fino*, excused himself, retreated to the extraordinary luxury of Manilla's city centre garden, and phoned his daughter.

'Daddy! How are things going? We saw you on the telly – with Manilla at the airport. He phoned here a billion times and said that Mikey and I could go and stay at Portopetro.'

'Yes, he told me. He seemed quite put out that you'd decided to stay on with Stumpf at his bomb site – especially in view of his somewhat anti-American broadcasts on CNN.'

'Well, he's been in shock since O'Connell's news conference – eating humble pie doesn't come easily for him. I say, what a bloody palaver! I still find it difficult to believe that those beasts Chiffon and Klipper were prepared to bump us all off. It's not a pack of lies, is it?'

'No, I'm afraid not, darling. Anyway, we seem to have sorted things out down here in Palma, thanks to Manilla's good offices. It's been a bit of a sticky wicket at times – I must be careful what I say on an open line, but–'

'To be honest, we thought Manilla was an obnoxious little tick after that boat trip with him and Beatriz last week. Such a bigot!'

'That's a little harsh, darling.'

'Yes, I feel quite ashamed now. Mind you, Werner has been cursing him all day, but then he's in a rather negative mood at the moment, even though the Americans have been absolute bricks helping to tidy up all the mess here. I just don't know how they do it. They've even brought in panes of glass from that aircraft carrier and a corps of glaziers to fix the windows. Incredible!'

'It's called being a super power, darling. And how's er ... Michael?'

'Fine, fine – missing Hugo, of course. Thanks ever so much for arranging for one of the FO's minions to take him up to Derbyshire. It was a great weight off Mikey's mind, what with Mrs Babcock going up to Scotland and–'

'I could have got you out of here on an RAF plane, you know. Actually, we should have scheduled flights up and running by tomorrow morning. I'm sure I could arrange–'

'No, no! It's Mateu's funeral tomorrow – the young gardener that got killed. We owe it to him to be there – you said so yourself. Luckily, it's the custom to get these things over with pretty quickly here. Well, in the days before refrigeration, bodies in the fierce summer heat–'

'Quite. We're coming too, actually.'

'*Oh! At last we're going to see you! How wonderful! When are you coming down? The funeral's in the evening at seven – did you know? That's another one of the local customs. Werner says it's because the Mallorcans can't bear the thought of losing a single hour of earning potential. Anyway, who's "we"?*'

'Manilla and I.'

'*Ah.*'

'Plus the King by all accounts.'

'*Good Lord!*'

'And most of the PANABA top brass.'

'*Hypocrites!*'

'And Gary Streisand.'

'***Who?***'

'Washington's man in Madrid. He's been here all afternoon. He's from Wyoming. He wears cowboy boots.'

'*Yuck! ... Oh, I forgot to tell you – we've finally got news of Margalida.*'

'Who?'

'*Margalida – Mateu's mother. Werner wanted to go up the road to her farm yesterday as she hadn't made an appearance and isn't on the phone, but the Yanks said it was jolly dangerous and wouldn't trot up themselves because it was "outside their exclusion zone" or something. They really do take political correctness to extremes, don't they? I mean, it's only a five-minute walk. Anyway, they got satellite photos emailed instead, but they showed no signs of life. Eventually, some of her family from Felanitx – a town nearby – got the* Guardia Civil *to search the place. Apparently, they found her in the pigsty – with the dogs.*'

'Dogs? She keeps dogs in a pigsty? Heartless brutes, these Spaniards.'

'*It seems she tried to kill herself.*'

'Oh dear. ... Were they rabid dogs?'

'*Don't be silly! No doubt she was consumed by grief. Well, Werner claims she worshiped him – Mateu that is. He was all she had. ... Actually, she'd drunk gallons of her home-made* hierbas. *Werner says it's positively lethal.*'

'Some kind of fertiliser? – a disinfectant?'

'*A liqueur. There were empty bottles all around her. She's in hospital being treated for alcohol poisoning, but she should be OK for the funeral tomorrow, so you'll get to meet her.*'

'Oh ... good. ... Ah, there's Manilla shouting for me. Dinner must be ready.'

'Werner's arranging a sort of post-funeral supper here tomorrow evening. Lionel and Jeanne will be coming. You'll come too, won't you? He's so anxious to meet you.'

'Tourny?'

'No, Werner.'

'Ah. ... I should think so.'

*'Splendid! Can't wait to see you. It's been **ages**.'*

'Must dash, darling. Give my regards to – to ... er–'

'And Mikey sends his love.'

'– Werner – *Michael* too – naturally. You've been very brave, darling – *both* of you. *Au revoir!*'

CHAPTER 24

'Well now, Werner,' said Sir Douglas, scanning *Ca'n Pau*'s idyllic courtyard as the sun dipped below the horizon, 'one would hardly think that a veritable battle had taken place here only three nights ago. Incredible! Splendid champagne by the way.' A steward from the *Hoover* dressed in whites materialised and offered to refill his glass. 'And awfully decent of the Admiral to help out with the catering for this shindig.'

'*Ja, ja*,' agreed the host, 'awfully decent. It's Jacques Selosse by the way – a present to me from the late King of Jordan.'

'Present? ... Sorry? I thought the Admiral's name was–'

The champagne ... it's Selosse.'

'Really? ... Jolly decent chap, Hussein. He was at Eton, you know.'

'The Admiral thought that Mr Streisand and the King might have joined us after the funeral. It's a pity they had to leave straight away.' Werner willed himself to continue smiling.

'Well, they do have a *rather* important meeting in Madrid with the acting premier.' Sir Douglas pictured the thick file that Streisand had shown him in the strictest confidence that morning, and the photographs of intertwined naked bodies. 'So, Werner, the Americans have done a pretty damned good job of clearing things up here, eh?'

'*Ja, ja*, Douglas. They have been ... *incredible*. It is good because my housekeeper, Margalida, will be unable to resume her duties for some days yet. I mentioned it to her at the church when I handed her the draft schedule. She thought she might be able to come back to work on Monday. She makes very good whitewash.'

'Oh? ... Jolly good. ... Your wife was telling me that the Americans have even flown in a piano tuner to fix your Steinway. I understand from Jane that she's a damned good pianist – good enough to be a professional.' He turned his head. 'Where is Jane, by the way? ... Ah, there she is, talking to–'

'I know Margalida was very touched by your presence, Douglas, and your kind words in Catalan – very touched indeed.'

'Yes, well seeing how the Catalans are so dynamic on the old business front – not at all like the lazy buggers in the rest of the dammed country – my God, the Andalusians! So, as buttering up the Catalans is frightfully important for British trade, I thought it would be politic to learn a bit of the beastly lingo. I say, do you think Heidi might play for us later on? If truth be told, I'm not too hot on the highbrow music front, but I suggested a few appropriate pieces to her, including Ravel's *Bolero* and–'

'I did ask Margalida to join us, you know, Douglas, but she declined. I think she would have felt out of place with people of our class. I doubt she has even heard of boarding schools! She wanted to be with her family ... peasants ... salt of the earth. I never realised she had so many relatives. They came from all over the island.'

'Yes, well they're Roman Catholics, aren't they? I thought there was going to be a riot at first when the American marines wouldn't let them into the church ... Calonge?' – Werner nodded – '... but it was a very *small* church – that ghastly heat! – and they were understandably concerned about the security implications for Streisand and the Admiral.'

'And the King too, I suppose ... and yourself.'

'Ha! Still, they were jolly decent about it, weren't they? – and all the other local mourners. They think of everything, don't they, the Americans? That huge TV screen in the square relaying CNN's live coverage! And all the refreshments! Free too!'

Werner's sigh was almost inaudible. 'Yes, I've never heard of a sponsored funeral before. I wonder how much Budweiser and Burger King had to pay.'

'I wonder. I feared the bereaved and weeping Margalida would object.'

'I don't think she was in any state to notice.'

'No, that alcohol poisoning had certainly taken its toll.'

Across the courtyard, as the exclusive champagne ran out and the bronzed stewards resorted to the Admiral's donation of California's best sparkling, the conversations from the various groups of mourners were becoming more animated. The Karpfen-Pinsels, Heidi and the Oakhearts had just been joined by the Admiral, who proceeded to stun them with revelations of the *Herbert Hoover*'s cultural activities, which included several choirs, a chamber orchestra, a string quartet, and an annual opera festival. The Admiral was reluctantly forced to admit that he was responsible for inspiring all these activities, with the exception of the choirs, which had predated his appointment to the Mediterranean Fleet. It didn't take him long to get round to suggesting that von Karpfen might like to come aboard and do 'a spot of conducting'.

Mike's thoughts drifted away. He couldn't help peering out of the corner of his eye at the trestle table in the centre of the courtyard covered in crisp white linen, from which the stewards in their equally crisp white jackets were dispensing the refreshments. He wondered what Werner had done with the bullet-riddled wrought-iron table that Mateu had desperately attempted to use as a shield. But try as he might, he couldn't in all honesty feel much grief for the death of a man he'd only seen once, and then for only a few seconds. And when Jane had gone for that walk on the afternoon of their arrival and bumped into him down in the olive grove, she'd said he was 'a bit creepy' – or words to that effect. And then there were Jeanne's sordid revelations.

And yet, the lad's horrible death had affected him deeply. So many seemingly fixed points in his own little universe had suddenly disappeared, leaving him confused, bewildered and thoroughly disillusioned. He'd never been so naive as to believe that all politicians of the great European democracies were angels: they were only human, and, therefore, prone to the occasional sexual deviancy, bribe or ruthless backstabbing of an opponent. Nevertheless, he'd always believed there were moral boundaries beyond which the likes of Chiffon and Klipper would never go. And yet, if the Americans were to be believed – and indeed his own prime minister – they'd been prepared to sacrifice the lives of innocent fellow Europeans to further their own squalid political ambitions. So, how could he ever trust *any* politician again – including O'Connell and Sandra Cork? Indeed, bearing in mind Cork's own notorious coolness towards the European Union, could it be that Chiffon was actually telling the truth – as Jeanne had so fervently argued – that the Franco-German Special Forces were in the vicinity of *Ca'n Pau* to protect Werner and his guests, only to be cut to pieces by 'the American invaders'? After all, the Americans were wholly mercenary in all things, weren't they – business, politics, even the law? Well, he'd had enough dealings with American lawyers to know they were prepared to break almost every rule in the book to advance the interests of their own clients. And on the political front, who really killed President Kennedy? What about Lee Harvey Oswald's bizarre slaying?

Absent-mindedly, Mike sipped his wine and thought of Vietnam and Agent Orange, of Nixon and Watergate, of Bush Junior and all the claims about Saddam's massive arsenal of 'Weapons of Mass Destruction'. Or had he just watched too many cynical European documentaries, read too many cynical European books and newspapers? Maybe the Americans really were like children, seeing everything in simplistic black and white terms – good guys and bad guys. But when all was said and done, and whatever the motives of Washington or Wall Street, hundreds of thousands of Americans had died in two World Wars to defeat despots and tyrants and to keep alive the flame of democracy. And even in Vietnam, where they'd ended up in such a murderous war of attrition, hadn't they been trying to stop the cancer of communism spreading from China, where countless millions had lost their lives just because evil old Mao had wanted to conduct some mad social experiment?

Around him, Mike detected the Admiral's educated Boston accent: he was now explaining to Karpfen that the *Hoover*'s 'Opera Festival' was, in fact, devoted to such works as *The Pirates of Penzance*, *West Side Story* and *South Pacific*. Karpfen was, nevertheless, smiling with just a hint of a superior sneer. He remained polite and charming, however; there were no diatribes against 'Anglo-Saxon pseudo-culture', or lectures on the genius of Stockhausen, Boulez or Schönberg. Instead, he mentioned a very busy schedule of engagements – his diary was usually booked up at least two years in advance – but promised to have a word with his agent as soon as he got back to Berlin. Then he winked at Mike. It was like a secret sign, as though they were parents indulging the naive notions of a precocious child, keeping a straight face so as not to hurt its sensitive feelings.

Mike didn't acknowledge the sign: the sense of gloom that had been festering ever since Monday afternoon's sunbathing session down by the pool was beginning to overwhelm him. He wanted to go home, to hold Hugo in his arms, to listen to some 'wallpaper' music, to go for a pint down at his local. He glanced again at the table. They'd all acted shamefully – himself included: they'd known Mateu was alone on 'guard duty'; they'd abandoned him. The tanned stewards were opening more bottles. Doubtless, they knew nothing of Stockhausen, Proust or Cervantes, but Mike felt sure that every one of them would have unhesitatingly risked his life to help Mateu. Or was that just another Hollywood myth?

Jane moved closer to him. She seemed to read his thoughts. 'We'll be home tomorrow,' she whispered in his ear, '– away from all these bloody Germans and Americans. Sorry, but I can't take much more of them. Actually, Daddy says he can get us on a British Mercia flight to Derby. We could be with Mummy – and Hugo – by early afternoon!'

Across the courtyard, Anna Kommis nodded in the direction of Lionel. 'They seem to be having an argument,' she said in French to Jeanne Moineau. 'What did you say they were called, those two ghastly Americans? They even talked all the way through the funeral.'

Jeanne's lips turned downwards. 'I don't give a shit. They're probably telling Lionel that time is money – you know how Americans are – and that he shouldn't have wasted the precious studio's time by staying for the funeral instead of turning up for the screen test with that brainless whore, Pine Stein.'

'Oh, are they going to star in something together? I quite liked her in that film–'

'The fat one is his agent, Mel Snook, and the even fatter one smoking the huge penis substitute is the head honcho at Cyclopean, Bill Klamp. They plan to get their treasured possession out of here and back to Tinsel Town tonight. He's all packed – not that he ever travels with much.'

Anna trembled. 'Oh, does that mean you'll be leaving the island too, Jeanne?'

'Well, I'm certainly not going to hang around here surrounded by the armies of the Anglo-Saxon imperialists. Anyway, I'm starring in a touring-company season of Corneille, Molière and Racine across Francophone West Africa – Sénégal, Chad, Niger. The French Ministry of Culture is very good at funding that sort of thing.'

Anna looked rather crestfallen. 'Oh ... right. Things will be rather dull here without you and Lionel. Manfred's treatment in Vienna is expected to last at least a month according to Dr Zimmermann. The Americans have offered to fly him out tomorrow. That's assuming I can persuade him to leave the house. He's still locked in the study.'

Jeanne continued to glare in the direction of Lionel. 'Zimmermann?' she mumbled.

'The psychiatrist. He's *very* good. He's helped Manfred before. Well, it's the height thing, of course.'

'Of course.' Jeanne suddenly turned to face Anna. 'I know! Look, *chérie*, we start in Marrakech with a performance of *Le Bourgeois Gentilhomme*. I have a little house there – had it for years. Nothing grand, mind you, but quite heavenly. You'll love it. Why don't you come and stay?'

'Oh – oh, I couldn't. I mean there's the dogs and – and–'

'To hell with the dogs! You've got bloody servants, haven't you?'

'Yes, but–'

'You're coming, and that's that.'

Then Jeanne embraced Anna and kissed her on the lips, and the stewards realised why the Admiral had got nowhere with them.

Europeans!

*

'Look, Leo,' bleated Bill Klamp, 'you saw all those media folk down at the funeral. They weren't there for that pissing king guy or our ambassador – or for any of the other big noises – but for *you*, baby. And that's just the tip of the iceberg. Wait until you get to the States! This revolution thing is only news because *you* were at the centre of it, see? Jesus! The more I think about this project' – his voice was building up to a crescendo – 'the more, I like the sound of it!'

'Me to,' boomed Mel.

'It's absolutely perfect for a movie, Leo. It's got *everything* – blood, guts, romance, sex, politics – even the U.S. cavalry rescuing you all from the bad guys, those Arab-backed Islamic terrorists and those French and German assholes. Hell, it's got aristocrats, Nobel scientists, a washed-out European movie star – a sort of Dietrich or Bergman character – the gorgeous Latin hunk dying heroically in a hail of bullets. It's got–'

'Lionel, baby, Bill's already spoken to Ronaldo Albóndigas. He's free and *very* interested. He'd be perfect to play this Mat guy. *Albóndigas*! You've always wanted to work with him, baby.'

'It's got *you*, Leo – *you*. Oh, let me get down on my knees and praise the Good Lord for this manna from heaven.' Mr Klamp tried to descend to the cobbles, but his girth made the manoeuvre impracticable, so he settled for a kind of curtsey and almost dropped his glass of champagne.

'Here – let me help you,' said Lionel.

'That's my boy!' said Mel. 'Such perfect manners.'

'Can you see the billboards at the theatres, Leo, can you? – "**TOURNY IS TOURNY!**" – like "**GARBO SPEAKS!**" Oh, Mary Mother of Jesus, I think I'm gonna wet myself. I can hear those fucking box office tills zinging away already!'

'It's the perfect part for you, baby. I mean who else could play Tourny? *Who*?'

'But–'

'Yes, I know what you're going to say, Leo – what about *Betsy*?'

'No – yes – well–'

'We dump it on the back burner for a while. We do this movie first, and it'll be such a sensation that the public will be fighting to see *Betsy*, OK?'

'Bill's right, baby.'

'But–'

'Don't worry about Pine, Leo – you're such a gentleman!'

'No, I–'

'There's probably a part for Pine. ... Maybe she could play that – that ... "Jan"? ... "Jean"? ... "Jane"?' Mel glanced nervously at Moineau: it really would be better for Lionel to have a younger girlfriend in the movie – much younger – and not one who was clearly addicted to both booze and cigarettes.

'No, no Mel! I want Brioche. I'm waiting for that agent of hers to return my call.'

Lionel whistled. '*Brioche*! No kidding?'

'Ha! I thought you'd like the sound of that, Leo. Yeah, just picture it – Albóndigas and Brioche ... and *you* ... working *together* ... side by side ... *here*.'

'Here?'

'But of course, Leo! Imagine the sensation of filming in the very location where the real drama took place!'

'Cool!' enthused Mel. 'And at the *Villa Tourny* too?'

'Sure! Why not?'

'But–'

'Leo, Leo … *Lee-o*. For Christ's sake, no more of these "buts", baby, OK? I–'

'There are laws and stuff,' Lionel finally managed to say, '– privacy, libel. I mean, for a start I don't think most of the guys who were under attack here would agree to all this – a movie being made of it an' all. There were kind of embarrassing things. … And I don't think Werner would *ever* agree to *Ca'n Pau* being used for–'

'Werner?'

'"Can *what*"?'

'The owner of this place – *Ca'n Pau* – Werner Stumpf – the famous writer. He's standing overed there.'

'He's some kinda Nazi, isn't he?' sniffed Mel.

'Nazis too! Even better! The name'll have to go – Stump! Jesus! … On the other hand, I don't suppose he'd want to be portrayed as a Nazi, and as we want to use this place for shooting … Hell! Oh well, you can't have everything. Mind you, we'll have to change a *lot* of things round here.' Sighing and shaking his head, Klamp surveyed the house and courtyard. 'It just doesn't look Spanish, does it? … More kind of … French? … Italian? The whole place will have to be whitewashed for a start.'

'Werner will never agree–'

'Oh, don't worry your pretty little head about all that, Leo! This Stump guy will do whatever we want once he sees those greenbacks in front of his greedy little Nazi eyes.'

'He's not a Naz–'

'Now, Lionel, baby, Bill has got one teensy-weensy little problemette, but we talked about it on the flight over, and I think we came up with the *perfect* solution – for you, your long-term career … and us.'

'Yes?'

'Well–'

'Let *me* explain, Mel. … Leo, *baby*, you're a great, great star, and this movie – *Betsy* too – will put you up there with the greatest – Chaplin, Peck, Grant, Wayne … But – and believe me, Leo, it pains me to say this – but at the present moment in time your country and your nationality are … well, they're not exactly flavour of the month back home, see?'

'Oh.'

'He's right, Lionel.'

'Of *course* the kid knows I'm right, Mel! Now, don't get me wrong, son, I love France as much as the next guy, but you have to understand that this movie – and boy, what a movie it's gonna be! – will get a much better reception from the great unwashed of Middle America if ... well, if the big star was sort of not ... French.'

'Lionel, baby, what Bill is saying – trying to say – is that it would do your career one helluva lot of good – propel it into the stratosphere, if you will – if you could see your way to becoming an ... American.'

While Klamp and Snook continued their hard sell of the benefits of U.S. citizenship, Lionel focused on Jeanne as she and sweet Anna Kommis chatted away so enthusiastically. She'd go ballistic; she'd smash the house up. So, it would be better not to tell her until ... No, that wouldn't work. She'd have to be told – like everyone else who'd been at the party, if only to get their consents to the screenplay. Otherwise – and he knew damn well what he was talking about – there'd be a mass of litigation. And it was all very well Klamp talking about money, but *he* didn't know Jeanne ... or the Oakhearts, or Werner – *any* of them. Well, maybe *they* could be bribed, but Jeanne? She had principles – principles chiselled in granite. And she had a hate list as long as his arm, and at the top of it was Hollywood and 'The Anglo-Saxon Conspiracy'.

And yet ... and yet ... well, he respected her principles even if he didn't agree with many of them. And although she drank too much and smoked too much, she'd looked after him for the last couple of years, not letting the fame go to his head, making sure he didn't throw his money away, keeping him off hard drugs, and, above all, teaching him everything she knew about acting – and that was a hell of a lot. 'A has-been actress'! What the fuck did these two idiots know? He should have butted in straightaway and set the record straight. She was a brilliant actress – the best. And she was still beautiful ... and sexy – so, so sexy.

Under his breath, Lionel began to hum Haydn's *La Poule* theme. He chuckled inwardly and then his eyes began to feel moist.

I love her. I love her more than anything in the world. I can't live without her. She's my rock. We're magic together.

And then he pictured Jeanne scampering on all fours under the tablecloth, clutching her bottles of *eiswein* like proud trophies.

'... for me, Mel? Shit! Of *course* the moron would! I can twist O'Connell round my little figure whenever I want – and that Secretary of State bitch. Leo will have his papers by the fall, no problem.'

'So, baby, what you say? Is it a deal?'

Lionel inhaled deeply: 'It's a deal–'

'Great!'
'That's my boy!'
'– on one condition.'

*

Sir Douglas and the Oakhearts were standing on the terrace adjacent to the dining room. With dinner over – the *Hoover*'s chefs had impressed even the French with their commendable efforts in *Ca'n Pau*'s galley kitchen – they'd withdrawn, at Sir Douglas's diplomatic suggestion, for a brief exchange of views on 'a family matter' before coffee was served and Heidi commenced her recital.

'Sorry about that,' said Sir Douglas as he terminated yet another call on his mobile. 'Blithe-Blister – as you probably guessed. Now look, you two, I know this is all a bit of a shock and, to be honest, I too find it a bit distasteful, but–'

'"A bit *distasteful*", Daddy! Talk about understatement! It positively stinks. Hypocrites, the lot of them. Jesus! Poor Mateu is still warm in his grave, so to speak, and they're already plotting to transform his horrible death into some kind of political travesty just to line their miserable pockets.'

'Well, I–'

'I completely agree with Jane, Douglas. It's grotesque. I mean, it's bad enough Werner selling his soul to the devil after all he's said about the Americans over the last week, but for these two French gits falling over themselves to sell their nationality for leading parts in that fat slob's crummy film ... well, it's beyond my comprehension.'

'Moineau won't dare set foot in France again. I bet you anything she'd get her head shaved, just like all those collaborators after the War.'

'I hardly think that's fair, Jane, dear. I thought her reasons for agreeing to collaborate – *take part* – albeit with great reluctance – were perfectly convincing. First, the film would be made in any event – with her character completely removed from the plot if she doesn't ... um ... cooperate. Secondly, she's insisting on a degree of editorial control to ensure that our American friends don't take too many poetic licences.'

'Ha! If you believe that you'll believe anything.'

'Don't be unkind, dear.'

'Look, Daddy, how on earth can we trust anything that Klamp chap says when it transpires he'd already spoken to Margalida before he'd talked to us? God only knows how much that vulture's going to be paid for her 'approval' – plus the filming at her horrid farm. And I bet they don't show those two dogs chained up all day.'

'And now she's going to be a hero *too*! I mean, Douglas, all this cock and bull about her coming down here with sandwiches for her beloved son on guard duty, only to find herself caught up in a murderous attack by the French and–'

'Jane ... Michael, *please*. I know it's monstrous, but dear Jeanne Moineau is absolutely spot on. If we – *you* – don't ... cooperate and sign those contracts, Cyclopean Productions are going to make this blasted film anyway, and you and all British involvement in the project will be expunged. Is that what we – *you* – really want? Confidentially, old things, the PM is pretty keen on the whole idea.'

'Daddy! You've already told her?'

'No. O'Connell tipped her off. Klamp is very close to the President.'

'Good God, Douglas! Whatever next?'

'The point is, you two, I think we're all agreed that the French and Germans have behaved very badly.'

'If our lot – *your* lot, Douglas – are telling the truth, that is. Frankly, I'm beginning to have doubts.'

'Michael, I have to say that the implication of your remark is somewhat hurtful. I can give you my word that what O'Connell has told the public is absolutely pukka. Which is why we have to expose these whiter-than-white Euro-rotters for what they are. My dear boy, do you really want to see any further drift down the dark road to a United States of Europe?'

'No, but–'

'So here is a heaven-sent opportunity to bowl the blighters out.' Sir Douglas raised his eyes to the stars. 'I hate to mention this, but, as I understand it, all of you – the Stumpfs, those gay chaps, mad Professor Whatsit and his dizzy wife ... and yourselves – will be portrayed as *heroes* – in your own very different ways, naturally. With stars like de Tourny, Moineau ... this Albóndigas person – and I'm sure there'll be big names playing you too – well, there'll be an *awful* lot of publicity – for *years* to come. And I doubt that could do your careers *any* harm ... do *you*? And then there's the money Klamp has mentioned for your co-operation. I should think you could buy quite a decent house with that ... something Georgian maybe ... in Belgravia even.'

The Oakhearts stared hard at each other, neither wishing to be the first to crumble.

'Daddy, I–'

'Douglas, we–'

Lionel came running out of the French windows. 'Jane! Mike! You'll never believe it! Bill's done it! He's almost definitely got Camilla

Fitzroy-Grosvenor to play you, Jane. And you'll never guess who's lined up for your role, Mike?'

'Who?'

'Guess!'

'I ... Wait a minute! I haven't even agreed–'

'*Guess*!'

'I haven't the slightest idea.'

'Camilla's Oscar-winning co-star in their blockbusting remake of *Sense and Sensibility* – Toby Farquhar!'

PART II
CHAPTER 25

It was April and Mallorca was experiencing yet another gloriously warm sunny day. In view of the weather, one might have expected Werner Stumpf to be toiling in his large and demanding garden; as always, there was certainly a great deal to do. But although it was just coming up to five o'clock in the afternoon, Werner was sat upstairs in his study, watching BBC World and awaiting the news bulletin 'at the top of the hour', an expression he despised.

Apart from the television, the chair he was sitting on, the desk and his PC, the room was bare. Everything else – including his thousands of books, his eighteenth-century engravings of Potsdam, and an entire wall of framed photographs of himself with heads of state and government – had already been packed away by the German firm of removers which, he hoped, would soon be shipping *Ca'n Pau*'s entire contents to Namibia's capital, Windhoek. His emigration was one of the reasons why he wasn't working in the garden – indeed, why he'd not undertaken any gardening for some months.

The arrival of the 'Edict of Compulsory Purchase' from the government of the brand-new Federal Republic of the Balearic Islands had plunged Werner into such a state of mental crisis that Heidi had postponed announcing her desire for a divorce: she'd feared pushing him over the edge and into the care of Dr Zimmermann in Vienna. The Ministry of Culture, Heritage and Sport was polite but firm: *Ca'n Pau* was a building of 'national historic importance' in view of the role it had played in the 'Great Leap Forward'. Consequently, it was the considered view of all 'interested parties' that the property should be purchased by the State for preservation 'in perpetuity' as 'The National Museum of Liberation'. Reasonable compensation based on the property's market value would, of course, be paid.

Needless to say, the Ministry made an offer which Werner regarded as derisory. He tried to pull strings: he appealed to the Conde de Manilla, to Sir Douglas Trench-Foot, and, finally, to Mr Bill Klamp of Cyclopean Productions; Cyclopean were about to start filming *Infernal Paradise* at *Ca'n Pau* – 'The True Story of a People's Heroic Struggle for Freedom', as the studio's publicity department was already describing it. Everyone, however, professed that nothing could be done. Werner said he'd rip up the contract permitting Cyclopean to film at his home; he threatened to take the fledgling republic before the European Court of Human Rights, only to be told that it had yet to sign up to the relevant treaty. Then Cyclopean got an injunction from an extremely cooperative judge in Palma – she was angling for the job of Balearic Chief Justice – which threatened Werner with contempt and imprisonment should he fail to honour a single provision of the contract.

An insidious evil, Werner concluded, oozed out of every rock and crevice of Mallorca and the pores of its sinister people. From the moment he'd first set foot on the diabolical island more than twenty years earlier, his fate had been sealed. In fact, now that he thought about it, he was struck by the alarming proportion of 'foreigners' with whom he'd been acquainted over the years who'd either succumbed to a fatal illness or had fled the island with every shred of life force sucked out of them.

Then, one day over coffee, Anna Kommis reported to Heidi that Manfred had resolved to get as far away from Europe as possible: the Karpfen-Pinsels were vicious peddlers of gossip, and 'the Bangkok revelations' were now common knowledge throughout German society's upper strata. Manfred had identified Namibia, where a significant ex-pat colony existed, thanks to its former status as the German Protectorate of South West Africa, one of the few overseas outposts of the Kaiser's Reich – prior, that is, to its capture by the British in 1915.

'Apparently,' Anna informed Heidi, 'the place ended up in the hands of the South Africans, and you know what racist fascists those Dutch Boers were. Well, like-minded Germans flocked there, and the Afrikaners gave them almost a free hand in running the place. A former colleague of Manfred's beetled off there some years ago after a rather nasty medical negligence claim. He loves it. He says quite a lot of his crowd still celebrate Hitler's birthday.'

'How awful!'

'Indeed. Anyway, everything's dirt cheap, so you can live in a palace and have armies of black servants for peanuts and lord it over the natives – a bit like Mallorca used to be fifty years ago. Manfred can't wait to go. He's already put our house in the hands of the agents.'

'God Lord! *You're* not going to Namibia, are you, Anna? You'd hate it.'

'Of course not! I was going to divorce Manfred, but the lawyers said the tax implications were just too awful. So, he's buying me an apartment in Los Angeles and a house in Marrakech – both just around the corner, so to speak, from Jeanne's places. Well, we thought it would be a bit more discreet, what with Lionel's career ... you know. Actually, he seems thrilled that I'm going to be around.'

Later that day, Heidi had attempted to amuse Werner by relaying Anna's news, but although she failed to generate any semblance of interest, he was soon searching the Internet for every reference to Namibia.

So, with completion of the Compulsory Purchase Edict fixed for 1 May, and armies of studio personnel arriving from Hollywood in advance of the 'stars', Werner had retreated to his study. Occasionally, he would emerge to make the lives of the removal men a nightmare as they prepared his possessions for storage in Palma, pending shipment to the Southern Hemisphere. He also made a nuisance of himself ridiculing – justifiably – the studio people's 'refurbishments' of *Ca'n Pau*'s principal rooms, including the hall and dining room: they conjured up a Mexican hacienda. Though bound by his contract with Cyclopean to permit the whitewashing of the exterior's rich yellow stone, nothing, it seemed, could silence Werner's incessant reminders that the thieving new owners would undoubtedly require restoration of their putative museum to the status quo ante.

He fired off several increasingly strident emails to Mr Klamp himself at the New York headquarters of his worldwide entertainment conglomerate. Mr Klamp did not send emails: he used the telephone. His midnight call to Werner some weeks back came as a surprise; the information communicated proved almost fatal. Mr Klamp used many obscenities. He told Werner – 'Stump' as he insisted on calling him – that he didn't want to hear any more whining. He knew 'a lot of big noises' in Namibia, and if Werner didn't shut his 'big Kraut mouth' he'd find his residence visas revoked. And if he upset 'his' stars when they arrived, 'Stump' would wish he'd never been born. As for the whitewashing, he'd cleared all that with 'the guys in Palma' through 'the Margalida dame.'

'My housekeeper,' Werner had replied, 'has no authority to negotiate anything. Even you must realise that. She's just an illiterate peasant.'

'Ha! Wake up and smell the coffee, bozo! She's a "Hero of the Revolution"! Your place is her family's old homestead. She's been made the Honorary Curator of this new museum scam and the hacienda comes with the job. We were told last week when we realised we probably wouldn't finish shooting before the end of May and that we'd need a fresh contract with the government boys. She moves in the minute you clear out, buddy. We assumed you knew. Jesus! I guess the old witch just didn't want to hurt your feelings, Stumpy.'

Despite Heidi's protests and the lateness of the hour, Werner had promptly marched up to *Ca'n Xet*; trotting behind, Heidi repeatedly begged him not to do anything rash. Alas, he banged on the door until he got Margalida out of bed. Then, in no uncertain terms, he told her what he thought of both her and her island race. She gave as good as she was given. Unwisely, Heidi sprang to her spouse's defence, shouting that a pig would have done a better job of cleaning *Ca'n Pau*. Then Margalida spat at Heidi, and Heidi slapped her across the face. When Werner finally managed to separate them, he summarily terminated Margalida's employment, whereupon the dismissed servant cackled jubilantly, for it was exactly what she'd hoped for.

The next morning, Margalida phoned her top-flight Palma lawyers on her recently acquired mobile. She'd already instructed them to file a redundancy claim against Stumpf in respect of the three months' notice she'd been given shortly after his receipt of the Compulsory Purchase Edict, which would bring to an end her 'twenty years of loyal service as housekeeper, cook, and social secretary', to use the wording of the draft claim. And in this connection, as security for both their client's anticipated compensation and their own costs, the lawyers were well advanced with the necessary papers for an injunction to prevent the removal from the island of any item of the Stumpfs' property. But Werner's reckless summary dismissal of Margalida opened up a veritable Aladdin's cave of additional juicy claims, including unfair and unlawful dismissal, with potential damages of scores of thousands of euros. And then there was the statutory holiday pay to which she was entitled in respect of all the holidays she'd never taken, plus the decades' worth of Social Security contributions that Werner should have paid to fund her state pension. The writs were served on Werner personally by a young and supercilious legal clerk, in whose presence the Defendant threatened to murder Margalida after inflicting the vilest tortures imaginable.

Perhaps it was unsurprising, therefore, that Werner rarely left his study these days. In any event, now that 'the stars' had arrived at *Ca'n Pau*, he couldn't bear meeting Tourny and Moineau as they rehearsed and performed Hollywood's risible script, and were fawned upon like royalty by the sycophantic studio minions. Oh, the Franco-Americans were polite enough and very understanding, but it was all too obvious to their ostensible host that they were clearly relishing his fall from grace. Well, there was a limit to how much humiliation any man could tolerate.

Heidi had tried her best to lift Werner's spirits. She repeatedly reminded him that the script which he so volubly scorned and ridiculed did, in fact, portray everyone who had attended his Sixtieth Birthday Party as a hero – not least himself. And he should be positively thrilled that, thanks to his departure from Texan politics, Anton Schuflicker – no less – had jumped at the opportunity to return to the movies and play her husband – this urbane, polyglot, polymath Renaissance man who, by the end of the movie, also proves himself more than capable with a pump-action shotgun when the going gets tough and the forces of darkness threaten decent folk. And wasn't it wonderful that when 'Anton' first arrived at *Ca'n Pau*, he'd been so charming, that he'd bent over backwards to be kind to her husband, to get to know him, to see into his heart, to portray him on screen as accurately as possible – and in the very best traditions of the Method?

But it was all to no avail. Werner was not flattered. There wasn't the least possibility that the black clouds engulfing his world had even a square millimetre of silver lining. Heidi tried another tack. She pointed out that the publicity from the movie would do wonders for his books; already his publishers were reporting increased sales. They were even planning fresh editions of those books which had been out of print for years. There were requests for meetings to discuss an autobiography and a magnum opus on the history of the Second World War, told at last from a 'wholly objective perspective'. Werner, however, refused to return his publisher's calls; he wouldn't even see the representatives who turned up uninvited at his door.

*

Just as the countdown to the 'Top of the Hour' news broadcast on BBC World reached its dramatic zero, the director's near-constant hysterical shrieking erupted in the courtyard.

'Bloody Moineau again, no doubt,' Werner muttered, '– improvising!' Almost immediately, her inimitable rasping roar exploded. He viciously pressed the remote control's volume button to maximum:

'The headlines at the top of the hour. The President of the Federal Republic of the Balearic Islands–'

'Terrorist bastard!'

'– is greeted at the White House in Washington by President O'Connell.'

'Lying bastard!'

'Rising sea levels due to global warming will result in the extinction of at least ten species of wading birds within the next decade, say scientists at Kabul University.'

'Who gives a damn?'

'The discovery yesterday of a severed head in a Disneyworld hotel room takes another bizarre twist.'

'Ha!'

'And Bolivian sex goddess Juanita Sanchez denies being the mother of Baby Sophia, the baby claimed by Dr Stavros Protopapas to be the world's first clone.'

'Jesus Christ!'

'Hello, I'm Shanta Kumar–'

'Good for you!'

'– and you're watching the news on BBC World.'

'You don't say!'

'In Washington a few minutes ago, President O'Connell welcomed to the White House for the first time the newly elected president of the world's youngest nation, the Federal Republic of the Balearic Islands. For a full report, we go live now to our Washington Bureau Chief, Kanu Agabi. ... Kanu.'

'Yeah, hi, Shanta. As you were saying, the Balearic President, Tomeu Grimalt–'

'Murderer! Terrorist! It's common knowledge!'

'– and his ambassador to Washington, Count Manilla–'

'Two-faced midget!'

'– were greeted here by the President with all the trappings – military bands, national anthems, guards of honour and a twenty-one-gun salute. Down at the railings there were a few demonstrators from Spain with banners calling the new nation an American puppet state and chanting "Death to the Traitors", but I doubt that either president heard them.

'In his speech, O'Connell again reaffirmed his commitment to stand up for little people fighting for freedom and democracy wherever they may be in the world, while urging all democracies to settle their differences by peaceful means and in accordance with international law, a reference, I would suggest, to the ongoing recriminations between the USA and France – in particular, with President Chiffon, who remains adamant that the so-called Tournygate Tape is a fabrication and undaunted in his efforts to get an EU-wide ban on all American movies.

'For his part, Grimalt, a former Palma restaurant owner, was generous in his praise of what he called "the extraordinary efforts of both the USA and Britain" to secure his nation's independence from Spain, and to provide financial assistance while it copes with the loss of EU grants and subsidies.'

'Yes, Kanu, on that point, do we know yet how much the Americans are going to pay for their ninety-nine-year lease of the former Spanish naval base in the north of Mallorca?'

'No, Shanta, that's still not clear. The Pentagon are saying it's a very complicated package, but unofficially I'm reliably informed it will be about a hundred million dollars a year. In fact, as I'm talking to you, Shanta, the formal signing of the treaties between the two nations is taking place inside the White House.'

'And I understand, Kanu, that tonight it will be the turn of the British to play host to President Grimalt and his wife.'

'That's right, Shanta. The recently appointed British ambassador, Sir Douglas Trench-Foot, who, you may remember, was our man in Madrid at the time of last July's crisis and subsequently spent a spell in Palma as civil administrator, will be rolling out the red carpet and pulling out all the stops with a slap-up banquet featuring roast beef and all the trimmings. And what's particularly interesting, Shanta, is that his daughter, Jane – who's eight months' pregnant, by the way – and her husband, Mike, are spending a brief holiday with Sir Douglas and Lady Trench-Foot at the Official Residence. You'll remember that they were two of the guests who almost lost their lives when Mr Stump's mansion–'

'Stumpf! Stumpf!'

'– was attacked by the ENABA terrorists in Mallorca last July.'

'That's right, Kanu.'

'By all accounts they never lost their heads, and risked their lives to try and rescue the heroic local lad who'd attempted to defend millionaire Mr Stump's–'

'STUMPF!'

'– luxury villa single-handed with just an old shotgun. Which is why President Grimalt will be investing both of them tonight with the new republic's highest honour, the Order of the Olive Tree.'

'Well, they deserve it, Kanu.'

'Absolutely! And soon we'll be able to see it all at the movies, Shanta.'

'That's right, Kanu. I understand that, as we speak, they're still filming on location at Stump's–'

'STUMPF, you fucking moron!'

'– exclusive retreat, but the latest from Cyclopean is that the movie should be released here in the States just before Christmas.'

'Well, Kanu, I know I'm looking forward to seeing it. And maybe we'll find out from Oscar-winning stars Toby Farquhar and Camilla Fitzroy-Grosvenor just a little bit more about that Oakheart pregnancy! By my calculations, Kanu, eight months ago takes us back to July last year, and–'

A tremendous explosion, followed by bursts of automatic gunfire, drowned out the sound.

'Not *again*!' thundered Werner, jumping up from his chair. 'How many more takes of that bloody scene are they going to film?' He marched over to one of the study windows and stared into the courtyard. According to the *Infernal Paradise* script, the treacherous siege of the house by the French and German Special Forces had dragged on through the night until dawn, when the American liberators finally arrived on the scene after battling their way over from the mysteriously deserted *Villa Tourny*. This poetic liberty had been taken when the producers vetoed the entire action taking place in the dark.

And so, as Werner glared at his whitewashed courtyard – the thick smoke from several thunderflashes was slowly dissipating – the long shadows cast by the early evening April sun were supposedly equating to first light on a July morning, even though they were in completely the wrong positions. In the centre of the courtyard, where his wrought-iron table had once stood, a two-wheeled mule cart – the conveyance by which Mateu had frantically transported himself from his mother's farm when last night's biblical storm burst upon the locality – was burning furiously. Suddenly, Lionel, who'd by now discarded his elegant white dinner jacket and black bow tie, was zigzagging at breakneck speed across the corpse-strewn cobbles towards the cart – Mateu had risked life and limb to unhitch the terrified mule during the hours of darkness – under which a gruesomely injured Ronaldo Albóndigas lay, albeit his unshaved face bore barely a scratch.

Meanwhile, according to the screenplay, Werner *von* Stumpf – the name Klamp had finally agreed to accept after Werner had vetoed all fifty of the writers' suggestions, above all Klamp's 'Schmidt' – was 'covering' Lionel from the roof of the 'guest cottage' with one of the three pump-action shotguns he'd managed to purloin from those members of the Special Forces he'd 'taken out' while battling his way to the cottage via a medieval subterranean secret passage. On the other side of the main house, 'Heidi' – together with the rest of the guests – were causing a diversion by hurling Molotov cocktails out of the dining room's French windows; Werner's Austrian *eiswein* certainly did have a kick to it.

Werner knew the script by heart: during the halcyon Indian summer days of last October, before threats of compulsory purchase and before Margalida had become a vexatious litigant, he'd enjoyed many hours meticulously amending the drafts sent to him by Cyclopean; his own location filming contract had suffered the same treatment. Although very few of his innumerable amendments had been accepted, it had been a most pleasurable occupation; he'd even convinced himself that he had all the necessary skills to be an accomplished screenplay writer. Indeed, during the winter months, he'd made considerable progress on transforming his seminal *Rommel: A German Hero* into what he thought would be a truly wonderful screenplay. Then the Ministry of Culture, Heritage and Sport's missive arrived and all work ceased.

Werner watched 'himself' blasting away on the guest cottage's roof with no less than three lethal weapons, and had to admit that Herr

Schuflicker was inspiringly courageous by rejecting a stuntman – except, of course, for the really dangerous stunts. In truth, he did look remarkably like himself in so many ways. They were even the same height and build – almost: he'd let himself go a bit since the Letter of Doom, but as soon as he got to Namibia he'd quickly get back into shape, what with all the gardening they'd need to do and–

'No, no, Anton,' Werner hissed, 'you *drop* the grenade into the courtyard – the remaining French are right below you – don't *hurl* it like a discus! It'll go right across the courtyard and blow up bloody Tourny and–'

Like a dam bursting, the seemingly endless words of comfort with which Heidi had tried to lift his spirits over the last few months suddenly filled his head. She was absolutely right! With so many stars, *Infernal Paradise* was going to be a fantastic box office hit, and, in consequence he, Werner *von* Stumpf – well, with hundreds of millions of cinemagoers across the globe repeating that name, the 'von' would surely stick! – he was going to become a celebrity in his own right. Out in Namibia he'd be the number-one socialite that every German ex-pat would sell their right arm to meet; he was presuming they had cinemas out there – and television. ... Of course they did! Oh, those colonials would be all over him – *and* Heidi, bless her! She was adamant that she'd only stay until he'd found a house to buy and got settled in, but he knew Heidi: she'd knuckle down. Secretly, she loved being ordered about: she was that type of woman. And yes, he had made a mistake: the piano routine made a good impression. It reflected well on him in the long run. People – the *right* people – didn't respect a man who had a bimbo or drudge for a wife.

My God, as a team we'll absolutely dazzle the Germans in Windhoek! I can just picture them. 'Did you really meet the King of Spain? Do tell us about Anton's teeth. Are they truly so menacing? Is it true Jeanne Moineau is an alcoholic? Was she drunk all the time they were filming? On the screen, your villa was so wonderful. How many bedrooms did you have? Chamber recitals on you terrace – with Gudrun Schluck and von Karpfen! Oh, how wonderful! That's what we miss out here – Culture. Is Heidi really going to give weekly recitals? Oh please, please put us on the invitation list.'

And really, if he was honest with himself, he hadn't done too badly out of the old house. Sixty per cent of two million euros was better than a kick in the teeth, especially as he hadn't paid a damn pfennig for the place! And whatever 'compensation' he might have to pay to that old crone in the end, the sums he was due from Cyclopean would no doubt cover it. Then there were all those royalties from his publishers, an autobiography – the family history might be a bit of a problem, but he could skim through that. ...

Well, maybe he should put the autobiography on the backburner until he'd completed the *History of the Second World War* – and the Rommel screenplay. Which reminded him: Herr Schuflicker would be perfect for the part! And as Rommel wasn't a Nazi – Hitler had even forced him to commit suicide – dear Anton and all those Hollywood Jews shouldn't have the slightest qualms about–

Christ! He should sound him out as soon as possible – tonight – over dinner! The dear man was always inviting him round to dine at his rented villa – or at his favourite restaurant down in Cala d'Or. Perhaps he'd appreciate some home cooking. … He'd almost begged Heidi to play for him – Schubert, he seemed to remember … Schumann? … Schönberg? – whatever. She could rustle up something – to eat that is. And the Bechstein which the studio people had dumped in the living room had sounded pretty good from up here when Heidi had had a go on it.

Within seconds, Werner was flying down the stairs in search of his wife, wondering whether Herr Schuflicker liked big-game hunting. Doubtless, there was plenty of that sort of thing in Namibia.

CHAPTER 26

In the elegant ballroom of the British Ambassador's Official Residence, Michael Oakheart was winding up his brief yet touching speech.

'And in conclusion, Senyor President,' he said, turning to Tomeu Grimalt and hoping that he'd pronounced two more Catalan words – Esperanto as his father-in-law called it – with the correct *Mallorquí* intonation, 'from the depths of our hearts, my wife and I thank you and all the people of your magical islands for the great honour that has been bestowed upon us. The symbolism of the Order of the Olive Tree' – with his fingertips, Mike brushed the silver medal embossed with a highly stylised olive tree which Grimalt had earlier pinned to his dinner jacket's lapel – 'will always be in our thoughts. Words alone cannot convey the emotions Jane and I experience whenever we contemplate – as we so often do – the events of that tragic yet historic night last July, and remember how close we, and so many of our dearest friends, came to sharing the very same fate suffered by that ancient and noble olive tree. But although the tree was destroyed, the beneficent life force which once flowed within it was not. I understand that around the crater where it once stood, saplings are now sprouting from the ripe black olives that dropped from its boughs before disaster struck. And there lies the important message for all those evil men – and women – wherever they may be – who want to destroy the values that *we* all hold most dear. Goodness is indestructible. ... Thank you – *moltes gràcies* – Senyor Grimalt.'

The applause was enthusiastic and heartfelt.

There were tears in Jane's eyes as she kissed Mike on the cheek. 'I'm so proud of you,' she purred.

'Well done, my boy!' roared Sir Douglas. 'Absolutely first class!'

When the applause died down, Jane approached the media's battery of microphones and said a few words of thanks herself, while deliberately avoiding an oration that might compete with her husband's performance. Then she smiled coyly, saying:

'Well, Your Excellencies ... ladies and gentleman, you've probably noticed' – she gently rubbed her stomach – 'that I've had to have a ball gown made especially for this occasion due to having put on a little weight recently.' There was polite laughter. 'And before I get inundated by scolding emails and the like, I would like to point out that Michael and I came over by *ship* and shall be returning by *ship*. Cunard cruise liners have fully equipped hospitals, so if the little sprog decides to pop out before she's due, we'll be in very good hands!'

There was more polite laughter and a crack from Sir Douglas that he hoped Cunard were paying her commission.

'Actually,' Jane continued, adopting an earnest expression, 'there is, Senyor and Senyora Grimalt, a serious reason for mentioning my pregnancy.' She paused and looked straight at the CNN camera. 'I've just let the cat out of the bag, so to speak, about the results of the ultra-scan. When Michael and I discovered we were going to have a little baby girl, like all parents we began thinking about what to call her. Goodness knows how many "final decisions" we've made! Well, earlier today, we reopened the issue all over again. We knew how much we owed our own families for all their love, kindness and generosity over the years, but as we watched the extraordinary events taking place at the White House this morning, Senyor President, it suddenly occurred to us that, but for the single-mindedness of one man, our baby' – she tapped her stomach again – 'would not exist at all.'

It was an enigmatic statement of the obvious, and with bemused expressions, the throng before her all gazed at Michael.

'I am, of course, referring to Mateu Obrador,' – there were gasps from some, and sighs of apparent comprehension from others – 'the heroic young Mallorcan who saved our lives. But for his courage in holding at bay for so many bloody hours the ... the treacherous forces despatched to assassinate us, well, in all probability, the mission of our American liberators would have been in vain.'

'Hear, hear!' boomed Sir Douglas. Grimalt nodded gravely, proving that his English was better than he admitted.

'And so, if our baby had been a boy, we would have called him Mateu.' She smiled at Mike. 'I hope that one day we will have that honour. ... Mateu's mother, Senyora Margalida Palmer Obrador, has lost her only child, but we hope that in her continuing grief, our decision to call our little girl "Margalida" may be of some comfort to her as a heartfelt gesture of our gratitude for Mateu's selfless sacrifice – and thank you so much, Mummy and Daddy, for your support.'

As the applause erupted, President Grimalt abandoned his frozen smile and bounded forward, embracing and kissing Jane, and then Mike, before positioning himself between them and putting his arms around their shoulders for the benefit of the jostling cameramen and photographers.

'What a girl!' blasted Sir Douglas proudly to Manilla, who laughed nervously.

'Yes, isn't she?' he said. 'I'm so lucky to be sitting next to her at dinner.'

The top table was long and positioned at right angles to all the others, the VIPs being seated along one side only and facing the less important diners. The menu bore all the hallmarks of Lady Trench-Foot: Scottish smoked salmon, roast Welsh lamb – not beef as misreported by the BBC – a variety of English cheeses, and an extremely alcoholic trifle made with lashings of Irish whiskey. All the wines were English, including a rather acidic sparkling and a very thin red labelled Badger's Burrow Pinot Noir, none of which were to the liking of the Grimalts, who said so candidly and without any hint of embarrassment. They were also somewhat perplexed by both the language of the menu – French – and their hosts' explanation – tradition.

'Well,' said President Grimalt in Catalan to Sir Douglas, 'if you ask me, it's the sort of tradition you ought to get rid of, now that the French are formally laying claim to those tiny islands of yours.'

'Ah, the Channel Islands contretemps,' sneered Sir Douglas, reverting to English but pronouncing 'contretemps' like a Frenchman. 'Mere bagatelle, Senyor President! Just another case of sour grapes. The French have got about as much chance of getting those tax havens back as the Argentineans have of ever getting their grubby little hands on the windswept, barren Falklands. So wise of you to shun the EU like the plague.'

'Hmm,' said Grimalt vaguely, not understanding any of the Ambassador's vernacular.

Sir Douglas took another sip of the Badger's Burrow, and, despite its vegetal bouquet and metallic aftertaste, beamed at Grimalt, for he was secretly relieved that the President had raised the issue of the Channel Islands: it was a topic about which he knew a great deal. So far, making conversation with the Mallorcan had been a nightmare: despite his time in Madrid, Sir Douglas knew little about restaurants that specialised in rice dishes. Unfortunately, it was just such an establishment that Grimalt had run in a Palma seafront location for most of his adult life. He'd tried to impress his host with the names of all the local celebrities who'd patronised *Arrozeria Grimalt* over the years, but apart from the Condes de Manilla, they meant absolutely nothing to Sir Douglas. Nor did he have the least interest in Palma Football Club. The Ambassador had hoped for better things when he learned that Grimalt had a boat and was a keen weekend fisherman. But Trench-Foot had no experience of fishing for sardines, whitebait or squid, and Grimalt was clearly disinterested in the finer points of fly-fishing. Indeed, his knowledge of rivers appeared to be confined to the dried-up variety.

'Jolly interesting place, the Channel Islands,' said Sir Douglas. 'Ever been there?' Grimalt had not; nor had he the slightest knowledge of where they might be. After the geography lesson came history, from William the Conqueror to the German Occupation during the Second World War.

'The only bit of British territory that lot ever occupied,' said Sir Douglas proudly.

In the hope of drowning his sorrows, the President downed another glass of Badger's Burrow. Trench-Foot was beaming at him, obviously expecting some kind of intelligent response. 'And ... er ... your king is duke of these little islands?'

That's right! – well, Duke of Normandy to be precise. That's why they're *his* – why they're *British*. And *that*, Senyor President, is why we have every confidence that, along with all our other true allies across the globe, your new nation will wholly support our position and tell the French where to get off, eh? Anyway, the Channel Islanders would rather die than be handed over to the French and lose their tax haven status – like the Gibraltarians and the Spanish, if you get my drift.'

Tomeu Grimalt did get Sir Douglas's 'drift', and bristled. Despite the Republic's rift with its former masters, it was impossible for him to forget overnight the propaganda on which he had been fed all his life. He nodded cautiously. 'Ah yes, Gibraltar. The EU blockade is hurting, yes?'

'An absolute scandal! I blame Chiffon. Left to their own devices, we're almost sure the Spanish would have reopened the border yonks ago.'

'Hmm. ... We are ... *sympathetic*, Sir Douglas. Of course, for obvious reasons so much of our trade is still with the Peninsula – mainland Spain – and our citizens must travel there all the time – for doing the business, the universities, the special doctors–'

'Yes, quite.'

'And now we no have the travel subsidies Madrid was to paying us, it is all *so* being expensive.' Grimalt shook his head gravely and sighed. 'The inflation!'

'Quite – damned bad show! Thank goodness you've got all that dosh flowing into the treasury's coffers from the Yanks, what? – for the naval base and everything. By the way, how's the ice hockey stadium coming along?'

'The American "dosh", Sir Douglas, is but droppings in the ocean, as you English say.'

'Oh? Maybe you should ask them for some more?'

'I have.'

'Ah.'

A waiter refilled Grimalt's glass; he stared at it gloomily. 'We *do* want to go on supporting you over Gibraltar,' he said without looking at Sir Douglas, as if hypnotized by the Badger's Burrow, '– we really *do* ... and the Chunnel Islands.'

'*Channel* Islands.'

'Hmm. ... Did I mention that the Spanish Interior Minister came to see me the other day, with the EU Commissioner for something?'

'Oh?'

Grimalt shook his head and laughed. 'You won't believe this, but they said that if we would be joining the EU after all, the new headquarters for the Harmonisation of Television Advertising Standards Directorate would in Palma to be built – not Córdoba, and that we'd get fifty per cent rebates on the cost of *all* air and sea travellings to *any* place in Spain, *and* to *any* place on, or within fifty kilometres of, the French Mediterranean coast! Pure briberies!'

'You rejected the offers, naturally.'

'Well, almost.'

'"Almost"?'

'I am a democrat, *senyor*. I said I must be referring their extraordinary proposals to my cabinet's colleagues and to the Parliament, but I thinks I am knowing what their response will be! By the highways, we receive very nice quotations from some British companies to supply us with the new boats we need for our coastguarding, and helicopeters for our new airplane force. They are clearly the best. ... If only they were not so ... *expensive* ...'

For an instant, Grimalt's expression reminded Sir Douglas of Hugo, the over-indulged Dalmatian, whenever he placed his spotty head on his son-in-law's knee and visually pleaded to be fed.

By contrast, Senyora Grimalt had no difficulty making conversation with Mike Oakheart, or rather, maintaining an endless monologue about her and Tomeu's new homes, the Marivent and Almudaina Palaces. She spoke in English and with all the confidence of one who is self-taught and has benefited from serving beer and snacks to British package tourists over many summer seasons, as indeed she had – at her brother's Palmanova 'pub', The Black Bull – before marrying Tomeu twelve years ago and joining him in the *arrozeria*.

As she impatiently awaited the extra ration of lamb she'd vociferously demanded from a stunned waiter, Senyora Grimalt appeared to run out of things to say about her zealous changes to the decor and furnishings of the former royal palaces. She paused to take breath, and Mike opened his mouth to change the subject to breastfeeding, the topic he'd thought long and hard about while 'Neus' – as Senyora Grimalt insisted on being called, a name he found impossible to pronounce – had droned on. He felt that in view of the impending birth of his daughter, it was a subject about which he should be fully conversant – preferably from someone who'd had practical experience. He had, however, felt unable to broach the subject with either his own mother or Jane's; Betty Trench-Foot was rather like the late Queen: one could not imagine her performing any kind of bodily function. On the other hand, Mike knew that the Spaniards – and for him that still included Mallorcans – loved children, and that Neus had three of them, aged eleven, nine and four. And he'd seen enough public breastfeeding in Spain to know that it was not something that caused the slightest embarrassment.

But before Mike could utter a single word, Neus was off again.

'You know, Mike, all this talk of my palaces is making me think that you and Jane really ought to have a holiday home, especially now that you is famous and everything. I mean, when that movie *Infernal Paradise* comes out, you'll be dead important – you'll be on TV and everything. You'll have *¡Hola!* begging you for interviews.'

'We've already had *Hello!* – the British equivalent – at our Richmond house – last summer, in fact – as soon as we got back from Mallorca.'

'*Hombre*, me and Tomeu are in every *week*! Anyway, *chico*, once that film is on at the flicks, you'll have the media round you like flies around a pile of dog dirt. And believe me, they ask the most cheekiest questions. And I bet you anything what you likes that they'll want to know how come you and Jane, what with all that money what you gets from the movie company to use your names and characters and all in the movie, and all your "love" for Mallorca – like what you just said in the speech thing before dinner – and the medals like what Tomeu gave you ... Anyhow, they'll want to know why you don't have your own place in Mallorca.'

'You think so?'

'You bet! – or they'll say you're only pulling the woollens over our heads. And of course, Mike, now that we've got all them laws and things making it difficult for foreigners to take their money out of our country – and them laws making it impossible for a foreigner to buy any house without the government saying it's OK, or to own more than one house, well, the prices of villas and flats have dropped like a brick.'

'So I've heard. I understand quite a few Germans have gone bust because they've had to sell up so cheaply. Some have even committed suicide.'

'Yes, isn't it sad?' Neus's face was a picture of grief. Then she burst out laughing. '*Hombre*,' she continued after wiping her eyes, 'you can pick up some great places for peanuts! It would be a dead good investment. I mean, prices will go up again once things settle down.'

'Well, I don't think–'

'Oh! I've just thought! We've got this wonderful old house right on the beach at Colònia de Sant Jordi – it's been in Tomeu's family for generations. You'd *love* it. We've had such wonderful times there every summer, and we can hardly bear to think of selling it, but now that Tomeu's President and we've got them palaces and big nobs to entertain all the time, the Colònia house is far too small, and we can never find the time to drive all the way down there – even with the chauffeur. But it would be perfect for you and Jane and little Margalida – what a lovely gesture! I know the old girl will be thrilled – she's a Hero of The Revolution, you know – and I'm sure it will give her something to live for – knowing that she'll be able to see her god-daughter regular like ... just down the road from Alqueria Blanca ... at Colònia. We'd do you a fabulous price, seeing who you are an' all.' Her eyes rolled around the great room and then she nodded in the direction of Sir Douglas. 'Have a word with Tomeu, after like. You do know she's moving into *Ca'n Pau* as soon as that Stump moves out ... Margalida, that is, don't you?'

'"*God*-daughter"? – "*moving*"? – *Ca'n*–? ... We knew about the Museum, but – but ... What do you mean, "god-daughter"?'

'Well, you're not going to give the kid Margalida's name and not ask her to be a godparent, surely? I just assumed – me and Tomeu – that was what you meant. I bet *she* does too – the whole island by now. I bet they was all watching you on TV back home, even if it was only four o'clock in the morning in Palma. Do you suffer from jet lag? I bet it's been one long fiesta there all day, ever since we was met at the White House this morning. Isn't Patrick tall? Mind you, that Caronia's a stuck-up cow. The White House is ever so titchy, isn't it? Our palaces make it look *really* pokey. When you come to Mallorca you'll have to come to stay. I bet you've never stayed in a palace, have you, Mike? Oh, I can see it now – all of us having drinks and nibbles on the terrace at *Marivent*, with Margalida playing with the kiddie like she's her real gran and everything. And every time we shout "Margalida! – no! – don't be naughty!" them two won't know what one we was shouting at! *Hombre*, there'll be some great photo opportunities for *¡Hola!*, won't there?'

The Balearic Republic's First Lady continued to regale Mike with her visions of Margalida Palmer Obrador's new role as Godmother and Honorary Grandmother – a welcome counterfoil to her more onerous duties as Honorary Curator of the National Museum of Liberation – but he couldn't share in her unbridled enthusiasm for the bonds between the

Oakhearts and 'her' island, which, she confidently believed, would be cemented in the very near future. Instead, his head began to ache, and with every sip of Badger's Burrow it got even worse.

Some distance away, at one end of the long top table, Jane Oakheart's equilibrium had also evaporated. The English wine industry, however, could not be blamed, for in view of her pregnancy, she'd stuck to Malvern water all evening, albeit she was planning to take a sip of something alcoholic when the toasts were proposed. Her problem was that the bigotry and snobbery which Manilla had revealed almost a year ago on his 'yacht' moored off Cabrera, had manifested themselves yet again. Almost from the moment they'd sat down, the odious little man had started. He seemed neurotic, his short fat body and disproportionately large head in constant motion, while other mannerisms suggested to Jane that he'd seriously underestimated the strength of English sparkling wines.

He started on the Americans, who, he thought, were no more civilised than the 'Red Indians' they'd almost wiped out in the course of settling their vile country. Fortuitously, the only Americans on the top table, Secretary of State Dralon Schwartz-Rodriguez and Defense Secretary Buck Goosepepper, sat well out of earshot, while on his other side he only had Betty Trench-Foot as a potential eavesdropper. But she was wholly engrossed in trying to comprehend the occasional barks and grunts emanating from somewhere behind the Balearic Foreign Minister's thick black beard. In any event, Manilla spoke in French, not because of his assumption that the Americans present had little or no knowledge of the language, or because of his absolute certainty that the Grimalts did not, but simply to show off. Having well and truly lambasted the Americans, he turned his sights on 'Tomeu' and 'Neus' themselves, names he pronounced with concentrated derision.

'They won't last long,' he sneered. 'The masses got carried away in the heady days after "independence" and the "amnesty", when so many of the ENABA top brass "came out" in order to cash in on their half-witted and misguided adulation. I tried to warn the voters that all this republicanism would be a disaster, and of the short-sighted antagonism towards the EU. I predicted the inflation, the collapse in the property market – I mean how can you have a healthy economy without a booming construction industry? I predicted tourism would decline even further. I said that without the Royals at *Marivent*, Mallorca would lose all its cachet – no *Copa del Rey* regatta for a start! Well, that was one of *the* events of the European summer season, Jane.

'Indeed, since the Royals' boycott, social life for all the nouveau riche in Palma has gone down the pan – and they're *livid*. And now the plebs have finally realised what an awful bloody mistake they've made, what with their first real taste of unemployment in years – and having to pay the full cost of getting to the mainland. And – this just goes to show how hypocritical the working classes really are – what they hate more than anything else is to see their own kind – two vile, common little oiks – living like royalty in the King's palaces, *and* giving the impression abroad that Mallorca is full of people like them – which it is, of course, but that's not what they want the rest of the world to know. It's the worst possible image for an island that relies almost entirely on tourism for its very survival.'

'I see,' said Jane stifling a yawn. 'So, Grimalt won't have a hope in hell of being re-elected next time round – when? – in another three or four years?'

'Ha!' snapped Manilla. 'Those two won't last that long, thank God! If it were not for that damned film *Infernal Paradise*, we could boot him out tomorrow.'

'Oh?'

Manilla tapped his nose slyly. 'I have a lot of friends, Jane, a lot of *contacts* ... in every corner of the island – of the Balearics – of Spain – of the world. My family has been part of Mallorca's ruling class for a thousand years. Our network is labyrinthine. There's *nothing* I can't discover about *anyone* on the island, sooner or later. And it may not surprise you to learn that I've had my sights on Grimalt ever since he crawled out from under his stone. And to think that Beatriz and I used to go to his restaurant for a *paella* now and then!

'Oh, he was clever, with his little friends – clerks and the like in town halls, changing dates on documents here, forging birth certificates there – but in the end I unearthed the truth about "Tomeu Grimalt", all right.' Manilla glanced down the table toward his President and hissed like a cat.

'And what is "the truth"?' asked Jane hesitantly.

A few seconds passed. '"The truth"? ... Oh, the *truth*! He's Jewish – and your average citizen of the risible "Federal Republic of the Balearic Islands" won't be amused by a Jewish "president" masquerading as a devoted Catholic.'

Jane stared at him incredulously. 'I – I don't understand. What on *earth* are you talking about? Are you mad?'

'Mad? Why should I be mad? He's descended from Jewish tailors in Palma – converted to Catholicism in the sixteenth century. I've got it all in black and white.'

'That doesn't make him Jewish, for God's sake – not that I'd give a damn if he were. I think you're just projecting your own vile anti-Semitism onto–'

265

'Shush! Don't shout it from the rooftops! Believe me, Jane, for a Mallorcan, it's enough. Of course, we won't impeach him on the basis of being a Jew. For a start, that would really louse up our relations with the Americans – the new base at Pollença is such a major source of income. And naturally, we don't want to rock the boat until *Infernal Paradise* has finished its run at the box office – Cyclopean and their protégé, O'Connell, wouldn't be at all happy. Anyway, once the great unwashed have stopped queuing to watch all those brain-dead hams in that Hollywood fantasy, we'll arrange for Grimalt's colleagues in the government to learn all about his ancestry, and they'll ask him to stand down – illness or something. He and that tart – the whole nationalist gang – will do anything to avoid *that* kind of scandal.'

'You *are* mad,' Jane muttered, shaking her head in disbelief.

'And I've sounded out a lot of the people who matter, and we think we can nip all this republican nonsense in the bud. We can't really ask the King to be head of state – we'd sort of end up united with Spain again and the hoi polloi won't have that, but a certain *Royal Highness* – no names – still highly confidential – would be *delighted* to accept the noble and venerable crown we have to offer. So, Jane, we'll restore the ancient Kingdom of Mallorca, which will be rather nice, don't you think? – a sort of Monaco but on a rather larger scale. Yours truly could be in line for the post of Lord Chamberlain, and Beatriz would be an admirable Mistress of the Wardrobe. And just think of the boost to tourism! Believe me, the peasants know which side their bread is buttered on. They'll love the idea. And before you know it, we'll be back in the EU on the old gravy train.'

'Why are you telling me all this, Alfonso? Perhaps Daddy would be a more appropriate recipient of–'

'Talking of scandals, Jane, brings me to–'

'Alfonso, I really don't want to hear *any* more. To be honest–'

'– *brings me* to you and Mike and–'

'*Me*? *Mike*? What the hell are you–?'

'– *and* Margalida,' he added portentously.

'The *baby*?'

'No, no, *no*!' He threw back his head and sniggered. 'Not the *baby* – the other one – "the Hero of the Revolution" – "the Honorary Curator of the National Museum of Liberation" – *and* the baby, I suppose … in a way. Let me explain …'

Like her husband, Jane knew of the 'nationalisation' of *Ca'n Pau* through her regular chats with Heidi on the phone, but Manilla's sardonic account of the good fortune of the Stumpfs' housekeeper came as a shock. 'Poor Heidi and Werner,' she said sadly. 'It must have been the final straw, and too painful to admit – assuming, that is, that they know. They *do* know, don't they, Alfonso?'

'Oh, I'm sure they do ... by now.'

'But I don't understand. How can Margalida be a museum curator? She's just a bloody cleaner? Frankly, I can't imagine what there is to see from the "liberation" point of view – apart from a thumping great hole in the ground.'

Again, Manilla sniggered. 'Exactly, my dear Jane – that *is* all there is to see. And that's all the visitors *will* see – along with those parts of the grounds between the front gate and the Olive Terrace – when, that is, the "Museum" is open, which I understand will occur only on "Liberation Day" and at such other times as dear old Margalida decides. Incidentally, did I mention that she'll have the run of the *whole* house – rent free – for life, with the State picking up *all* the utility bills and maintenance charges?'

'Good Lord! I know she lost her son, but that's incredible. Anyway, that's your "scandal", is it? But what the hell has it got to do with me and Mike and ... the baby?'

'"*Incredible*", Jane? No, I think the word is "fraudulent". The "Museum" is a "scam", as our American friends would say. Oh, Jane, Jane, Jane, I *do* so wish you'd had a word with me before making that announcement earlier – such a fine gesture, but alas *so* misguided. All through dinner I've been dreading this moment, but ... Well, I'm afraid Margalida is not the sweet old lady you thought she was – well, not all that old really – she just looks old, but then she did gravitate from toiling as a peasant to toiling for the likes of Stumpf.'

Suddenly, Manilla leaned so close to Jane that his cheek touched hers. 'You see, Jane,' he whispered into her ear, 'Margalida was one of *them* – an ENABA agent. And whatever the French and Germans were up to that night, the bomb that went off up there on the Olive Terrace was planted by Margalida – to kill Stumpf and all his illustrious German guests. If it's any comfort, the terrorists only became aware that there would be an Anglo-French contingent at that ghastly Kraut's party once the wheels had been set in motion. Anyway, in so far as those lunatics had any clear idea of what they were doing, it seems their hope was that the uproar in Germany would be so violent that Berlin would force Madrid to impose martial law and finally provoke the Mallorcans into violent opposition and a unilateral declaration of independence. In any event, they'd get the worldwide media attention that all these fanatics crave for.'

'I don't believe a word of it,' Jane finally croaked. 'It's – it's as crazy as your story about Grimalt being Jewish.'

'Oh no. She told me herself – just some weeks ago. You see, Jane, another one of my hats is Chairman of the Balearic Historic Buildings Board, and, unsurprisingly, I wasn't prepared to sanction Grimalt's incomprehensible proposals for *Ca'n Pau*. Well, the next thing I know, an "invitation" arrives via Grimalt's secretary to join the old *tricoteuse* for a *frito* at her hovel – God, how I loathe greasy peasant food! – it being made quite clear that to decline would be rather unwise. So, she and I had a truly ridiculous clandestine meeting, and I heard the whole bizarre story.

'Apparently, on the night in question she even arranged to get her son out of harm's way by sending him down to the bar in Calonge – she claims he didn't know she was in ENABA. Then the storm broke, and, realising Stumpf's party would be moved indoors, she crept down to move her bomb from the Olive Terrace – it was timed to go off at eleven – only to find the place swarming with foreign "gunmen". Well, Mateu never made it to the bar. She suspects his scooter broke down. He must have returned home, found his mother out in the storm, and rushed down to *Ca'n Pau* – God only knows why. And the rest, as they say, is history.

'Well, canny Margalida told me in no uncertain terms that she wanted her family's house back – it once belonged to her uncle … brother? … brother-in-law? – no matter. She threatened to scupper *Infernal Paradise* unless she got it – and my goodness, wouldn't it be embarrassing for you *and* the Americans – *all* of us – if it had come out that there really was an ENABA plot to kill the lot of you, just as Klipper and Chiffon – and that pillock Azucena – have always alleged? … So, Jane, mum's the word.'

Without waiting for a response, Manilla turned to Lady Trench-Foot, who was twiddling a wine glass and nodding to something the Foreign Minister was mumbling. 'My dear Betty, I've been neglecting you! *Do* forgive me, but Jane and I have had *so* much to catch up on. How are the Labradors, Alcock and Brown?'

But as Jane's mother launched into one of her favourite topics of conversation with obvious relief, Manilla could only think of his wonderful triumph. The Oakhearts had behaved abominably on that trip to Cabrera: as soon as those French mountebanks turned up, he and Beatriz had been snubbed, humiliated, abandoned. Well, he who laughs last laughs longest. Oh, it was glorious! For the rest of their lives, every time Jane and her bourgeois spouse looked at, or thought of, their daughter, they'd see a bloodthirsty assassin!

CHAPTER 27

After toasts to Britain's monarch and President Grimalt had been drunk, coffee and liqueurs were served; in the ballroom, a small but raucous band began playing *When They Begin The Beguine*. Feeling decidedly unwell, Jane wanted nothing more than to escape to her room and lie down, for the prospect of telling Mike that their baby would bear the name of a cold-blooded murderer filled her with terror. And so, pleading exhaustion and barely able to maintain a forced smile, she escaped a lively exchange of gory hunting anecdotes between Manilla and her mother, and then proceeded along the top table repeating her excuse. As she approached Mike, Jane noticed that he looked rather pale himself. She'd just placed her hands on the back of his chair and was leaning forward to whisper in his ear that she needed to speak to him privately, when Senyora Grimalt suddenly stopped talking and finally tuned in to the Latin-American medley emanating from the ballroom. Supercharged with Badger's Burrow, she shot out of her chair, almost knocking over both it and Jane.

'*Para Vigo Me Voy*!' she shrieked. 'One of me favourites! Come on, Mike, let's dance! Oh, Jane, you look terrible! No dancing for you. You'd better lie down.'

'Darling–' Mike began.

'Mikey–'

'*Vamanos*!' blasted Neus, pulling Mike out of his chair with her formidable arms. 'Oh, Jane, Mike's got some great news for you, but it can wait until after we've danced a bit.' She embraced Jane with an almost life-threatening bear hug. '*Hombre*, we're going to be one big happy family in Mallorca, what with the kiddie, us Grimalts and Granny Margalida just up the road from your new house! And when she hears about being a god–!'

'Darling–!' cried Mike, causing heads to turn as he was dragged away, grimly aware from Sir Douglas's expression that it would be a diplomatic disaster should he decline the honour of dancing with the President's wife.

It was more than two hours later when a dishevelled Mike gently opened the door to the bedroom and began to tiptoe in. But he pulled himself up with a start: Jane was propped up in bed, staring oddly at the opposite wall, where a portrait of Lord Halifax – Britain's wartime ambassador to Washington – hung incongruously. Lady Trench-Foot had removed it from the hall immediately upon moving in: it was a quasi-abstract work in the style of Picasso, and the American artist had given undue prominence to Halifax's tragically withered arm. The canvas had not soothed Jane's fevered brow: it reminded her of Kaiser Wilhelm II, who'd suffered from a similar disability, and her mental images of his notorious pomposity, hauteur and paranoia had only served to remind her of Werner Stumpf. Which brought her back to 'Granny Margalida', a term she'd intoned almost continuously like a witchdoctor's curse since her escape from the festivities below.

'Oh,' said Mike, 'I thought you'd be asleep. I'm really so sorry, Footy, but that bloody Now-oos – Nay-us – Nee-ows – or however you pronounce her bloody name – just wouldn't leave me alone all night. The proceedings have only just ended downstairs, with the Grimalt woman leading a conga around the garden. From what I could see, only her miserable husband didn't take part.'

Mike sat down on the bed and took his wife's hand. 'Are you feeling any better, Footy? Betty told me she'd popped up earlier on to make sure you were all right. She just said you were feeling a bit queasy and needed some peace and quiet. ... Darling, have you been crying? Oh, Footy, my poor baby, what is it?'

Jane finally stopped staring at Lord Halifax, and, lowering a shaking head, wailed: 'Oh, Mikey! *Gran-ny Mar-ga-lida*! It's – it's too hor-rible for wo-ords.'

Mike put his arms around her. 'Oh, honey, I feared you'd be fretting about that – and a house in Mallorca – of all things! I wanted so much to talk to you there and then, but that great tub of lard just wouldn't let me off the dance floor for one second, even though I'm a bloody awful dancer, especially with all this Latin-American stuff. Mind you, I think I've just about mastered the tango, and even though I say so myself, I'm not too bad at the bossa nova now. Actually–'

Jane's shoulders heaved as she began wailing again. 'Oh, Jesus Christ, what in God's name have we done? It's a nightmare! I don't want this baby. I never wanted a baby. If only we'd never gone to that bloody island. If only we'd never had all that vile cheap rosé. If only we hadn't gone skinny dipping in the pool. If only–'

'Footy, baby, *darling*, what are you saying? We've wanted a baby for ages. This is a dream come–'

'No! *You* wanted a baby. I – I–'

'You're getting this out of all proportion, honey. Naturally, I was horrified when that Nay-us – Nee – bugger it! – Noose started rabbiting on about buying their bloody beach house. But don't worry, I didn't agree to *anything*. Jesus, I'd rather die than have any dealings with that bunch of crooks! And anyway, I think the last thing either of us wants is another house at present – and certainly not one on bloody Mallorca. And yes, I felt sick too when she started talking about old Margalida being a godmother, and that the islanders would assume–'

'"Godmother"? ... *Godmother*! What are you talking about?'

As Jane battled against her sobbing, Mike related Senyora Grimalt's grim prediction of what the entire Balearic nation would assume about Baby Oakheart's name. 'But,' he concluded, 'I gave it a lot of thought during all that bopping, and I think I can see a way out on religious grounds. I dare say we can pull the wool over their eyes with some mumbo-jumbo about our little Margalida being a Protestant and having to be baptised in the Anglican Church, and so as "Granny" Margalida is a Roman Catholic ... well, I assume she's a Catholic. ... I seem to remember her doing a lot of genuflecting and crossing herself at Mateu's funeral–'

His reference to the deceased Hero of The Revolution set Jane off once more. 'Oh, Mikey,' she wailed, 'it's far worse than you could ever imagine – far, *far* worse.'

*

It was after four in the morning and the big house was silent. Although Mike had removed his jacket and bow tie, he was still dressed and pacing the room, two fingers drumming on his lips. 'There is the possibility that Manilla is lying,' he suggested rather unconvincingly.

'A remote possibility.'

'Remote or not, you have to concede it's possible – that he's just a vicious old git getting his own back – or trying to.'

'For what?'

'For us pissing off with Lionel and Jeanne that day at Cabrera, of course.'

'Don't be ridiculous. He can't be that paranoid.'

'I don't see why not. I–'

'We're going over the same old ground yet again. We have to assume he's telling the truth. And it does have a ring of truth about it. That bomb had to be an inside job. How else could ENABA have known about the party?'

'Hundreds of ways. Or it was indeed a Franco-German bomb as the Americans–'

'Oh, for God's sake!' After a few seconds' silence, Jane added: 'Mikey, we have to consider the worst-case scenario. Manilla is a gossiping bastard. So is Beatriz. God only knows what they might say when in their cups. My God, the way he drank that filthy wine tonight! And then there's that murdering crone herself. She's already used her "secret" to get Werner's house. She might get even greedier. And then one day she'll be senile ... perhaps quite soon ... who knows? Oh my God, it'll be a sword of Damocles hanging over us for the rest of our lives.'

'And over the head of our daughter too, I suppose.'

'Yes ... naturally.'

'Perhaps we could call her something else after all. I mean, she's not even been born yet. We have every right to change our minds. We–'

'Don't be such a bloody fool! We announced it on TV – *live – worldwide*!'

'Hmm.' Mike considered querying the 'we', but then thought better of it. Instead, he said: 'And you also indicated that when we had a son, we'd call him Mateu.'

Jane gave a little shriek of horror. 'Oh, Christ! I'd forgotten that.'

With a twinge of conscience, Mike began tapping his lips again. 'Maybe they were a mother-and-son partnership. ... Maybe they were in it together – the bomb and everything.'

'Thanks for that comforting thought. That's not what Manilla said though.'

'Maybe she was being economical with the truth when she met with him – to protect her son's glorious image.'

Jane's thoughts, however, had already raced on. 'It would completely wreck the film – the truth – wouldn't it? – if it came out before it was released? They'd have to abandon it. Bloody hell, Cyclopean would lose *millions*! Do you think they could ask us for their money back – force majeure – a total failure of consideration or something? And if they found out that we'd found out–!'

'They'd be in an even worse pickle if the truth came out *after* the release – while it was still showing. And they must anticipate TV screenings for years. The reputations of the stars would be pretty tarnished too, wouldn't they? Those scenes when Lionel goes up to her farm to give her the bad news, and she thinks Mateu's been out all night with his girlfriend after boozing down at the bar, and–'

'Never mind *them*! What about *us*?'

'"Us"?'

'Of course – *us* – the Oakhearts – as portrayed on screen doing all those heroics to rescue "brave" Mateu, the son of the murdering bitch behind the whole night of terror – maybe her accomplice. *Us* welcoming the American liberators. *Us* commiserating with hysterical Margalida as she lies weeping over her son's mangled corpse.'

'Oh hell! I've already got quite a few new and very prestigious clients on the back of all the reports of our night of heroism.'

'I know. Me too.'

'And my partnership. And the new corner office.'

'I know. And there's the textbook on website domain names I've been asked to write.'

'My editorship of *European Copyright Review*!'

Jane shook her head. 'No, no, no! We're getting hysterical. None of them has the least incentive to spill the beans – Margalida – God, how I hate that name now – Grimalt or Manilla.'

'Grimalt?'

'Well, he proudly boasted being ENABA's head honcho during his election campaign – the "I-only-ever-blew-up-empty-German-second-homes-campaign" – so as Mad Marga's boss, he must have known all about the assassination.'

'Oh yes. You're right.'

'So, he and the crone have to keep quiet or risk prosecution for–'

'There was an amnesty for ENABA.'

'That only applies in the Balearic Republic.'

'Oh yes.'

'And Manilla sees a glittering career ahead of him as ambassador, royal flunky, and all the rest of it. He doesn't want it to come out that he, as Chairman of the Historic Monuments Board – or whatever it's called – approved her pay-off as a loyal ENABA assassin with this *C'an Pau* museum and curator scam.'

Mike finally sat down on the edge of the bed. 'So, what the hell are we worrying about then?'

'Sod's Law,' Jane snapped back, 'Murphy's Law – whatever. Somehow, some time, the terrible truth will come out – Margalida does go senile, Grimalt seeks revenge for being thrown out of office – he goes to the Americans and asks for ten million dollars – or else, little fat Manilla blots his copybook as Lord Chamberlain of this naff new kingdom and decides to write his memoirs – God, *I* don't know! Maybe half of ENABA's membership know the truth about Margalida and her bloody bomb factory.'

'That island's a curse,' Mike hissed, 'just as Heidi said on the phone when you two last spoke – that Werner was convinced of it. My God! Can you imagine what his reaction would be if he found out about all this? He'd be in front of the cameras before you could say ... "Manfred Kommis". For a start, he'd have a field day ridiculing all talk of a "National Museum of Liberation". He'd get his bloody house back – and a whack of compensation, I bet. He'd say he was right all along – about the French and the Germans being sent to rescue him from an ENABA assassination plot. Chiffon and Klipper would be completely exonerated – that buffoon Azucena too. Nobody would believe the Americans.'

'Or us – the British ... Sandra Cork.'

'Bloody hell, your dad would look a right chump – the great diplomat negotiating the islands' freedom from EU-backed Spanish tyranny – all those fine speeches at the UN – all those–!'

'You don't need to gloat. ... You really don't like Daddy, do you? You never have done.'

'Don't be ridiculous!'

'I feel sick again.'

After Jane had vomited what was left in her stomach of Betty Trench-Foot's culinary tour de force of the British Isles, she sat on the bathroom lavatory for a while. 'I wish Margalida were dead,' she whispered, '... all of them.'

Everything was so utterly unfair she told herself. Although she didn't regularly attend church or say nightly prayers, Jane believed herself to be a good Christian. She was not at all sure that Jesus had been the Son of God, but she was in no doubt that His teaching was pure goodness. And ever since her days at boarding school – if not before – she'd striven to live according to His principles – in all things. In point of fact, she also had a great deal of respect for the Ten Commandments. She'd never indulged in proselytising, however: faith, she believed, was a very private thing. Indeed, she'd never even discussed Christianity in any detail with Mike, who, she'd concluded, was something of an agnostic.

And thus it was that she'd never committed adultery, or done anything remotely unprofessional in court. Furthermore, even before their marriage, she'd convinced Mike that they should donate a fixed proportion of their joint income each year to charitable causes. And from time to time, they offered their legal expertise gratis to the local Citizens Advice office. In truth, and although she didn't like entertaining such vain thoughts, she was a good person – certainly better than most.

Which was why all this Mallorca business was so horribly unfair. To be blunt, the cow Margalida was a criminal of the very worst kind: she'd been prepared to murder a dozen people in order to further a vile political cause. Oh, Jane had no problems with self-determination, if that was what a community wanted, be they Palestinians, Kurds or Mallorcans. But to kill innocent people in the belief that the end justified the means ... well, that was beyond the pale, particularly in a country that already enjoyed all the privileges of democracy. And what did people like Margalida and Grimalt want this 'freedom' for? – to be the big fish in a very little pond, with the power to throw out of it any and all fish of a species different to their own.

They were, in brief, totally motivated by hate and chronic inferiority complexes.

And now Margalida had got Werner and poor Heidi out of their house – the house that they'd transformed from a hovel into a paradise after years of toil – forcing them into exile thousands of miles away – in Africa! – in the middle of a desert! And Grimalt – another murderer – was living in former royal palaces and enacting blatantly racist laws. Even Manilla, with all his airs and graces, was nothing more than a vulgar, bigoted snob – hating Jews, hating Americans – even despising his fellow Mallorcans below the rank of aristocrat.

These, then, were the people who held her future – and Mike's – and her unborn baby's – her parents' too – in their criminal hands. It was unthinkable that such miserable vermin should have such power: Daddy was probably in line for a life peerage; by his side in diplomatic missions across the globe, Mummy had done more than enough for charity to be made a Dame Commander of the British Empire. Six months after the birth of Elizabeth Gwynedd Margalida Oakheart – trust Mike's mother to have such a bloody awful name, and they'd never said 'Margalida' would be her first name! – she herself would be back in chambers ploughing on steadily towards her ambition of taking silk – a King's Counsel, Jane Oakheart, KC. And then, in due course, wouldn't she be elevated to the Chancery Bench as 'Mrs Justice Oakheart'? And surely if she played her cards right, she'd be in with a good chance of becoming a Lady Justice of Appeal – perhaps even a Justice of the Supreme Court ... Baroness Oakheart!

But all these dreams would come to nought if this beastly scandal should ever leak out. Dear God, the cynical, conspiracy-mad media might even try and float the theory that all those who'd attended Werner's birthday party had been part of some dastardly O'Connell-Cork conspiracy to undermine the European Union – that they were all in league with ENABA!

Alone in the bedroom, Mike had slowly and very deliberately undressed. Now wearing only a pair of Pinsel brand body-hugging cotton and lycra under shorts, he was still pacing up and down. He was not thinking of the Stumpfs' sequestration or Namibian exile, or the honours which his parents-in-law might or might not receive from their monarch, or his wife's putative judicial appointments in the decades to come. All he could think about was the Office. It was the centre of his universe; everything of any importance in his life flowed from it, above all his self-respect – his ability to hold his own with Jane. Indeed, it was no exaggeration to say that but for the Office he would never have met Jane: it was the Office that had sent him to that high-powered intellectual property seminar. It was one of the leading IP specialist practices in the country – in the Top Five – all the reputable legal directories said so – and had an enviable international reputation. And now he'd been made a partner, the *Infernal Paradise* kudos having made him quite a star in his own right. Secretaries who use to treat him like a leper, now couldn't do enough to help him; young assistants invited him to their parties in studio flats in Camden Town; stuffy partners who once wouldn't give him the time of day because he hadn't been to a public school or Oxbridge, now almost fought to sit next to him at the weekly partners' lunch in the boardroom.

And after years in that gloomy sardine can of a room with that depressing view of the central courtyard, he now luxuriated in a lovely corner room with a Georgian fireplace and a panorama of Lincoln's Inn Fields from his three – yes *three* – sash windows. It had taken a lot of hard work – and money – to find all those original engravings to replace the previous occupant's IKEA Corot prints: Haydn in profile; the Palaces of Eszterháza and Eisenstadt, where the great man had spent so many years as *Kapellmeister*; Haydn receiving his Honorary Doctorate in Oxford's Sheldonian Theatre in July 1791.

No, losing all that was too painful to contemplate!

It was in moments of crisis that Mike would normally seek comfort from Hugo. He would nestle up to him and press his head against his spotty flank and inhale deeply, for the aroma and the velvety softness of the dog's fine hair always calmed him and raised his spirits. But Hugo was almost four thousand miles away, being spoilt by Mrs Babcock, and all he had was a pregnant wife vomiting in the bathroom.

Mike sighed and listened. Actually, all that horrid puking seemed to have subsided. He was about to go and investigate, when Jane came waddling out of the bathroom. She took in his near-naked body, and for a fraction of a second lust exploded within her. Then, silently, she cursed her pregnancy.

'I've been thinking,' she said.

'Me too. Feeling any better?'

She ignored the question. She'd rehearsed her speech and was not going to be deflected. 'I've been thinking. ... Well, for a start, we didn't make any promises that "Margalida" would be the baby's first name, did we?'

'No ... we certainly did *not*.'

'So, I think we'll be home and dry on that issue if we call it "Elizabeth Gwynedd Margalida".'

Mike nodded slowly. 'Ah-ha.' He pondered both the name and Jane's use of 'it'. 'I suppose that's a possibility. ... Hmm. ... Her initials would be

E-G-M-O ... "EGMO". I wonder if that means anything unpleasant in any major language ... or computer jargon. We need to Google it. The other possibility is Gwynedd Elizabeth–'

'That would spell "GEMO", which sounds like a lavatory cleaner, or a silver polish. Perhaps there is such a brand. It certainly sounds familiar.'

'Hmm. We'll Google that too.'

'Anyway, she'd end up being called "Gwyn". That's a Welsh boy's name, isn't it?'

'Jane, we've had this discussion – and the "Liz-Lizzy-Bet-Betty" one – a million times.'

Jane tried to smile sweetly. 'Well, I think we're in agreement about the *principle* – the Margalida thing being bunged at the end.'

'Oh yes. It was obvious really.'

Again, Jane smiled sweetly. 'And we're agreed about the christening thing, your Anglican Church stuff.'

Mike nodded.

'Good.' For some moments there was silence as Jane stared at Lord Halifax. Mike followed her gaze and appeared to become mesmerised too. Finally, in a faraway voice she said: 'Then there's the other problem.'

'Hmm? ... "*Other* problem"?'

'Sod's Law ... Murphy's Law.'

'Ah.'

'I think we need to talk to Daddy – privately – first thing in the morning.'

'Oh?'

'He'll appreciate the possible repercussions – if it came out.'

'Yes?'

'He has channels ... to the people who'd need to know.'

'Ahhh. ... You mean the PM ... O'Connell?'

'Well, I was thinking more along the lines of Blithe-Blister and Sir Richard Shaddock. They were at school together ... with Daddy.'

'Who the hell is Sir Richard Shaddock?'

'He's the head of the Secret Intelligence Service ... MI6.'

'Oh. ... What's it got to do with him ... *them*?'

Jane turned to face her husband and stared into his eyes. 'She's evil Mikey, pure unadulterated evil, that woman, that murderer. You do agree, don't you?'

'Of course, but–'

'But for a chance storm – an amazing stroke of luck – an Act of God – she would have killed us all – blown us to kingdom come,' – she patted her stomach – 'including our little baby girl.'

'Yes ... yes, she would have ... *all* of us.'

'And now she's laughing and sneering at us all. And soon she'll be installed in that house, like the lady of the manor – the woman who's had her dogs chained night and day out in the yard for years and years and years.'

Mike was nodding. 'Yes, she's a monster.' He pictured Hugo curled up in his bed, and tears began to well up.

'Mikey, darling, having failed in her murderous mission, we can't allow her to have a second chance of destroying us. Without her, everything would be just hearsay. ... They'd make it look like an accident – they're experts – or the work of a German fanatic seeking revenge – one of the thousands who's lost everything thanks to those bigots.'

Mike was still nodding. 'Like Werner.'

'Like Werner – exactly! Of course he'll have an alibi, being in Namibia.'

'Of course.'

'And ... well, I know it's a terrible thing to say, but that woman's "tragic" demise could ... well ...'

'Yes?'

'Well, it could make *Infernal Paradise* an even bigger sensation.'

'Yes,' said Mike with studied solemnity, 'that *is* a rather gruesome thought – her death promoting the film.'

After a moment, Jane once more fixed her gaze upon Lord Halifax and said: 'Actually, depending on how fast these people move – and they may need to liaise with the Americans – Werner might not yet have left for Africa by the time ... you know?'

Mike followed her gaze, and once more appeared to fall under the former ambassador's spell. 'Ah ... I suppose so. ... You know, I'm surprised that bloody awful painting is in the Residence at all – let alone our bedroom. I mean, he was the bloke who, as Chamberlain's Foreign Secretary, bent over backwards to appease Hitler. And then when France capitulated, he wanted to give in too, allowing Hitler a free hand in Europe so that we could hold on to the Empire. No wonder Churchill exiled him to Washington for the duration.'

Jane managed a smile. 'You never cease to amaze me, Professor. I wish you'd given me the history lesson when we first arrived. I always thought there was something sinister about that face.'

'I ... I didn't like to say anything ... critical.'

Jane closed her eyes and sighed almost imperceptibly. 'I'll ask Mummy to have it removed.'

'Good.' Without standing up, Mike removed his Pinsel underwear, and, as he did so, began to hum Haydn's jolly hen theme. After a few bars he stopped. 'You know, he may be crazy, but Heidi does love Werner very much. ... We'd better wait until they're off the island before saying anything to your dad.'

THE END